And Then There Was GOLF!

The Lost Legend

Published by
Cavalry Publishing

And Then There Was GOLF!

The Lost Legend

Dr. Jason E. Holmes

Concept by

William 'Bill' Greenleaf
Senior Master Professional, PGA

And Then There was GOLF!

The Lost Legend

Dr. Jason E. Holmes

Cavalry Publishing

Published by Cavalry Publishing, St. Louis, MO

Cover and Interior design: Davis Creative Publishing Partners, CreativePublishingPartners.com

Credits: Ball (on cover) - Hickory Lane Featherie, 106 East Faulkner Rd. East Peoria, IL 61611, hickorylanefeatherie.com

Photos (author bio and ball) - Dr. Nancy Rathjen, iPhone 13

Names: Holmes, Jason E., author.

Title: And then there was golf! : the lost legend / Dr. Jason E. Holmes ; concept by William "Bill" Greenleaf, Senior Master Professional, PGA.

Description: St. Louis, MO : Cavalry Publishing, [2023]

Identifiers: ISBN: 979-8-9874974-0-1 (paperback) | 979-8-9874974-2-5 (hardback) | 979-8-9874974-1-8 (ebook) | LCCN: 2023903098

Subjects: LCSH: Golf--Scotland--History--Fiction. | LCGFT: Historical fiction. | BISAC: YOUNG ADULT FICTION / Historical / Medieval. | YOUNG ADULT FICTION / Historical / General.

Classification: LCC: PS3608.O4943543 A54 2023 | DDC: 813/.6--dc232023

2023

Dedication

To my family,

My children, Jason III and Kim, Sean, Aaron and April, Travis.
To my 'adopted children' Erin and James, Alan and Angela.
All the delightful grandkids in my life.
May they discover a passion for golf and experience #joyinthejourney!

To my partner,

Dr. Nancy Rathjen. In our careers as educators, she is my sharer.
My fellow traveler, who gets me to the right place at the right time,
prepared and properly fed. Thank you for helping me take care of the details.

Papa

Table of Contents

And Then There Was GOLF!
The Lost Legend

Writers prefer for their books to be read by starting at the beginning and reading to the end. They labor to build a guiding sequence. If you plan to read from beginning to end, you may skip the rest of this map and proceed to the beginning.

Readers select a book for various reasons. I realize that readers freely choose a book to match their own specific interests. For some, reading from beginning to end may not suit their purpose. Other pathways to read this book are available.

Regardless of the pathway chosen, before reading any other parts of the book:

Carefully read and think about the Prologue.

Carefully read and think about the Foreword.

Read the Table of Contents. The Table was carefully crafted to function as a map for the reader. Use the Table of Contents to determine your chosen pathway. Each Chapter Title contains a Heading to identify the main idea for that Chapter. Each Chapter Title also contains a year:

1399, the lads and lasses invent golf.

1458, Brother Tanner composed the legend.

2000s, discovery, provenance and translation of the manuscript by the Professors.

Readers can follow any pathway to enjoy the book. They may select a single thread. Or they may wish to combine two threads. Readers may even read all three threads and follow a different pathway than produced by the writer.

Preview the Appendix. If you have questions about ancient golf, about medieval St. Andrews, about how adolescents work and play together, there are resources to access. Most of the resources are available free on-line.

The Voices. Character descriptions are contained in this section of the Appendix. Use this section as you would use the Dramatis Personae for a play.

This Reader's Map is offered to guide individual readers to meet their purposes, needs and understanding. Enjoy learning about golf, about medieval Scotland and about historians.

If you find golf interesting to read and learn about, a short list of books is included that you might enjoy.

Any game known to date prior to the invention of the printing press which continues to grow and expand in popularity every year deserves its own origin story.

My first memory in life was the 'sparkle' of sunlight on a golf ball. I was almost two years old when my fascination with golf began. From that moment I began to see sparkles everywhere, especially in the eyes of kind people.

My dad shortened a 7 iron for me. From that day on every dandelion in our yard was destroyed as I imagined it to be a ball. One time I crushed a nice sized rock. Much to my surprise and horror, it flew about fifty feet through my younger brother's bedroom window. He was in his crib. That was the first time I got punished by having my golf clubs taken away.

As I grew, neighbor yards were fairways with driveways and sidewalks serving as water hazards. By 5th grade, I was old enough to ride my bike to Norwood Hills Golf Club. I went nearly every day. Spring, summer, fall and winter, I was there.

I watched professional golfer Bob Cochran hit golf shots for hours. He could paint the sky with graceful and powerful golf shots. I imitated Bob and other golfers as I taught myself how to play the game. (My first lesson was when I was 25). I was a kid, so it was fun for me to imitate fluid motions and to imitate awkward motions. I hit more good shots with a fluid motion which naturally became the foundation for my swing.

At age eleven, I read Ben Hogan's *Five Lessons*. The pictures were clear and easy to imitate. As I look back, that was a lucky choice. I began with one of the great golf books of all time. As I look in the rearview mirror, it's clear that I learned golf by using my imagination, putting myself mentally in winning ways. My love affair with golf continues to grow at age seventy-four. It's often said: "Golf is a game for a lifetime." and that's what I've experienced.

When I reached back into my history, I could easily imagine an origin story for golf that would be a fun bedtime story for my kids. Our children loved bedtime stories and an idea came to me one night. Since golf has no written history and no origin story, I could make one up.

The possibilities for telling my kids a bedtime story about the origin of golf came to me from studying the changes in the game. Improvements in golf balls from the 'featherie' to the gutta percha and then to modern balls. I learned about changed course design and equipment innovations.

To imagine sailors playing their way into town from where the long boats were stowed on the shore was not a big leap. I knew that the origin of bunkers was simply cows or sheep digging into a sand dune to get cover from a fierce storm. The towns were built far enough in land so as to avoid damage from large tides during big storms. The land between sea and town is called Linksland for the very reason it connects the town to the sea and it's not good for farming while being fine for herding animals to graze.

So when I imagined how the Scots got introduced to the game, I took the factors: two mile walk to town…Sailors having fun with a game on the way to town (ships anchored and disembarked crew on long boats in 1300's)…Scottish lads and lasses out on the Linksland tending their herd observing the commotion the sailors would make playing with a stick and ball game.

While my imagination was churning, I also saw a natural development of the ball from wood to a pouch stuffed with feathers, a 'featherie'. The club required some imaginative engineering 14th Century style. It quickly became a game that involved the different trades and the citizens of the area.

Jason Holmes and I met in the fourth grade at Camp Viking (a summer day camp sponsored by our Normandy School District). We enjoyed each other as friends and appreciated each other as intense competitors who wanted to excel as players. When we reconnected a few years ago on social media, we realized how much we had in common. Jason and I had played different sports with equal passion. After our competition days passed, we both gravitated to coaching. Our passion for empowering a student with self-realization questions filled our time together with many subjects to explore.

Our connection created a permanent bond. When Jason and Nancy came to visit Marta and me on Maui, it was like no time had passed between us. Jason loved my kids' bedtime story. Ever the historian, he began his research into the origin of the game of golf. What his research uncovered is woven into *And Then There Was Golf!: The Lost Legend*. Jason has created a real feel for the people, the land, and the conditions that were perfectly suited for the creation of a game that spans the Earth.

As a historian, Jason is one of those engaging people whose stories turn history into a living experience. I asked him to help me finish my kids' story and before I knew it, he was planning a trip to St. Andrews to research the history of the origins of golf. For anyone who loves golf, *And Then There Was Golf!: The Lost Legend* is a treasure.

Imagine St Andrews in the 1300's. Imagine shepherds watching foreign seaman play a ball and stick game walking to town. Next, imagine the club and ball being developed to play a game across the land that links the town to the sea. Jason brings all of the above to life in the golf origin story.

The story is historical fiction with an emphasis on history and on golf. *And Then There Was Golf!: The Lost Legend* will take you on a journey that bridges golf now with the origins of golf in a most elegant manner.

William 'Bill' Greenleaf
Senior Master PGA Professional

INTRODUCTION

When we are challenged to think back 600 years to a time when there was no electricity, no social media, no mass communication, or printed materials, it is easy to imagine that life was drudgery, and that people were simple compared to today. Nothing is further from the truth! In the late 14th century serfs, or neyfs, as they were known in Scotland achieved freedom. Society could evolve to the benefit of all rather than a few.

In those new days, people worked together. They collaborated to provide for the needs of the community. While most farmed, other families would develop special skills such as carpentry, shoemaking, weaving and so on. Children's schooling in those days consisted of the skills needed for survival and for their trades. By their early teens children could become skilled artisans.

Despite laboring to produce necessities for living, people of all ages still found time for relaxation and fun. This book tells the story of a group of young friends, all skilled at individual trades, who combined their skills and worked together to create a game that all could enjoy.

This is the story of golf in the beginning.

Michael Finkel, M.D.

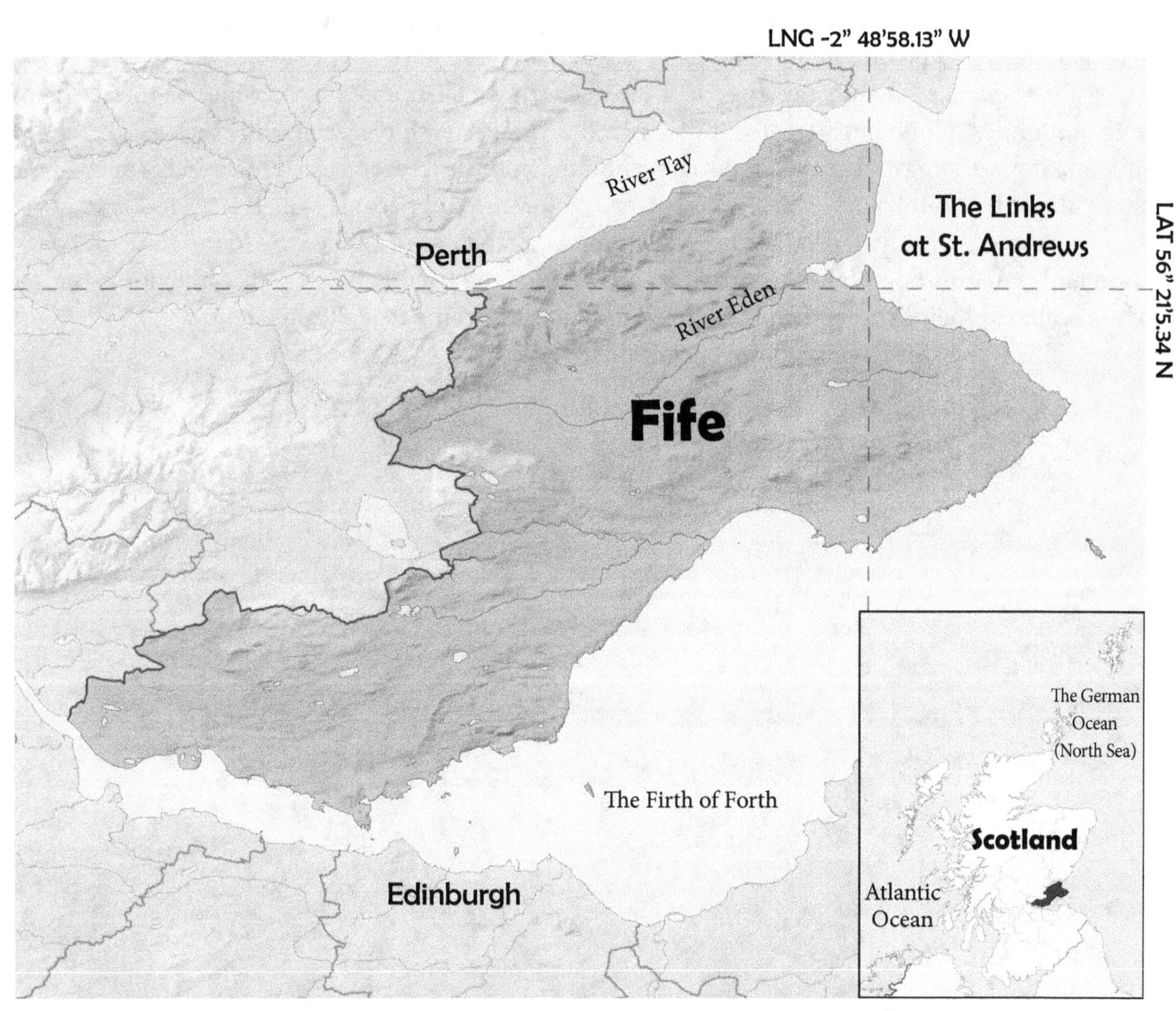

LNG -2" 48'58.13" W
LAT 56" 21'5.34" N
River Tay
Perth
River Eden
The Links
at St. Andrews
Fife
The Firth of Forth
Edinburgh
The German
Ocean
(North Sea)
Scotland
Atlantic
Ocean

Location

Latitude:	56° 21'5.34" N
Longitude:	-2° 48'58.13" W
Elevation:	27'

Place

THE LINKS, ST. ANDREWS

FIFE, SCOTLAND

Time

Lammas Day, Sunday 11 August (Old Style or Julian Calendar) 1399

9th year in The Reign King of Scotland, Robert III

14th year of His Excellency, The Most Reverend Walter Trail, Bishop of St. Andrews

The beginning of the Harvest Season

The Royally Chartered Lammas Festival

"THWOCK!"

A thunderclap crackled the still, stifling August heat. An explosive percussive resonation rocked two young shepherds. The sound startled! The sound shocked! It was a strong, solid, satisfying sound!

Two shepherds tended their flock on the Links. In the moment before the sound reached the shepherds' ears, the new Cathedral clock called the faithful to noon prayers. Simultaneously, the Shepherds responded involuntarily to the sound. Both tucked their heads below their shoulders. They flapped their arms up and bent their elbows over their heads. Danger lurked on the Links. For shepherds and for their flock, survival demanded high alert from all senses.

By instinct, each sibling first checked the safety of the other. Bessie and David located each other's eyes. Their faces answered the unspoken question, 'Are you alright?' They satisfied each other of their safety.

The two looked to the sky. No clouds. Clearly, this thunderclap was not sky formed. After their initial physical reaction, the shepherds quickly concluded that this sound indicated no immediate danger. Instead, the resonating sound filled them with a sense of awe. Intense excitement and wonder overpowered the shepherds' emotions. The thunderclap took their breath away.

The Shepherds knew the sound of metal striking metal. Repair work on the metal roof of the Cathedral sang the rat-tat-tat of hammers starting a nail. Hammermen and tinsmiths performed a percussive rhythm while they installed the new metal roof. After hammermen accurately started a nail, their strokes built to a crescendo. Controlled power drove nails through the surface to lock the tin sheets permanently. They knew the sound of church bells from the towers of St. Andrews churches and Cathedral. Metal striking metal produced a unique pinging, ringing.

Both Shepherds knew 'THWOCK!' was not the sound of metal striking metal.

The Shepherds knew the sound of stonemasons at work. The sound of the hammer driving a chisel shaped the stone. Masons shaped stone to exacting dimensions. Stones fitted snugly to construct great buildings. The Cathedral and the Castle were stone structures.

'THWOCK!' was not a sound produced by stonemasons.

The two knew well the sound created by wood striking wood. Many times, during a normal day in town, they heard carpenters at work. Carpenters swung wooden mallets to pound dowel rods into tight holes drilled in wood. To produce kindling for the daily fire, young men swung a huge, heavy wooden maul. The maul smashed a wooden spike. The carefully aligned spike split the wood along the grain for kindling. The two shepherds were well acquainted with collisions of wood striking wood.

'THWOCK!' did not match the sound of wood striking wood.

The shepherds recognized that the musical resonation of wood produced one side of the new sound collision. What created the other part? What did the wood strike?

"THWOCK!" sparked curiosity. The first encounter with the striking sound signaled the birth of new possibilities. The thunderclap promised drama and passion. The sound enchanted Bessie and David. Right away they knew that this sound must be shared with their friends.

Curiosity etched both faces. Silently, they stared at each other. A question formed. Finally, Bessie broke the silence, "What caused that sound?"

Chapter 1 | 2015 | Edinburgh Evening News

Edinburgh Evening News

Trusted News since 1873

29 July 2015 (New Style)

Antiquarian Trunk Uncovered at City Construction Site

While removing articles from a stone foundation basement today, workers discovered an ancient trunk. Construction of a new parking lot in the downtown area of Edinburgh required removal of the foundation for a ruined building. When workers attempted to lift the trunk, they realized that substantial items were contained inside. Rather than opening the trunk on site, the construction supervisor contacted the History Department from University of Edinburgh. Original ownership of the trunk remains unknown. The current owner of the property donated the trunk to the University.

A University archivist carefully opened the trunk and found two linen wrapped wooden boxes of identical size. The linen wrapping tightly covered a chained codex, the historical ancestor of a modern book, in each box. Prior to printing books on paper, scribes hand lettered ink onto parchment, a writing surface predating paper, made from specially processed animal hides. In addition to each codex, several loose parchment fragments were also found. Near the top of one fragment, the archivist read the notation, "Anno Domini 1458, St. Andrews".

A University spokesman reported, "First, we wish to express how very grateful we are to the workers and supervisor who contacted our History Department so that we could remove this artifact from the site. Such precautions are crucially important to document the entire process of discovery to verify information as accurately as possible when we interpret history. The packed codices indicate careful preparation for safe movement and long-term secure storage. Even though the ancient parchment is quite brittle, there is much that we can decipher. Based on preliminary observation, this codex seems to be a cartulary rather than a religious book. Cartularies are medieval manuscripts which often contained information including transcriptions of original source documentation.

We transported the trunk and the codex to our university laboratory in order to preserve the condition of the parchment. Our laboratory environment allows us to control exposure to temperature, sunlight, and humidity. One of our first tasks will test to determine the age of the document. We are very hopeful that the codex is authentic and does indeed date to 1458, which predates the Protestant Reformation in Scotland by more than a century. St. Andrews was then one of Scotland's most important towns. While the date is written in Latin, as was most church writing, other script appears to be in Middle Scots. Middle Scots was a language contemporary with the Middle English in which Chaucer wrote 'The Canterbury Tales'. In 1458, St. Andrews Cathedral drew faithful Scots to make pilgrimage, the same way that Canterbury attracted Englishmen. Pilgrims came to view religious artifacts housed in the Cathedral. All information we can verify and transcribe will contribute to our understanding of 15th Century Scotland."

Chapter 2 | 2015 | St. Andrews Pilgrims

The Professors — Lecture Notes

Dr. McGregor –"Clergy and townspeople expected large numbers of Pilgrims to arrive on Lammas Day in Medieval St. Andrews, Scotland. Pilgrimage fulfilled a sacred Christian obligation. Men and women journeyed great distances in order to pray to sacred artifacts housed within the Great Cathedral. The faithful believed the reliquary contained a tooth, an arm bone, a kneecap, and fingers belonging to Andrew the Disciple, the Patron Saint of Scotland.

The St. Andrews Lammas Festival is the oldest Royally Chartered Fair in Scotland. In 1153, King Malcolm granted Royal status to the festival. The term, 'Lammas' derives from the Anglo-Saxon language for 'loaf mass'. August 11, Old Style, marked the date which fell at the exact middle point of summer. Halfway between the summer solstice and the autumnal equinox, the grains ripened. The grain harvest, which included barley, rye, wheat, and oats, opened the harvesting season."

Professor Greenwood – "Millers ground the new harvest grains into flour. Folks baked the new flour into bread loaves. To give thanks for the first harvest of the season, Christians brought the first loaf baked with flour from the new harvest to church for a blessing ceremony. The blessing celebrated both the survival of the old year and a promise for the community to prosper in the new year. Harvest season continued for approximately sixty days, from Lammas (Loaf Mass) through Michaelmas. October 11, Old Style. Michaelmas, the Mass for St. Michael, marked the final harvest of the year. At that time old debts and rents were paid. People negotiated new deals for the next calendar year. In this new, post-feudal, time, elections for town offices were held at the time of Michaelmas."

Dr. McGregor – "Construction of The Great Cathedral proclaimed and celebrated the power of Christianity. St. Andrew's Cathedral was the largest and grandest building in all Scotland. The soaring shape and overwhelming size offered a glimpse into the faith promised to believers. The arches pointed congregants' eyes and hearts toward heaven.

To house the relics of St. Andrew, Christ's first disciple, required a grand building. Christians came to the shrine, which they believed contained relics from St. Andrew. The reliquary, an elaborate container for the relics, occupied the prominent position within the Great Cathedral. Pilgrims moved in single one-way file. The line entered from the North Gait. The ritual procession brought them close to the reliquary. They exited at the South Gait."

Professor Greenwood – "Pilgrim's displayed badges. Official badges were affixed securely to clothing, often a hat, or a shawl. The badges identified the particular pilgrimage undertaken by the wearer. The badges proclaimed that the traveler exercised his/her Christian obligation to embark on the pilgrimage experience. Most pilgrims who came to St. Andrews came from Scotland or neighboring England. Pilgrimages to St. Andrews from Continental Europe were not rare occurrences, however. Royalty and common folk, women and men went on pilgrimage. Pilgrims traveled hundreds or even thousands of miles. They journeyed to seek grace from a particular saint. Rome enticed many pilgrims. Some pilgrims traveled all the way to the Holy Land. There they wished to experience the place where Jesus walked and taught."

Dr. McGregor – "The badge served as identification that this traveler journeyed on a sacred mission. Badges were intended to provide protection for the pilgrim along the sometimes, dangerous way. The display of an official badge promised safe passage across borders. When the pilgrims arrived at the reliquary in St. Andrews Cathedral, authorized pilgrim's badges served another function. Augustinian canons protected the reliquary. Canons checked the badges. An authorized pilgrimage badges enabled a special privilege to the pilgrim. Possession of an authorized badge allowed the pilgrim to 'touch'. Pilgrims were allowed to lightly contact the badge with the jeweled and elaborately decorated box which contained the holy artifacts."

Professor Greenwood – "Touching performs a powerful human connection. Christians believed that touching their badge to the reliquary, generated a religious force which moved directly from the Saint to transform the badge. When pilgrims approached the reliquary, powerful holy emotions triggered their feelings. Some pilgrims experienced overwhelming emotional reactions. Christians believed that touching the reliquary could empower prayers, heal infirmities, or soothe their worldly troubles. Authorized badges were usually formed of pewter. The molds for the badges were carved into limestone. Molten pewter was poured into the limestone molds. When the pewter cooled, the molds were tipped over. The pewter badges were removed. A very few pilgrimage badges for royalty and the very rich were made of gold."

Dr. McGregor – "Pilgrims cherished the badges. Most pilgrims kept their badges for the rest of their lives. For a few pilgrimages, other rites followed. In the case of Pilgrim badges for Thomas a Becket, for example, badges were thrown into a river. It was a ritual for pilgrims to break the badge and throw it into the river to grant a wish or as a sign of thanks. Pilgrims received support from the Christian world. Free food, free lodging, and free passage across waterways via ferries were often provided to pilgrims who displayed official badges. Near Edinburgh, St. Andrews pilgrims received free passage across the Firth of Forth via Queensferry. Queen Margaret, who died in 1093, paid for construction of the free ferry for pilgrims to St. Andrews to cross the Firth in perpetuity. The ferry crossing saved several miles and many hours of walking. After crossing the Firth of Forth, St. Andrews pilgrims often stayed in a hospital, or hostel. At Dunfermline, the building was also constructed for those on the 'Way to St. Andrews' by Queen Margaret. The hospital provided shelter, rest, and nourishment."

Professor Greenwood – "Elevated slightly higher and to the right of the Castle, two magnificent towers framed the view from the Links. As a result of an accidental fire in 1378, the Great Cathedral required extensive repair. His Excellency, The Most Reverend William Landallis, Bishop of St. Andrews (1342-1385) initiated the project to restore the Cathedral to its former glory. Massive renovations of Castle and Cathedral required many skilled workers. High demand for skilled workers meant high wages. High wages attracted many new workers and their families to migrate to St. Andrews. In addition to the lure of high wages, the clergy made a promise to the workmen. The workers were told, 'If a man should die in an accident while working on the Cathedral, his soul would immediately ascend to heaven.'"

Chapter 3 | 1399 | The First Day

Psalm of Bessie the Shepherd

Scores of miniaturized white and gray robed angels

Rapturously ascended

Into the bright, clear, cerulean heaven.

Above the Links,

Graceful acrobatic flights

Animated the atmosphere.

Gulls and fulmars

Glided and fluttered

Amidst invisible rising thermals

Crossed by dynamic wind currents.

Fragment

Along North Gait, one of three nearly parallel east to west thoroughfares within the busy burgh of St. Andrews, pilgrims assembled into a long single file. The devout neared completion of their sacred journey. As they shuffled the final steps to fulfill the commitment their hearts nearly burst with joy.

On the Links, Bessie the Shepherd engaged in her daily task to mind the flock. While at work, she often paused in grateful acknowledgement for moments of exaltation. Bessie shared the day with joyful flying companions. Adroit skilled flyers controlled their passage through often unpredictable, invisible winds. Bessie marveled at the acrobatics effortlessly executed by the feathered creatures.

Bessie daydreamed. In her mind the antics of the chattering flyers reminded her of the multitude of holy men; brothers, priests, friars, and canons who blanketed the Cathedral town throughout pilgrimage season. Townspeople called the holy men 'gray friars' or 'black friars'. The names acquired from the color of robe worn by the men. Sometimes people referred to the friars as 'gray robes', or 'black robes'. Distinctive clothing identified the order to which each holy man belonged.

In overstuffed beaks, opportunistic flyers lugged large parcels of freshly baked loaves. To celebrate their feast, the birds cackled blatant, raucous, piercing conversations. Bessie imagined that the gray gulls and black birds gossiped the daily news to their colleagues in a manner similar to the chattering among men wearing 'gray robes' and 'black robes' encountered in the holy town.

"Do animals talk?" Bessie pondered, "I wonder. Would a bird tell her friends the best place to find a feast to share?"

Grey and white gulls and fulmars grunted, purred, squawked, crooned, and squealed. "Only a short flight from here! See where the stones are piled high! Many, many walkers there today. So much food! People hold chunks of bread out for the taking. An easy feast. All the bread you can clutch. Hasten to the high stones."

"Caw! Caw!" Black robed rooks interrupted the seabirds' confabulation. The dark wings counterpointed the cacophony. Jabbering calls alerted other birds on the Links. "The great feast is on. Dinner time! Let's go to town! Let's get bread!" Seabirds and ravens hovered, floated, glided, climbed, and dived through the scouring winds. For birds, the flight traversing the distance from the Links to the Great Cathedral required mere moments.

Bessie snapped out of her daydream. She shook her waist length, wavy, light brown hair. Bessie blinked. She resumed her daily assignment. To check on the flock she scanned her eyes over the familiar landscape. The lass stood watch on shoreline bordered by the River Eden estuary. From her location, near the northern most point on the triangular shaped peninsula, Bessie gazed. An overwhelming feeling of pride warmed her heart when she viewed her town. Bessie easily identified the nearly completed rebuild of the castle tower which sustained serious damage during a storm. His Excellency, The Most Reverend Walter Trail, Bishop of St. Andrews ordered that renovation.

Just after sunrise each morning, Bessie, and her one-year younger brother David, began their daily routine. Shepherds and collies worked in tandem. The team guided the flock out from the security of the fenced barnyard to open pasture. North point was the place on the Links farthest away from the town limit. Bessie and David carried L-shape shepherd's crooks, their most important tools. Crooks helped shepherds manage the flock by extending the reach of their hands. Since Old Testament times, the essential shepherd's crook remained recognizable to working herders. Crook designs differed. Shepherds selected crook design based on personal preference. From the time Bessie left the croft, her crook remained within reach.

The St. Andrew's Shepherds managed a large flock. Bessie and her brother David directed two collies who gently herded and secured the sheep. The team responsibly performed an important task for the family. All four worked together closely. During the day the team minded the grazing flock. The flock numbered three hundred. One hundred sheep owned by the Shepherd family, fifty sheep owned by the Weaver family, and one hundred and fifty sheep owned by the Diocese of St. Andrew. Throughout the kingdom of Fife, several flocks owned by the Diocese generated substantial annual income.

At the end of the day the shepherd team returned the flock to the security of the barnyard. From North point, the route to the castle required more than an hour's walk. To arrive in less than an hour meant traveling unencumbered by sheep. Every evening the good shepherds counted each valuable animal. After all three hundred sheep were counted, the shepherds closed the gate. They secured the flock safely for the night.

Parents infused older sisters with a powerful sense of responsibility. In addition, mothers and fathers strove to ensure that eldest daughters developed a generous, loving spirit. Mother charged Bessie to nurture her younger brother's curiosity. Father challenged Bessie to advance David's leadership qualities. Bessie took both charges seriously. She strove to fulfill her responsibilities consistently and lovingly.

To respond to changing, challenging problems, Bessie and David adhered to a proven process. To help them make smart evidence-based decisions, they learned process from their parents. Throughout each day Bessie and David acquired many facts. The siblings continuously sorted through the data. Each one updated, organized, and processed the data into useful information. Bessie and David loved to solve problems together. Problem solving worked best when they communicated clearly and concisely. The two discussed their ability to perceive the data. They tested the veracity of their observable evidence. They explored how to organize verified facts. Confidently, each one prepared, presented, listened to, analyzed, and evaluated logical presentations based on accurate factual evidence.

During flock supervision, Bessie and David honed their observation skills. Daily practice developed acute powers of scrutiny. They worked together to truly understand their issues.

"THWOCK!"

Excitement crackled over the Links. That sound filled David with a feeling of drama. He twisted his body in an attempt to ascertain the direction of the sound's source. David turned. He stared fixedly toward the direction where he thought the strange sound originated. Then, David's eyes skimmed over the silent, feeding flock. He searched with purpose. David sought his sister. Of all his peers, David most trusted Bessie's guidance. At least once every two hours the two shared a situation report. Updates helped alert them to any issue that might arise.

Instantly, David noticed Bessie's posture. The tilt of her head indicated that she stood on full alert. Bessie's facial expression mirrored the question etched on David's face, 'what was that?' Her silent stare confirmed her answer to David's quiet question. David knew Bessie heard the same sound because she leaned into the same direction his hearing pointed. Without speaking, both gestured towards the direction of the sound.

Bessie and David flanked opposite sides of the flock. From respective vantage points neither immediately determined the sound's source. Nor could either offer a satisfactory answer to explain the sound. Both wondered at the magical sound. Curiosity sparked brother and sister. Both relished the surprise. David felt thrilled to share the experience with Bessie. The distinctive sound promised possibilities.

"What was that?" The lad pondered, "what could make such a sound?" David gazed out over the triangular shaped peninsula to the sea.

Bessie signaled David to join her. Quietly, so as not to disturb the feeding flock, David established eye contact with his collie. Without moving or making a sound, the collie locked and focused large, brown luminous eyes with David's. Collies and shepherds communication depended powerful eye contact. The collie awaited David's explicit command. Smoothly and efficiently the dog gently controlled the flock. David raised his hand. He held his hand palm down. Then, he kept his hand still. The collie recognized the command. Immediately, the dog responded and acknowledged receipt of David's signal, "Stay". The collie held position. David calmly walked around the flock. He approached Bessie and her collie.

"Did you hear that, David? I don't recognize that sound," Bessie pronounced. "I do not remember having ever heard such a sound before."

"Aye. Nor have I. I am curious to learn the cause." David agreed. "Obviously, one of us must stay with the flock," Bessie observed. "We can't both go investigate the sound at the same time. I believe I should be the one to remain here with the sheep. Both collies will help me manage the flock. Even though I am older, you are taller. You are stronger. You run like the wind blows across the Links. Do you agree that I should stay with the flock?"

"Aye. Your reasoning is sound. I should go."

"In my opinion the sound came from the direction of the Ocean. If I am correct, I believe it probably has something to do with sailors. Yesterday afternoon we watched the cog anchor there. Remember? Do you think the sound came from that direction, brother?"

"Aye. I agree that the sound probably has something to do with sailors from the cog."

"Are you willing to go by yourself to find out what made that sound, David?"

"Aye. I am. I know you and the flock will be fine. Besides, I will not be far away."

"Alright." Bessie acknowledged. "I will wait. I will keep watch. As soon as you return, you must tell me everything you see and hear."

"Aye. Agreed. It pleases me how we trust each other in everything we do, Bessie. As soon as I determine the source of the sound, I promise to return swiftly. I will report what I saw and heard."

"All right then, brother. Our collies stay with me. We will manage the flock safely. You will be on your own, alone. If we are right and the sound was made by sailors, don't let them see you. Do your best to stay hidden. Be very careful. Return safely to me. Return quickly." Bessie restated their plan.

David and Bessie looked over the flock. They checked the collies. The obedient animals maintained tight control. Under careful watch the grazing sheep herded safely and calmly.

Still, David worried. He wanted to be certain of Bessie's feelings. He decided to ask one more time. "Bessie, are you sure that you are okay for me to get closer to the sailors? I really want to see what I can learn about that sound."

Bessie assured. "Go on, brother." She smiled. "There is no need for you to worry. But remember everything you see and hear. You must tell me everything you learn about the sound."

David answered, "I want to know what makes that sound. I want to know what the sailors are doing. I want to learn what they are using. I want to understand why the sailors responded the way they did to that sound."

Chapter 4 | 2019 | The Cog

The Professors — Lecture Notes

The meaning of words changes over time. Originally a 'links' was any rough grassy area between the sea and the land and the word itself is derived from the Anglo-Saxon word 'hlinc', of about 931 A.D., meaning a ridge. Later the word was used to denote any common grassy area and today the term 'The Links' is commonly used to refer to any golf course. **"Scottish Golf History"**

Professor Greenwood – "Throughout the fourteenth century, single-masted commercial cargo vessels, called cogs, sailed the waters surrounding Europe. From all directions the shipment of cargo and trade connected people who lived in coastal towns. Cogs carried shipments containing various types of cargo. Overseas trade encouraged merchants to expand their businesses. Shipping added new markets and expanded existing partnerships. Market growth significantly increased wealth for merchants who traded goods. More markets also increased wealth for those who produced goods. At anchorage, the cog rocked quietly on the lulling waters. The crew efficiently rolled and wrapped the cog's single sail. Tightened ropes bound and secured the sail to the crosswise spar. The spar crossed the tall vertical wooden mast.

Among the most important products produced for export in St. Andrews, fine sea salt rated high demand at faraway markets. Salters boiled sea water in copper kettles using fires fueled by local wood to evaporate the sea water. The salt water boiled away until only one substance remained in the bottom of the kettles, the extra fine sea salt.

Many of St. Andrews' most valuable trading products resulted from the shepherds' labor. Scotland's wool was in high demand. Fleeces were shorn, cleaned, and bundled to sell to wool merchants. Wool merchants shipped the wool fleeces to contracted markets. When loaded with new cargo from St. Andrews, the cog sailed on to the next port of call."

Dr. McGregor–"To harbor the ship safely from strong swirling winds in the bay presented a daunting task to sailing crews. Painstakingly, ships' captains and crews practiced careful sailing procedures. To guide the cog into safe harbor, captains employed local pilots. Harbor pilots continuously updated their specialized detailed knowledge of depths, channels, currents for their specific port. The ability to find secure anchorage was crucial to bring the ship into port. Every safe port of call contributed significantly to the highly profitable successful completion of the voyage. Before resuming the voyage, sailors worked diligently. After sailors unloaded the cargo, they performed a variety of necessary chores. Those necessary jobs maintained the vessel in seaworthy condition. Maintenance began with a thorough sweeping. The sailors meticulously cleaned the empty ship. From inside, sailors examined each and every part of the hull and frame of the empty ship. They searched for the tiniest breaks, cracks, and leaks. Sailors made necessary repairs. Following cleaning and repair, officers inspected the ship. The officers decided to declare when the cog met ship shape standards. After the ship shape declaration, the crew loaded the new cargo.

Town merchants employed workers to deliver cargo to the cog. Upon receipt of the new cargo, sailors work recommenced. First, sailors loaded the new cargo onto the ship. Next the crew carefully balanced the load. After balancing, the precious cargo was lashed securely into place. When sailing the German Ocean, ships frequently experienced rough seas. During rough seas, unsecured objects posed problems. Loose cargo presented a significant danger to hull and framework inside the ship. During storms, unsecured items often caused serious injury, up to, and including death to sailors. After a thorough check of the safely secured cargo in the fully loaded cog, the officers signed a receipt to certify that the ship was ready to depart. The crew stood ready to set sail. Soon, the ship sailed to another port city. There, another market waited. That meant another opportunity for merchants to increase their wealth when their merchandise was sold or traded. The destination could be Edinburgh, London, or Dublin. Maybe they would sail across the German Ocean to Flanders, or through the English Channel to Paris. The crew may even journey all the way through the Straits of Gibraltar, across the Mediterranean to the eternal city of Rome."

Professor Greenwood –"After sailors finished their assigned tasks, cleaning, routine maintenance, and necessary repairs, sailors secured the ship. There was time before the sailors loaded the new cargo. During the in between time, crew members often disembarked from the empty cog. Sailors enjoyed some well-earned, albeit too brief, free time, also known as 'liberty'. Cogs brought more than new cargo and new wealth to coastal towns. Cogs also brought new people. Sometimes new people only stayed in port for a short while. Sometimes new people migrated to work and live in the new town."

Dr. McGregor –"New people brought new ideas to towns. While the crew members enjoyed their liberty, they usually spent a portion of their pay at the festival in town. Often, sailors spent a sizeable portion of their hard-earned wages. Town merchants welcomed the influx of money. However, quite often there were some citizens did not care much for the sailors."

Chapter 5 | 1399 | Magic Wands

From where David stood on the Links, he observed the cog closely. The ship floated where the fresh river water from the Eden estuary mingled with the salt water of the ocean. David noted the cog rode high on the lazy waves. High riding hulls indicated empty ships. David deduced that from this ship the cargo had been unloaded. At anchor, the empty cog waited for the new cargo load from St. Andrews merchants.

Sailors meandered across the Links. The men laughed, joked, teased, and boasted. David watched them walk toward St. Andrews. He could see they headed across the Links to join in the Lammas Fair festivities. The men sauntered at a leisurely pace. The sailors seemed in no rush to join the throngs at the Fair. While walking the sailors engaged in more than laughter and joking. They played a strange game. The game captured their interest totally.

"THWOCK!"

That was the sound! David recognized it. That same sound David and Bessie heard earlier. Several times David heard "THWOCK!" Each time he heard it, he felt explosive excitement. The sound carried magic.

David also heard other sounds. Sounds voiced by sailors accompanied the striking sounds. Whenever he heard, 'THWOCK!', David noticed a gasp from the crew. A manly cheer of appreciation and congratulations quickly followed the gasp. The men cheered in unison. Congratulations showered the hitter.

David climbed. He wanted a good look at the sailors. He positioned himself to observe.

A sailor gripped a stick which bore a remarkable resemblance to David's L-shape shepherd's crook. However, the sailor held his stick differently from any way that David ever saw shepherds hold their crooks. First, the sailor took a well-balanced stance. He spread his feet apart a wee bit more than shoulder width. He centered the stick on his body. The sailor wrapped his fingers near the bottom end. He positioned both hands so close together that the bottom finger of the top hand contacted the top finger of his left hand.

Then, the sailor rested the L-shape end of the stick on the ground slightly forward of center between his legs. When the sailor moved his hands, the stick transformed. No longer did the stick resemble a mere shepherd's crook. Of its own accord, the stick rose. Like a sorcerer's magic wand, the stick levitated. On a smooth pathway the wand continued to extend behind the sailor. He extended his arms. He paused. His hands stopped even with his head. Gracefully and effortlessly, the wand curled. Continuing in a smooth, slow rhythm, the sailor allowed the stick to descend softly to the original position.

The sailor stilled. First, he lifted the stick slightly above the ground. He waggled the wand backwards. Then he waggled it forwards. He took a breath. He repeated the process. Throughout the routine the wand seemed to control and guide the sailor's hands. During the waggle, the magical incantation created momentum. Slowly, the wand returned to a precisely measured spot. It rested. The sailor lifted his head briefly. He located a target. Satisfied, the sailor resumed his downward gaze. He settled his body. His eyes refocused. He took another deep breath. He exhaled slowly. In slow motion, as if of its own accord, the magical wand again rose. Ever so briefly the wand settled into a slight pause exactly behind the sailor's shoulder.

Down the wand stroked. At first, the L-shaped end of the stick dropped. Suddenly, the speed of the descending stick accelerated and exploded. The wand beautifully extended the motion of the sailor's arms. In concert, sailor and stick performed a choreographed movement. David studied the motion of sailor and stick. The beauty completely captured him. During the ritual, David believed that sailor and stick magically melded into one entity.

David's imagination conjured others who waved wands. In his mind's eye, David recalled the sorcerer at the Festival. His magic wand moved as a graceful extension of his right hand. David recalled watching the magician rhythmically wave the wand. He heard magic in the voice. The sorcerer chanted an incantation. Precise movements of the wand punctuated the voice. Throughout the performance, sight and sound combined to establish a hypnotic aura. The magical incantation followed the beat of the wand. The wand directed the sorcerer's speech rhythmically. David remembered the sorcerer chant magic words, 'Hocus Pocus! You must focus!' The magic wand directed viewers' to rivet their eyes on a specific spot. Like a pair of skilled dancers, the sorcerer and the wand blended together to make magic. A successful performance of magic tricks required precision timing. David felt that the sorcerer's magic wand directed heartbeats and breathing rates in the audience to blend harmoniously.

David's mind leaped. He pictured the Cathedral choir. Heavenly sounds awed all who heard their song. The choir harmonized angelic notes which assured the congregation that heaven is real. To gain the singers' attention, the choir director rapped his baton. The crisp staccato quietened the disciplined choir. In the choir director's right hand, the baton floated. The baton reminded David of how the sorcerer used his wand to control his audience. The choir director stilled the stick. From the choir and from the congregation, all eyes focused on the baton. For the briefest of moments, the director paused. He took a deep breath. In unison with him, all singers synced their intake of air. In the choir director's right hand, the baton lifted slightly, then accelerated into the downbeat. The synchronized movement of the wand directed the choir to produce the first notes. When the baton fell, voices sounded. Magically, joyful music burst forth.

Throughout the song, the choir's eyes followed the wand. The moving wand commanded musical magic to live. Music demanded precision timing. Knitted together in perfect time, the baton intertwined melody and harmonies. Throughout the entire performance, the director brandished his baton. The baton kept the magical music beating. Sacred sound flooded the sanctuary. David thought. Upon hearing such sounds, who wouldn't believe, that in the hands of a skilled master, a wand could command magic? Or, in the year of our Lord 1399, who could possibly doubt that magical sounds existed? Faith reigned.

David continued to observe. On the downstroke of the sailor's magic wand, David recognized the now familiar magical sound.

"THWOCK!"

For the first time, David realized that the magic sound accompanied the movement of the wand. The sailor finished the swing. A well-balanced final flourish completed the motion of the sailor's stick.

Immediately, more powerful magic shocked David! As wonderful as the sound was, the sound was not the real magic!

Far, far more magical than the splendid sound explosion was the rapture that captured David's eyes! David witnessed! Magic became visible! At astonishing speed, the lad observed a bright white tiny sparkle launch into the sky! The sparkle ascended rapidly into a long, soaring, flight!

David focused. His eyes followed the flight. He witnessed the glorious vision! The tiny sparkle soared. It flew high! It flew fast! Higher and higher! Save for an arrow, the bright white sparkle flew faster, and flew higher than any object David ever saw fly through the air. The beauty of the flight took David's breath away. He gasped. The sparkle climbed to a rapturous heavenly height.

Slowly the sparkle began to descend. Down it came. Faster and faster the sparkle descended. From the heavens it returned to the bonds of earth. David identified the sparkle. It was a tiny white ball. The ball struck the ground and bounced. It bounced a second time. Then, it rolled and slowed. Finally, on the brownish green grass the ball stopped.

The sight hypnotized David! His eyes opened wide! He stared at the sky in wonder! David pictured the arcing pathway the sparkling sphere inscribed across heaven. The vision of the sparkle in flight marked the most compelling sight David ever witnessed. He believed he observed something truly magical! David experienced a feeling of joy!

David wondered, "When the sailor waved the wand, what kind of magic did he conjure? How did the compelling sound connect with the magic in the sailor's stick? What magic enchanted that sparkle into such a beautiful soaring flight?"

Each sailor took a turn. Each sailor waved his own stick. David noted a wide range of varying sounds accompany each sailor's turn to wave his stick. Several times the sounds contrasted sharply with the satisfying sound of solid contact, "THWOCK!"

One sound seemed cracked and disappointing. David thought the cracked sound more like a '*thunk*'. The disappointing '*thunk*', bore little resemblance to the crisp, joyous resonation, "THWOCK!"

Whenever the wave of a sailor's stick produced the disheartening sound '*thunk*', the others groaned in collective empathy. Along with the group groans, David noticed voices of a few louder sailors. Deep manly voices good naturedly taunted and teased any unfortunate sailor who produced the sad, '*thunk*'.

The lad asked himself, "What caused a group of sailors to engage in such activity? How were those two different sounds '*thunk*', and "THWOCK!' created? Why did the men have so much fun when they connected the stick and ball?"

David followed his sister's safety directions explicitly. He kept the low ridge between his body and the sailors. The tactic concealed him. Sailors meandered along. David followed in a stealthy creep; he moved like crouching collies silently worked sheep. Unlike the collies who deliberately made themselves visible however, David hid and peeked. He slithered quickly, quietly, and purposely.

Over centuries, flocks of sheep hollowed steep, deep bunkers from the sandy soil base on the Links. Huddling flocks dug protective shelters to escape from howling horizontal winds. Inside the bunkers, all the animals—even the tiniest lambs, found safety from the elements. When gusting powerful winds rolled across the surrounding German Ocean to blast the peninsula, the bunkers, scattered around many different points on the Links, provided life-saving shelter.

The deep sand bunker provided a perfect position for David. From its confines he studied the crew of rowdy young men without being seen. He did not want the sailors to suspect that they were under surveillance. Nor did David want the sailor's knowledge of his presence to affect the observation. Bordered by a steep high wall, the perfectly positioned deep sand bunker allowed David to carry out his mission.

Cautiously, David raised his head. He peered over the hillock. Sufficiently steep and deep, this bunker allowed David to stand comfortably. In order to continue his investigation, he leaned into the side of the bunker. Should a sailor turn his head towards his direction, David immediately ducked. He remained obscured from the sailors' view.

To the front of the bunker an impenetrable bramble thicket grew. Sheep avoided these densely interwoven brambles. Of all grazing animals on the Links only goats braved the bramble thicket to browse.

David maintained his observation as the men continued to enjoy their game. They were deeply involved. David, Bessie, their family, and their friends, loved games and contests. A different game might prove interesting to the young friends.

David wondered. "What kind of game might be fashioned with a stick striking a tiny ball in such a way as to form an explosive sound?"

<u>club</u> (n.) c. 1200, "thick stick wielded in the hand and used as a weapon," from Old Norse *klubba* "cudgel" or a similar Scandinavian source (compare Swedish *klubba*, Danish *klubbe*), assimilated from Proto-Germanic *klumbon and related to clump (n.). Old English words for this were *sagol*, *cycgel*. Specific sense of "bat or staff used in games" is from mid-15c.

Chapter 6 | 1399 | The Lost Ball

David watched the next sailor take a turn. David noted the sailor gripped the stick in a specific manner. Carefully and deliberately the sailor aligned the fingers of both hands together. He secured the stick with two hands.

While gripping the stick loosely, the sailor willed his arms to hang freely. He positioned his feet precisely. He accurately measured the end of his stick from a spot on the ground. With the stick stilled, the sailor took a deep breath. He paused. The stick floated and coiled behind his body. The stick dropped into a beautiful accelerating motion. The sailor's wrists threw the stick into a powerful stroke. The swing exploded the stick down. He finished the swing with his hands around his opposing shoulders. The pathway of the L-shaped end of the stick carved a beautiful arc around the sailor's body.

Then, across the distance from the sailor to the bunker, David heard.

"THWOCK!"

There it was! That same seductive, solid, satisfying sound! A sound so pleasing to the ear. David felt joy. That was the sound which initially captured his and Bessie's attention.

Speeding away from the strike, David delighted in following the flight of the small white sparkle! Now he knew it was a ball. Higher and higher the sparkle soared to its highest point. Then slowly began to descend. The arc of the sparkling ball painted the sky with beauty. Down, down the ball fell to the ground. Creeping bent grass formed a carpet changing in color from bright green to mid-summer tints of brown and gold on the Links. The ball bounced and bounced, again. Then rolled to a stop.

David looked to the sailor's face. He noted the look. The expression went beyond satisfaction. He saw a feeling of joy! He saw a feeling of exhilaration! David wanted that experience! Surely, that feeling must be magic!

"Hooray!" shouted the other sailors.

"Bravo!"

"Great hit!"

"That's the way to hit it!"

David itched to hit the ball for himself.

"Where can I obtain such a ball?" David wondered.

David continued to monitor the sailors. He studied their movements carefully. He recalled his promise to Bessie, to deliver a complete and accurate report. David noted that each sailor possessed his own ball. Each sailor carried his own stick. To strike the ball, the men took turns. When it was a man's turn, he unleashed a mighty stroke. David watched each man swing the club.

The sailors took turns. They hit the balls towards town. They continued to walk across the Links. David realized the sailors played a game. As far as he could tell, their game consisted of taking turns, hitting, talking, and walking across the Links. Then repeat the entire process. At one point the sailors walked close enough for David to hear them converse. Even over the howling wind David found if he strained his ears, he could comprehend significant amounts of their sentences.

The background noise contained faint sounds of instrumental music wafting from town. Melodies and harmonies interrupted the sailors' conversation. Immediately, the sailors' concentration veered away from playing the game. Tantalizing music captured their attention. Happy festive rhythms invited young people to come together. When young men and women grouped together accompanied by such music, there would definitely be dancing to enjoy.

"Do ye hear that, mate?"

"Aye! I do. I hear lively, happy, music! What a distinctive rhythm! Such rhythmic music means dancing!"

"Aye, and dancing means bonnie lasses!"

"We haven't seen a single lass in weeks. I fancy finding a bonnie lass who will dance with me. What say ye?"

"I say, 'let's stop the game!' Let's move along towards town faster now. What say the rest of ye?"

"Aye." Echoed the sailors in unison.

"I want to take one more stroke with my club." The last straggling sailor in line declared.

"All right then, Lad! Go ahead. Put a good stroke on the ball!"

"THWOCK!"

The last sailor made a strong, powerful swing. The ball launched high and flew far. However, instead of following the intended path straight towards town, the precious ball deviated sharply from the intended line of direction. The high-flying ball veered to the sailor's right. The ball carved an arc in the sky. The misdirected ball sliced farther and farther away from the straight pathway. Down the ball zoomed.

David watched the ball fall. It found the center of the dense thicket of thorny brambles. The thicket so very close to his bunker hiding place.

"Waesucks!" cursed the sailor who struck the ball. "Did you see where my ball landed, chief?"

"Aye. Waesucks is right. Indeed, I did see where your ball landed." Laughed the leader. "Do you see that big thicket of brambles to your right? Your ball landed right smack in the middle of the thicket. You're on your own finding that ball, lad! Anyone venturing in that bramble thicket will be sure to come out cut and bleeding from those thorns. You'll find no help from me to dig into that thicket of stickers to look for your ball. Right now, I aim to make my way straight to town. The festival, the music, and the dancing with bonnie lassies. That is what is calling my name."

"Aye, the music and the dancing, but most of all the bonnie lasses are calling my name. Lad, you're on your own to find the ball in that thicket." Chuckled another.

"Good fortune searching in that mess of thorns." Smirked a third.

The other sailors snickered. Briskly, the crew members marched away. They strode towards the sounds of Festival music. They accelerated their pace. They could no longer wait to get to town.

The last sailor looked at his mates speeding away. "Hey! Wait! Wait for me! Wait a minute! Let me at least look for my ball! Perhaps it will be easy to find!" The lone sailor trotted towards the bramble bush thicket, to see if he could find his ball.

Immediately, David dropped his head below the rim. He hunkered down in the bunker. He stilled. He willed himself to be small, to appear invisible. He issued no sound. To breathe silently, David forced himself to inhale slowly through his nose, and exhale silently through pursed lips.

"Go on, then. Look quickly, Lad. We will wait just a moment. But we are not waiting all day." shouted the sailors' leader.

"Aye. I will just be a moment. I promise to be quick."

David felt his heart thumping. He hoped his heart did not beat loud enough to alert the sailor of his presence.

"Come on, Lad!"

"Let it go, mate!"

"Aye, let's get a move on!"

"Och! I'm convinced. My ball is long gone. The stickers are way too numerous and way too thick. Those thorns are wicked sharp. I will not waste more effort to look for my ball in there. I'm coming now. Wait! Wait up! Wait for me!" The saddened sailor jogged to catch his mates. The crew moved briskly towards town.

Chapter 7 | 1399 | David's Problem

David waited. And waited. He continued to wait until he no longer heard any sailors' voices holler any shouts, sing any songs, or fashion any other sounds. He hoped the sailors were almost to town. Slowly, quietly, smoothly, David raised his head just high enough above the rim of his hiding place to make certain all the sailors were gone.

No sailors remained visible. Quickly and quietly, David scrambled to the bramble thicket. When the ball flew offline on the slicing curved trajectory, David watched attentively. Employing eyes trained from tracking precious arrows launched from his father's longbow during weekly archery practice sessions, David easily tracked the flight of the ball. Into his memory, he filed the exact spot where he saw the ball enter the bramble thicket. David assumed the ball penetrated the thicket all the way to ground level. It did seem unlikely a hard covered ball of such small size would catch in vines and branches without falling through to ground. David decided that should he fail to locate the ball at rest on the ground, he would restart the search. During the restart he would look for places the intersecting vines and branches might have captured the sphere.

Peering into the thorny patch, David started a systematic search. He scanned through the bramble thicket all the way to the ground. In his mind David divided the thicket into square grids of equal size. Forward, back, left, right, his highly trained eyes searched. David searched each imagined square thoroughly. Until he was certain that no ball rested inside the square, he did not stop searching. Then, he mentally checked off that grid and systematically moved his search to the next square. Shepherds conducted searches every day. While they kept track of the entire flock, they looked for likely hiding spots. The daily responsibility required them to develop remarkable self-discipline.

David spotted his prize. "Aha! There you are!" David said aloud. Nestled on the sand, underneath the thorniest, thickest trunk, he located the 'lost' ball. Even though David 'found' the ball, he did not yet hold a ball in his hands. To actually possess the ball, required David to solve more thorny problems. How would he recover the prized ball? How would he avoid being stabbed and blooded by the sharp thorns entangling the dense thicket?

David knelt. He studied. David focused his attention to solve the problem. He fastened his eyes squarely on the ball. He concentrated. He considered how to solve the problem. Exposed needle sharp thorns protecting entangled branches presented prickly problems. David needed a good plan. To position the end of the crook just beyond the ball, he needed to negotiate his way under, around, and through the stickered vines.

David realized that he must successfully solve two issues. Problem one: retrieve the ball. Problem two: avoid injury from the wicked sharp thorns. To solve both problems simultaneously required extreme caution. If David's calculated movements were off, he could accidentally push the ball. Then the ball would be out of reach. If he accidentally pushed the ball beyond his reach, the ball would be lost.

David postulated that he needed to lay his stomach flat on the sand to stretch his six-foot-tall frame to full length. Next, he would slide the shaft on the sand. He needed to stretch his right arm as far as he could reach. At that point, David would carefully extend his hand. He would lift the L end of his Shepherd's crook. Carefully, he would guide the L end into a hover. He must position the end of the stick just over the precious ball.

David slid his crook smoothly across the sand. When the crook neared the ball, David would need to lift the end of the crook and move it another two inches beyond the ball. He must not touch the ball until the L end of the crook hovered beyond the ball. That way, when he lowered the end, he would be able to cradle the ball on the inside bend. If, by accident, his crook nudged the ball away from him, even a wee tiny bit, the ball would roll hopelessly beyond his reach. To execute the plan, David must coordinate each movement. He needed to execute each step precisely. He visualized a pathway for the L end of his crook to attain the ball.

David stretched his body to full length. He paused momentarily. Slowly, he expelled his breath. He gathered himself. He quietened his muscles. He settled his nerves. David planned to slide the crook in a straight line. He envisioned a pathway to roll the ball slowly to his grasp. That was David's plan to secure possession of the ball.

Three briar stalks blocked a straight-line retrieve for David's crook as he slid it along the sandy ground. Strong, flexible vines threatened to take control of his crook. Springy branches nudged it out of the intended pathway. Slowly and cautiously, David guided his crook. Then, he scooted to reposition the angle of the crook. He worked tediously. Cautiously, David pushed his crook along the sand. David threaded his crook through the branches, thorns, and around the stalks along a successful pathway. He eye mapped the pathway to the ball. David maneuvered his crook to the spot he believed to be the perfect position. Slowly he lifted the L - end of his crook. He believed the crook hovered just above the precious sphere. The lad summoned his limber body to stretch an additional two inches. The final stretch of his body was all he could give. He stretched as far as he could reach. To achieve those final two inches, forced David to lay his head flat on the sand. With his head flat on the sand, David could no longer see the ball. The moment of truth arrived.

David self-questioned, "Have I successfully calculated the correct distance from my hand to the ball? Have I successfully positioned the crook beyond the ball?" The lad hoped his calculations were correct. He prayed that that he positioned the end of the crook behind the ball. To have accidentally pushed the ball farther away from defined is worst fear. If the ball was out of his reach, when he lowered his crook to the sand, his efforts would fail. Agonizingly, David pulled the crook back slowly. Very slowly. He hoped to catch a slight tug. A catch would indicate resistance when the crook contacted the ball. David wanted to feel the weight of the ball.

"No!" David said to himself. "Nothing! No, no." He felt nothing. No catch. No extra weight added to the end of the crook.

And then, "Yes!" David felt something. At last, success! He felt the slightest change in the weight added to resistance in the crook. That slight change in weight confirmed that the crook cradled the ball. He pulled. He knew he needed to control the slowly rolling ball. Slowly and carefully, David retrieved the crook. He brought the precious ball in. David felt his excitement intensify. "Stay calm." He thought to himself. "Keep steady. Just keep the ball rolling slowly." David lifted his head just enough to look for the ball. He saw it. "Aye! There it is!" Finally, David grabbed the ball in his hand.

David could not wait to share what he saw the sailors doing! David remembered his promise. He needed to return to Bessie.

Chapter 8 | *1399* | First Aid

David raced over the rolling rises as fast as he could run. Through the grassy dips he sprinted. He sped past the sand bunkers. He hustled over the final large rise. Bessie pastured the flock at North point. David streaked to his older sister. Breathlessly, David approached.

"Well, that took a while. Tell me everything you saw, David. I want every detail." Bessie commanded.

"David! Your right arm is bleeding. Go right down to the water and wash your arm immediately!"

"Oh my! I didn't even feel it! I will go wash it after I tell you what I saw."

"No! You will go wash the blood off your arm now! I refuse to listen to you until you show me a clean right arm. I will get my bag. Now go!"

David knew Bessie was right. On the Links, bloody arms or legs required immediate care. It didn't matter if the arms and legs belonged to sheep, collies or humans, bleeding injury needed immediate treatment! They needed to know the extent of the bleeding. Open wounds invited infections. Infections were dangerous. David obeyed Bessie's command.

David trudged to the water. He submerged his right arm. He wiped his left hand over his right arm. Only then did David notice the scrapes and stab wounds inflicted by the thorns. He was so excited he didn't feel them before. Some stickers remained embedded. David knew they required removal. Those he could reach, he pulled out. He could feel others. He would need Bessie's aid to remove the rest.

David returned to Bessie.

"You did a good job of washing the blood off. I can see each wound. Turn your arm over, please!"

"Bessie, there are some stickers I can feel but I cannot reach them to pull them out."

"Aye, I see them. I brought my bag."

Shepherds carried a woven woolen bag with them each day. Bessie and David wore bags with attached shoulder slings. Slings allowed them to carry the bags and keep their arms free as they maneuvered the flock. Usually, they found a convenient place to hang the bag, for example on a nearby post, or a tree.

Each morning Mother Shepherd packed food in the bag. A small wooden box contained sliced porridge. She included a hunk of bread and a hunk of hard cheese. If season, she packed apples, peaches, or pears. For condiments each bag contained two stoppered pottery vials. One contained honey. The other, vinegar. Knitted covers helped protect each precious pottery vial from breakage. The bag also contained a pile of wool and a drop spindle to spin yarn, a knife, tweezers, a flute, and a pad of clean spider webbing.

"My tweezers will help me clean out every sticker."

"Are the stickers bad?"

"Not really bad. But if we don't remove them, your arm could become infected. There is still some bleeding. I will use the pad of clean spider web to daub the wound. If the bleeding stops, it should be clean and good."

"What if the bleeding doesn't stop when you daub it?"

"That is a good question. Should the wounds continue to bleed I have two more answers."

"What is your first answer?"

"The most soothing choice is to dribble enough honey on the wound to cover it. Covering the wound will help it to heal. We could use honey on the collies when they get a bleeding wound except they have a tendency to lick the wound. Usually, the collies keep their wounds clean by licking. Promise you won't lick the honey off?"

"I don't know. I love honey. Honey flavored blood might be tasty." David joked. "I promise not to lick the wounds I can't reach."

"Remember, I said I have two extra treatments."

"Aye. I remember. What is the second?"

"It's not as soothing as honey. However, to stem the blood flow it is also effective. The second option is to douse the wound with vinegar. Rather than soothe the wound, it might make it sting a bit. And you will not be as tempted to lick the vinegar from the wound as the honey."

Bessie treated the wounds with honey. She was satisfied.

Chapter 9 | 1399 | The Ball

"Now David, tell me what you saw."

Excitement colored David's report. He illustrated how the sailors readied themselves. He described how the sailor focused before he took a swing. David told how the stick seemed to transform into a wand. He explained how the stick poised before it performed magic the same way that a sorcerer's wand delivered magic. He compared the magical stick to the control exerted by the Choir Director with his baton.

Then, David demonstrated. He explained the sailors used sticks shaped much like their shepherd's crooks. He showed Bessie the balanced stance with feet spread apart a wee bit more than shoulder width. He illustrated how the sailors gripped the stick. He showed the way the sailors swung the stick. He described how the swinging stick collided with the ball. He positively identified that the collision of stick and ball was the source which created the sound, "THWOCK!"

Bessie appreciated David's glowing enthusiasm. She knew her brother was excited by what he saw. David's report impressed Bessie. "You did a great job, David. I applaud your report. The details helped me feel that I stood right beside you."

"Thank you, Bessie. I wanted to deliver the most detailed report that I could. I only regret that you could not be there, too. I want you to see the magic of that white sparkle flying through the air. I wanted to make my best report for you. I wanted you to feel what I felt."

"I wish we had such a ball." Bessie mused.

David smiled.

"David… why are you smiling?" Bessie intoned.

David reached inside his tunic. He pulled out the sparkling white ball.

"David, I thought you told me that the ball was hopelessly lost in the bramble thicket."

"Bess, listen carefully. I said, 'the sailor said, the ball was hopelessly lost in the bramble patch.' I think the sailor didn't really want to climb into the brambles. I don't think the sailor wanted to take a chance on getting either himself or his clothes torn by the thorns while looking for the 'lost' ball, like I did. Really, I believe that sailor felt rushed by his mates."

"How did you get this ball?" Bessie questioned.

"Getting the ball required time and effort. None of the sailor's mates wanted to help him find the ball. Once the sailors heard the music, they hurried their pace into town. Obviously, each sailor wished to find bonnie lasses to share a dance. I know the last sailor felt pressured to give up looking for the lost ball. His crewmates urged him to leave the ball behind to join them at Festival. Really, I think that sailor hoped to find a bonnie lass to dance with, too. He gave up looking for the ball rather hastily. That was good news for us. I managed to see the ball rather quickly. Retrieving the ball was another matter, however. To actually acquire the ball in my hand required me to engage in some challenging problem solving."

David recounted the steps he employed. He described how he lay prone on the sand, guided his crook carefully through the brambles and branches, stretched his arm to position the crook to where he thought the blade passed over and beyond the ball, then finally, how he retrieved the ball carefully to his free hand.

"So, dear Bessie, your magical brother grants your wish for such a ball." David crowed.

"Aye, David," Bessie smirked, "you are indeed a truly magical brother. You have learned much of the magic your older sister taught you." she laughed. "May I see the ball?"

"Of course."

The size of a medium chicken egg, the ball was colored like snow under a noonday sun. The weight felt similar to that of a chicken egg. An extremely hard leather shell covered the ball.

David stepped onto a patch of creeping bent grass. The grass extended some 25 yards beyond where Bess stood. After the reapers completed mowing the rye and fescue grasses, creeping bent grass blanketed the Links. Rather than hand the ball to Bessie, rather than toss the ball to her, David dropped the ball on the ground.

As if to address the sphere, David positioned the end of his crook beside the raised ball. David drew the stick back slightly. Then, he gave the ball a slight tap. That tap propelled the ball. The leather covered sphere hopped off the crook. It rose in a low arc into the air, then descended to bounce once. Then it rolled and slowed, until right before it reached Bessie's foot, the ball came to a complete stop.

"Ha!" Bessie laughed. "What a novel way to share the ball with me, David. Although, I didn't hear the 'THWOCK!'"

"True." David chuckled. "Look, Bessie, you can see that the cover of the ball is made from hard leather. The hard leather shell helps the ball to maintain its round shape."

"Interesting," observed Bessie, as she reached down to grasp the leather sphere. "Indeed, the leather shell is very, very hard. One would hardly believe that leather could be made quite that hard. I can see that such a hard ball would withstand quite a hard strike from a wooden crook. I can also see how such a hard ball, struck with sufficient power could travel a far distance."

David explained, "The special sound we heard earlier this morning is created when a wooden stick strikes the hard leather ball. The sound of a wooden stick striking a hard leather ball makes magic. However, the sound occurs only when the hitter takes a big swing. But a big swing does not assure the sound. To make the 'THWOCK!' requires solid contact between the stick and the hard leather ball. To see the ball fly high and far after a powerful stroke from the stick solidly strikes the ball is far more amazing, far more magical than the sound we heard."

"I do like the way the ball flies when you strike it. I want to hit the ball also." Bess stated. "Here, let me hit the ball back to you the way you hit it to me. The ball rolled smoothly and accurately when you hit the ball." Bessie repeated David's action. Using a short smooth stroke, Bessie tapped the ball back toward David. The ball rolled right to his feet and came to a stop.

"That is a fine shot, Bessie. You made the ball stop right where you wanted it to stop." David praised.

"Let's hit the ball back and forth to each other," Bessie offered.

"Aye, Bessie. Hitting the ball back and forth sounds like fun." David replied. "I think I will try hitting one time with the ball resting on the grass, rather than make a sand cone."

David struck the ball. This time the ball did not ascend into the air. It rolled to Bessie.

Bessie repeated David's stroke. The ball rolled back to David.

After each took five strokes, David asked, "Bessie, how about we each move one step back from each other, following each stroke? Let's continue to aim the ball to rest at each other's feet. Does that sound like fun? Stepping back each time we take a turn will add a little challenge because we add distance."

Each time the lass and lad took a step backwards, they realized that they needed to add just a wee bit more force to guide the ball to stop at the other's foot.

"Hitting the hard leather ball with my stick is even more fun than it looked when I watched you hit the ball." Bessie observed. "I can understand why the sailors enjoyed striking the ball so much. Each time we stroke the ball with a wee bit more power, I notice the sound of wood striking a hard leather ball gets louder. Would you like to take five steps back this time, David? I think I would like to take a more powerful stroke."

"I thought you would never ask, Sis. I look forward to using a swing with full power. I want to make the sound, 'THWOCK!'

I want to experience what it feels like to deliver a solid strike from my crook to the ball." David answered.

Bessie and David stood some thirty yards distant from each other. They found that the greater the distance the more difficult it became to stop the ball at a precise point. From thirty yards away, rarely did one stop the ball right at the other's feet. Making the ball stop right on target presented a challenge. To a young Scottish lad and a young Scottish lass, challenges equal fun.

Likewise, the farther the ball flew after Bess and David hit, the more they discovered. Directing the ball to fly and roll to the target demanded concentration and skill. Ironically, the lass and lad realized that the more challenging targets also provided more satisfaction. Each time they executed an accurate strike they felt joy. The more times they struck the ball the more success they experienced and the more fun they enjoyed.

Every time Bess and David hit the ball they collected new information about how to strike the ball. Bess and David learned how hard to swing the crook. They learned to maintain control of the crook through the swing. Applying that information helped them to send the ball in line. They found a precise spot on the ball to strike. They discovered a 'sweet spot' on the stick to contact the ball. While they took turns hitting, Bessie and David experimented. They tried to apply the correct amount of force for the distance they wanted the ball to roll before complete stopping. Learning how hard to swing, plus learning how to keep the ball in line with the target, led them to develop new skills.

Each time they sent the ball the right distance in the right direction, David and Bessie enjoyed success. It was a powerful feeling they wanted to repeat. When they did not stop the ball at the target, they thought about what they wanted to change the next time they hit. They thought about what they could control to hit a more accurate shot next time.

Taking turns to hit the ball to each other offered joy to the sister and brother. By taking turns they took far more swings compared to hitting alone and then chasing the ball. Hearing praise from each other after a well-executed shot brought a satisfied feeling. Bessie and David loved the sound each time they connected with a solid hit. The wooden stick created the magic sound when it connected to the hard leather ball. Every time they watched the ball soar into flight, they experienced joy. The Shepherds agreed. Hitting the hard little leather sphere with their wooden crooks was just plain fun. Even when they failed to hit the target, they enjoyed striking the ball. David and Bess also enjoyed their practice time together. They talked and joked with each other. They realized there was no assurance they would perform a perfect stroke every time they swung their sticks.

To make the ball roll 30 yards, neither Bessie nor David executed a full swing. The farther apart they stepped, the closer the sound approached, "**THWOCK!**" Both wanted to create that sound.

"Bessie, there is ample space. Would you like to move back ten more steps? I think we can control the ball well enough. We can take a full swing." David inquired.

"Okay, David. Let's do it!!"

Chapter 10 | 2015 | Provenance: Laboratory Report

The Professors – Lecture Notes

Dr. MacGregor – "When working with ancient artifacts, provenance (the origin, the source of the artifact) is supremely important. To establish provenance means that the object first passes visual examination. Then the object passes a battery of tests. To evaluate this manuscript in laboratory testing we followed protocols suggested in a paper by Diane L. van der Reyden. The paper is outlined below. Alongside the outline, the lab test results for the manuscript are italicized."

From *Identifying The Real Thing* (Prepared by D. van der Reyden of SCMRE, for School for Scanning, Sponsored by the National Park Service and Managed by the Northeast Document Conservation Center, September 11-13, 1996, New York City).

INTRODUCTION – THE POWER OF "THE REAL THING"

Why is "the real thing" so important to people? Objects are valued not only for their appearance, but also for their tremendous symbolic power. Any object can have symbolic and visual power. However, only "the real thing" contains the evidence to support both symbolic and visual importance. Evidential artifactual value depends on the material composition of the object. Reconciling the symbolic, visual, artifactual and evidential value of "the real thing" requires the convergence of stylistic, historical, and scientific analysis. Such expertise is often the result of collaboration among many experts found in museums like the Smithsonian, or the British Museum.

Professor Greenwood – HOW TO IDENTIFY, "THE REAL THING" To determine whether an object is "the real thing," that object must be analyzed in different ways. (2) Three important ways to examine objects for authenticity, illustrated in Table 1, include: Stylistic Analysis, Historical Analysis, Scientific Analysis

Dr. MacGregor – Stylistic Analysis "Stylistic analysis compares the style of an unidentified object to a known body of work. Stylistic analysis may provide three important aspects concerning the origin of 'the real thing' (3)

Place of Origin – Style of codex matches style produced in and near St. Andrews, Fife, Scotland.

Materials: *Parchment, leather, and metal consistent with other materials present in St. Andrews at that time.*

Period of Origin – Style of codex matches similar artifacts produced during the time of Bishop Thomas Kennedy.

Document contains the signature of a scribe at the end of the document. Placement of a signature by the scribe is consistent for that time. Document contains an imprint of the verified and known Seal of Bishop Thomas Kennedy. Use of a seal on a written document is consistent with late Medieval times.

Purpose of Origin – Purpose of the manuscript is to record the creation story of how twelve young people invented a new game written by the sole remaining survivor and witness to the events.

Materials, stitchery techniques and leather work verified for the period."

Professor Greenwood – "Historical Analysis – To be 'the real thing', the object must be made with materials and techniques consistent with the style of the object and the history of materials and techniques associated with the time and place of origin of the object.

Materials and Techniques of Paper or Parchment Making – *Parchment determined to match parchment known to have been produced 1455, to within ten +/– years. Parchment material identified as from sheepskin source. The age of the manuscript parchment matches known sheepskin parchment from that era.*

Materials and Techniques of Media – Ink, a term originally derived from encaustic by way of "inchiostro"(7) has often been used as a writing, painting, and printing medium, although it is usually applied in thin washes rather than thick impasto.

Ink matched the composition of ink known to be produced in the middle of the 15th century on verified documents."

Dr. MacGregor – *"Scientific Analysis"* Objects can be characterized qualitatively and/or quantitatively by using destructive or non-destructive chemical or physical analysis of formation techniques or furnish materials (both organic and inorganic).

Qualitative analysis – reveals what materials (elements or compounds) are present.

The parchment came from sheepskin. Matches other parchment known to be made from sheepskin St. Andrews in mid 15th century.

Quantitative analysis - measures how much of the elements or compounds are present. The quantity can be measured numerically, and the numbers can be organized into tables or graphs.

Destructive analysis - implies that a sample (removed from an object) is destroyed in the process of analysis, as opposed to non-destructive analysis, where the sample (either still on the object or even if removed from the object) is not destroyed but remains available for further testing.

A sample was removed though not tested at this time. Sample remains available at University of Edinburgh."

Professor Greenwood – "Otherw tests are necessary. The following information is from a pamphlet published by usgs.gov, entitled, *pH and Water."*

'Chemical analysis–"requires a test which, "measures an object's chemical properties, including composition or pH. pH is a measure of how acidic/basic water is. The range goes from 0 to 14, with 7 being neutral. pHs of less than 7 indicate acidity, whereas a pH of greater than 7 indicates a base. pH is really a measure of the relative amount of free hydrogen and hydroxyl ions in the water.

Water that has more free hydrogen ions is acidic, whereas water that has more free hydroxyl ions is basic. Since pH can be affected by chemicals in the water, pH is an important indicator of water that is changing chemically. pH is reported in "logarithmic units". Each number represents a 10-fold change in the acidity/basicness of the water. Water with a pH of five is ten times more acidic than water having a pH of six. ***For a solution to have a pH, it has to be aqueous (contains water). Thus, you can't have a pH of vegetable oil or alcohol."***

Composition of the ink in the manuscript matched pH for ink used in mid-15th Century St. Andrews.

Physical analysis-measures physical properties such as gloss or strength.

The gloss of the parchment matched expected gloss level compared to known 15th century parchment.

Strength of parchment of parchment, though sometimes brittle, matched expected strength compared to other known 15th century parchment. Leather cover of codex matched leather of known 15th century cover. Iron closures securing codex matched strength of known iron materials from 15th century."

Dr. MacGregor – **"Organic analysis"**-identifies the carbon compounds (like hydrocarbons) derived from formerly living organisms, such as plants for paper or petroleum products for synthetic adhesives.

Carbon compounds found in the parchment via organic analysis found carbon levels consistent with 15th century origin.

Carbon compounds found in the ink via organic analysis found carbon levels consistent with 15th century origin.

Carbon compounds found in leather cover tested via organic analysis found carbon levels consistent with 15th century origin.

Inorganic analysis-identifies elements and compounds derived from minerals (like oxides of carbon).

Oxides on iron chain and lock identify as a match with iron oxide levels from known 15th century iron manufacture."

Professor Greenwood – "Scientific analytical techniques can fall into several broad categories:

Illumination-*The illumination was found to match similar known 15th century artifacts*

Radiography-not tested

Magnification-*used for visual inspection. No anomalies were noted under magnification to 10 times normal compared to known 15th century materials nor techniques.*

Elemental Analysis-*No anomalies noted compared to similar 15th century elemental measurements.*

Property Measurements-*The codex measurements were within limits of known 15th century manufacture."*

Chapter 11 | *2017* | Translation: Medieval Manuscript to Modern English

The Professors — Lecture Notes

Professor Greenwood – "Our team completed the laboratory analysis of the trunk and contents and published the report. Conclusion from the laboratory report confirmed provenance for the origin of the artifact to fit the period around mid-15th century at a 99% confidence level. Laboratory analysis finished the first step in our process to document authenticity and interpret the manuscript accurately.

Next, our research team scanned the entire document. The scan produced an accurate and readable digitized copy. We reproduced a copy for each team member. Digitized copies allowed us to share the manuscript with all members in real time. We found this feature especially advantageous when we worked on different sections simultaneously. We decided to limit access to the manuscript to members of the research team. All work occurred under our supervision. To preserve the physical condition of the original manuscript, we placed the fragments in a vault in a secure location. We installed a secure connection between both campuses. Our translation teams shared communication of their insight, their interpretation, and their questions, so that they could offer or receive immediate feedback."

Dr. MacGregor – "Translation is an involved process. The Middle Scots, Middle English, Middle Flemish and French vernacular mixed with church Latin language in which the manuscript was written presented a challenging opportunity to medieval scholars. Effective interpretation required mastery of the medieval languages. In addition, the local dialect of the vernacular presented a puzzle to the translator. Before we signed off to publish, we aimed to obtain consensus agreement on the interpretation of the entire document.

Some similarities existed between our modern 21st century workrooms and the Medieval 15th century St Andrews Scriptorium. Like the 15th century canons, our team would talk, analyze text, ask questions of each other, form hypotheses, and test our ideas together. That way we could work together and provide immediate feedback. Our work rooms were designed to be much more conducive to productive efficient work than the original scriptorium."

Professor Greenwood – "Fifteenth Century scribes labored for six hours every day. The weather of the day determined the temperature, humidity, and light inside the Scriptorium. Certain select scholars and scribes worked longer hours. They were provided more candles so that they could continue their work when darkness descended on the workday.

Our rooms were far more comfortable than the St. Andrews Scriptorium. Modern rooms were temperature and humidity controlled. Each team member accessed the latest technology at her/his own work desk. Each workstation featured a large screen. Scholars worked from a digital copy of the manuscript. Digitalization allowed us to enlarge the image to perform minute examinations. We could all view the same image on our own large screens, simultaneously. Our university libraries provided immediate access to collections of rare books and references (books, maps, articles, documents)."

Dr. MacGregor – "Before sitting our team down to work at their translation desks, we believed it was important to call them together to re-evaluate the role of translation especially for this manuscript. We asked our team to read Maria Camarota's article, "Translating Medieval Texts: Common Issues and Specific Challenges", so that we could discuss the concepts contained therein. We reiterated our desire to pursue consensus. From Camarota's article, we highlighted theoretical and practical issues inherent in presenting manuscripts, which were conceived in a culturally and historically distant past, to modern readers. The subject of this unique manuscript possessed incredible potential to produce a translation of high interest for the modern world. We focused on how we could translate an ancient text so that the new generation of readers who lacked a rudimentary knowledge of old stages of modern languages understood the meaning and the nuances contained in the translation."

Professor Greenwood – "We engaged our team with the puzzle of how to produce an accurate translation from an artifact produced in the Middle Ages to Modern language. As a team, we worked to combine historical-philological (the study of literary texts and of written records, the establishment of their authenticity, their original form, and the determination of their meaning) methodology.

We agreed to investigate the impact of our translation on our modern audience. Particularly, we wanted to engage that portion of the audience who possessed a passion for golf.

It is important to analyze an image of the Middle Ages for us to deliver to present day. Over time, we know that translations change. Definitions are overhauled. Translation is a form of rewriting and manipulating a source text."

Dr. MacGregor – "Edwin Gentzler offered 'translation is one of the most vital forces to introduce new ways of thinking and inducing significant cultural change."(2017). The translation of a literary text from the distant past provides largely the same problems as any other translation. Translators cope with all the peculiarities of the manuscript culture, in this case, 15th century St. Andrews, Scotland. The Middle Scots vernacular remained an open question, particularly variations and stability within the manuscript.

Translators will never be neutral, and they may function as editors. Variations in quality and quantity of conjectural (to conclude or suppose from grounds or evidence insufficient to ensure reliability) restorations may limit verification. Throughout our work we needed to keep those concepts in mind."

Professor Greenwood – "All translators cope with encyclopedia/world knowledge. Our text is from a remote time. There are allusions to events, habits and people that can be irredeemably lost. To determine the meaning of words, phrases, sayings, and proverbs often presents a problem.

Translators depend on dictionaries. Dictionaries result from literary processes and provide selected meanings. Dictionaries cannot correspond to all actual uses of a term in all the contexts it may appear. These issues are particularly true for historical dictionaries. Often the meanings in the dictionary represent hypotheses of the scholars who compose the definitions. For medieval texts, translators can rely on a very limited set of instruments. There is little opportunity to check on the veracity of one hypothesis against other reliable sources.

Sometimes metaphor is used to obtain the translation to a modern word. For example, 'hwhaol path' or 'whale path' becomes the modern word, 'ocean'. When the translator solves a combination of words problem, the results help to clarify understanding for the modern reader."

Dr. MacGregor – "Finally, translators must consider the response of the primary audience. Sometimes the literal meaning is clear. However, the translator cannot go beyond a superficial understanding of the content. Most ancient texts contain a high degree of complexity. In addition, several levels of opacity, both linguistic (of or belonging to language) and cultural exist. For the translator awareness of these issues is fundamental. Readers should also possess the same awareness."

Professor Greenwood – "There will be no clear-cut distinction between the original writing and the translation. We acknowledge the dignity and the creativity of the translated text. For the translator, the challenge is to decide how faithful the translation mirrors the original manuscript. The decision liberates the translation. The distinction of the line between the original and the translation becomes blurred. Translators strive: to establish the original form, to determine meaning, and to allow scholars to possess a reliable source to investigate into the past (society, language, and insight into the mind-set). We believe it is time for a more balanced way to consider the two ends of the translation process. To manage the identified issues and concerns, our interpreters employed a series of translation strategies. The series involved an intricate chain of decisions throughout the translation process. Each separate decision depends on several factors.

1. **Function of the target text.** In our case, we presented a translation of the manuscript to a modern audience. The translation is aimed at those who love golf.
2. **Literary texts may legitimately possess different, legitimate purposes.** Our purpose is to inform medieval scholars and golfers of what we learned about the contents of the recently discovered 15th century manuscript.
3. **May aim to introduce new ideas** (certainly an important purpose for our manuscript)
4. **May be main object of interest.** (The topic contained within our manuscript is paramount interest).
5. **We need a translation that responds to this specific purpose.** (This is our guide)."

Dr. MacGregor – "Translations help modern readers encounter the culture of a distant age. Helping modern readers is increasingly important. Only a few experts possess the competency to read works in medieval languages. Over time the number of people who pursue knowledge of ancient languages and cultures continues to decrease. To reach wide readerships, translations represent the sole access to vernacular languages from the Middle Ages. Translations are strongly needed to interpret original texts. To a lesser or greater degree, all translations transform their sources. American poet and translator Burton Raffel stated, {Translations aim to}…re-create something roughly equivalent in a new language, something that is good (writing) and that at the same time carries a reasonable measure of the force and flavor of the original.

Professor Greenwood – For translation of this manuscript, our task is to… "Write…readable, lively, and interesting for the general reader." One way to reach our goal is to employ simplification. To simplify the original, we decided to omit all features that in our (translators') opinion were relevant only to the historical author and his audience. We eliminate features because they are not relevant to modern readers. With a combined audience of scholars and golfers, the decisions may be tricky. We employed the simplification strategy to help resolve the issue. In the future, scholars will have access to study the digitized copy.

Entirely literal or entirely free, entirely source oriented or entirely target oriented translation can hardly ever be created. The juxtaposition of two opposite strategies serves as a useful idea. The juxtaposition idea downplays the freedom of each translator during the selection process concerning textual levels (syntax, lexicon, rhetorical figures, rhythm etc.) Then translators decide how to transpose each textual level."

Dr. MacGregor – "Several theorists claim that to write a version for the present time, translators of works from the distant past must employ creative powers. They argue that cultural bound phenomena (facts, observations, occurrences) should be transformed into the modern target language. If translators do not write for the present then the translation may appear ridiculous, awkward, or absurd. The only viable option is to rewrite the text in a way that reproduces the response intended for the original audience in such a way that the translation essentially induces a similar response from new readers. To translate a work which was conceived in a culturally and historically distant age with a specific function, to make it accessible to a new generation of readers who possess no training in the dead phase of modern languages, poses a significant challenge for translators. However, we believe such translations can peacefully coexist with other ways of representing a medieval work to modern readers."

Professor Greenwood – "One particularly useful way to approach the task of translation from a culture distant in time seems to occur by the construction of parallelism between a reader of the original text, and a reader of the translation. To understand the semiotic (the study of signs and symbols as elements of communicative behavior; the analysis of systems of communication, as language, gestures, or clothing) system that a medieval author shared with his readers, translators face many obstacles.

A successful translator must be ready to accept limits of understanding. Effective translations guide successful readers through a similar journey into a different world which sometimes remains inexplicable."

Chapter 12 | 2019 | Edinburgh Evening News

Edinburgh Evening News

Trusted News since 1873

9 November 2019

Scottish Medieval History Publication Announcement

Scholars from the University of Edinburgh and St. Andrews University jointly announced publication of a paper today. The paper described and interpreted the findings from a codex that was secured inside an old trunk. The Edinburgh Evening News reported discovery of trunk and codex in 2015. University of Edinburgh Professor of Scottish Medieval History, William Greenwood, and St. Andrews University Dr. Christine MacGregor, Ph. D., Scottish Medieval History, spoke publicly about the information contained in the codex for the first time today.

Professor Greenwood – "We were surprised to find writing dated from 1458 that was definitely neither church related nor government related. Originally, we suspicioned that we discovered a cartulary. Finding writings about church and state is always important, but this finding is truly unique."

Dr. MacGregor – "We believe this codex to be created by an Augustinian brother who worked as a scribe. He grew up in St. Andrews during the decade of the late 1390s. The writer came from the Tanner family there. After Brother Tanner took his vows, he learned to read and write in Latin, Gaelic, Middle English, and Middle Scots. Several Medieval Scottish words used phonetic spellings which are often similar to the Middle English spelling style Chaucer employed.

It is our opinion that Brother Tanner created the story recorded in the codex. He wrote the story as he recalled it late in his life. The codex tells the story of twelve friends, who shared a vision, to design and develop a new Scottish game. To invent the game, the friends, an equal number of six lads and six lasses worked cooperatively and collaboratively. They wanted to create a fair fun game which would present challenges for all participants. Regardless of size, strength, speed or gender, participants possessed an opportunity to succeed in equal competition while playing the new game. They wanted a game that would combine elements of physical skill, mental strategy, and emotional discipline. They intended for the game to be enjoyed in a natural outdoor setting."

Professor Greenwood – "We suspect that this codex was removed from the Cathedral sometime prior to the destruction of the Cathedral at St. Andrews during the Protestant Revolution. We do not know how the trunk and the codex were moved to Edinburgh where they were recovered. We believe that in this codex, Brother Tanner recorded the actual creation of the game we know today as golf. It is our considered opinion that Brother Tanner's writing confirms that the Game of Golf originated at the Links, St. Andrews, Fife, Scotland during the late 14th and early 15th centuries."

Chapter 13 | *1457* | Act of Parliament (Extract)

6 March 1457

Transcription

"Item it is ordanyt and decretyt that Wapinschawing be haldin be ye lordis and baronys spirituale and temporale four tymes in ye yeir. And [th]at ye futebawe and ye golf be uterly cryt done and not usyt And [th]at ye bowe markes be maid at all parochkirks a pair of butts And scouting be usyt ilk Sunday … And touchand ye futebaw and ye golf We ordane it to be punyst be ye baronys unlaw. And if he tak it not to be tain be ye kings officars.'

Translation

'Item, it is ordained and decreed that the lords and barons both spiritual and temporal should organise archery displays four times in the year. And that football and golf should be utterly condemned and stopped. And that a pair of targets should be made up at all parish churches and shooting should be practised each Sunday ... And concerning football and golf, we ordain that [those found playing these games] be punished by the local barons and, failing them, by the King's officers.'

The Professors - Lecture Notes

Dr. MacGregor – "The preceding paragraphs represent the earliest known written reference to the Royal and Ancient Game of Golf. Prior to our discovery, nothing is known to exist in writing about golf which could be authenticated before 1457 Common Era or C.E. Today, historians use the term C.E. to refer to the same time period as the term A.D. used by Brother Tanner in the extract.

One must speculate, of course, that in order for the king to take the step to ban the game, golf would surely have been played for a significant period of time prior to 1457. Our opinion is that in order to inspire such enthusiastic pursuit of the game of golf that it would cause adult male citizens to neglect performance of their civic duty, (that of attending required practice of archery, for example) must have required several decades. It probably took more than one generation of golfers for Scotsmen and women to become so addicted to playing the game of golf."

Professor Greenwood – "As historians who specialize in Scottish Medieval History at University of Edinburgh and St. Andrews University, respectively, our job is to unearth secrets of the past.

Then, we share the evidence we uncovered and collected. What we learned about this important time is based on the historical evidence. With our team of graduate students, who share our passion for this time and place. We studied and deciphered the available fragments of parchment discovered in the trunk in 2015 C.E. In this book, our aim is to share our discovery with you. In order to truly appreciate the impact of this discovery, it is important to understand the context of time and place. That is, the when, and the where, our narrator, Brother Tanner lived."

Dr. MacGregor – "In many ways, the surroundings of modern day St. Andrews remain the same today as it was in 1399. The River Eden continues to flow into the Eden Estuary, then merges with the North Sea. Although the body of water now named the North Sea, possessed a different name then. Until World War I, the North Sea was called The German Ocean. During the Great War, the Allies changed the name for propaganda reasons.

The peninsula of land north of the town, which connects the mainland to the sea, is still called the Links. The sun continues to describe the annual cycle of seasons. The Swilkan Bridge, sometimes called the old stone bridge, still arches over the Swilkan Burn. The burn never ceases to flow through the Links. Strong winds continue to persist in scouring the Links. In many other ways, which we plan to share with our readers, the late Medieval burg of St. Andrews differed markedly from the St. Andrews in our modern world. The great Cathedral that served as the Center for the Holy Church in Scotland, now stands in ghostly ruin, deliberately dismantled during the Protestant Reformation, 1559-61."

Professor Greenwood – "Scotland united with England to form the United Kingdom. The Union ended the wars of conquest between the peoples of the two lands. The flag of Great Britain, the Union Jack, combined two crosses, the Cross of St. George, the patron saint of England and the Cross of St. Andrew, the patron saint of Scotland to symbolize the confederation."

Dr. MacGregor – "The Museum at the University of St. Andrews, displays a famous map of St. Andrews drawn in the 16th Century. The map is surprisingly similar to a map of the present-day town. According to Dr. Bess Rhodes in, "Augmenting Rentals: The Expansion of Church Property in St. Andrews, c. 1400-1560", however, St. Andrews in early 1399 differed substantially from that map. The three main east-west thoroughfares, South Gait, Market Gait and North Gait were constructed centuries before the map was drawn. "The extent of the pre-fifteenth-century development along these thoroughfares is uncertain. By 1400, South Gait was divided up into burgage plots (a rental house and strip of land in a town) at least as far west as Logies Lane, and probably beyond. Some sections of North Gait and Market Gait were also divided into the small strips of land typical of medieval towns, although these streets were probably less densely inhabited than South Gait."

No University was located in the burg in 1399. The University officially appeared in 1413. Upon the delivery of a Papal Bull the University opened officially. Unofficially, however, teaching began around 1410. All the church buildings were located at the East end of the old town of St. Andrews bordering on the Sea. Clustered together, "the cathedral, the collegiate church St. Mary on the Rock, the parish church of Holy Trinity, and the hospitals of St. Leonard and St. Nicholas," formed a zone of religious buildings. By the time the map was drawn, the parish church moved out of that zone."

Professor Greenwood – "The fourteenth century brought many changes to the people of St. Andrews. To the people who dwelled in St. Andrews when the new century opened, those changes seemed rapid. Knowing about a few of those changes helps to understand how the people reacted to and adapted to their changing world. Our perspective of time and place will differ markedly from theirs. Nevertheless, learning how the people approached their lives and their world, enriches our own perspectives, and adds to our understanding.

Our narrator will do his own introduction."

Chapter 14 | 1458 | Introducing Brother Tanner

In the year of our Lord, 1457, the King of Scotland decreed a ban against our fair game. Folks find it difficult to understand such a ban. Golf is fair. Golf is challenging. When folks immerse themselves into the game, they develop a passion to pursue excellence. The story of the genesis of golf has not been written. I write to assure readers that golf is not an invention by the devil. I am the last of the Twelve who constructed the game. Only I can share the story. The others are gone. I believe our story is important. I want to share the story.

Brother Tanner is the name I am called. My Christian name is Thomas. For more than 50 years no one called me Thomas. Here at St. Andrews, the great Cathedral, located in the town of my birth I took my vows. After I made my vows, the parishioners, as well as the holy men and women with whom I served, called me Brother Tanner. The name Thomas was forgotten.

In the Great Cathedral of St. Andrews, I learned to read and write. Eventually, reading and writing became the work of my life. For decades and decades, I copied the Holy Books. To copy the Holy Word demands slow, tedious labor. However, copying the Holy Word is manifestly important to the life of the Holy Church. The Church depends on access to the Holy Words. The words must be copied with perfect accuracy. It is necessary for the holy men to read the gospel accurately and truly. When people hear the true story, they must hear the words of the Holy Spirit perfectly. Then they will know comfort. Then they will believe the gospel. When the folk hear the Holy Word, they may understand the message in order that their immortal souls might be saved. I performed my holy task with thorough diligence. Over the course of my life, I earned a sterling reputation as an exacting scribe. I know that pride is one of the deadly sins. Nevertheless, I humbly and honestly confess to the sin. I do possess a level of pride regarding the manner I performed my sacred task.

Now, my age is three score and a dozen years. When I walk, I illustrate the final answer to the riddle which the Sphinx inquired of Ulysses. What creature walks on four legs in the morning, two legs during the day and three legs at night? The answer to the riddle is man. As a baby, he crawls on all fours in the morning. On two legs during the light of a healthy life, man walks. In my knees and hips, the arthritis inhibits my ability to move. No longer do the nerves below my knees provide the information from my feet and legs I require to maintain my balance. If I am unable to look directly at the ground where I stand, I will stumble. I fear that I may fall. In order for me to walk now, requires that I employ a stick. The stick serves to make a third leg for a man of 72 years. By evening, as I approach the end of my earthly life, I am that creature. My joints are stiff always. They pain me continuously from within. Some days the pain is sharp like a knife. Other days the pain is dulled and throbbing. Debilitating pain also resides in my shoulders. Some nights, I can find only one position in which to find relief from the pain so that I may rest. On those nights I count myself fortunate because I may be able to sleep for a few hours. Other nights I can find no position in which I may find the comfort of pain free rest. I suffer.

My sacred Augustinian Order no longer requires me to copy the Holy texts. My superiors at The Great Cathedral declared that I earned my keep for the remainder of my mortal life. Some days, when the pain permits, I assist other scribes. When a scribe requires a rest, or succumbs to an illness, or should the canons fall behind schedule to complete a task, I can still fill in to help. I revel with joy when I assist with the sacred work. But now, I do the work so slowly. No longer am I able to maintain the pace at which I once performed my sacred work. In recognition for my lifetime of service, and in appreciation for assisting my brother scribes, Bishop James Kennedy granted use of a desk in the copying room reserved for me. I stay connected with my brother scribes. Along with the desk, I possess ready access to a supply of writing utensils, new quills, new parchment, and ink. The bounty is a gift from Bishop Kennedy.

Yesterday, I walked by my reflection in a glass window. I was shocked by what I saw. I realized that in the reflection, my back formed the shape of a surprised cat's tail.

Once upon a time however, I was young and strong. When I was a lad, my circle contained twelve friends. Those were golden days. As children, we learned and played together. We worked and played so hard that each night we welcomed sleep. We looked forward to the joy we would find tomorrow.

It is impossible for me to imagine that any children anywhere or anytime could have grown into adulthood with better friends than our Circle of twelve. Nor can I conceive that there could ever have been a better time to be young than our time. Our youth coincided with turning the calendar to a new century. I cannot remember a time when my sister and our friends were not part of my life. Our Circle of twelve included:

Barbara and Russell, the Bowyers;
Heather and Robert, the Carpenters;
Marion and Jonathan, the Shoemakers;
Bessie and David, the Shepherds;
Rhona and William the Weavers;
my sister Margaret and me, Thomas, the Tanners.

My friends departed earthly life. Even my sister, Margaret is gone. Only I remain. I am the last. I have not forgotten the lad, Thomas, nor the friends from my boyhood. It is my duty to write our important story. Memories of my friends require a written record. To preserve how we twelve conceived and shared a vision, I must transcribe my memoir. I will tell how our shared idea came to life. We pooled questions, ideas, and skills. To complete our vision we created a new game.

This manuscript chronicles events which occurred at St. Andrews between the time of Lammas and Michaelmas in the year 1399. For us, the excitement extended from the months when the old century closed, on into the new century, our new time. Auld lang syne, (Scots for 'a long time ago') my sister, our friends and I shared a vision. Together, we twelve friends brought our vision to life.

Chapter 15 | *1458* | The Accident

Brother Tanner

Mystery infects life. Power manifests within the unfathomable. Many believe that the most horrible event in one's life, the worst tragedy to ever befall a man, can change his fortune. Ironically, the worst tragedy becomes the transforming moment to guide his life. The concept contains a mystery. The belief that the worst tragedy can power a mighty transformation offers empowerment.

As adults we learn to realize that an encounter with severe adversity may reveal previously unknown strength. The ability to face and overcome adversity can serve as the driving force when a man struggles to construct the remainder of his life. Overcoming adversity can guide one toward a direction completely opposite from the original intended pathway for his life.

Personal tragedy, no matter the degree of horror contained, is never what truly matters. Of most importance is the man's reaction to adversity. When confronted by the horror of a tragedy, we want to see how the man answers such questions as:

How does a person respond when confronted by the most horrible tragedy in his life? How does one think about the tragedy? How does one react to tragedy?

To believe that the worst event in a person's life can power a transformation presents a mystery some find difficult to grasp. Sadly, the truth revealed within such mystery many may never appreciate. For many, comprehension of such mystery fails to arrive until the attainment of maturity and wisdom. A person must grasp the concept of irony to fathom deep mystery. One must acquire awareness of how irony interweaves within the fabric of human life. Awareness of irony combined with acceptance of mystery enhances understanding. Appreciating the great transformational ironies offers the opportunity to achieve inner peace. I accept the existence and power of mystery. I witness irony. I believe transformation exists.

What seems at first to be a man's greatest tragedy can, by exertion of will, combined with the caring support of family and friends, mysteriously transform. That which first appears to be unbearable tragedy provides the seed. Should the seed fall upon fertile ground, and should the seedling receive proper tending, the potential exists for the response to adversity to blossom into life's greatest blessing.

To support my thesis, I offer my own story. Before I held conscious memory my story began. My parents told me that I was born with two normal hands. Father and mother recounted the accident I suffered. I was not yet two years of age. I possess no memory of the calamity. However, I heard the story many times, from my parents and from the townspeople. So often did I hear the story, I recollect the events they described. This is the story they told.

One day, a cart loaded fully with fresh hides from the butcher backed into the vats room at the Tannery. Carts backed into the room often. The first step to begin the treatment process at the tannery, was to unload the animal hides. The process to convert simple cheap raw hide into valuable finished products, like leather or parchment began in the vat room.

Deep slick muck covered the wet vat room floor. Father carefully placed two parallel oak planks in the room as rails to guide the driver when backing the cart. The rails enabled the driver to keep the wheels safely out of the muck. Each time a cart left the vats room, father swept the muck off the planks. Father marked a spot on the plank for the driver to stop the cartwheels. By stopping at the marked spot, the driver delivered the cart to the best place to load the raw hides directly into the first vat. It was an efficient system.

I was but a wee toddler. I wandered into the vat room to play but no one saw me. I slipped in the wet muck and fell into the danger zone. In an attempt to regain my balance, I flung out my arms. My left arm reached for the oak rail. My wrist found the rail at the precise marked stopping point for the massive oaken cartwheel. Before anyone knew of my whereabouts, a giant wooden cartwheel rolled onto my left hand. The heavy wheel nearly severed my crushed hand. Father heard me scream in agony. He ran to me. He found me pinned beneath the cart. The cartwheel rested on my crushed left hand.

Father quickly pushed the cart from off my hand. He picked me up and hurried to the surgeon's office. When the surgeon examined my hand, he determined that to save my life the best choice was to amputate my tiny, mangled hand. The surgeon severed my hand. On my left arm, he fashioned a stump. Our surgeon saved my life. I am forever grateful to the surgeon's skill.

Mercifully, I possess no memory of the accident. Neither do I remember having two hands. For all my life, I remember having only my right hand. I learned to live with only one hand. Two handed people could not teach a one-handed person like me to perform tasks in the same way they taught other two-handed people. My parents encouraged me to teach myself to perform nearly every task that my two-handed friends performed. I didn't always solve problems the same way my two-handed friends solved them. Many times, I needed to learn a completely different approach. But I usually figured out how I could get the job done.

My friends and my family always treated me in the same manner they treated any other two-handed lad would expect to be treated. Growing up, I participated in nearly all the games the other lads and lasses enjoyed. Only a few games put me at a disadvantage. For example, I never learned how to balance the caber successfully.

Because of the superior strength in my remaining hand, I experienced no disadvantage when throwing the shot put. To compete in the shot put everyone had to throw the shot with one hand. I excelled at the game of shot put. I also negotiated the hammer throw with one hand. Even though I possessed only one hand, my strong hand served me well. I did not win the competition in the hammer throw. However, I often finished among the leaders in these events.

Over the years, something strange occurred. In addition to superior strength, I learned ways to develop superior control in my right hand. I possessed more precise control in my right hand than any of my friends. The control I developed in my right hand seemed to compensate for the loss of my left hand.

My father believed an ample supply of beggars already patrolled the streets in St. Andrews. Father refused to allow his only son to join the legion of beggars. His love nurtured me. He also challenged me. Father's confidence in my ability to solve problems guided me to learn his honorable and important trade. The occupation of tanner offered a respected living in St. Andrews. To become a tanner, I mastered the many tasks required to produce the variety of leathers offered in our tannery. In addition to producing leather, our tannery produced fine parchment.

My daily focus guided me to acquire deep knowledge of the tanning craft. I strove to learn everything about the goods we offered in our tannery. There was much to learn. I wanted to know how to deliver the finest leathers and the best glues to our customers.

To make up for my missing hand, I learned many ways to adapt my left stump. To hold an object in place, I used my stump to pin it against the leather work apron I wore. That procedure allowed me to 'work' leather and parchment.

Our tannery provided valuable commodities to the people of St. Andrews. All the skills that went into two hands for other tanners, entered into my right hand. I believed that I was on my way to continue the family tanning business.

Chapter 16 | *1458* | The One-Handed Artist

Brother Tanner

Warm sunny Sundays St. Andrews invited families outside. We loved to gather on the beaches attached to the Links. There we relaxed and enjoyed a few hours at play. Smooth sand on the beach invited children and adults to draw. All the folk, young and old, enjoyed the pastime. We created many likenesses in the smooth wet sand. At first, we used our fingers to draw. Later, to draw in the sand, we changed to sticks. Often, we laughed at our attempts.

Frequently, our parents used the wet sand as a slate is used for chalk. To illustrate ideas to their friends, adults drew pictures in the sand. Sometimes when we gathered around to see the design, the artist told a story to accompany the drawing.

Stories combined with drawings entertained everyone, especially children. Illustrated stories helped teach children important ideas about living in our community. We squatted or sat on the sand. So that even the smallest audience member could view the drawings while we listened to the story, we carefully arranged our seating. Children were completely enthralled by the stories and the drawings.

In addition to developing superior strength in my right hand, I discovered something new. A far different and more important talent than strength, blessed my single hand. Like many others who enjoyed the smooth St. Andrews beaches, I enjoyed drawing in the sand with a stick. I discovered I possessed a gift for drawing likenesses. My talent for drawing was first acknowledged when I was a wee lad at play on the beach.

To create my drawings, first I thought about the picture I wished to create. Whenever I worked on a sand drawing, I concentrated deeply. While engaged in the process of drawing, I retreated into a world of my own creation. Deep inside my mind I discovered a powerful ability. My ability to concentrate fully enabled me to visualize any object I wanted to draw. My skill in drawing brought me great satisfaction. My hand accurately translated my visualization into my drawing. In my right hand, my superb control to draw served me well. To illustrate my thought pictures, my hand delivered accuracy and clarity.

Folks acknowledged beauty in the drawings I created. Frequently, grownups complimented my illustrations. They appreciated the pleasing proportions in the drawings. My confidence grew. I knew I could draw better likenesses than anyone else in all of St. Andrews.

My friends enjoyed the drawings I made. They asked me to create special drawings. When my friends saw my creations, they always reacted with delight. I learned that the more often I practiced drawing, the better my illustrations became. My friends informed their parents about my ability to draw likenesses. Eventually, whenever other parents needed clear detailed drawings for work, they employed me to create drawings.

In addition to producing all types of leather for customers, our tannery transformed the raw material of animal hides into other important merchandise. Glue was among the most important products from tanneries. Glue permanently fastened objects together. Glue was in high demand. Shoemakers, carpenters, bowyers among the customers who acquired glue from our shoppe. In order to extend the life of wooden objects, raw wood needed to be finished and protected. Carpenters applied lacquer to protect wood surface from moisture and dirt. Lacquer also protected wood from scratching and abrasion. In our tannery, we also worked with stains and dyes. Stains protected leather. Stains also made leather beautiful. Customers desired different color stains for leather and wood. Stains enhanced the beauty and durability of wood products.

Tanners produced one more commodity valued by our community. Eventually, I built my life on that commodity. That product provided me the opportunity to make my contribution to the community led by the Holy Church. Our shoppe produced and sold fine parchment. The Cathedral purchased nearly all the parchment we produced. The scribes became our most important parchment customers. For their important writing tasks, the Cathedral scribes demanded the finest high-quality parchment. All the codices in Scotland were written on fine high-quality parchment.

Animal hides furnished the raw material for parchment. Any type of hide could produce parchment. However, to produce the finest parchment, sheep hides were preferred. Shearing the valuable fleece did not remove all the hair from the hide. Not all sheep hides were sheared before the hide was removed from a carcass.

The tannery contained huge vats. The vats were constructed to be large enough to submerge several entire hides in the chemicals for days. The soaks usually required a fortnight, (or fourteen days). The first vat held a chemical to remove all the hair from the hide. Each day we stirred the contents in the vats two or three times. After soaking, the wet hide was draped over a frame. Tanners used a long knife to scrape the hide to remove all the hair. To make leather, the hides soaked in a solution mixed with vegetable matter that contained tannin. Though most vegetation contains tannin, tree bark is the preferred source. Different varieties of tree bark, nut shells, even leaves, determined the color of the leather.

Hides destined to become parchment also began treatment in vats. But the chemical solution in the parchment vats differed markedly from the tannin vats. To make parchment, hides soaked in a solution of lime and water. The soak required an additional ten days. Upon removal from the lime and water vat, the hide was secured to a wooden frame. The tanner stretched the wet hide until taut. Using a large, rounded knife, workers 'punched' the wet skin. The rounded knife blade scraped the rough spots away. Removal of all rough spots produced a smooth surface. Both the hair side and the skin side received similar processing treatment.

When satisfied that the skin surface was smooth, the tanner moved the framed hide to the drying room. They stood the rack, frame, and skin on edge until the skin dried completely. Workers spread chalk dust on the dry parchment and rubbed lightly with a pumice stone. When the hide dried completely, the tanner cut the material out of the frame using a sharp knife. The process transformed wet, smooth skin into high quality parchment. Parchment presented the best surface for writing and drawing. Parchment accepted and permanently locked ink, paint, dye. Even metallic liquids, like gold leaf bonded to parchment. Drawing and writing on parchment preserved the message clearly and accurately for as long as the parchment was properly cared for. Books made with parchment have lasted more than a thousand years.

After cutting the standard sized sheet of parchment out of the frame, some scrap parchment remained in the frame. Father saved the larger parchment scraps for me to practice ink drawing. When Father saw my drawings in the sand, he decided to see if I could draw as well with ink on parchment as I could with a stick in wet sand. First, father created a supply of quill pens from the flight feathers of geese. Since I use only my right hand, I needed the flight feathers from the left wing to produce my quill pens. Father showed me how to mix ink from carbon. Wood fires produced a plentiful amount of carbon. Father showed me how to load a small, but sufficient, amount of ink in the quill pen. I used the ink in the quill pen to draw on the parchment surface.

Creating a drawing on parchment in ink offered far more challenge than creating a drawing with a stick in the sand. However, whether drawing in the sand or drawing on parchment, the act of drawing remained similar. I liked drawing. I wanted to get better. I knew the way to improve my skills at drawing was to practice drawing. I practiced drawing every day. As my drawing improved, Father presented larger, more valuable pieces of parchment to me. The first time he gave me a full piece of parchment I was nervous because I did not want to mess it up. I also felt very excited. I wanted to create a beautiful drawing

Father arranged for me to visit the scribes in the Cathedral. The scribes invited me to view the extremely valuable and awesomely beautiful, illuminated manuscripts. What I saw on the manuscripts made a deep impression on me.

For my first full piece of parchment, I decided to create a drawing that used the illuminated manuscript as a model. On my first attempt I was not completely satisfied with the results. I knew I could do a better drawing. Father saw my work differently than I did. He praised the work. When I pointed out one of my mistakes in the drawing, Father reminded me. "You made mistakes on parchment before, Thomas. You know how to fix mistakes. You fixed your mistakes by very carefully scratching the ink out of the parchment with a knife blade. But you might have to rub a wee bit of chalk powder where you scratched in order to repair and smooth the parchment again. Then, fix the mistake." Following that reminder, as I continued to work with ink and parchment I gained confidence.

Our tannery contracted to supply parchment on a regular routine schedule to the scribes at the Cathedral. One of the elder canons who worked as a scribe came to the tannery. He came to gather the standing order of parchment. While there, the canon saw my work. He asked Father if he could borrow a sample of my work on parchment. Father agreed.

The canon showed my drawing to the Bishop, Henry Wardlaw (Bishop from 1403-1440). That was how the bishop learned about the drawings created by the little one-handed Tanner lad. After Bishop Wardlaw saw my work, he visited our tannery. The bishop's visit surprised Father and Mother. An in-person visit from the bishop, brought great honor to our tannery. He stated that he visited our tannery to fulfill a specific purpose. He desired to speak directly with my parents and me together. Bishop Wardlaw proclaimed to Father and Mother that 'God touched my right hand'.

Chapter 17 | 1458 | The One-Handed Scribe

Brother Tanner

I remember the exact words the bishop delivered when he spoke to my parents. Nearly sixty years later, I still hear the tone of Bishop Wardlaw's voice.

"God has chosen Thomas to perform a sacred holy task."

I remember complicated feelings. I felt strange. I felt humbled. I felt honored. I felt all those emotions at the same time.

The bishop's statement pleased Father and Mother. My parents appreciated that Bishop Wardlaw recognized my talent as a gift from God. Mother and Father also believed that my talent came from Heaven.

Bishop Wardlaw issued a formal invitation. He asked me to join the canons who worked as scribes. My task would be to use my talents to illustrate the holy books as illuminated manuscripts. The priests who read the Holy written word shared my illustrations with their congregations.

If I accepted the invitation, I would eventually wear the long, wide sleeved black woolen tunic, the black leather girdle, and the shoulder cape connected to the long-pointed hood. Those were the garments worn by the Augustinians. They were the Holy men in St. Andrews called the 'black robes'.

Neither my parents nor I could imagine refusing an invitation from Bishop Wardlaw. When I became of age, I accepted the bishop's invitation to join the Augustinians. For the remainder of my mortal life, I observed the rule of St. Augustine. (Purpose and basis of common life, prayer, moderation and self-denial, safeguard chastity and fraternal correction, care of community goods, treat the sick, ask for pardon, forgive others, governance and obedience and observance of rule). I adopted the Augustinian charism (gift from the Holy Spirit) which guided our community. My service began by illustrating pages for the illuminated codex copied at the Cathedral. "Make the illuminations beautiful." Bishop Wardlaw's words of instruction guided me as I drew and painted the designs and illustrations.

I felt blessed that I found the proper place for my talents to spread the Word of God. My love for drawing and painting served the people in God's community. The scribes produced Holy books for the churches in Scotland. The illuminated manuscripts enabled priests to illustrate readings from the Holy Word when they shared the message with their parishioners. Bishop Wardlaw continued, "We know that beautiful illuminations require time to create. You will need time to plan, time to design, and time to create the important illuminations we expect. We grant you the time you require. We want beauty. Create illumination that is as close to perfection as you can achieve. We have no concern about how fast you work. We want the illumination to accompany the words to be beautiful."

I now know that Bishop Wardlaw intended to remove pressure from me to produce the Holy work assigned to me. I appreciate his intention. However, I suffered a painful lesson. I learned that perfection is truly unattainable. Regardless of the amount of time available, perfection always eludes humans. My work satisfied my superiors. They were thrilled with my creations. I heard their praise. At first, I felt ashamed. I knew my work failed to achieve perfection. I saw the imperfections in my creation. I criticized the illustrations I produced harshly. Certainly, I was more critical of my work than others. Each imperfection mocked me. I struggled. I felt compelled to make each illustration perfect.

I attempted to fix my imperfect work. Unfortunately, I learned that even though parchment is repairable, there exists a finite number of times that parchment may be repaired. The amount of scratching, sanding, and powder that parchment can tolerate does exist. When the limit is crossed, that piece of parchment is damaged. It is beyond repair. At that point, the only option remaining is to cut off and remove the damaged piece. Then stitch a partial page on the remainder of the page to replace the damaged piece. Stitched repairs are far from seamless. Stitching parchment produces an ugly repair. The stitches form a permanent scar across the hand lettered page.

I humbly confess that when attempting to fix my own work, during my pursuit of perfection, far too often I destroyed the work of others. I destroyed pages my fellow scribes already completed. To see the painstaking work that my brother scribes completed get destroyed, hurt them deeply. When I realized I had hurt my fellow scribes I felt ashamed. I also hurt. I felt so bad that I was the one who had damaged the work they produced.

My pursuit of perfection haunted me. I said many prayers. After a long, long time, I begged forgiveness and I humbled myself. I discovered a more effective pathway to serve my Lord while illuminating the manuscripts. Eventually, I learned. I must accept my own humanity. I must accept my human limitations. When I realized that no human ever attains perfection, I felt enlightened.

Rather than pursue perfection, I followed a different pathway. To guide my passion, I discovered a different pursuit. For an illustrator, perfection provides the wrong target. I abandoned my pursuit of perfection. In its stead, I began the pursuit of excellence. I learned that the right goals to pursue are excellence and goodness.

While I worked in the scriptorium, I experimented. I began to copy the letters inked on the pages. Copying the letters compelled me to study. I committed the patterns I observed to memory. Memorization of each letter enabled instantaneous letter recognition. I ascertained that the letters were not the words. Soon, I realized how each letter combined with other letters. Seeing the ways that letters combined with others formed a critical step to understand the formation of words on parchment.

My fellow scribes helped me learn to read. Patiently, they explained how the letter combinations represent sound. At first, I watched the scribes point to individual letters using their fingers. They moved their fingers from left to right under the letters to keep their places while reading. They modeled the process of reading for me. I heard the scribes vocalize sounds which were associated with the letters. The scribes read the sacred text to me out loud. Their reading helped me to acquaint sounds with patterns of letter connections and combinations. I realized my brothers made a sound for each letter combination. The process of seeing letters, then recognizing the sounds connected with the letters excited me greatly. I hungered to learn more about how the process of sound representation on parchment worked.

When the scribes read from the texts, they always said each word out loud. Their fingers indicated which word they were reading. The pointing finger also helped them keep their place on the page. Sometimes the canons spoke loudly enough for everyone in the room to hear what they were reading. When we all worked in the scriptorium, the scribes did their best to keep their voices soft. They did their best to read at a low volume. They attempted to read softly enough so that only the reader could hear the words he formed. Several scribes read aloud at the same time. All scribes read as softly as possible. They did not want to interfere with the concentration of other scribes. So many different soft voices reading different words blended together to form a humming buzz. The many voices of active reading combined to form a backdrop for scholarly study.

For a certain period of time each day I watched and listened to one of the canons read aloud from the text. I paid close attention to where he pointed. I wanted to say the words he spoke. As I observed, I listened. Something clicked for me. The combinations of letters and patterns began to connect with the sounds the canon uttered. I experimented. I realized that I could use my finger to point at the word. I made the sounds that were represented by the letter combinations. I experienced a joyful epiphany. That was the moment I realized that I could read.

After I received the explicit instructions for reading from my fellow canons, I began to understand the letters. I began to understand how the letters formed the words. Even though my job was to illustrate the manuscript with my drawings, within a year of my arrival in the scribes' room, I realized that I could read. My fellow canons expressed excitement upon seeing that I possessed the ability to read text. They were astonished at how quickly I picked up the process. They decided to further my learning. They engaged me with direct instruction for more patterns to practice. I understood each explanation. I memorized every pattern. The canons invited me to ask questions. They wanted me to inquire about any point I did not understand.

Learning excited me. The canons glorified knowledge. I continued to imitate their behavior. I sounded out the words, the same way the scribes modeled. The scriptorium was never silent. As the scribes copied each letter they said each word out loud. Another canon compared each word on the copy to each word on the original. Seldom would a mistake be found during the copying process. The aim of giving our best effort was to ensure that each copy obtained perfect accuracy. However, when a mistake was found, the scribe fixed it. First, the scribe scratched the ink mistake out of the parchment. Second, the scribe rubbed chalk powder on the scratched spot until the parchment was dry and clean. That two-step process fixed the mistake. We used the same two-step process my father taught me how to fix a mistake when I began drawing on parchment.

In 1408, Bishop Wardlaw announced the opening of a new university. St. Andrews University became the first university in Scotland. My fellow scribes and canons circulated a petition. Without my knowledge all signed the petition to recommend to Bishop Wardlaw that I, Brother Tanner become admitted as a student at the new University.

I became the one-handed scribe, Brother Tanner.

Chapter 18 | 1458 | Lammas Day Memories

Brother Tanner

I remember the final Lammas Day Festival for the old century as clearly as if it occurred yesterday. All the people in St. Andrews looked forward to the new year. The new year would bring a new century. The new century promised a new time for Scotland. St. Andrews developed into a center of learning. Many gathered to study and listen to learned men discourse on subjects like mathematics, philosophy, and religion. In all Britain only two recognized universities existed. Oxford and Cambridge rarely admitted young Scots. To receive a university education, Scots travelled to the continent of Europe, usually France. We held high hopes for a letter from the Pope to establish a university. A university in St. Andrews would complement the Great Cathedral. When the Papal letter arrived, St. Andrews opened as the site of the first university in all Scotland.

Among our group of twelve friends, only Bessie and David, the Shepherds, were absent that Lammas day. They performed their daily work outside of the burg. They shepherded the flock on the Links. David and Bessie were unable to attend the festival that day.

In Scotland, Pilgrimage Season began in the last half of spring, the months of May and June. Pilgrimage continued through the first half of summer, July, and August. Then the Pilgrimage Season waned. Lammas marks the middle day of summer, exactly halfway between the Summer Solstice (the first day of Summer) and the Autumnal Equinox (the first day of Fall). Large crowds attended St. Andrews Lammas Festival.

Ten of the twelve friends, including my older sister Margaret and I, manned our families' trade booths. On Market Gait trade booths clustered tightly together. Due to the proximity of booths, customers could easily visit several shops. Market Gait lay between the two main streets in the burg, North Gait and South Gait. We worked long hours during festival. All family members took a turn. During one part of the day, we worked in our family Shoppe. Other times, we manned the booth on Market Gait. We sold our goods to fair goers and pilgrims.

Our families wanted us to experience the Lammas Festival. As often as possible, our parents freed us from managing the booth or securing the shoppe. Our families granted us free time. Parents encouraged us to explore. They insisted that we enjoy the festival. As long as we remained together in a group, consisting of up to twelve friends, our families believed we were quite safe. In fact, with so many pilgrims, there were many strangers roaming around St. Andrews. Our parents demanded that we band together, with any other available members from the circle of friends. We wanted to experience the festival. We loved to explore the activities together with friends.

As we grew older, all of us enjoyed the entertainment at the festival. Later in our lives, some of us participated in the many activities. We all loved dance. Most of us competed in the games.

Usually, during a festival, we reveled in the experiences available along Market Gait the sights. We loved the sights. To celebrate festival, many people arrayed themselves in richly colored attire.

Sounds punctuated the activities of Lammas. Songs featured voices and instruments. Bagpipes blared, drums rolled and beat. Only three years before, the pipes and drums summoned the Clan Chattan and Clan Kay to battle. King Robert III invited the Clans to settle their feud once and for all at the Battle of North Inch, an island in the River Tay near Perth. Both sides began the contest with 30 men. At the end, Clan Chattan claimed 10 survivors. Only one man from Clan Kay lived. The horrified King Robert granted royal honors to the victorious Clan. The lone Clan Kay survivor received a pardon.

Songs from bagpipe and drum stirred us. The powerful music moved our bodies and inflamed our souls. To drive men into the blood lust violence of battle, Scots sounded the pipes and beat the drums. We recognized how bagpipe and drum affected our emotions.

The aroma of fresh cooked meats and fresh baked breads wafted over the town. Delicious smells beckoned Pilgrims and fair goers to buy. Sweet succulent scents whetted our appetites. The breads were plentiful. Usually, the Baker's family found fresh hot bread for us to enjoy.

For nearly two hundred and fifty years, the Royally Chartered Lammas Day Festival enlivened our royal Burg of St. Andrews. In the year 1153, it was recorded that King Malcolm granted the original Royal Charter to the Lammas Day Festival. We celebrate Our St. Andrews Lammas Market as the oldest Fair in all of Scotland. To express thanks for the first harvest of the year, families journeyed to celebrate at our Fair in St. Andrews, from all around Scotland.

Lammas Day marked the harvest of the first wheat crop for the season. The wheat crop harvest meant that people would eat freshly baked bread from this year's harvest. No longer would folks be forced to subsist on scarce, too often rancid, and rotted remnants from the previous year. People celebrated the successful crop with an important traditional rite during Lammas. From each household, someone brought a fresh baked loaf of bread. The fresh loaves were baked using flour milled from the newly harvested grains. A priest blessed the fresh bread. The loaf was broken into four pieces. One piece of the fresh loaf was placed in each of the four corners of the church building.

By early August the summer grass no longer continued to grow tall and fat. Reapers worked to complete the final hay crop harvest for the year. Long summer daylight hours enabled reapers to work extra hours each day, if required, to finish the job on schedule. By the time the Lammas Festival begins, August 10th, (Old Style), reapers celebrated completion of their annual task. The final crop of hay is the most critically important crop of the summer growing season. To make the hay crop, reapers must harvest, process, and store enough hay in order to supply feed that will last throughout the winter for the cattle. Storing a sufficient supply of feed to maintain healthy livestock throughout the winter is crucial. Each household kept enough dairy cattle to produce the dairy products throughout the cold and dark time of the year.

The process of hay production embodied a sequence of several steps. First, reapers mowed the fat grass using their long, sharp scythes. Second, workers raked the new mown grass to spread the fresh grass carefully. Spreading the grass hastened the drying time. Warm sunlight, combined with powerful gusting winds quickly removed the moisture from the grass. The dried grass transformed into hay. Once dried, the hay needed to be moved to safe, dry storage areas. Moving the hay meant it must be gathered, then stacked. Stacking the hay was an important step. Stacking protected the hay from rotting in the field if exposed to a sudden, soaking rain. To thoroughly dry and complete the harvest of the summer 'fat grass', workers constructed haystacks. Then, the hay was loaded onto carts to be delivered to barns and storage sheds.

Harvest of the lush hay marked an important date in the calendar year. To find grass suitable to nourish the St. Andrews milk cows required other pastures. The people of St. Andrews knew that the cowherd would drive the cattle herd to other pastures. For the next nine months only sheep and goats would graze there. When the fat grass greened anew the following Spring, cattle returned to graze on the Links.

Way out past the Swilcan Burn, across "The Old Stone Bridge", on the far side of the Links away from town, David and Bessie managed the flock of three hundred. In the flock, sheep belonged to three separate entities. Parts of the flock were owned by the Shepherd family, the Weaver family, and the Cathedral. Sheep did not know there was a Festival in St. Andrews. Quietly, the flock grazed on the stubble remaining from the newly mown grass covering the Links. Wherever sheep graze, shepherds watch over their safety. On the Links that Lammas day, two shepherds, accompanied by their two collies, tended the flock.

David and Bessie knew that the rest of the Shepherd family worked in town. They also knew that all their friends and their friends' families worked and experienced The Lammas Fair. The Shepherds thought everyone in the vicinity of St. Andrews attended the Fair. The two did not believe any other people were on the Links with them while they tended the flock.

Chapter 19 | *2019* | Festivals and Games

The Professors - Lecture Notes

Professor Greenwood – "In Scotland, we call boys, "lads", and girls, "lasses". Together, lads and lasses participate in games, compete in sports, feel the music, and dance. They perform with great enthusiasm. Games guide lads and lasses to learn how to compete. The spirit of competition requires athletes to train in order to build their muscles and strengthen overall fitness. Lasses and lads practice athletics and dance. Practice enables athletes and dancers to develop their skills, improve their timing and hone their sense of rhythm."

Dr. MacGregor – "Dancing enhances the sense of balance. Dances challenge the body and the mind to perform intricate movement. Music mixes rhythm and harmony. Music and dance practice sharpens precision timing. Devotion to the dance guides young Scots to develop strategic thinking skills. Games, training, practice, and dance enable Scots to develop their wit. Lads and lasses learn the value of always playing to win. For all these reasons, Scots love and appreciate festivals filled with dance and music. Often, festivals featured athletic games and contests early in the day, followed by music and dance into the evening."

SCOTTISH GAMES

Professor Greenwood – "Scottish folk love games. Difficult games are held in special favor by Scots. They passionately track games that challenge strength, require stamina, command skills, reward speed, demand accuracy and test intelligence. Men and women first learn to participate and compete in a variety of games at early ages. They enjoy the spirit of competition with their friends and countrymen. As spectators, Scots especially relish a tough, evenly matched contest. Contests which offer both sides a fair chance to win bring out the kind of competition Scots' favor.

Scottish parents watch their young people develop skill and strength with great pride. Parents encourage children to practice for and compete in the games. Scots enjoy contests which pit the athletes from their burg versus athletes from another burg. Scottish parents expect lads and lasses to practice with passion and train hard. Lads and lasses listen to their coaches. Coaches teach athletes to improve skills. Coaches instruct athletes to develop specific techniques. Athletes learn how to set strategy to compete in every event.

Dr. MacGregor – "Scottish lads and lasses grow up together. At play, from very early ages, they learned to compete and to win. Races marked their first contests. Sometimes they raced on flat smooth courses. They raced were at various distances. Sprints covered only a hundred yards to test maximum speed. Long races, sometimes several miles in length, demanded stamina. Other races, like the Steeplechase possessed degrees of difficulty. Steeplechase offered more demanding obstacles than merely running. The obstacles included hurdles, water puddles and jumps.

Scots also love other types of contests. Some contests feature objects flying through the air. Lads and lasses like to throw many different objects. For example, in the games, one object which participants propel to fly through the air is called the caber."

Professor Greenwood – "The caber is formed from a huge pine log. First, the thrower must lift the caber vertically. After completing the lift, the next task is to balance the caber. Once balanced, the thrower then runs while carrying the caper in order to build up enough momentum. The thrower utilizes momentum from the run, in order to throw the caber in the prescribed manner. The caber must be launched so that the bottom of the caber completely flips over the top end. The bottom flips over the top while the entire caber is airborne. Judges determine the winner of the caber throw. Judges observe the pathway for the completely flipped bottom end. The caber which lands closest to a direct line from the launch was declared winner. To successfully throw the caber, demanded an exceptional combination featuring strength, balance, timing and accuracy."

Dr. MacGregor – " The hammer is another object Scots love to see fly through the air during their games. The hammer is a heavy iron sledge attached to a long wooden handle.

The thrower spins around and around, faster, and faster. While spinning fast, the thrower whirls the heavy hammer around the shoulders. The thrower whirls the hammer faster and faster in an effort to reach maximum speed. At the point of maximum centrifugal force, the thrower releases the hammer. Up, up, and away! The hammer flies through the air. The winner in the hammer throw is determined by which hammer flies the farthest distance. The hammer throw tests strength, balance, and timing. Both men and women compete in the throwing the hammer. The hammer thrown by men weighs 16-20 pounds. For women, the hammer weighs about a quarter less than the weight of the hammer the men throw."

Professor Greenwood – "The shot-put event uses a heavy stone. Both men and women compete in throwing the shot put. Propulsion of the shot actually occurs by a push, not a throw. Without going over the line, the thrower pushes the shot as fast as possible in order to launch it to fly through the air. The shot that flies the farthest distance is the winner.

Scots love to see athletes 'paint the sky with beauty'. Hammer throw, the shot put, and the caber toss are examples of objects that fly through the air, from the Scottish Games. When Scots witness an object 'paint the sky with beauty', the phrase illustrates a feeling and describes the joy Scots feel from the throwing games. To see an object fly through the air continues to fascinate spectators."

Dr. MacGregor – "Scots also love the competition in another game, a team game called 'Tug of War'. Eight people form a side. A large rope was stretched between both teams. Each team member grips the rope. A line is drawn midway between the two teams. The judge tied a ribbon at the midway point between the first contestant on each team. The object of 'Tug of War' is to pull the other team until the ribbon crosses your line. In 'Tug of War', a successful team possesses superb strength and power. The teams are evenly matched in order to provide a spirited competitive contest for spectators to enjoy. Strength is a requirement but because the teams are matched, however, strength alone is insufficient to win top level 'Tug of War' competition. Winning teams must work to pull together in rhythm. Successful teams must possess determination to prevail, even while they endure aching, straining fatigue in every muscle fiber.

'Tug of War' rewards teammates who learn to focus on the positive. Even when the team can only gain, or lose half an inch, during the contest, the team that is able to remain positive, acquires a significant advantage. Often, the 'Tug of War' looks like a stalemate. To spectators, it may appear that neither team is working. At those moments, teammates must dig in with determination to maintain position. Then, the team must find some advantage, some way to overcome the inertia of the stalemate. If, and when, the advantage is opened, the team must press the advantage on to victory."

Chapter 20 | 1399 | Friends Discuss the Games

"I do love watching the Games." Margaret the Tanner announced.

"Aye, attending the Games is joyful. It is thrilling to watch athletes display their strength." Heather the Carpenter agreed.

During Lammas Festival, the friends enjoyed watching the Games. Like all the other audience members, the competitors' exhibition enthralled the friends. Skill, strength, and speed displayed by the athletes testified to the amount of time they invested in training. Throughout the games the performances demonstrated commitment to the pursuit of excellence. Men and women, lads and lasses competed in the games. While the friends watched the competition, they shared their delight in the games. In order to build strength, to gain speed, to enhance stamina, and to develop skill, athletes trained diligently.

William the Weaver added, "I love the races. The runners are so gifted. They glide easily and smoothly. Their legs stretch so far. They run so swiftly their feet barely seem to touch the earth. I love to run, but I could never run as fast as the champions."

"Watching the men throw the caber is exciting! That log is incredibly big and heavy. I am amazed anyone can lift a log as long, as heavy and as unwieldly, as a caber. After lifting, the competitor must hold the caber upright. He must maintain balance in that same position until the judges signals. To hold the caber upright demands exceptional strength. But that's not all that is required. Maintaining the log in an upright position, adds the element of balance to the element of strength. At the judge's signal the athlete throws the huge, heavy log up in the air. The log must be thrown so that the bottom flips over the top of the caber. Wow! The contestants are so strong and so well balanced." Jonathan the Shoemaker marveled.

Rhona the Weaver continued, "True. Yet strength and balance are not enough to win the caber contest. Accuracy determines the winner. The winner tosses the bottom of the log over the top end so that the caber lands in the straightest line from the launch."

Barbara the Bowyer offered, "I like to watch the shot put. Both men and women compete to see who will win the championship. Sixteen pounds of iron sphere for the men. Eight pounds for women. The shot put is a contest for the strong. Did you see how far that big heavy ball flew through the air when the champion shot putters threw?"

"When I saw that big iron ball fly through the air, I felt thrilled. There were times, that the ball travelled more than 20 paces before thudding to the earth." David the Shepherd noted.

Robert the Carpenter explained, "I noticed that after the shot putter lifts the heavy ball, she or he carefully balances the heavy shot on the fingertips of the throwing hand. At first glance, I thought that the throwers must place such a heavy ball in the palms of their hands. I believe I would need to place the heavy iron sphere in the palm of my hand, in order to just hold the shot-put."

"My fingers are far too small and much too weak to hold the heavy shot put in one hand on my fingers. I am sure that I would have to place it in the palm of my hands, also." Bessie the Shepherd observed.

Russell the Bowyer responded, "Interesting observation, Bess. However, if you put the ball in the palm of your hand, do you think you could throw the shot? I don't believe it would be possible to throw it from your palm. I believe you will not be able to throw the shot from your palm. I know you will be unable to guide the iron ball into the air."

"Aye, I believe Russell is correct, Bessie. In order to throw the heavy iron ball, just like throwing the caber, you must use your fingers." agreed Robert.

"If I am ever going to learn to do any of these contests of strength, if I ever hope to propel an object into the air, I will need to develop powerful fingers. For champions, strength and control work together." Jonathan concluded.

"True." agreed Thomas.

Russell interjected. "I was just thinking about what we do when we shoot an arrow. To pull the bow string to full draw on the longbow also requires strong fingers. I recall when I first learned to draw an arrow on the bow. I first tried to pull the bow string back. I tried to use my whole hand to pull the string. That was a disaster. I rapidly discovered there was no way to control the arrow nock while simultaneously pulling the bowstring with my palm. Father taught me how to pull the bowstring to full draw using three fingers."

David continued, "The accuracy we expect to attain when we launch an arrow demands far more upon skill than upon strength to pull the bow string to full draw. To shoot an arrow accurately the archer holds the bowstring steady at full draw. At full draw the archer controls the nocked arrow so that it remains perfectly still. The archer holds the bowstring at full draw long enough to aim the arrow precisely on target."

"With the target sighted in, the archer releases three fingers in a smooth equal motion. An accurate shot requires that all three fingers release the string simultaneously." William added.

"If the release is unbalanced, the arrow will sail off target." David stated.

"An arrow that misses the target is wasted. To shoot arrows accurately, archers practice regularly. Skilled archers invest many hours in practice. To maintain their accuracy and rhythm archers need to train. Training aids archers to develop the necessary power to draw the heavy bows consistently. Archers must deliver arrows reliably. Regular training helps archers to maintain deadly accuracy. The combination of precise accuracy, rhythm, and timing to launch a flight of arrows simultaneously, plus the knock down power of war arrows helps to win the King's battles. Training develops confidence in the archer. Archers develop confidence in the other members of the company." Russell emphasized.

"Physical strength is important for a competitor to compete successfully in the shot putt. However, to become a champion requires more than strength. In addition to power and strength the best throwers possess balance and timing.

The champion thrower also needs body control. Judges watch to see that the thrower's foot does not go over the line. If the foot goes over the line even by a part of an inch, the throw is judged a 'scratch'. When the thrower 'scratches', that throw is completely disallowed. To become a champion shot putter, takes talent and strength certainly, but champions practice for many days. Like archers, the strength, skill and close to perfect timing to release the iron ball makes the difference." William expounded.

Robert stated, "I thought Hammer Throw was the most exciting event. Throwers swung the hammer round and round their heads. They twirled the big heavy hammer, faster and faster. Around and around the throwers twirled and turned their bodies. Their muscles bulged and strained. At the precise right moment, the thrower released the hammer. And away the hammer flew. It sailed high and far. Farther and faster than anything else that was thrown at the games. The only things that flew farther through the air than the hammer were the arrows."

"The Hammer Throw is exciting and very dangerous. Throwers hurl a heavy hammer at deadly speed." Heather said.

"The hammer throw demands great strength. Champion hammer throwers learn to harness their strength into controlled power. The throwers possess an incredible sense of balance. They hone and develop exquisite timing. Through practice, champion throwers learn to feel the instant to release the hammer during the throw to attain maximum velocity. Judges measure accuracy as an element of a successful hammer throw, also."

"To lift the hammer, I would have to use the palms of my hands. I know I could not lift a hammer using just my fingers." Heather confessed.

"But Heather, when the hammer throwers lifted the heavy hammer, they did use their fingers." David stated. "Let's think about how the hammer throwers performed their sport.

"To lift and hold the hammer, the hammer throwers could use their palms. Even whirling around the throwers could use their palms. But, like the caber throwers, the shot putters, and the archers, if hammer throwers attempted to release the hammer from their palms, there is no way they could release the twirling hammer with accuracy." Bessie explained.

"To throw the hammer successfully, throwers must develop strong fingers." Jonathan judged.

William summarized, "I see a pattern in all the Games. Especially the games we enjoy so much. I know we all love to watch the games where we can watch an object fly through the air."

"I see a pattern as well. To send an object through the air for accuracy and distance requires speed, power, and accuracy. Winning any event where an object flies through the air demands control. To control an object before and during a throw depends on strong fingers." Barbara stated.

"People say athletes perform with their hands. And they do, but only with parts of their hands. The parts of the hands the athletes use are the fingers. To achieve accuracy, the most important part of the performance, athletes guide an object by controlling part of their fingers. The more accuracy the sport demanded, the more skill the athletes train to develop the ends...the tips of their fingers. Think of the work we perform every day. To spin yarn our fingertips carefully draw wool from the pile and guide it onto the spindle. In the specialized trades, weaving, leather craft, carpentry, shaping bows and arrows, pottery, the touch of our fingers shapes the product. People say we work with our hands, but we know better. The 'feel' in our fingertips produces the professional quality workmanship. While people compliment us on our 'handiwork', we know our work is done with our fingers. The work should be called, 'finger work.'"

Margaret added, "The skill to send an object accurately flying through the air demands timing, rhythm and balance."

"There is more to the festival than Athletic Games." said Heather.

Agreed Rhona, "That's right. Didn't we all love the dancers, too?"

Robert reminded the Circle of Twelve, "While we were watching the dancers, it seemed like we all laughed and smiled."

"We laughed. We smiled. We clapped along with the beat of the music. Fiddlers, drummers, and the bagpipers played music. Their music makes everyone want to get up and dance." Russell recalled. "We felt the music as much as heard it. When we 'felt' the music we wanted to move."

"The dancers' steps matched the rhythm and beat of the music." Rhona observed.

"While dancers execute the steps and body movement for each dance, they must sustain their balance. Maintaining balance throughout the dance demands strength and stamina." explained Marion.

"Successful dancers and athletes develop a sense of balance, a feel for rhythm and exhibit superb timing." Bessie compared.

"Dancers and athletes acquire strength, develop skill, maintain balance, move in rhythm and execute with perfect timing because they practice and train." Russell concluded.

Chapter 21 | *1399* | A Roundtable Discussion Meeting

"We need a new game!" exclaimed Marion the Shoemaker, the youngest lass.

"Who said we need a new game?" inquired William the Weaver, the eldest lad.

"I did." answered Marion, proudly.

"What is wrong with the Scottish games? Why would we need another game? Marion, Why do you think we need a new game?" asked Margaret the Tanner.

Marion answered, "Don't get me wrong, Margaret. Don't misunderstand what I am saying. The Scottish games are wonderful. The games are thrilling. I love every one of the games. I appreciate the skill the athletes possess. I marvel at the strength the participants display. I never want the people of Scotland to stop a single one of our ancient traditional games. Every time we gather to observe athletic competition the games provide a joyful celebration of our Scottish heritage. However, we only see and share the experience of the games during Festival."

Russell the Bowyer continued, "Aye. Opportunity to compete is an issue, Marion. I agree with you. I support you. May I offer evidence that there is another problem with our traditional Games. I love that strength is celebrated. But it is impossible for every man, every woman, every lad, or every lass, to become the strongest athlete at the Games. For any given event, only one man, or only one woman can be crowned the champion."

Bessie the Shepherd continued, "I truly do love the races. Running is so important. Running an important part of the games. Sometimes we need to run when we manage the sheep. Running is also fun. But only one lad or lass can become the fastest runner."

Robert the Carpenter explained, "Becoming the fastest runner seems more to be a function of who was born to be the fastest. Running speed does not seem to be a skill, which can be nurtured and developed, as much as it is natural born talent, in order to be acknowledged as the fastest runner. True, a person can practice. And a person can improve physical conditioning by practice and training. But, as we experienced while growing up, playing, and competing together, the person who is the fastest runner, is the person who was the fastest runner. Barring injury, at a given distance that runner simply continues to be the fastest runner."

"We do need a new game." reiterated Barbara the Bowyer.

Jonathan the Shoemaker confirmed, "Aye. A new game is a grand idea."

Looking around to gauge each other, all twelve friends observed agreement in their friends' eyes. A consensus to invent a new game took root in their fertile minds.

"Okay, we are all in agreement. We need a new game. So," William inquired, "from this discussion we already know much of what we do not want in a new game. Let's turn this discussion around. Let's not focus on the negatives. Let's re-focus. Let's share our thoughts on positive outcomes. What is it that we do want in our new game?"

"I want our new game to be a physical game. I think we ought to design the game to test physical skills. Unlike a game like chess, where the competition is a contest of wills, yet chess competition offers no test of any physical skill." David began.

"Aye! I want a game that features a test of physical skills, too." Russell seconded David. "I think we can add more elements to our new game in addition to constructing a game which contains only physical skills. In most athletic contests we watched, we observed a measure of physical strength. I like the idea of combining physical fitness with the element of control which utilizes the combination finger strength and skills in a new game. Instead of a contest of brute strength, like lifting or throwing a heavy object, or pulling against a team of opponents in the 'Tug o' War'. I would like a game which rewards skills."

"I love the 'Tug o' War.'" William stated.

"William," Margaret questioned, "What is it that you love about 'Tug o' War'?"

"Thank you for the question. By responding, I can share my thoughts and feelings about 'Tug of War' with everyone. A couple of components come to mind, Rhona. I love best that 'Tug of War' is a contest of winner take all. 'Tug of War' functions like a trial. The competition tests a combination of elements. First, 'Tug of War' is the ultimate team competition. Every person on the team makes a commitment to give their all in the effort to win. The match tests strength, endurance, and commitment to work together. The team must exert explosive physical strength. Teammates face a serious test of their resolve, their determination. They take that challenge in front of the whole village. 'Tug of War' offers a strength of will power as an emotional strength.

At the conclusion of a great 'Tug of War' match, all participants are completely drained of strength. 'Tug of War' may provide the most intense team competition in the Games. Rarely do you see anyone celebrate at the end of a 'Tug of War' contest. All participants are totally spent. They can barely move. Often the winning contestants just lay flat on their backs in place. You can see their chests heaving up and down. They gasp for air. They are so tired they remain motionless until they recover. We see the participants give what looks like their last ounce of strength to win."

"Aye. Winning is surely great fun." Barbara agreed.

Robert observed, "I believe that winning is most fun when you are challenged. Standing up to some feeling of danger or facing a fear of failure provides challenge. When we face the fear of failure and we triumph over the feeling of danger in a tight contest, winning feels most exhilarating."

"What I love most occurs at the end of the match for 'Tug of War'. Everybody can see who won, and who lost. To determine who won the 'Tug of War', there is no need for a judge. Winning is exciting and fun. Losing feels excruciating." I hate losing. And I know everyone here hates losing too." William added.

"Aye. I hate losing. When I lose, it almost feels as if I succumbed to the danger." Jonathan continued.

"No one ever wants to lose at 'Tug o' War'. The competition is ferocious. Athletes want to win so much that every participant on both teams digs deep to summon every ounce of strength." William explained. "I wonder. Perhaps the athletes give their all in an effort not to lose."

"One competitor alone cannot win 'Tug o' War'. You are right, William. The effort demands a total team commitment to pull together. You can only taste winning the contest when all teammates completely commit. You must work together. Winning requires each team member to work as a part of a committed functioning team." Russell interjected.

"Winning a contest by working together as a team is the other reason, I enjoy the 'Tug o' War'. You win as part of a team. Or you lose as part of a team. Working together toward a common goal is critically important. And in 'Tug o' War', the entire team concentrates throughout the entire game on one single goal." William concluded.

"During the 'Tug o' War' contest there is often a time of stalemate. Sometimes, during the fierce struggle, it seems that there will be a tie between the opposing teams. But every time there seems to be a stalemate, there is always one person, on one team or the other, who refuses to give in. I hear that voice. 'No. We are not going to tie! We are going to win! No ties! Never give up!'" Robert added.

Barbara wondered. "Perhaps we can incorporate teamwork in our new game, as an important element."

"I like the idea of being part of a team!" Marion exclaimed.

Margaret refocused, "Aye. In addition, it seems to me that we might consider that the new game should incorporate something like the finger strength required to develop a skill in order to launch an object to fly through the air. Everyone enjoyed seeing the beauty of an object flying through the air. If we could find, or perhaps if we could invent, a set of skills to compete with each other in a game, that seems preferable to me. Especially when we compare our new game to a brute strength contest, like the game of the 'Tug of War'. We already noted that very little skill is involved in 'Tug of War'. Because there is so little skill, anyone can participate."

"I agree. I want the new game to reward that type of finger strength. I want the game to require the same type of finger skill, that same type of timing, that is so necessary to display mastery and control of an object flying through the air. I find that preferable to a contest of brute strength." Thomas argued.

Barbara wondered, "Our new game might be fun if the playing of the game lasts long enough to reward endurance. For example, we might design a game that requires maybe a morning, or an afternoon, to complete. I do not want to design another contest that ends quickly, like some of the throwing events, or running the shorter races, the dashes. For example, I submit that our game should require a significantly greater amount of time to complete than the amount of time to complete the one-hundred-yard dash, or the time for an arrow to reach its target, or a caber to flip over, or a hammer to launch and land."

"Do you believe we really can design a game that might last, say a few hours to complete?" Robert asked.

Rhona answered, "I believe we could. If we design a game that requires a few hours, there is another advantage we could consider. A game of such duration would invite us to talk with our friends. It would be so much fun to talk with friends at the same time we participate in the game."

Heather responded, "Aye. A game that incorporates walking and talking with friends is a great idea. Walking and talking with friends while playing outside sounds fun. Any day when I invest a morning, or an afternoon, with good friends offers the opportunity to create a memory that I know I shall treasure."

"I would enjoy a game that invites us to walk and talk with friends while we play." Marion said.

"Then this new game definitely needs to be played outside." stated Jonathan.

"I like to play games which require me to think, don't you? By that I mean, I enjoy a game that challenges me to examine a problem. I want to acquire accurate information. Then, I need to realize exactly what the problem is. Once I define the problem, I know my next step. I need to formulate a plan or choose a strategy, to solve the problem. I also need to execute tactical movements." Robert challenged.

Robert's sister, Heather, agreed. "Games that make me think, are the most fun. When a game engages me to think throughout the entire game, I pay close attention. To succeed at games that make us confront and face up to problems, requires us to determine a strategy. We think about possible solutions, then we select what we think will be the best solution.

Games invite us to think and help us to learn something about ourselves. When we immerse ourselves in games with friends, we learn more about our friends. Games engage us, stretch us to solve problems, and challenge us to improve and grow."

"Solving problems creates a more challenging game. Games that are challenging, are also more engaging, more compelling. Every time I solve a problem, I enjoy feeling successful." Rhona stated.

"Every time I solve a problem, or help someone solve a problem, I feel good." added William.

Margaret continued, "A game which continually presents new situations, forms a more challenging and interesting game. As we encounter new situations the game challenges us to reconsider our strategy. During the course of a two to three-hour game, players will need to adjust and to readjust strategy. Challenges from new situations will motivate players throughout the entire game."

"We definitely want our game to be interesting. If we do not build high interest, people will not want to play the game very long. If we want a game that requires a few hours, the game must build and maintain a very high interest level for every player." Thomas added.

"I agree completely that challenges are important. I wonder what types of challenges we can design into our game." Rhona said.

"I believe we can build a two to three-hour physical game which incorporates mental planning, selecting a strategy, problem-solving, tactical execution of physical skills, high interest and compelling challenges. I think we can add one more test to the game experience. The test to control emotions is part of the will power I admire in 'Tug of War'. Players commit to exert all their strength because they don't want to lose. A challenging game will test our emotions." William added.

"That is an interesting concept, William." Margaret pondered.

Chapter 22 | 1399 | Fear Of Failure

"What if we make challenges in the game border on feeling like danger? For the individual player, the reaction to danger will threaten on an emotional level. If we build challenges that seem like danger, I believe we will make the game test a player's emotional strength." David continued.

Bessie stated, "I don't think we want real physical danger in our game."

Rhona reinforced Bessie, "Nor do I."

David responded, "I apologize. I do not mean to imply that we want a game which includes real physical danger. We certainly do not want to create the real danger of death and life which occurred three years ago in Perth. That horrifying contest which the King witnessed from a grandstand. We want to create serious competition in a fair and challenging game, not the bloody resolution of a feud between clans."

The other friends acknowledged David's apology.

The memory of the Scottish tragedy in nearby Perth remained fresh in their young memories. They recalled hearing about the futile attempt by King Robert III to resolve a long and deadly feud between Clan Chattan and Clan Kay. The King ordered a staged battle. Thirty men for each side. Armed with swords, axes, and maces, the men competed for the winning Clan to march into battle as the right flank of the King. The men fought to the death. On the 'winning' side only ten men survived. On the 'losing' side, the last man lived only by leaping into the river. From the grandstand, the horrified King watched the bloody horror of men dying on the field.

All the friends recalled the mesmerizing sound of the pipes during Festival. The bagpipes stirred their blood. Stimulated by the pipes playing martial music, the friends experienced a feeling of willingness to march together into danger. Recollection of powerful feelings sent shivers up their spines.

"We want no situation in our game where someone might face the prospect of serious injury. Certainly, none of us desire deadly danger in a game. No, friends, I am thinking about a different kind of danger. Think about when we are pushed to our mental and physical limitations. What I think we want for the game is to construct that 'feeling'. The feeling that accompanies danger." David offered.

Margaret continued David's inquiry. "To establish this 'feeling of danger' offers an interesting aspect. David, are you suggesting that rather than life threatening danger, or perhaps serious, even debilitating injury, this other type of danger for us to consider is the 'feeling of danger'?"

William interjected, "Perhaps if we can inject this 'feeling of danger' as a 'fear of failure', there is an opportunity for us to add challenge to the game. Let's consider how to add a test to control emotions during the game. Think about the feelings we experience when we are confronted with the 'fear of failure'. The 'fear of failure' tests a player's ability to control emotions when confronted by a situation perceived as dangerous. The feeling from 'fear of failure' increases when danger seems more apparent as a part of the decision-making process. If somehow, we can design opportunities to incorporate the 'fear of failure' feeling, I think we might be able to make the game more challenging, more exhilarating, and much more exciting."

"Our game should reward those who approach problems by employing a process. Players who consider alternate strategies, and then select a smart plan, are most likely to successfully problem-solve. Participants who successfully utilize the physical skills they developed to overcome the emotional fear of failure should experience a rewarding feeling." Barbara summarized that aspect of game construction.

Bessie offered her insight to the group. "Players who remain clear headed, who control their emotions and overcome the 'fear of failure' should be rewarded. Players who lose control of their emotions should pay a price."

Margaret evaluated, "I really like these ideas. I want us think about some more ideas for the new game. Most important, I want the game to be structured so that our new Game and all of its rules are equally fair to all participants."

"There should be no advantage to being tall or being short, fast or slow, strong or slender in our game." Heather challenged.

"However," Rhona countered, "our game should incorporate rewards to players who invest in developing and improving skills."

"Likewise, physical fitness and endurance should play an important role to compete successfully in our new game." Robert continued.

Russell began the summation. "We all agree that we want a game that lads and lasses can play together. Each gender stands a fair chance to win our new game. We want a game that invites a player to develop control over a variety of different physical skills. The person who invests time and effort in practice to master a variety of physical skills, will be rewarded in our new game.

"We want a game that will reward the player who maintains mental clarity to solve a problem. Our new game will challenge a player's ability to manage and control emotions when confronted by a fear of failure." Bessie continued to summarize the ideas.

"New challenges should be faced every time one plays our game. Facing an element of danger provides a thrill. Finding solutions, should be rewarded by a feeling of satisfaction." Russell made the concluding statement for the group discussion.

The friends agreed that, like the physical Scottish games the friends observed, the new game should demand players to respect the necessity of challenging their balance. In addition, they wished for their new game to continue another of the traditions included in the traditional Scottish games. They wanted to include another joyous element so loved by Scots. They wanted to launch an object into the air. A flight they described as, 'painting the sky with beauty'.

Was there a way to launch an object to fly? Was there a possibility of seeing an object inscribe a parabola through the sky?

The twelve agreed that players should experience a thrill. They envisioned the feeling of satisfaction that accompanies the beauty of a well-executed shot. They believed that the game should interest players to strive continually to develop and improve rhythm and timing.

"The game will be played outside. We want to take advantage of the unique physical geography of the Links. The characteristics of the Links should come into play. The grassland, the Burn, the sandy soil, the bunkers, and the water will all be important elements in our game." William restated.

"Then we all agree to commit to work together to invent new game. Is everyone on board to work together? Are you as committed to this task as if you participated in a 'Tug of War' contest?" Margaret asked.

All the friends silently connected eyes with each one. From each friend, they found the same answer. They were committed. They were all in on their mission to create a new game.

William spoke, "If anyone doubts your desire to provide complete cooperation to complete this mission, now is the time to speak. As a group, nay, not a group. As a team, we must bring our own best effort and we must trust that each team member brings her/his best effort throughout this process."

"I am so excited. When I said, 'We need a new game', I meant it. But honestly, I had no idea the feeling would connect so deeply with all of you." Margaret observed.

"Aye. Nor did I believe we would connect on this idea so rapidly." Robert added.

"We have quite a list to consider!" Marion observed

"Before we leave, I believe we must agree on one more crucial element?" Barbara asked.

Chapter 23 | 1399 | Setting A Deadline

"What would that be?" Russell questioned.

Barbara continued, "Hear me out. Our fathers and mothers all run businesses."

"Aye. That is true." Jonathan answered.

Barbara explained, "To run a business, women and men are no longer serfs. Serfs were assigned to do their work every day. They were to finish their job for that day. Serfs worked for others.

To run a successful business, a man or a woman must manage time. For those businesses whose products require more than a day to manufacture, managing time effectively is crucial to make a profit. Reward comes to the business owner who completes the promised product at the contracted time.

Running a successful business is difficult. It is also satisfying. All our parents run their own businesses. They commit to provide the goods to the customers which they produce on time. They deliver the work as promised on schedule. When they deliver the product to the satisfied customer, on time, they receive the reward for a job well done."

"Our parents receive the reward of the payment for which they contracted." Jonathan added.

"Aye. Completing the sale allows the business to remain in business. Even better, successful owners can expand the business." Marion interjected.

William observed, "This seems to be a delightful digression. May I ask, why have you brought up business while we are discussing our commitment to invent a new game, Marion?"

"Thank you for getting us back on track, William. I was getting lost." David appreciated.

"I remember. I think Barbara mentioned something about a contract. Don't contracts have a due date? The product must be completed by a specified and agreed upon time. Our fathers and our mothers contract with the patrons to complete and deliver the product at a mutually agreed upon date." Rhona reminded.

"Aye. That was the original point Barbara made." Russell agreed.

Barbara proposed, "Michaelmas is about 60 days away. Michaelmas is the time of the year that people settle their accounts. The rents are due. New contracts are let. Even elections are held to serve the people for the next year. I think we need a due date. We need to set a deadline, like a contract. We agree unanimously in our commitment to complete the structure for the new game by a certain day. What do you think about using Michaelmas as the date for us to complete our new game?"

"Do you think we can invent our new game by Michaelmas?" Thomas asked.

"Does anyone think we are incapable of completing this mission in 60 days?" Margaret presented the null. "If we are in agreement, we set Michaelmas as our due date to complete the formation of the new game."

Bessie then added. "If we play our new game on the Links, there will be another crucial element."

"What is that?" Robert asked.

"The wind!" responded David the Shepherd. "The weather, the rain, the sun, the hail, the fog. And did I mention, the wind?"

Chapter 24 | 1458 | Shepherds' Idea

Brother Tanner

Children of St. Andrews, like lads and lasses all over Scotland, loved to play outside. At the end of the workday, following completion of our chores and lessons, my friends and I who lived and worked in town met.

Then, ten friends headed out to find our friends, the Shepherds on the Links.

We loved to compete. Nearly every day, we enjoyed a race from town to the Links. We ran races. Also, we raced by hopping, galloping or skipping. We loved to dream up new ways to race. In addition to inventing new ways to race, we loved to invent new ways to compete in many different activities. The Shepherds waited impatiently for us to arrive.

David the Shepherd and Bessie the Shepherd looked forward to our time of the day. They recognized us running from town towards the Links. Whichever Shepherd first spotted the friends, shouted to the other, "Race you!"

The sound of those two words challenged both Shepherds to race. They grabbed their crooks. Off they sped to the old stone bridge. The sister and brother ran from the oceanside towards the town side. For our races, we agreed that the old bridge crossing the Swilkan Burn, always marked the 'Finish Line'.

'Stay!' The Shepherds' faithful collies immediately obeyed. The dogs remained to watch over the flock. Easily and naturally, the two collies exerted gentle control. Disciplined collies freed David and Bessie to enjoy time with their friends. They ran to the Bridge.

In the spirit of friendly competition, we agreed upon a different kind of race for each day's contest. We took turns. Each day a different friend decided the kind of race.

There were racing contests: Who would win a race of 100 steps? Of 200 steps? Of 400 steps? Sometimes we ran, sometimes we skipped, sometimes we galloped like a horse, sometimes we hopped like a rabbit. Every once in a while, when Jonathan chose, we even ran backwards. Laughing and giggles accompanied funny falls when we ran backwards. Whatever the race, we all committed to compete as hard as we could.

To determine who first crossed the old stone bridge in the race from town the Shepherds served as judges. David and Bessie stood at the bridge, laughing. Enthusiastically, the two cheered us to exert maximum effort in the race. With arms and fingers lightly grasping the shepherds' crooks, the siblings stretched their arms. Two crooks reached completely across the old stone bridge to serve as the finish line. Whichever racer first grabbed a crook won that day's race.

Games and contests seemed to spring to mind every time we gathered. Whoever thought of a game or contest immediately shared the idea with the group. In addition to races, we enjoyed many types of throwing contests: Who could throw a rock the size of a chicken egg the farthest? Who could throw the most rocks to land in a hole from 10 steps? from 20 steps? from 30 steps? from 40 steps? Who could make a rock skip the farthest on the water? Who could make a rock skip the most times on the water? Whatever idea was chosen, we played hard. Once the contest began, every one of us competed. We exerted our best effort in each contest. In our competition we prized honesty and integrity. Every friend made certain to congratulate and to appreciate the winner for that day's contest.

As we grew taller, we realized that some of us matured at different rates. Our individual maturation differences provided some friends with exceptional physical advantages for some contests. Likewise, the differences meant that other friends would have no chance to win in other games. Some grew tall. Some developed powerful muscles. Some transformed into swift runners. Some developed agility and flexibility. Some could jump high. Some could jump far. Some friends could throw a rock farther than all the others. Some friends won the one hundred step race, every time. Some friends won the four hundred step race, every time. Some friends combined speed and endurance when running and jumping over obstacles while they maintained balance without falling and without slowing. As lads and lasses, we appreciated the strength, the speed, the balance, or the stamina required to win. For those reasons, we loved to compete in a variety of contests.

Already we knew that often we could most effectively solve a difficult problem by viewing the problem in a completely different way than the way that the problem first presented itself. Thinking about the process of problem solving led to Jonathan's idea of running a race backwards. By inventing a variety of ways to race, we discovered that we were able to expand opportunities for different friends to excel in a competition. We decided that we could enjoy more competitive fun if we created other contests besides racing and throwing. Some contests became quite creative. Who could stand on the right foot the longest? Who could stand on the left foot the longest? Who could do the most push-ups? Who could hold the plank position the longest? Who could hold the plank position on one hand the longest?

We strove to find and invent contests which would present each friend with an opportunity to excel. Perhaps, the variety of competitions we designed could provide every friend an opportunity to experience the joy that accompanies winning. We knew that every lass and every lad loved to participate and enjoy a fair opportunity to excel.

Deep in our hearts, all the friends knew that the main reason we loved competition so much, was because when we played, every single one of us played to win. We believed that when all friends put forth their very best effort, we all won. We all won by giving our best effort. Also, we all won because we all improved. Each friend truly believed that during competition, all friends also gave their best effort. Never did one friend ever 'let' someone win.

We realized that an equal opportunity or an equal chance, for each friend to win a particular race no longer existed. We already knew the fastest runner at each distance. In order to make the outcome of the races more competitive we attempted several possible solutions. For example, we instituted a 'head start' of several yards for some runners during some races. The head starts did manage to make the races more competitive. The fairer competition encouraged each runner to exert maximum effort. Head starts succeeded in making the races closer than when all the friends used the same starting line. However, even though the end of the races were more competitive, and the runners exerted maximum effort, the question remained: "Is a head start the best way to be fair to all participants?"

Eventually, we realized that what we missed most about carefree younger days was something different. We missed not knowing who would win a contest. Back then, almost every day a different friend won that day's contest. We agreed that we wanted quality competition. We wanted our contests to provide a fair chance for any friend to emerge victorious any time we played. We desired contests that presented a challenge for every single person. We meant to maintain a high degree of interest for each player. We wanted to keep the contests fun. Our new game design must encourage competition. We shared the belief that close competition would inspire all players to want to participate. A fair, competitive game would compel each participant to put forth the best effort throughout the game. We committed to design our game to provide a fair and equal opportunity for each participant to excel.

The race that day recalled our initial desire when we explored the concept of an entirely different game. We reviewed what we wanted in a new game. We began by remembering that the game should offer no advantage to a big and powerful person. There would be no advantage to the swift or lithe. Though strength would be important, the contest would not be determined by who was the strongest. Strength would be helpful in the new game, but strength alone does not win the game every time. Fitness, the combination of strength, stamina, and flexibility would also be tested.

We reminded each other that we wanted a physical game because physical games are exhilarating! Scots love physical games and challenging dance. We wanted a game which would demand the application of intelligence to solve problems. In our world, we thought smart choices ought to be rewarded. Likewise, the game should punish unwise decisions.

We were always sure that we wanted to play the game outside in the full grandeur of our Scottish landscape. We reminded ourselves that we put a premium on a game to enjoy as part of a team. Like boys and girls all over the world, the St. Andrews lads and lasses loved to talk with each other. And we loved to talk about games.

On this particular day, David and Bessie were very excited. All the lads and lasses sat talking. David blasted his whistle! The whistle blast signaled that we should stop talking immediately. Ten friends responded in exactly the same way to the whistle blast that the collies responded. Immediately, all lads and lasses quietened. We looked closely at David's face. We paid strict attention. Excitedly, we waited to hear from David and Bessie.

Chapter 25 | 1399 | Shepherds Share and Show

"Lads and lasses!" Bess began, "David and I have something to tell you. We want to share something new with you. Today, we heard something that we never heard before. Then, we saw something we never saw before. We thought about our new game, the dream we shared. Remember, we talked about wanting a game that is fair to all of us, regardless of size, strength, or speed. Though we don't yet know what the game will be, we feel compelled to share with you what we heard and what we saw. We want to share this experience with you now."

David told us about watching the sailors walk across the Links. David described the sailors as they waggled a stick shaped like an L–shaped shepherd's crook. Then, the sailors took a full swing with the stick and hit the ball.

Bessie described the alluring, compelling sound, "THWOCK!"

David told us about hearing the cheers when they heard, "THWOCK!" He told about viewing the swings and listening to the sounds. He reported that the "THWOCK!" was followed by cheers and congratulations.

Bessie told the circle of friends about the cracked sound, "*thunk*". She told us about hearing the moans from the sailors when they heard, '*thunk*'. That sound, she said, was followed by a loud combination of moans, coupled with good natured teasing from the other hitters.

David told us about seeing the ball fly through the air. He described how the soaring ball seemed to 'paint the sky with beauty'. When the stick and ball made the alluring sound of solid contact the group of sailors applauded and cheered. It was the contact that sent the ball soaring up, up, and away. While the ball soared through the air, loud cheers appreciated the effort. The sailors applauded the sheer beauty as they watched the arcing flight of the ball through the sky.

"The ball in flight", Bessie continued, "is a magical sight. The ball in flight reminds me of when we watch our fathers release an arrow from their longbows. I love to watch the arrows as they fly through their arc to the target. During Sunday archery distance practice contest, following the flight of an individual arrow as it soars so fast, so high and so far, is among my favorite sights. The flight of the arrow through the sky is simply beautiful.

"And", Bessie added, "it did not matter how big and strong the sailor was who swung the stick and hit the ball, to launch the ball into flight. What mattered was, when the stick connected with the ball, did we hear the solid sound, 'THWOCK?'"

"Sometimes a big sailor hit the ball. We heard the 'THWOCK'! And the ball flew".

David spoke. "Sometimes, a big sailor hit, and we heard '*thunk*'. Then the ball did not soar. In fact, then the ball didn't travel far at all.

Sometimes a little sailor hit the ball, 'THWOCK!' Then the ball soared just as the ball flew when we heard the solid hit sound from the big sailor.

And sometimes the small sailor hit the ball a '*thunk*'. Then the ball didn't go far at all."

"Hitting a ball with a stick does sound like something fun to do." Marion the Shoemaker wished.

"I can think of many things I would like to hit with a stick." Her brother Jonathan snickered.

"I would like to hit you with a stick, right now." Marion countered.

Jonathan teased, "Aye! I bet you would. But how would you like it if I hit you with a stick?"

"That I would not like." Marion laughed.

David resumed the conversation, "Aye, so let's concentrate on the idea of hitting a ball with a stick. Forget about hitting your sister or your brother with a stick, please."

"Och! I suppose you are right. I am all in on the idea of hitting something with a stick. But I want no part of being hit by a stick. Hitting a ball with a stick does indeed sound like a smarter, better choice than hitting a person." Jonathan agreed.

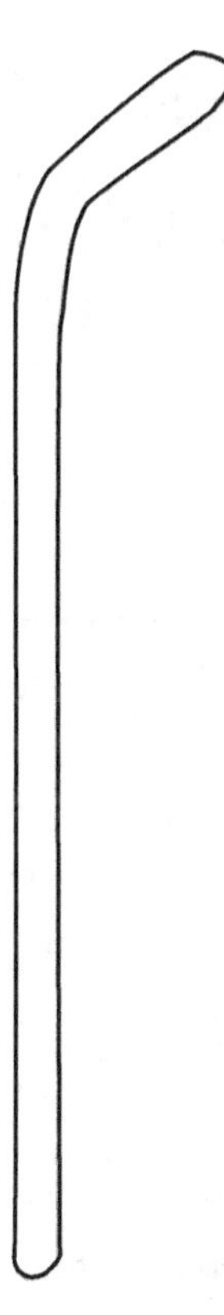

Chapter 26 | *1399* | First Group Lesson and Hitting Exercise

"So, what do we need to play this game?" asked Barbara the Bowyer.

"A great question, Barbara." David answered, "The shape of our shepherds' crooks is quite similar to the sticks the sailors used. Look!" David pointed to the end of his crook. The end of David's crook was shaped like a long nose club.

"I found one of the balls the sailors used. Bessie and I have been playing with it."

Bessie added, "Even though my crook is shorter than David's, the shape is the same. David and I experimented. Like the sailors, we hit the ball with our crooks. We learned that both crooks work the same as the sailors' sticks. Already, we both strike the ball as well as many of the sailors did."

"We have been hitting the ball to each other with our crooks."

"Watch this!" David commanded.

Bessie and David stood approximately 10 yards apart and faced each other. Both held their own shepherd's crook. David dropped the ball onto the creeping bent grass patch. He took a measured stance. His feet inscribed an imaginary line parallel to an imaginary straight line drawn from the ball to Bessie.

David stood comfortably balanced. He approached the ball. To reaffirm the accuracy of his line, he glanced at Bessie. Then, David made a practice swing. The purpose of the practice swing was to help calculate the best speed to swing the crook to send the ball right to Bessie.

David used the crook to measure the distance from his shoulders to the ball. He took a small backswing. In perfect rhythm, David dropped the crook into a down swing. The stroke flowed into smooth contact through the ball. A short, soft follow through finished the stroke.

When David's crook made contact the ball jumped. It flew through the air in a soft slow arc. Then the ball descended. It touched down about five yards in front of Bessie. The leather ball bounced, bounced, then rolled to Bessie's feet.

The friends absorbed the sequence: Lad, stick, swing, contact, ball, flight, roll and stop near the lass.

Then, Bessie took her turn. She readied to hit the ball back to David. Bessie repeated her brother's actions. She took a strong, balanced comfortable stance. Her feet stood on an imaginary line parallel to an imaginary line from the ball to David.

Bessie made a practice swing. She established a feel to decide how hard to swing. Then, she measured her stick from the ball. She stepped up more closely.

Bessie made a short backswing. She loosed a smooth forward downstroke. The crook contacted the ball. The stroke guided the ball. The ball bounced, rolled, and stopped at David's feet.

The two repeated the exercise. Bessie said, "Okay David, let's take three steps backward. Then we will repeat the exercise."

David and Bessie each took three steps backward. Now, rather than ten yards away from each other, they were sixteen yards apart. The practice swings and the velocity of the swings were a wee bit faster than at ten yards.

After two more strokes for each sibling, David asked, "Do you want to take five more steps back and repeat now, Bessie?"

"Aye!" Bessie and David stood some twenty-five yards away from each other. With excitement, the friends watched the two Shepherds hit the ball back and forth to each other. The two guided the ball back and forth to each other with astonishing accuracy. At the longer distances, the ball did not roll perfectly to the feet of the target as often as from closer distances. However, the receiver seldom needed more than a few steps to retrieve each ball.

"Alright. Does anybody want to try hitting the ball with my crook?" Bessie asked.

"Aye! I do!" Shouted ten friends in answer.

"It is fun!" David chuckled. "We can all do the activity. Bessie and I planned a way for each of you to hit the ball today."

"Let's show our friends what we planned for them to do, can we David?" Bessie asked.

"Alright. We just need you to share the ball and the crooks. To share, we need you to take turns." David explained.

"Aye. David and I talked about how to share this exercise with all of you at the same time. We have two sticks and one ball for our equipment. By taking turns you can all share equally as we hit the ball. So, here's what we want you to do. First, we need you all to move. We want to get you to stand in two lines. Stand facing each other about ten yards apart. Come stand here with me, lasses. Stand in a straight line facing the lads."

"Lads, come stand here with me." David said. "Just like the lasses, stand in a straight line facing the lasses."

"We will start with the oldest today. Tomorrow, we will start with the second oldest and so on." Bessie ordered.

"I am the oldest lad." stated William the Weaver.

"I am the oldest lass." added Margaret the Tanner.

Together, we reiterated our insistence in our game for absolutely everything about to be completely fair and scrupulously honest. Immediately, we all agreed to take an equal amount of time and an equal number of turns to strike the ball. We also believed that we should rotate who goes first each time we played. The lads and lasses knew what was fair. We took turns. Each one practiced hitting the ball just the way we saw Bessie and David hit. All the friends found great pleasure hitting the ball. We agreed with Bessie and David that hitting the ball with the crook required skill. Quickly, we realized that adding the challenge to hit towards a specific target offered even more fun. When we took our turn, we learned how much more difficult it was to hit a target with the ball, rather than merely hit the ball.

The friends rapidly realized that to stop the ball near the target, in this case, the foot of a sibling, added to the challenge. It was far more difficult to stop the ball at the target than it appeared when David and Bess hit the ball to each other. All the lads and lasses received several opportunities to hit the ball. Taking turns worked for all the friends. We were all satisfied that we received an equal number of opportunities to hit the ball.

"To stop the ball where you want it to stop was fairly difficult to do when we were ten yards apart. But each time we stepped back a few paces, that became far more challenging." Marion the Shoemaker observed.

"I agree, Marion." Russell the Bowyer replied. "At the same time, when we succeeded at the more challenging, the longer distances, the feeling of satisfaction greatly increased. Success from 25 yards felt far better than succeeding from 10 yards."

Robert the Carpenter noted, "Aye, when we hit the ball for the longer distances, I discovered that hitting for a longer distance is much more fun. At the same time, the farther I hit, the more difficult I found it to hit the ball on a line to the target."

Rhona observed, "When we stepped back further and further away, I could hear louder sounds each time the crook struck the ball. We needed to add more and more power each time we struck the ball. But I have yet to hear the sound that you described. I have not heard the "THWOCK!""

"Oho, Rhona! So, you want to hear the 'THWOCK!?'" Bess asked.

"Aye!" Rhona responded. "You started your story by telling us about the two of you hearing a strange new sound. The sound was so unique and sharp that you could hear it out on the Links in all that wind. You described the special sound as 'THWOCK!' Of course, I want to hear the same sound."

David asked, "Does anyone else wish to hear the sound we heard?"

"Aye!" roared the chorused reply from nine friends.

Bessie commanded, "David, stay where you are. I will step off forty paces. Lads, you stay with David. Lasses come with me. I will give a signal when I am ready for you to hit. We will retrieve the ball. Then, I will hit the ball back to you." Briskly, Bessie paced off forty yards. The other lasses paced right along with Bessie and confirmed the measurement of her strides. When the lasses counted forty, they spun around. They waved to David and their brothers. David stepped into a quiet, balanced stance. Carefully, he measured off the length of the crook from the ball. Then, David pulled the stick back behind his right shoulder as far as he could turn. And then, in a free, fluid motion, David swung the crook down.

"THWOCK!"

The crook collided with the ball solidly. David swung the stick all the way through the arc. He finished his swing. His trailing right arm contacted his left shoulder. That touch of arm to shoulder signaled to David that he completely finished his full powerful stroke. David's hands slowed to a complete stop. The finish of his swing brought the right hand, which held the end of the crook just past his left shoulder.

The ball leaped off David's stick! Up, up, and up! Much, much higher than any ball even the strongest lad ever threw a rock. The leather ball soared into the air! Until it reached the apex. Then, the ball began to descend. Down, down, down. Over the heads of the lasses the ball continued in the air. Bounce! Bounce. Roll.

"How far did the ball go?"

"Bessie, step off the distance the ball traveled. The lads want to know."

Chapter 27 | 2019 | Archery Practice

The Professors - Lecture Notes

Dr. MacGregor – "Early in life, Medieval Scottish children learned to measure distances to an astonishing degree of accuracy. During medieval times, accurately estimating and measuring distance formed a crucial life skill. Under close supervision from their fathers, uncles, and older brothers, young Scots developed the ability to estimate accurately from stepping off distance.

On Sundays, following completion of church services, Scotsmen obeyed the King's special orders. All able-bodied males, age twelve and over, practiced archery. The King's Law decreed that each adult male should own, and maintain in good repair, his own custom fitted longbow. Each archer received a sheaf containing two dozen standard length practice arrows from the King's representative. All over the land, archers mastered the longbow."

Professor Greenwood – "The archery officer divided practice time into three parts. In the first part, archers practiced accuracy. Archers carefully aimed and shot specific targets. In the second part, the archers shot arrows at various prescribed distances. Shooting arrows at specific targets located at differing distances helped archers to sharpen their aim. In the third part, archers practiced shooting speed volleys simultaneously.

On the first command from the sergeant, "Load!" all archers nocked an arrow to the bowstring at the same time.

On the second command, "Aim!" the archers raised the longbow into shooting position. Using the first three fingers, the archers pulled the bowstring with the nocked arrow to full draw. They held the bowstring steady. The archers calculated the angle of elevation, aligned the windage, and judged the point of aim to send the arrow to the target.

On the third command, "Release!" Simultaneously, all archers straightened their three fingers. They released the bowstring. Arrows launched into the air as a wave! Dozens of arrows rained down on a bracketed target. Timed, accurate, coordinated flights comprising dozens of lethal arrows formed a deadly weapon. For nearly three hundred years, archers using the longbow effectively helped to defeat their enemies."

Dr. MacGregor – "In addition to shooting for accuracy, archers practiced shooting for distance. Knowing the measured distance is crucial to an arrows lethal range in battle. To measure how far an arrow travelled accurately, archers stepped off the distance from where they launched the arrow to the exact point where the arrow struck the ground or the target.

On Sundays children enjoyed accompanying their fathers to archery practice. When fathers walked out to retrieve the practice arrows, the children stepped alongside. Fathers taught the children to take even, consistent steps. They practiced diligently to match their steps to their fathers'. Children learned to make a step exactly one yard long. To determine distance, they counted the number of steps they took. On the archery range, there were known distance points. Comparing their number of steps to the known distance poles, children achieved a high degree of confidence in their ability to estimate distance accurately."

Chapter 28 | *1399* | How Far Did The Ball Fly?

"48, 49, 50, 51. Wow! That makes 51 yards!"

"I want to hit the ball next", pronounced Marion the Shoemaker.

"Sure, Marion". Bessie offered her stick to Marion.

Marion stepped up to the ball. Using Bess's crook, Marion mimicked the way Bess measured the distance to the ball with the stick. She took a mighty backswing stretching to the tips of her toes. Then, closing her eyes, Marion swung down as hard as she could, "*thunk!*"

Marion looked at the ground. She saw that she had buried the head of the stick in the sand. "Ugh!" she grunted. "Hitting the ball as far as you hit it, is not as easy as you made it look, Bessie."

"Aye, Marion, you are right!" Bessie grinned. "David told me about watching the sailors. David said the sailors made the swing look easy. The first time I swung the stick I did the same thing you just did, Marion. David hit the ground the first time he took a full swing also. I was there and saw him. '*thunk!*' We both laughed in embarrassment when we buried the stick right into the ground.

By watching David I learned so much about how to hit the ball. When I first began to swing, I learned that hitting the ball solidly is not easy. I also learned that taking a full swing with the stick is so much fun. After practicing many swings, I learned how to measure the head of the crook in order to center a spot right on the L–shape to strike the ball. I learned the best spot of the ball to strike. Then, I learned how to pull the stick back to just the right place, far enough to get power, though not too far to lose control. Next, I learned to swing the stick down to strike and continue the path of the stick through the ball.

David coached, "Take another swing Marion. This time, before you swing, measure the center of the club head to contact a wee tiny spot just below an imaginary line circling around the center of the ball. After you determine your point of contact on the ball, then, slowly pull the stick behind your right shoulder. When you swing, make sure to swing down in such a way that the crook seems to go right through the ball. I know you will see just how much fun it is to hit the ball with this sweet spot on the club solidly."

"I do want to make another attempt." Marion verbalized her task, "I have two new ideas to consider. This time I plan to swing the stick using more control while applying less power. I want to make sure I strike that central spot of the stick just below the imaginary line around the center of the ball. This time I intend to keep both eyes wide open. I will keep my eyes focused on the ball. On my first swing, I swung so hard that I closed my eyes."

"Aye, Marion. It is vitally important to keep your eyes wide open when you swing through the ball." Bessie acknowledged.

Marion relaxed into a comfortable stance. To measure the distance to the ball she rested the stick to the exact place just below the circumference on the ball she intended to strike. She determined the center spot on the stick. She visualized the exact spot where she wanted the stick to contact the ball. This time, Marion pulled her arms back only about two thirds as far as she did the first time. She swung the stick down. This time the pathway of Marion's swing guided the stick to travel directly through the ball.

"THWOCK!"

Marion barely felt the solid contact of club to ball. But the sound was glorious! The ball leaped off the club. Up, up, up! The ball flew to the apex of a parabola painted by its flight in the sky! Then down came the ball at a mirrored accelerating pathway.

"Oh my! Hitting the ball felt really good!" Marion exclaimed! "The ball traveled a long way!!"

"Let's step off the distance!!" Shouted Thomas, the Tanner. "30, 31, 32 yards!"

"And I barely swung the stick." Marion observed.

"Who wants to hit next?" asked Bess.

"I do!" In unison, the nine remaining friends sang a response to answer. The unison response sounded similar to the way the children sounded when they chanted a response during the singing at choir. The friends all laughed together.

"Our response to your successful strike, Marion, sounded just like the way we sound when we sing as a choir in unison. Remember at choir practice when we all sang the exact same note at the exact same time." observed Thomas the Tanner. "A fitting observation, Thomas. I shared the same thought." Heather noted.

"Aye, I agree." Russell added.

"We have only one ball." Jonathan noted.

"Aye, Jonathan, that is true. But we do have two sticks. I think the lasses should stay here with me. Lads, why don't you go with David? Step off thirty yards. We will take turns. First, we will hit the ball from the lasses to the lads. Then, the lads will take turns to hit the ball back to the lasses. We just need to make sure that everyone gets the same number of turns." Bessie suggested. "Does that sound like fun to you?"

"I believe it is a fair way for us to practice." Robert stated.

"Aye. It truly does sound like a fun activity. And I agree. The plan sounds reasonable. I think sharing and taking turns is a good plan. I believe the plan is fair to each of us." Thomas added.

"Sharing and taking turns creates a fair plan. We will all experience an equal number of times to strike the ball. Having an equal number of turns to strike the ball, ensures that your plan is fair to each of us." Rhona stated.

David added, "Bessie and I will not hit today. That way, each of you can enjoy a few more swings before darkness sends us home. If you have questions, perhaps Bessie and I can offer insights we learned to answer. We will both gladly share with you whatever we have discovered from practicing so far. We can do that. Do you agree with me, Bessie?"

"Of course, David. We want our friends to enjoy the experience of striking a ball with a stick as much as we enjoy it."

Each lad and each lass took a turn. Each friend took swings until each one connected the stick to the ball for a satisfying experience. The goal was for each friend to hear the solid 'THWOCK'! David and Bessie wanted each fried to revel in the joy of feeling solid contact from the wooden stick to the leather ball. That joyous feeling accompanied the glorious sound of solid contact. Then, the lass or lad passed the stick on to the next friend.

For some of the friends, after only one or two swings they experienced the feeling when they heard, "THWOCK!" That was the way Marion experienced the successful stroke.

For Jonathan, the youngest friend, learning to make successful contact required a longer time, and quite a few more swings. Before Jonathan experienced a successful "THWOCK!", he took six swings. Jonathan really wanted to watch the ball fly through the air when he hit it. He wanted so much to see the ball fly in the same way the ball flew when David hit the ball.

Jonathan feared that he would miss seeing the ball fly. Because Jonathan wanted to see the ball fly when he hit it, he took a wee little peek up into the air, to see each time he took a swing. He failed to keep his head down. He neglected to keep his eye focused on the part of the ball he wished to strike.

Just before the stick was to strike the ball during his swing, Jonathan slightly turned his eyes up. He kept trying to look up into the air where he expected to see the ball fly. Each time Jonathan took that wee little peak, he lifted his head a wee little bit. Each time he lifted his head a wee little bit, he lifted the club a wee little bit above the intended pathway during his swing. Each time he lifted the club a wee little bit from the pathway one of two outcomes happened. He missed the ball completely. Or he struck the ball a wee little bit above the intended contact point. That produced a 'thunk', instead of a 'THWOCK!'. Each time that Jonathan failed to create the sound of 'THWOCK!" he felt frustrated. David, and all the friends, could hear and see Jonathan's frustration.

Jonathan was puzzled. He simply could not figure out what the problem was. Why was it so difficult for him to hit the ball solidly? Jonathan wanted so much to be successful. He wanted to produce the 'THWOCK!' He wanted to hit the ball. He wanted to make the ball fly up into the air.

David coached, "I want you to concentrate when you strike the ball, Jonathan. May I suggest that you consider this idea. First, pick out the spot on the ball that you wish to strike with the club. As I look down at the ball I pick out the widest part. Then, I visualize striking a point that is just a wee bit below the widest part. Throughout your swing, continue to look right at that spot on the ball. Let your trailing arm tell you when you can look up. When your trailing arm touches your chin, you will know that you kept your eyes focused directly on that spot on the ball all the way through your swing. When your trailing arm touches your chin, that is your signal. That is when you can look up. Then, I believe that you will hear the 'THWOCK!' You will see the ball flying."

Jonathan listened intently to David. Jonathan realized that when David struck the ball, he was successful very often. Jonathan possessed great faith in David's desire to help him succeed. Jonathan truly believed that his friend indeed told him the right things to do in order to accomplish the goal. This time when Jonathan swung the crook, he did his best to follow David's instructions. This time Jonathan did not look at the whole ball. Instead, he focused his eyes on a place just below the ball's widest part. Jonathan swung the club in a pathway fashioned to contact the stick precisely at that point, just below the widest part of the ball. Throughout the entire swing, Jonathan kept his eyes focused on that specific spot on the ball. He maintained focus. He kept his eyes on that spot of the ball until he felt his trailing arm touch his chin. Jonathan made certain that he did not take even the tiniest wee bit of a peek away from the spot on the ball.

And then,

"THWOCK!"

Jonathan received the reward. Jonathan heard the glorious sound! This time, he felt the thrill. Jonathan felt his trailing arm touch his chin. Only then, did he allow his eyes to search the sky. He saw it! At last, Jonathan saw the ball he hit fly through the air.

Each time one of the friends produced a solid 'THWOCK!', the others cheered. The lads and lasses then stepped off the yardage from the spot where the stroke was taken to the spot where the ball ceased to roll. The distances varied from 25 yards to 35 yards. No one came close to Bessie's 48 yards distance, nor David's 51 yards distance. Bessie and David knew that the distances the balls traveled, which their friends hit, would increase soon. When their friends practiced hitting the ball as often as the two Shepherds practiced, the lengths would improve dramatically. Soon, all the friends would reach similar distances to those Bessie and David demonstrated. The Shepherds knew that frequent practice would make a big difference to the frequency their friends would hear and feel a "THWOCK!"

Bessie and David remembered when they started to hit, the ball rarely traveled more than 25 yards. Everyday Bess and David practiced hitting the ball. Each time the two Shepherds practiced hitting the ball, they felt their strokes became smoother, stronger, more consistent, and more repeatable. Higher and higher, the ball flew. Each day the friends practiced, the ball flew farther and farther. Bessie and David realized that when their friends practiced hitting the ball daily, they too, would experience a similar learning pathway. The friends would learn how to strengthen the swing. The friends would learn what to do in order to develop control to land the ball at the desired target. The friends would learn to enjoy control and power when they stroked the ball.

stroke (n.)
"act of striking," c. 1300, probably from Old English *straw* **"stroke," from Proto-Germanic** *straik-* **(source also of Middle Low German** strek**, German**

Chapter 29 | 2019 | The Snag: Background Information

The Professors - Lecture Notes

Professor Greenwood – "We reached a spot in the narrative that initially confused us. It seemed that Brother Tanner veered off track from the origin of golf story. In 1458, he clearly stated the purpose for the narrative. We expected him to get straight to the story of the game.

At age 73, Brother Tanner realized his time to tell the origin story grew short. For nearly six decades, he drew illustrations and transcribed stories before he committed to document the creation of the game in this manuscript. His memory of twelve friends unfolded. Brother Tanner knew the story contained difficulties which required thorough explanation.

Brother Tanner knew we would ask, 'who'? We needed more than names. To see the friends as Brother Tanner saw them, we needed descriptions. His artist's eyes selected the defining details contained in his memory. He composed his description to access the recollection of his young friends. When we read the manuscript, we realized how successful he was. His writing transported the friends from that time between Lammas and Michaelmas in 1399, to life.

Brother Tanner knew we would ask 'why'? He created the manuscript in response to the king's ban of golf. He realized we would ask questions about the manuscript. When scribes read from manuscripts they often engaged in discussion about the meaning. He was familiar with how readers asked and discussed the question of why. Why did he tell us so much about how each family business worked? Why did he write in such detail about how the businesses functioned interdependently? Why did he tell us so much about the town of St. Andrews? We believe he addressed these questions in the parts of the manuscript we organized into the next several chapters.

Brother Tanner knew we would ask, 'how?' We believe that Brother Tanner developed a deep faith in the power of process contained with human interactions. He chose to accentuate specific conversations. Those conversations illustrated the deep communication levels in which the friends engaged while they created the game. His response to the question 'how' is critical. The friends use language in a most supportive manner. They speak with respect always. Their behavior is polite. They ask questions to show genuine concern, or indicate a sincere desire to understand. Responders always appreciate questions. Brother Tanner showed how friends value individuals.

Dr. MacGregor – "We trusted Brother Tanner's voice. He copied the greatest stories known. He was skilled at writing stories. Brother Tanner knew a great deal about telling stories. He understood that when people read and listened to a story they needed background. We delighted in the rich trove of details Brother Tanner provided. We endeavor to discover artifacts and records. To establish provenance, we work meticulously to test artifacts and records objectively. We labor to ensure that we present accurate factual details. Accurate details help establish credibility and offer new insight into the human experience."

Professor Greenwood – "Brother Tanner realized that readers required background information to accept how the game was created. He intentionally invested the energy to detail a lengthy report. He understood that readers might doubt that this incredibly complex, rich game could be fashioned by twelve adolescents. He knew the truth. In the manuscript, he wrote detailed descriptions for the same reasons he wrote rich details as a scribe. Detailed descriptions convince readers that testimony is accurate, reliable, and true. When the faithful heard the Holy Word they received assurance.

Brother Tanner shared a sincere report on each friend. Background reports on the twelve friends removed doubt and offered assurance. To establish that the twelve friends possessed all the necessary skills to produce quality equipment, Brother Tanner cited facts. He proved that the Carpenters and Bowyers held access to tools and materials to craft durable golf clubs. The Shoemakers, Tanners and Weavers possessed tools and materials to fabricate high quality golf balls. The Shepherds shaped and maintained a golf course on the Links. We trusted Brother Tanner's wisdom, and we were rewarded. We learned to trust him the way we trust a great teacher. He is the experienced teacher who knows what he is doing. Over a lifetime, he witnessed the power of well told stories to guide readers and listeners."

Dr. MacGregor – "As we continued reading and translating, Brother Tanner's reasons clarified. He guided us. He reminded us to offer guidance about his time in Scottish Medieval history for readers. Some may not possess a great deal of knowledge concerning the 'late Medieval period'. More specifically, they may not know much about 'Medieval Scotland'. Readers may even need to know the geography of present-day St. Andrews. Certainly, Brother Tanner and his friends did not know that they lived in a time now labelled 'late Medieval'. Historians use such labels to help explain the concept of time by identifying artifacts, ideas and people. For this manuscript, the 'late Medieval' period is important to understand. Late Medieval immediately precedes the time we label the 'Renaissance', also known as the 'rebirth'. It was a time when human knowledge exploded with inventions, discoveries, and new ideas."

Professor Greenwood – "During Brother Tanner's lifetime, Scotland's first university opened in St. Andrews. The Renaissance awakened. On a daily basis, Brother Tanner worked and communicated with literate men. To share the translation of Brother Tanner's story, we followed his guidance. In addition to the background in text translation, we offer background knowledge of late Medieval Scottish history focused on St. Andrews."

Our duty as historians requires that we inform readers that in the beginning, sheep and wool funded the nation which became Great Britain. The imprint of Great Britain around the globe included the export of the Royal and Ancient Game from St. Andrews to every land where the Union Jack flew."

Dr. MacGregor – "Prior to the invention and manufacture of mechanized mowers, only sheep pastures provided an acceptable site for a golf course. Sheep grazing 'mows' grass to an acceptably short and uniform height. Tiny spheres of sheep droppings rapidly dry in the short grass. Droppings fertilize and reseed the fairways. Cattle grazing simply fails to 'mow' grass to either a uniform or an acceptable height. In addition, for golf fairways, large wet piles of cattle manure are simply unacceptable. The creation of golf, and for the next four and a half centuries, the expansion of golf required sheep and shepherds to develop and maintain the courses.

Sources we consulted are listed in The Appendix. Most of the sources are available on-line, free of charge."

Chapter 30 | 2019 | St. Andrews An Important Town

The Professors - Lecture Notes

Dr. MacGregor – "Auld lang syne, (Scottish for long, long ago.) Far, far longer a time before anyone's twentieth great grandparents lived, people settled in a village on the East Coast of Scotland. Rivers attracted settlements because of the need for an adequate, dependable fresh water supply. Near the place where the River Eden met the Ocean, the residents called their little settlement, Kilrymont. On that same location stands the town now known as St. Andrews. Centuries before our story about twelve friends began, Kilrymont gained importance. The tiny village developed into the most holy place to all who lived in Scotland."

Professor Greenwood – "Hundreds of years before the settlement of Kilrymont, the story opened in a land far away. Jesus invited Peter and Andrew, two fishermen to join his twelve disciples. Peter and Andrew were brothers. Jesus offered them a mission that changed their lives forever, "follow me and I will make you fishers of men." Peter and Andrew accepted. For the remainder of their time on earth the two fishermen, Peter, and Andrew, dedicated themselves to share Jesus' teachings.

The Martyr – Andrew spread the joy of Jesus' good news. For his ministry, the faithful Andrew suffered martyrdom. Worldly men judged and condemned the Disciple to die on a cross. Andrew argued that he was unworthy to be crucified in the same manner in which the Romans crucified Jesus. He convinced the executioners to place him on a cross different from the Roman cross."

Dr. MacGregor – The Saint Andrew Cross "The court granted Andrew's request. Andrew suffered crucifixion on an X shaped cross, also called a saltire cross or a Saint Andrews' Cross. Andrew was crucified on a white colored cross. He wore a blue robe. The flag of Scotland consists of a white St. Andrews cross emblazoned on a sky-blue background.

In those distant days, centuries prior to the Protestant Reformation, only one Christian faith existed in the British Isles. In all of Europe, from Italy west to the British Isles only one Christian religion existed, the Roman Catholic (universal) faith. All Christians in the nations now called, Great Britain, France, Spain, Portugal, Italy and the Germanic nations practiced their faith as Roman Catholics."

Professor Greenwood – St. Rule "Around the year 340 CE, a Christian holy man, known by some as St. Rule, and by others as St. Regulus, served as bishop for the city of Patras, Greece. In a dream, an angel told him that the Emperor Constantine planned to acquire holy relics from Greece. Constantine planned to relocate the relics in shrine in Constantinople, the capital of the Eastern half of the Empire. The relics in Patras were identified as certain bones from St. Andrew, The Disciple.

The angel instructed St. Rule to protect the St. Andrew relics. Rather than submit the relics to confiscation and face being moved to Constantinople, he was directed to take the bones far away to save the St. Andrew relics for the Roman Church. St. Rule believed he was assigned a sacred mission.

St. Rule formed a plan. He resolved to carry the relics as far away from Constantinople as possible. He carried the relics and boarded a ship that sailed to west. Eventually, far away from Rome and Greece, the ship wrecked on the east coast of Scotland. At the site, St. Rule built a church, which bore his name. On the edge of civilization, St. Rule's church housed the relics of Saint Andrew. By the year 748 AD, the town which would become known as St. Andrews, was settled."

Dr. MacGregor – "In Scotland, around 1000 AD, festivals began to honor St. Andrew as Scotland's patron Saint. Believers made pilgrimages to St. Rule's church. Christians came from Scotland, from England, and from Europe. Travelers found comfort from viewing the holy relics of St. Andrew, the Apostle. Pilgrims prayed to St. Andrew. Because of the relics housed in St. Rule's Church, the town later became known as St. Andrew's town. More and more Christians made pilgrimages to the village. The residents realized that Saint Rule's church was too small to serve the many pilgrims. The townspeople thought that to house the important relics of Scotland's patron saint demanded a more substantial edifice than the little church. The citizens believed that they needed a great cathedral to house the sacred relics of the Disciple. Other Christians agreed.

In the year 1158, construction began to erect the largest, most magnificent cathedral in Scotland. From all around, Christians continued to pilgrimage to St. Andrews. Pilgrims and residents contributed resources to help pay for the construction. The cathedral required 160 years to complete. Dedication occurred in 1318.

Professor Greenwood – "In Edinburgh, Christians realized that many pilgrims traveled through their town on the way to St. Andrews. Citizens of Edinburgh provided food, drink, and shelter to the travelers. Queen Margaret of Scotland directed the people of Edinburgh to care for the faithful on the 'Way to St. Andrews Pilgrimage'. She financed construction of the Queen's ferry to cross the Firth of Forth from Edinburgh into Fife. She decreed that her ferry would never charge pilgrims for the ride across the Firth of Forth. The Queen's ferry saved many miles of walking and considerably shortened the time to complete the holy pilgrimage."

Dr. MacGregor – "After pilgrims crossed the Firth of Forth, they required lodging. For the night, they stayed in a hospital, sometimes called a hostel. In those days, the word 'Hospital' meant a building where pilgrims could stop, rest, and eat. Queen Margaret directed construction of a new hostel, a safe place to refresh, before they continued on The Way to St. Andrews. Queen Margaret died in 1193. In 1250, the Church honored the good works and miracles attributed to her. She was declared Saint Margaret. Since then, Queen Margaret was remembered as the Patroness of Scotland."

Chapter 31 | 2019 | St. Andrews-PLACE

The Professors - Lecture Notes

Dr. MacGregor – "Many folks still refer to County Fife, as 'The Kingdom of Fife'. At least 35 castles lie within the boundaries. Among the most well-known are: Aberdour Castle, the oldest known castle in Fife, dating from around 1200 C.E. Aberdour Castle may be the oldest castle in all of Scotland. Ravenscraig Castle, built for King James II of Scotland, another notable structure is probably the first castle designed to be defended by firearms rather than by long bows. The ruins of St. Andrews Castle offer a glimpse into the time before the Protestant Reformation."

Professor Greenwood – "The Firth of Forth marks the Southern boundary for County Fife. Edinburgh is the large port city located on the south bank of the mouth of the Firth of Forth, the River Firth. The River Tay defines the Northern boundary for County Fife. The town of Dundee lies on the North bank of River Tay. Between the Firth of Forth and the Firth of Tay, a smaller river, the River Eden, splits County Fife. The Eden Estuary mingles with St. Andrews Bay of the North Sea."

Dr. MacGregor – "Where the Eden flow empties into the North Sea, an isosceles triangle shaped peninsula located on the south bank, knifes into the estuary. On a map the peninsula resembles a compass arrow pointing true north. Residents of St. Andrews call this peninsula, the Links.

On the extreme eastern boundary of County Fife, the city of St. Andrews edges St. Andrews Bay. The city is slightly south and east of the Links. The River Eden and two burns (small creeks) supplied fresh water for St. Andrews. Settlements require a plentiful and dependable source of freshwater. People need freshwater to drink, to cook, to clean clothing, and household goods. During growing season, a reliable, plentiful source provides freshwater to grow fresh garden vegetables. To sustain farm animals requires a dependable supply of fresh water. The manufacture of products to offer at the town market demanded a reliable supply of freshwater. Manufacturing occupations including tanners, shoemakers, weavers, bowyers, and carpenters require freshwater. Fresh water is a necessary ingredient to produce the goods sold at market. A thriving market enables farmers and tradespeople alike to make a living for their families. The River Eden provided a reliable supply. The Kinness Burn runs along the Southern edge of St. Andrews."

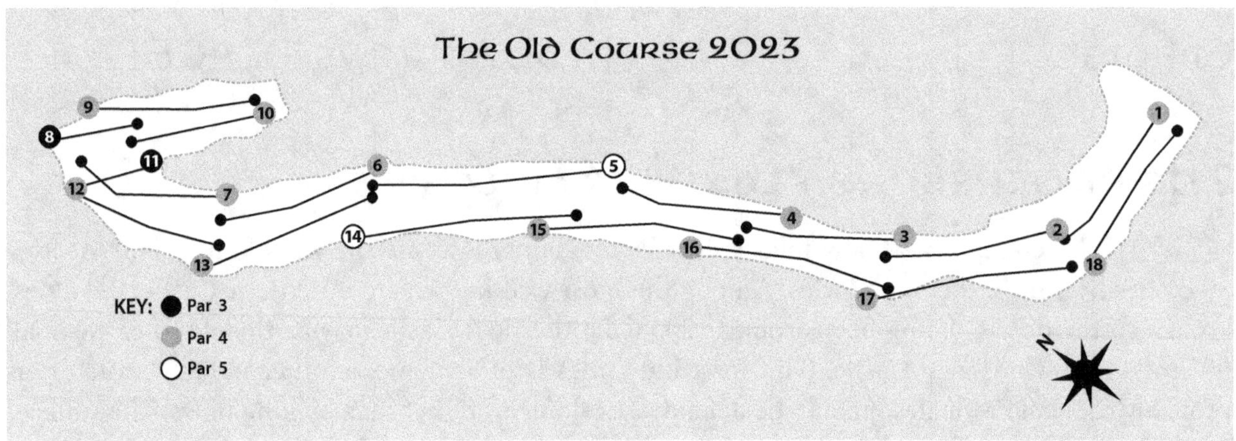

Professor Greenwood – The Links. "Between the town and the ships anchorage, the small triangular tree barren peninsula shaped around a low ridge. The total area of the peninsula is approximately 300 hectares. At a conversion rate of 1 hectare = 2.471 acres, that would measure approximately 741 acres for our American friends. The people in St. Andrews called the land, the Links, for a special reason.

The Eden Estuary is shallow and rocky. In Medieval times, large ships known as cogs, brought goods to trade in St. Andrews. To anchor, cogs require a depth shallow enough to secure a dropped anchor or to tie the ship securely to a stationary object. It was necessary to avoid the danger of damage to the ship's hull as a result from running aground. Cogs required water deep enough to float the vessel safely even in stormy conditions. Town buildings were constructed on higher ground. At the town's location, the water was too shallow for large ships to approach safely. So, the ships anchored in the safe, sufficiently deep water. To go ashore from cogs, passengers transferred to small boats. Sailors unloaded cargo from the merchant ship then reloaded onto small boats. Sailors rowed the small boats through the shallows to the Links, where they docked safely. Merchants, or their designated representatives, met the sailors to claim cargo. From town, people walked and rolled carts to the dock. At the dock, they transferred cargo into carts to wheel to businesses in St. Andrews."

Dr. MacGregor – "When storms arrived, fierce winds rushed over the Links. Frequently, winds blew sea water spray which saturated the Links. So strong were the winds, and so extensive the salt spray which scoured the Links, that only a few highly adapted plant species thrived there. The Swilkan Burn still meanders through the treeless peninsula known as the Links.

At the time of our story, the Swilcan Bridge, an arched stone construction, provided safe passage to cross the Swilcan Burn, the small creek that meandered through the Links, for more than a hundred years. Shepherds used the old stone bridge to move hoofed animals over the Swilcan Burn. Fish wives pushed carts filled with the days' catch across the old stone bridge to market in town. Sailors and townspeople rolled cargo laden carts from boat dock to town, or from town to boat dock."

Professor Greenwood – "During long, warm, sunny days in late spring and early summer, cattle grazed on the rich pasture grass growing lushly on the Links. In the mornings, cattle and sheep crossed the bridge to go to pasture. In the evenings, the livestock crossed the bridge in the opposite direction to return to the sheltered barn yards. The milk cows were led home to their respective shelters. At home, the cows were milked again. Then, they rested safely through the night.

Whenever the rich grass grew faster than the milk cows could eat, cattle pastured on the Links. At the middle of summer, the growth of fat grass ceased. People gathered to harvest the fat grass and make hay.

While workers performed their labor, they frequently, engaged in song. Music established a rhythm. When people worked hard rhythm increased efficiency. Rhythm established the appropriate tempo for reapers to swing their scythes. They mowed the rich grass using scythes with wooden handles and spines custom fitted to each reaper. The business end of the scythes culminated in a long curved razor edged steel blade."

Dr. MacGregor – "Each reaper carried a sharpening whetstone. Harvesting the hay crop required a smooth stroke to deliver the razor-sharp blade accurately. After each smooth stroke, live green grass remained at a level height of one-inch.

Following every thirty or so strokes, the reaper stopped. He inverted the scythe. Deliberately and carefully, in order to avoid slicing a finger open, he maneuvered the long, sharp curved blade. Then, he stroked the whetstone skillfully along the blade. The stroke of the whetstone set a razor-sharp cutting edge. By stopping to sharpen often, the reaper insured that to slice through the fat grass he always swung a super sharp cutting blade. Over the course of the day long labor, frequent maintenance of a sharp edge saved his energy. A successful reaper delivered the sharpened blade with an efficient, rhythmic stroke. That combination produced a smooth, nearly effortless cut. The proper tool, teamed with a skilled stroke, sliced hay grass far more effectively than anyone who attacked with brute strength. Skilled reapers mowed the fat grass evenly. Every time the reaper sharpened his blade, he purchased a few moments rest for his arms, his shoulders, and his torso. Moments of rest from the strenuous labor helped a reaper regain his strength. Frequent refreshening breaks allowed reapers to maintain a steady efficient pace. During the long sunlight hours of summer, one skilled reaper could mow ten or more acres in a day."

Professor Greenwood – "Reapers walked and mowed together in a row across the field. The newly mown grass fell to the ground. To spread the wet grass, workers employed long handled wooden rakes. New mown grass needed to dry quickly. Persistent winds coupled with long hours of sunshine accelerated drying time. Hay provided sweet, healthy, nutritious cattle feed for the winter.

If wet grass was baled into hay, moisture caused the grass to mold or rot. Moldy hay caused dangerous health problems. Rotten hay damaged vulnerable young livers or kidneys. Young calves could die. Moldy hay seriously compromised the health of dairy animals. It was a known cause of aborted pregnancies to cows. A lost pregnancy interrupted the cycle of milk production. An unhealthy cow limited food availability for families who depended on milk production during the long winter months. Wasted, rotten hay needed to be properly disposed, far away from healthy cattle.

After the grass dried, reapers gathered the final hay crop of the summer. Men loaded hay onto wagons and carts. Draft animals pulled vehicles over the old stone bridge to barns and shelters around town. Working together, each barnyard received the proper share of hay."

Dr. MacGregor – "'Fat' grass only grew during a relatively short time. The other nine months of the year, the grass growing on the Links was not suitable to feed cattle. Following the summer hay harvest, one grass species continued to grow on the Links. Though it continued to grow, that grass species did not contain adequate nutriments to serve as cattle feed. The species that continued to grow was the creeping bent grass. Only sheep could graze on the creeping bent grass. And the sheep thrived on it.

Because there were no mechanical grass cutters before the mid-nineteenth century, golf was predominantly played in winter when the grass was naturally short following animal grazing. The links area on the east coast was accessible to the golfers of the time and coincides with the area of minimal rainfall in Scotland. With its better drainage, links land is therefore more suitable for winter play and was less damaging to the early <u>leather stitched golf balls</u> that were used. –Scottish Golf History

Chapter 32 | 2019 | St. Andrews- NATURAL RESOURCES

The Professors - Lecture Notes

Professor Greenwood – "Free people knew the value of hard work. Scottish families also knew how to play hard. To solve problems, Scots employed collective knowledge and engaged their imaginations. St. Andrews folks believed in the importance of their town. They shared a vision that someday people all over the world would know about St. Andrews."

Dr. MacGregor – "During the 14th and 15th centuries, a multitude of valuable resources enriched the growing town. Animals, plants, the land, plentiful fresh water, the ocean, the climate, and the location combined to provide an enviable supply of raw materials. Abundant resources attracted people to a community where they could live free and prosper. Craftsmen migrated to St. Andrews to work. Master tradesmen employed journeymen, apprentices and laborers to generate more profit from their work. The abundance of freshwater and food, the availability of plants and animals, plus the geography and the growing population established an attractive, bustling market town.

When a family produced more goods than needed, they acquired a surplus. Through their labor and skills, folks produced marketable goods. Folks traded their surplus production with others. Merchants established reliable trade. Eventually, people created the means to trade with other places. Regular shipments of goods and products from St. Andrews brought favorable prices in distant markets. Trade routes connected producers and consumers in markets near and far. For the citizens of St. Andrews, trade delivered new wealth.

Professor Greenwood – "By boiling saltwater in enormous kettles near the ocean's edge, salters produced an extraordinarily fine quality sea salt. Salt enabled fishermen to preserve the fish they caught. Farmers and butchers rubbed salt into meat to preserve pork. Salters produced more salt than the people of St. Andrews required, so they shipped surplus quantities salt to trade in other European markets to make a profit."

Dr. MacGregor – Farm Animals "All around St. Andrews, men and women raised healthy farm animals. St. Andrews' families kept poultry or fowl (chickens, ducks, swans, geese). Swine (pigs) provided pork. Cattle provided dairy and beef to the diet. In addition to supplying food for the family, farmers could trade or sell surplus animals. Most families kept at least one dairy cow to supply raw milk. One or two cows produced a sufficient quantity to fulfill the needs of a family. Cows were milked twice per day, morning and evening as part of the daily chores. During medieval times most milk was not consumed in liquid form. If not immediately cooled and stored cold, milk spoils quickly. Farmers processed raw milk into other foods. Cream was separated, skimmed, and collected from the milk, then churned into butter. Cream, cottage cheese, farmer's cheese and other cheeses were made from the rich milk. In the Medieval world dairy made an important contribution to healthy nutrition."

Professor Greenwood – "Most cattle were raised for beef. Only a few bulls were needed to breed with the milk cows. Most young bulls were slaughtered, then butchered into beef. In addition to food, beef cattle produced hides. Families raised pigs for food. In the cool days of early winter, families gathered to slaughter, butcher, and process hogs. On hog butchering days, people congregated to work together for the entire day. Cuts of pork were salted, smoked, or brined. Preservation treatments insured that the pork remained safe and edible throughout the long, cold winter. Pork was ground, seasoned, and stuffed into natural casings as sausage. Tanners bought hides, hooves, and bones of beef and swine from farmers.

For farm work, Scots developed magnificent horse breeds. Farmers harnessed the large strong horses to plow, to plant, to harvest and to thresh their crops. Powerful horses were bred and trained to pull wagons and coaches. Some of those large horses were recognized for their bravery, strength, and agility. Armored knights searched for large powerful, brave and agile horses to ride into battle."

Dr. MacGregor – "In barnyards, townspeople also raised fowl or poultry. Almost every family cultivated poultry. Poultry included chickens, ducks, swans, and geese. Chickens, ducks, and geese provided fresh eggs and fresh meat. Unlike chicken feathers, duck and goose feathers were waterproof. Duck and goose feathers and down provided excellent light weight comfortable insulation to stuff into quilts and layered clothing to keep warm during the windy, cold winter season. Feathers stuffed pillows and mattresses, too.

Farm animals provided meat, eggs, and dairy products. Draft horses and oxen provided muscle power to cultivate fields. Horses and donkeys improved transportation of goods and people. Hides were processed into leather and parchment. The processed hides improved the efficiency of tools and made clothing more durable. Leather door hinges improved convenience in cottages and other buildings. Feathers increased accuracy and distance for arrows propelled by longbows. Duck and goose down and feathers sewn into comforters insulated body heat to survive long cold winter nights. The rich diversity of farm animals provided a steady, reliable high quality supply line for people living in and around St. Andrews."

Chapter 33 | 2019 | Sheep and The Wool Economy Medieval Britain

The Professors - Lecture Notes

Dr. MacGregor – "One farm animal brought the greatest wealth to the economy and development of Britain. In the article, 'Medieval Sheep and Wool Types', M. L. Ryder reported, that archaeological evidence indicated the arrival of domesticated sheep in Britain by about 4,000 BCE. Since Neolithic times, and continuously for over 6,000 years, sheep thrived in Britain. British wool exports to Europe began around 700 CE. The 1066 Norman invasion greatly expanded the sheep and wool industry in Britain. By 1100, quickly following the Norman triumph, wool drove the British economy. Most sheep from the British Isles produced wool. Wool furnished the most valuable product from sheep. For more than a thousand years prior to our story, merchants and weavers prized wool from Great Britain as among the world's finest. One Roman wrote that "the wool from sheep in Britannia was fine as a spider web". The finer the wool, the softer the yarn. The softer the yarn, the more comfortable the fabric."

Professor Greenwood – "In 1331, King Edward III encouraged Flemish master weavers to migrate and settle in Great Britain. The 1349 Black Death decimated the human population on the island. The resulting shortage of farmers to cultivate tillable land spurred a dramatic change in the agrarian society. The availability of cleared land dramatically increased the amount of pasture acreage available for grazing animals. The area around St. Andrews included abundant pasture. Flocks were raised in large numbers. Sheep produced a significant amount of food for Medieval Great Britain. Meat from sheep is known as mutton. Spring lamb was a seasonal delicacy.

Ewes deliver lambs once per year in the Spring. At an average rate of about a half-gallon of milk per day, ewes continue milk production for about four months. Since lambing occurs in the spring, usually March, that means ewes lactate into July. March may provide temperatures cold enough that milk will not spoil. So that the ewe's milk production is not wasted from April through July, milk must be processed and converted into other foodstuffs. The most common and delicious processing converts the raw milk into cheese. In medieval St. Andrews, farm families and monks processed most of the surplus ewe's milk into cheese. Today, there are more sheep in Scotland than there are people. Breeds of sheep in Scotland include, Cheviot, North Ronaldsay Sheep, Scottish Blackface, Shetland Sheep and Soay.

Dr. MacGregor – "During the time of our story, separate breeds were not yet recognized. Instead of modern breeds, sheep were classified by the length of the wool fibers from the harvested fleece. Wool created a miracle fabric. Wool could be woven into light, medium or heavy weight. Heavier weights provided warmth and protection from severe weather conditions. Wool "breathed", that means that the wool fabric allowed air to circulate next to the body. Even when drenched with water, which could occur often in the Scottish climate, woolen fabric enabled the retention of body heat. Wearing wool, people stayed warm in the cold even when they were wet. People continued to work and to travel during uncomfortable, even life-threatening, dangerous weather conditions.

Wool held dye well. As a result, woolen cloth could be produced in many colors. Wool could be woven into solid colors. Weavers fashioned bright colored dyed woolen yarns into the famous Scottish plaids. Originally, plaids identified specific weavers who crafted within a local geographical area in Scotland."

Professor Greenwood – "Through trade, wool brought wealth to Scotland. People in other lands wanted clothing made from Scottish wool. For all the same reasons that Scots prized the wool from the sheep raised in their land and climate, people all over Europe wanted to wear clothing made of wool from Scotland.

Sheep hides also provided a source of income to shepherds. Tanners bought sheep hides, also called, 'Woolfell'–the skin of a sheep with the fleece still on it.' Dictionary.com 2019.

Tanners processed some of the sheep hides into leather. However, most of the sheep hides produced another valuable product from the tannery. In St. Andrews, the tannery supplied parchment to the scribes at Cathedral scriptorium. Parchment formed the pages for the hand lettered books before the invention of the printing press and the advent of paper.

Chapter 34 | 2019 | Fleece to Wool Cloth

The Professors - Lecture Notes

Dr. MacGregor – "By 1399, many tradespeople migrated to St. Andrews. To repair and maintain the Great Cathedral required skilled workers. Craftsmen possessed a variety of valuable skills. They earned sufficient wages to bring families to live in the town. Medieval St. Andrews evolved into a truly urban center. Citizens dealt with craftsmen who owned their own shoppes. These businessmen and businesswomen steadily increased the number of commercial products to sell to customers.

Some craftsmen worked together especially closely with those from one other trade. Even though one craftsperson may have provided a majority of another's business, the two did not always trade exclusively with only one other shoppe. In our discussion we wish to connect the six families identified in the manuscript. Lasses and lads from the six families possessed and pooled a sizeable volume of diverse knowledge and manual skills. They committed to work cooperatively to bring a shared vision to life. Together twelve young people developed the design, the skill to construct, and the imagination to invent all the necessary equipment. They conceptualized how to modify the Links. They laid out and built an ideal course in the sheep pasture."

Professor Greenwood – Sheep Shearing "In the cool wet Scottish climate, successful year-round human habitation requires warm clothes. For centuries, people knew that wool produces the best fabric to keep humans warm. To produce and provide quality wool cloth, shepherds and weavers developed an interdependent partnership. The two occupations provide materials to clothe people in St. Andrews. Sheep provided the raw material to produce fine wool. Raising sheep continued an activity in Britain known since the time of the Romans, over a thousand years before our story. The best long wool is removed from the body of the sheep in one complete piece, called a fleece. Shepherds and weavers gathered to harvest the fleece. Shearing (cutting the wool fleece away from the sheep) demands skill and hard work. Removal of the fleece does no harm to the animal.

To separate the fleece from the live animal requires shears, a special two bladed tool. Examples of shears dating to the Bronze Age are displayed in European and Asian museums. One hand controls the two opposing blades. The design of shears closely resembles scissors. To cut the wooly hair, shears are operated similarly though not quite the same, as a skilled barber."

Dr. MacGregor – "Expert shearers need extremely sharp blades. No more than two fleeces are harvested before they resharpen edges. Whether made from bronze, more than 2500 years ago, or from high-grade carbon steel today, the design of hand shears remains essentially unchanged. Today, many shearers use electrically powered tools to perform their work. However, sheep continue to be raised in many remote places where electric power may be unavailable. Or if available, it is prohibitively expensive. Therefore, a substantial amount of shearing continues to utilize the traditional hand shear design.

To produce a quality uniform cut of the fleece, shearers practice a technique perfected over centuries. One shearer handles and controls each individual animal. The shearer effectively immobilizes the animal by resting it's back against her/his own legs. Holding the sheep in this position calms the animal and permits the shearer to make the first cut in the wool across the belly side, also known as the dirty side. Clean high-quality fleeces bring premium prices at market."

Professor Greenwood – "Strong, skilled hands guide the shears. The first cut formed a straight, diagonal line across the belly stretching from one shoulder to the opposite side back leg. To make the cut, the shearer pulls the wool up and away from the skin with one hand to expose the skin. Following cuts continue the pattern. With the fleece pulled back securely, the shearer safely maneuvers the blades for the next even cut. Similar to peeling an orange in one piece, the shearer continually pulls the fleece up away from the skin. With the wool pulled up and away, she slides the dull side of the shears safely along the skin to make the next cut. Cuts were repeated until finally removing the entire fleece as one large piece. From a compliant sheep, expert shearers remove the fleece in a matter of minutes. The sheared sheep exits the table and returns to the pen or pasture. Each fleece is stuffed into the bag until it is full. The full bag of fleeces is called a 'bag full'. Men and women work together to shear and bag the fleeces. Shearers and baggers repeat the entire process with each animal until they complete the harvest."

Dr. MacGregor – Steps to Process Fleece into Wool Pile. "However, several steps are needed to become cloth. The first step is a thorough washing. The fleece must be cleaned completely to remove lanolin, oily secretions from the live animal. Lanolin binds the fibers of wool together to protect live sheep. The next step is to separate the clean strands of wool fiber. Following thorough washing, the fleece is completely dried. To separate, the fibers are pulled apart during a process called 'carding'. The 'cards' comprise two similar tools made of metal studded 'teeth' on one side. The other side of the card is smooth so that the operator can firmly hold the card. Firm control of both sets of teeth on the cards is critical. Carders place a handful of clean dry wool between the cards and pull them away from each other. Pulling the cards apart separates fibers from attached wool pieces. The separated fibers are removed from the cards. The fibers are collected into a pile. Carding transforms the fleece into a pile of clean wool fibers."

Professor Greenwood – "A pile of wool fibers will not make clothes suitable for humans to wear in Scotland's cold blowy environment. Woolen cloth requires yarn. Yarn is made by a procedure that twists the wool fibers from the pile so that the fibers cling together. Twisting the separated fibers into yarn is a process called spinning. During medieval times, most yarn spinning used a simple tool, called a drop spindle. The spinner begins by hand twisting the fibers. Another way to begin twisting is to rub fibers from the wool pile in one direction across an apron or a pants leg.

Spinners tied the twisted fibers starter to the drop spindle. When dropped, the spindle twists. Twisting action spins, spirals, and binds the wool fibers together. Continuous controlled action pulls fibers out of the wool pile intertwines the fibers together to spin a single strand of yarn. The spinner controls both the amount of fiber pulled into yarn and the speed of the spindle."

Dr. MacGregor – Weaving Yarn into Woolen Cloth. "In medieval times, nearly everyone spun wool into yarn. Weaving cloth required hundreds of yards of yarn. Once children learned the feel of how to spin wool fibers into yarn, they spun yarn every day. While spinning, people talked with friends. Talking while spinning yarn created a term for sharing stories, 'yarn spinning'. When friends talk and spin together, they develop a working rhythm. When folks work together, they finished the job far more quickly.

Dyeing wool was optional. There were two distinct methods for dyeing. To hold dye, wool must be clean. One coloring method was to dye the fleece, the other was to dye the yarn."

To produce cloth, weavers operated looms loaded with the woolen yarns. Every village in Scotland boasted at least one weaver. Each weaver developed a unique pattern, a signature plaid design, (yarn threads woven into a distinctive pattern to identify the cloth produced in the shop). The signature plaid design pattern identified the weaver. Most of the folks who lived close to, or within a certain vicinity, obtained their plaid cloth from the same weaver. Since the weaver created a distinctive plaid pattern, those who lived near that business ended up wearing the same plaid in the village and surrounding vicinity. The woven plaid, also known as the Tartan, became the national dress for Scotland.

Chapter 35 | *2019* | Weaver Family

The Professors - Lecture Notes

Professor Greenwood – "During the 14th Century, some people emigrated from their native land to another. They moved to find a better quality of life for themselves and their families. People left their native land to find a more attractive economic situation. Unstable or unsafe political situation caused people to migrate from their homelands. Religious differences also drove people from their homes. Considerable economic and political disagreements took place in late Medieval Europe. Governments of Scotland and Flanders formed an alliance. The countries reached an agreement between King David II of Scotland and King Philip VI of France."

Dr. McGregor – "King Edward III needed money to finance England's armies. He maneuvered to monopolize control of the wool trade. Wool acted as the currency to pay English taxes. Edward based his royal budget on the value of wool promised to him by Parliament.

In 1340, Parliament agreed on legislation to standardize the weight for a sack of wool. From that date on, a sack of wool was to weigh 26 stones. The weight of a stone was fixed at 14 pounds. 26 stones, multiplied by 14 pounds = 364 pounds of wool in one sack.

In 1341, the Scots captured Edinburg Castle. King of Scotland David II returned from exile."

Professor Greenwood – "English leaders closed off access to education for Scottish lads at Oxford and Cambridge. To obtain a university education, the edict forced Scottish students to travel to Paris. Young men visited the region in and around the city. In the great European Cathedrals, students experienced awe and wonder.

The clergy believed that stories illustrated on tapestries which hung in the Great Cathedral, helped parishioners strengthen their faith. The vast majority of people were illiterate. However, they knew their Bible stories. Throughout their lives, in medieval times folks listened to Bible stories, acted out Bible stories, and enjoyed Bible stories during dramatic productions. From the beginning to the end of the church calendar, familiar stories were read aloud. Symbolic details and visual depictions illustrated the tapestry and served as memory aides."

Dr. McGregor – "Symbols and illustrations embedded in the tapestry guided believers. A picture needs a story. Visuals enabled parishioners to remember the sequence depicted in the story. Parents brought children into the Great Cathedral. Mothers and fathers carefully explained how the pictures on the tapestries told the Bible stories. They required children to explain the illustrations to clarify understanding. A beautiful tapestry brought joy and comfort to believers.

Weavers around the city of Arras produced the most striking tapestries. In fact, so exquisite were the images, their products acquired the name of the city to identify their origin. Rather than being called tapestries, the finest woven art acquired the name, 'Arras.'"

Chapter 36 | 1458 | Weaver Family Memories

Brother Tanner

William the Weaver, Age 15 – William stood the same full six feet height as David. Unlike David's slim athletic build, William carried massive shoulders. He outweighed David by two stone. The additional weight was all muscle. William's shock of hair shone like new fluffy snow on a bright cloudless day. A piercing deep blue colored his eyes. His clear complexion tinted copperish high cheeks. At age 15 years, William was the oldest. His voice sounded deep and manly, though not nearly as deep as David's. He spoke more slowly and softer than David as well.

William and David were best friends. Whenever David and William were present in the group the rest of us felt safe. We knew that they had our backs. Both were polite and respectful. Both tall lads demanded that respect and courtesy be practiced for every voice, and every idea whenever we met together. Respect and courtesy provided an opportunity for those of us who were younger and smaller to offer ideas. Together, William and David functioned as guardians for civility.

I always appreciated both of these young giants. I am sure that Jonathan and Russell shared my feelings. We spoke of William and David many times. Both were excellent athletes. David ran faster, although William also ran fast. William had stronger arms and shoulders. William was the best at the caber toss. He also excelled at the shot put and hammer throw.

Weavers produced woolen cloth in various weights, colors, and plaids. As a young man, William mastered every technique. In the shoppe, William set up the looms. His father inspected. Father taught the process to William.

The Weaver family worked closely with the Shepherds. Those two families shared ownership of the flock with the archdiocese. Owning sheep, reduced their cost of raw wool. During fleece harvest William and Rhona shared shearing duties with the Shepherds.

Rhona The Weaver – Rhona's hair refracted the color of light-yellow honey. Her hair glowed like light from the warm summer sun. She instructed her close friend Bess to keep her hair sheared to just shy of shoulder length. Frequently, Rhona pulled her hair up to secure it. When Rhona wore her hair up, I thought it looked like she wore the crown of a princess.

However, Rhona wore her hair up for a practical reason. She always wore it up when she worked on the looms. Wearing her hair up, kept loose strands away from the yarns in the looms. Her skilled fingers moved nimbly across, over and through the warps and wafts in the loom. Her fingers moved so rapidly that my eyes found it impossible to follow the tasks of ten fingers moving independently. Rhona explained her reasons to keep her hair short, "Weaving stray strands of my own hair into the tapestry was disadvantageous."

At age 13, and 5'9 height, Rhona towered over the other lasses. I know that her height sometimes made her uncomfortable. Only two lads were then taller than Rhona. Yet, in spite of the uncomfortable feeling, Rhona always carried herself regally. Like a queen, when she walked with perfect posture, Rhona floated above us.

Rhona's eyes were those of an artist who maintained perfect harmony with color. Some call the color of such eyes, hazel. Hazel eyes are sympathetic to other colors. When Rhona wore green fabric, her eyes appeared green. However, when she wore blue fabric, her eyes picked up the color blue. I found this attribute of Rhona's eyes especially endearing. As a fellow color artist, I recognized Rhona's true genius to color her tapestry.

Rhona produced tapestry masterpieces. She could transfer any cartoon to tapestry. She mastered the standard looms. Rhona was an expert on the new, large loom. She knew the secrets to weave metal threads of gold and silver into the tapestry. She created scenes which reflected sunlight filtered through the stained glass and shined with life.

The Weavers worked closely with the Shepherds. Rhona also worked closely with me as an artist. Frequently, we worked cooperatively to create artistic design in tapestry. Rhona maintained close contact with Bessie the Shepherd and Heather the Carpenter.

William maintained close contact with the Carpenters. The looms were constructed of wood. At times, the large instruments required repair and replacement. A close relationship with skilled carpenters offered an advantage when looms needed timely repair.

All the friends looked up to William and Rhona. Obviously, the first reason that we looked up to them was because the two Weavers towered over the rest of us. All of us except David, who stood eye to eye with William. The Weavers always maintained friendly relationships with everyone. Never did they look down on anyone. Nor did they look down on any good faith idea or proposal.

The Weavers were problem solvers. Both combined vision, imagination, patience, and skills whenever they confronted a problem. They loved to pitch in and help others. I suppose the daily practice of operating a loom prepared them well to overcome any problematic issues.

Chapter 37 | 1458 | An Immigrant Family History

Brother Tanner

William shared the Weaver family story with me. Sometime during the early 1340s, two canons recruited William and Rhona's grandfather and grandmother to come to St. Andrews. The Weaver family migrated from Arras, Flanders. Upon arrival in Scotland, Grandfather Weaver changed the family name from Fleming to Weaver. In addition to weaving fabric for clothing, some highly skilled weavers possess the knowledge and vision to create tapestry.

In 1332, following the death of Bishop James Bane, the office of the bishop remained vacant for more than nine years. However, the work of bringing souls to God never ceased. The canons continued to lead the Cathedral faithful. They carried on with their sacred work until the election of a new bishop occurred.

Church members desired to add glorious tapestries to the new Cathedral. In the late 1330s, two canons departed St. Andrews for Europe. During their time overseas the canons encountered enormous, exquisite tapestries. The beauty of the woolen masterpieces. enchanted the men.

Following consecration on February 18, 1342, the new bishop, William Landallis, summoned the two canons to return. On arrival, the three holy men discussed the bishop's vision. He desired to enhance the grandest building in Scotland with magnificent tapestries. Some tapestry designs indicated the season of the clerical year. Seasonal tapestry adorned the pulpit and the lectern.

Scenes and symbols which displayed stories from the Bible and from the saints were woven into kneeler coverings. Tapestry covered cushions. Brilliantly colored tapestries hanging along walls warmed and softened the stone expanse. Bishop Landallis believed that fine tapestry displayed in the Cathedral would glorify the Holy Word.

Bishop Landallis assigned the canons to find weavers capable of creating tapestry worthy of St. Andrews. If they succeeded in finding an acceptable candidate, the plan would move to the next phase. Bring a renowned weaver to St. Andrews.

On the continent, the canons scouted several cathedrals. Every time they discovered a fine tapestry, they interviewed local clergy. The canons searched diligently to find the weavers who produced such amazing beauty. Tapestries worthy of gracing the new Cathedral were produced in one vicinity. To report the results of their mission the canons requested an immediate audience with Bishop Landallis upon their return. They reported that they found weavers of superior artistic tapestry in Arras. Fine woolen creations produced there were no longer called 'tapestry'. Instead, the woven art earned the name, 'Arras'.

The canons persuaded the bishop to send a team to Arras to recruit a master weaver. Bishop Landallis agreed. He immediately dispatched the same two canons back to Arras. Their new mission was to bring the right weaver to St. Andrews, the man who would produce the legendary St. Andrews Cathedral artistic Arras (tapestry). A Scots wool merchant who was a childhood friend of one canon worked in Arras.

When the three men met they delighted in the recall of so many shared moments from long ago. The wool merchant recalled Cathedral Consecration Day, July 5, 1318. The men remembered sitting together. While the merchant spoke, the men shared intense feelings from that day. Chills ran up their spines. Once again, they felt like lads. On Consecration Day, Robert the Bruce rode his horse right into the Cathedral. The men recalled standing so close to Robert the Bruce they could reach out and touch his horse.

The canons informed the Scotsman of their mission to bring a weaver whose work would glorify God to St. Andrews. Fortune smiled on the canons. The wool merchant knew all the finest weavers around Arras. Local weavers and their families thoroughly enjoyed his jovial company. They also appreciated doing a profitable business with the Scotsman. He identified weavers who produced the highest-quality work. The Scotsman recommended and introduced the canons to Grandfather Weaver's Shoppe.

When the canons saw Grandfather Weaver's tapestries, they agreed. They found the right weaver. He created glorious Arras. His creations would be a stunning treasure to enhance the grandeur of the Great Cathedral. The work would glorify God. Surely, such beauty would bring souls to the Church.

The canons told Grandfather Weaver about the Cathedral. They sang the bishop's praises. The most sacred spot in Scotland, where the bones of St. Andrew the Disciple rested, deserved to be surrounded by the finest artwork. The canons extended Bishop Landallis' bona fide offer of a commission to Grandfather Weaver. To the Weaver family, the commission looked like a wonderful opportunity.

Grandfather Weaver accepted the commission. He felt inspired to create beautiful tapestries for the Great Cathedral. He agreed to bring his talents and his family, consisting of a wife and three sons to St. Andrews. Two economic advantages appealed to Grandfather Weaver. He wanted to take advantage of the high-quality wool produced in the St. Andrews area. He also wanted to avoid the high import taxes that he was forced to pay on Scottish wool in Flanders. Economic hardships resulting from high taxes made the family unhappy in Flanders.

Before departing, the Weaver family acquired improved technology. To produce the Cathedral sized tapestries required weaving with the new larger loom. The larger loom provided the family with the capability to complete special orders. The newly commissioned tapestries were double the size of any previous pieces the Weavers previously produced. Grandfather Weaver sold the family holdings in Flanders. He carefully disassembled the valuable looms. The family packed their goods. The Weavers said goodbye to Flanders and migrated to St. Andrews.

When Bishop William Landallis viewed samples of Grandfather Weaver's work, he was delighted. Bishop Landallis immediately commissioned three major tapestries to hang in the Great Cathedral. The newly commissioned tapestries featured gold and silver threads. Precious threads of gold and silver helped illuminate the tapestries.

Grandfather and grandmother Weaver arrived in St. Andrews around the year 1342. They arrived twenty-four years following completion and consecration of the great Cathedral.

In 1350, tragedy struck! The Black Death infected St. Andrews! People suffered. Within the Cathedral campus infection and mortality rates of the deadly disease were extremely high. More than 60 percent of the holy men and women died.

The Plague did not spare the Weaver family. Just as Grandfather and Grandmother Weaver neared completion of the first full tapestry both fell sick. Two brothers contracted the disease and passed in that same year. Father and grandfather suffered for a year before they recovered. The disease left the two Weavers so weakened that they were unable to resume work until 1351.

Years later, after I became a canon, I heard the story about how the Weaver family came to St. Andrews from the canons. Their version began shortly before the devastating arrival of the Black Death. The plague took more than half of those who lived at the Cathedral complex. Sadly, the dead included the two canons who recruited Grandfather Weaver.

Three canons who worked with me when I was a young scribe, still remembered by name the two canons Bishop William Landallis selected to go to Flanders in search of a weaver. The canons confirmed the reason for the Weaver family migration was to produce the treasures named the St. Andrews Arras (tapestries). I remember that the canons who worked with me told me the names of those two canons. Their names were Brother Daniel and Brother Peter.

Bishop Landallis led the Christian community from 1342-1385. William told me that he was born in the year that Bishop Landallis passed away. In a gesture that pleased Grandfather and grandmother Weaver, William's parents chose to honor the family patron and named him for the bishop.

The grandparents taught the master secrets of tapestry weaving to their son, William and Rhona's father. Father passed the secrets of weaving valuable gold and silver thread into the treasured tapestries on to his children. By age 14, William mastered known weaving techniques.

William was closer to becoming a grown man than any of the other lads in the circle of friends. We frequently sought William's experience, insight, and guidance. He planned to continue the family business. William listened intently. He showed us how to listen carefully to ideas. For success in business, he knew the advantage of listening carefully.

Both Rhona and William possessed a keen eye for detail. Their fingers were skilled and nimble. When they worked on the loom, I found it impossible to follow the swift movements of their hands and fingers. Their fingers moved at great speed when they reproduced a cartoon (a drawing of the image on parchment) into fabric. Manual skill and speed developed as a result of many hours of working on the loom every day. Their skilled hands and nimble fingers were also incredibly strong. At fourteen, William's bow was among the heavier draw weights the Bowyers produced.

William and Rhona brought much to our Circle. They were important contributors in our quest to invent the new game. In addition to skills, Rhona brought a pleasant, cheerful disposition. She loved conversation. Like her brother, Rhona demonstrated the attributes of a powerful listener. All the friends enjoyed talking with her. Rhona owned a knack for problem solving. To confront a problem she applied curiosity and creativity. She delivered great insight. When the group became enmired in a problem we counted on Rhona to find a different perspective.

Chapter 38 | 1458 | The Tapestry Artist

Brother Tanner

Color is integral to weaving fabric. Rhona's passion for color opened her mind. She strove to acquire knowledge concerning color production. Vibrant colors required quality materials. Tapestries feature rich vivid color. To produce a tapestry worthy of the Great Cathedral, demanded bright yarns. Rhona featured brilliant colors in the designs she created.

Dyes produced from locally grown plants transformed the yarns. Rhona established a close relationship with the litester, or dyer. The litester maintained a garden to cultivate mader, weld and woad. Mader was the source for red dye. Weld made yellow. The rich blues for which Scotland is so famous came from woad.

The plant harvest began in their first growing season. Strict procedures produced stunning vegetable dyes. Following harvest, sheep grazed on the remaining plant matter to ready the garden for planting the following Spring. Margaret joined Rhona to learn about the native plants to make dyes at the hands of the litester.

Wool held dye. Leather also held brilliant colors made from the plants in the litester's garden. Everyone knows that Scottish lasses are born with an eye for color.

The Cathedral commission designated that gold threads and silver threads were to be woven into their tapestries. Rhona possessed great skill on all the looms which paired with a wonderful eye for detail. Her nimble, talented fingers produced the highly prized designs. On the loom, Rhona and her mother performed the most intricate operations.

To fulfill the Cathedral orders for four new grand tapestries, the Weaver family invested in the acquisition of another large loom. The large loom, plus the other looms in the shoppe consumed massive amounts of yarn.

To keep the looms operating at high capacity, the weavers needed far more yarn than one family could spin. To obtain yarn in sufficient quantities necessitated exploring new options. To acquire a sufficient supply of yarn, one option came from trade. In exchange for yarn, the Weavers offered finished cloth from their looms. Trade provided the weavers with far more yarn than they could spin. However, even the increased acquisition of homespun yarn failed to produce a sufficient quantity to solve the supply of yarn problem for tapestry creation.

The Weaver family learned of a new technology to spin yarn. The new way offered the advantage of spinning yarn at a far faster rate and a more uniform quality than the drop spindle. To increase the supply of quality yarn, the Weavers sought to acquire a new large spinning wheel.

The Weaver close contact with the Carpenters paid off. The two families of skilled tradesmen worked together to repair looms. They also designed and custom-built new looms.

The Weavers asked the Carpenters if they would have an interest in producing a large spinning wheel. The Weaver and Carpenter families worked together to design and build the first big spinning wheel used in St. Andrews.

Compared to drop spinning, the large spinning wheel enabled a skilled spinner to produce a far greater amount of high quality yarn at a much higher rate of speed. In addition, using the wheel allowed the yarn to load directly onto skeins.

A skein is a length of yarn or thread wound on a reel or swift. Full skeins could load directly onto the large loom. The Weavers taught several women who lived close by to spin yarn on the big wheel. Because several skilled spinning wheel operators were available, the large wheel could be operated almost continuously. To keep the wheel spinning yarn all through the day, three ladies staggered their work. Their labor was paid for with finished cloth from the looms.

After the successful build and operation of the first large spinning wheel, the Weavers wanted more wheels. They contracted the Carpenters to construct two more large spinning wheels for their shoppe. When the Weavers placed three large spinning wheels in operation, the business maintained a plentiful supply of yarn for all their looms.

Chapter 39 | 1399 | The Cartoon

Rhona became among the first of her gender to master the new large loom. To work the large instrument, Rhona's height and reach provided a great advantage. Her eye for meticulous detail helped envision beautiful scenes during the design process. To dazzle viewers' eyes, she incorporated fine points from Bible stories. Particular details guided congregants' recall. Scenes woven into the tapestry connected memories to the church members' feelings. She created scenes which emphasized the important ideas contained within the story. Rhona and her brother wanted to provide the Cathedral with storytelling tapestries.

"Knock, knock!"

"Thomas, may I come in?" Rhona entered the tannery.

"Aye, Rhona, of course. Come in. Please, come in."

I thought Rhona came to the Tannery to pick up the Weavers' regular parchment order. While the canons bought the largest amount of parchment, we also maintained a standing order to supply parchment to the Weavers. For copying the Holy texts the canons demanded vellum, the highest quality parchment.

Weavers bought parchment of a quality lower than vellum. They did not use parchments for writing or illuminated manuscripts. Weavers used parchments to draw cartoons. Cartoons were detailed drawings. When Weavers created woven images, they used cartoons as guides. They copied the cartoon on their looms. Cartoons enabled weavers to visualize exquisitely detailed scenes before they were woven into fine tapestries.

"How may I help you, Rhona? Are you here to pick up your parchment order?" I asked.

"Aye." Rhona responded. "I am here to pick up the order. Also, Thomas, I have another issue. I think you are the only one in all of St. Andrews who can help me with this problem. Only you have the expertise that will help me. I don't really trust anyone else."

"How can that be, Rhona? What is it that only I, of all those who reside in our town can do?

"I need to create a panel featuring a lamb and an ewe. Look at this cartoon I drew. I am so disappointed with the appearance."

"Rhona, I think you have drawn a wonderful likeness of a lamb and ewe. What seems to be the problem?"

"Thomas, thank you for the compliment. I put in a considerable amount of time and effort to produce the cartoon. However, the problem is, I can see that the proportions are just wrong. I know if I reproduce this cartoon on the loom, Father and Mother will be disappointed. That will disappoint me. I don't know what the problem is. I just know that if I copy this cartoon on the loom, it simply will not work."

"Aye, Rhona. I am beginning to understand. I may be able to help you. Before I start to draw, let's talk some more. Help me to see the problem as you see it."

"Thomas, for this panel the lamb must be the most important part. The lamb is a symbol to represent Lord Jesus. I need to make the lamb shine. Yet, if I simply make the lamb large, it is all out of proportion compared to his mother ewe. The cartoon I created is simply inadequate. It fails to convey the right symbolism for the panel within the context of the story. There is no drama to my scene. The image just looks flat and cold. Does my explanation make sense to you?"

"Aye, Rhona. I understand your concern now. I do have an idea. Do you want me to sketch it for you?"

"Thomas, that would be wonderful. I have a request. If you might consider."

"What is it, Rhona?"

"Thomas, when you compose the cartoon, might I watch you while you draw?"

"Certainly, Rhona. May I ask you why you want to watch me while I draw the cartoon?"

"You draw likenesses differently than anyone else. The results are always so beautiful. I want to watch you while you are in the act of drawing. I want to observe your process. I want to see the techniques you employ. I hope to learn something about the process. Perhaps I can apply some of your drawing technique to the way I manipulate threads on the loom."

"Rhona, that is a marvelous idea. Now that I know why you wish to observe the drawing process, I can do more to help you. I can describe the techniques I am using. I can share with you why I choose a particular approach. If, at any point, you want to know what I am doing or why I do something, please stop me. Feel free to ask why I use that technique. Talking about my drawing helps me to think about my drawing process. I know that talking and thinking about drawing helps me to improve my own skills."

"I think watching you, talking with you, and thinking with you, will challenge me to improve my skills to create my art. I believe as I work to reproduce cartoons on the loom, I will do a better job. I don't know exactly what I expect to learn. I will observe you with a discerning eye and a questioning mind."

"Rhona, may I ask a personal favor? I wonder if I might observe you when you transfer my cartoon to the tapestry?"

"Of course, Thomas. All right then. When will you be available to work on drawing the cartoon?"

"Rhona, I have time right now. Are you available now?"

"I am."

Rhona handed me a sheet of parchment. She had previously trimmed the parchment to the exact size she needed for the panel in the tapestry.

"Where do you want to place the lamb and the ewe on the panel, Rhona?"

"I believe the Lamb should be in front. The body in the bottom left with the face in the center." Rhona explained. "Then, I wish to place the ewe in the top right. Do you think you can make that work?"

"I think I can. When you mentioned that you wanted the Lamb to shine before, did that mean you wanted a halo around the Lamb?" I asked.

"Aye, I wish to place a halo around the Lamb's head. I plan to make the halo using gold threads. What do you think of that idea, Thomas?"

"I think it a splendid concept. I look forward to seeing your creation featuring the golden halo. I have an idea for your cartoon. You can look over my shoulder if you wish. Perhaps you can see what I envision as I draw. Feel free to ask me questions at any time."

"Thank you, Thomas. I feel very comfortable watching you at work." Rhona added.

I began drawing the cartoon by placing the Lamb's face in the center of the panel. Lightly, I outlined the size of the face. Then, I visualized a perspective line. My use of perspective differed from the flat outline that Rhona had drawn. I placed the body of the Lamb in a comfortable reclining posture. The Lamb's body curled diagonally to the bottom left. The perspective guided the viewer to look down on a contented Lamb resting in the pasture.

Then, I shifted the perspective from the main figure. I focused on an outline for the mother ewe. I deliberately made the ewe smaller. However, I wanted the smaller size to represent a physical distance away from the Lamb. To make the appearance of distance work, I placed the ewe's body at an angle to enhance the illusion of distance. I asked Rhona what she thought about the sizes and the new perspective.

"Thomas, I think you have guided me to solve my problem. Those two figures should work beautifully to fit into this pattern. If you will complete your cartoon in ink on parchment, I already have some yarns and threads I envision. Please continue."

I completed the drawing. To accentuate the perspective on both figures, I added some subtle shading. I wanted the face to look three dimensional, rather than two. The shading and the lines focused on the Lamb's face. Rhona saw exactly what the shading did for the cartoon.

"Thomas, the perspective difference helped. When you applied the shading you provided me with just what I needed to understand the problem. Don't worry about drawing in the halo. I am quite pleased with the cartoon. I already know what I want to do about the halo."

We carried the parchment order to the Weaver Shoppe. I handed the cartoon to Rhona. She secured the cartoon behind the waft threads on her loom. She gathered skeins of various colors which she planned to weave into the tapestry. I watched her set up the loom. She began to weave the warp through the waft. Watching her at work was a glorious gift. She worked confidently.

Rhona wove a few strands of gold thread in the body of the Lamb. The gold threads truly did make the Lamb shine. The gold threads also served to direct the eyes of the viewer to the face of the Lamb. She surrounded the face with a heavy golden semicircle. The circle of the halo was broken only by the Lamb's body. Her tapestry was glorious!

Rhona thanked me for drawing the cartoon that guided her to the solution for her problem.

"All I did was draw a simple line perspective cartoon." I answered. "It was you who created this incredibly beautiful tapestry."

"Thank you, Thomas. However, I know that I needed you to help me solve my problem. You brought a new approach. You added the right perspective to help me solve my problem. Thank you so much."

Rhona was the true artist. She completed the treasured St. Andrews Tapestries.

I thanked Rhona for giving me the opportunity to contribute my talent. I offered to help her with cartoons anytime.

Chapter 40 | 1399 | The Compliment Circle

Rhona believed she sat alone. In the corner of the Weaver workshop, the tallest lass in St. Andrews drooped. Her shoulders hunched, her back curved and her head dropped. She held her face in her hands. Tears uncontrollably flooded her cheeks and fingers. Sobs punctuated the deluge.

Rhona was not alone. In the doorway, her dear friends, the other five lasses silently appeared. The lasses came to check on their friend, Rhona. They wished to see if she was available to join them in a group meeting consisting of all six lasses.

"Oh, Rhona, are you feeling sad?" Bessie the Shepherd asked. Her tone showed deep concern. "You seem to be sobbing."

"Are we disturbing you, Rhona?" Barbara the Bowyer gently questioned. "If you need to be alone, we can come another time."

"If there is anything we can do to help, we are all here for you." Margaret the Tanner comforted.

"Oh. I am so ashamed that you saw me crying. I thought I was alone. I was just indulging in what Mother calls a 'pity party.'" Rhona explained.

"What on earth do you mean by a 'pity party'?" Marion the Shoemaker queried.

"If I begin to feel sorry for myself and mother notices, she chastises me. She reminds me of the blessings in my life. What a joy it is to have a trade in which I can create beauty! She points out the joy of being part of a healthy family. And of course, she talks about the wonderful friends with whom I share so much joy.

It has become a family tradition to measure each lad and lass on the same date every year in order to determine how much taller we have grown. We place a mark on the kitchen door frame with our initials. Over the past year, I grew another two inches. Not only am I the tallest lass in St. Andrews, but I continue to grow.

I feel like I am destined to continue growing forever. Will this growing taller never stop? I feel like I will never fit in with the rest of you. Just look at you. You are all so dainty and so pretty. When I stand next to all of you, I feel like a giant clumsy freak.

When Mother sees me feeling sorry for myself, she makes a joke. She tells me that I am indulging in such a waste of time and energy. That is what Mother calls a 'pity party.'" While Rhona spoke, she attempted to cease sobbing.

"Oh Rhona, you are so beautiful. Being a tall lass is such a blessing. Whenever I see you gliding across the Links, I think of how regal you appear. It pains me to hear that you feel so sad about being tall." The tiny Marion stated.

"I agree with Marion, Rhona. When you stand up straight, when you walk or run or dance, you are so elegant. You are a pretty lass." Heather added.

"I am so envious of your height, Rhona," observed Barbara. "You can easily see things naturally. I am unable to see the same objects without climbing on a stool or up a ladder."

"In addition, you can reach things that I must ask Father or brother to reach. Sometimes asking for help from men makes me feel helpless. I don't care for that feeling of depending on men to get something for me." Said Heather.

"It is true, my ability to reach provides an advantage when I work on the new larger loom. I love to focus on weaving the tapestry assignments for the Great Cathedral. Making beautiful scenes and designs in the tapestry does bring me great satisfaction." Rhona sniffled. She began to regain some composure.

"When you stand up straight and tall, Rhona, you look so beautiful you take my breath away!" Marion pronounced. "It always seems like candlelight shines all around you whenever you stand tall showing your perfect posture."

"Honestly, I do understand the advantages of being tall. But look at me. Do I really need to be this tall? I am taller than most of the lads. Being taller than most of the lads is no advantage for a lass."

"Think about when we dance. There is not one single lad who doesn't want to take his turn to dance with you, Rhona. You are as fine a dancer as any of the other lasses." Margaret praised.

"I agree. I noticed that whenever we dance the lads look forward to their turn with the tall and stately Rhona." Barbara claimed. "Surely, you noticed that also."

"Oh Rhona, we all feel blessed that you are our friend." Heather added.

"Each one of us appreciates who you are!" Bess exclaimed. "We feel blessed to have a friend who is as tall you are."

Marion continued. "But being tall is only one part of what makes you such a special friend."

"You are so responsible. We know we can always count on you to do your share of the work for the group. You always help us make sure the work is correct and complete." Margaret appreciated.

"We know you always listen to each person, each idea, each presentation made to the whole group." Margaret said.

"The Tapestry you create will be admired and appreciated for many, many decades to come. It is stunningly beautiful." Barbara complimented.

"You are a wonderful dancer." Bess stated.

"You are a terrific runner. You run fast and you can leap over high hurdles. You win your share of races. Even when you don't win, you are competitive. You always run hard and often come in close to first place." Marion praised.

"Every time we compete in a contest, you give us your best effort. We know you will play to win." added Heather. "At the same time, you encourage the lasses and our brothers to do our best at all times."

"Honestly, we do not care if you continue growing, or if you grow no taller. We value you as a total person. You are our dear friend." Barbara reassured.

"Even though you are the tallest lass, Rhona, two lads are taller than you are right now." Bess counseled.

"Aye. And everyone knows that lads grow tall more slowly than lasses. Soon there will be another lad or two who will stand as tall, or even taller than you stand." Marion observed.

The lasses completed giving the compliment shower to their friend. Rhona smiled. A compliment shower from friends provides one powerful tool when a friend feels sad. Whenever the friends realized that someone was feeling hurt, or feeling bad, they wanted to help that person change that feeling. A compliment shower often helped. Reception of a shower of genuine sincere compliments from trusted friends, helped another person feel better and stronger.

It was time to determine the results of this compliment shower. The lasses asked themselves, "Did Rhona feel better? Or did she need more comments?"

"Ah. Aye. That may be true if I ever stop growing taller." Rhona conceded.

"Well, I think you just may have grown as tall as you ever will, Rhona."

"I hope you are right, Marion.

Chapter 41 | *1458* | Shepherd Family

Brother Tanner

The Shepherds family cottage fencing bordered the community ground on the Links. Proximity to pasture and shelter helped the family manage the large flock efficiently. The stable and fenced barnyard secured the flock.

The family consisted of Father, Mother, Bessie, and David. Shepherds worked hard raising, husbanding, tending and shearing the flock. Two important partners slept near the house. The "useful dogs", a male, named Boghan, and a smaller female, named Saighead, worked intimately with the family.

Bessie the Shepherd, Age 14. Bessie's hair, blending tones of russet and sienna with chestnut highlights, cascaded in long tresses to her trim waist. On the Links, she frequently wore braids. Bessie worked outside all day, all year. The sun kissed her face. Her complexion exploded in light freckles. Freckles enhanced her friendly, natural smile. Bessie stood 5'2. At age 14, Bessie was the oldest lass. Her favorite color was light orange.

Bessie combined athletic and musical talents. She played flute expertly. Since the times preceding the Biblical David, countless shepherds shared musical and athletic talents. Bessie asked reflective questions which challenged the friends to think and consider.

The many hours of loneliness inherent within shepherding invited Bessie to indulge in daydreams. She observed animals and plants on the Links continually. However, she knew how to keep herself and others on task. Bessie was responsible and trustworthy. She employed excellent communication into her managerial skills.

Bessie learned how her animals responded to different stimuli. When the flock grazed peacefully, she often pulled out her small flute. The sound her flute created soothed the flock, the collies, and communicated to David that all is well.

Together, Bessie and David directed the collies. The job contained two major goals:
1. To maintain a healthy flock
2. To keep grasses on the Links productive.

Bessie was devoted to David. Lovingly, she guided him to develop the skills of the profession. She listened. She served as a sounding board for his ideas and questions. She was so proud to see David develop into an accomplished speaker.

David the Shepherd, Age 13. David's light brown hair color mimicked dry straw. At age 13, light freckles spotted his smooth complexion. David stood an even six-foot. His height meant friends 'looked up' to him physically. We also looked up to David because of his integrity. He never cheated. A commanding speaker, David was blessed with a deep rich voice. He spoke clearly and deliberately. He never mumbled. His voice compelled us to listen. We always knew where David stood on any issue. David was also a wonderful listener. The combination careful listener and effective speaker always served David in the midst of any discussion. David focused. His power to focus helped keep others on task as well.

To solve problems, David applied creative approaches. He was observant and reflective. He never hesitated to ask questions. David valued facts. David changed his mind when he listened to a logical presentation of factual evidence. He expected the same of others. To build his arguments he cited facts. His ability to understand facts clearly, intensely listen, and speak powerfully made David an excellent communicator. Whether in a discussion or in a fight, David was one you wanted on your side. David was athletically precocious. His ability to run fast, coupled with amazing agility served him well, especially when the sheep required a guiding hand.

With so many hours of time away from other humans, David was a dreamer like his sister. But he did not dream as an escape, David welcomed and shouldered responsibility. His dreams often led to visionary solutions.

To stay in communication beyond the range of their own voices, the Shepherds employed various means. They developed clear communication using whoops, whistles, and arm signals. Like Bessie, David enjoyed creating music. Both played the flute and they loved to play duets.

David trusted Bessie completely, though the two enjoyed teasing each other good naturedly. The two worked together. They were on their own every day. They experienced the frustrating loneliness shepherds endure.

The Shepherds knew the geography of the Links intimately. They kept track of every square yard. They followed the calendar closely and knew which week to expect the appearance of the sweet grass. In their heads, they mapped out seasonal, weekly, and daily grazing patterns. To sustain a healthy and productive pasture, they adapted and rotated grazing patterns each day.

Both Shepherds continuously studied the sky. Weather on the Links could change rapidly several times during a day. When sudden storms appeared, they guided the flock into the safety of the numerous bunkers on the Links. Shepherds were no strangers to danger. To confront dangerous conditions Bessie and David adapted to manage the situation.

COLLIES Shepherds and their "useful dogs", tended the sheep on the Links. David named his collie, Boghan, the Scottish word for 'bow'. David chose the name because Boghan could send the sheep exactly where David wanted them. For similar reasons Bessie named her dog, Saighead, the Scottish word for 'arrow'.

So skilled at communicating with, and managing their collies were David and Bessie, that when folk watched the team at work, it appeared that all the lad and lass had to do was think. The collies seemed to read their minds. The dogs anticipated how to solve the problem. Usually, the collies anticipation was correct. They performed the task exactly the way that Bessie and David wanted.

To command collies, handlers master an ancient language shared between shepherds and working dogs. Collies respond instantly to specific signals. The two collies complemented the lad and lass. They reacted to each other in tandem, similar to the connection of a bow and arrow. To perform the function of delivering an arrow to the right target, the skilled archer controls both the bow and arrow expertly. Employing two collies to work together to control the flock is as important to the shepherd as it was for an archer to control the bow and arrow. Under clear commands from Bessie and David to Boghan and Saighead, the collies gently directed sheep precisely to the desired destination.

Chapter 42 | 1399 | Collie Commands

The sheep grazed calmly. David signaled Boghan softly, 'Come by!' The command 'come by' sent Boghan in a clockwise direction. The collie crouched and creeped smoothly. The animal made himself highly visible to the flock. Sheep responded to the collies. The herd tightened formation. David watched. Then, he whistled. Boghan continued to crouch and creep. The collie purposely circled around the flock in the clockwise direction until David issued a different whistle command.

At precisely halfway around the flock, David whistled the signal, "Stop!" Instantly, the collie froze. Boghan made direct eye contact with David. David whistled the signal, "Lay down!" Immediately Boghan responded. The dog dropped. He dropped so hard that the Shepherd heard the collie's bones crunch on the ground. The collie flattened his body to the surface.

Bessie watched Boghan drop. The dog remained motionless in the collie crouch. Bessie signaled Saighead. Bessie commanded, 'Away to me!' Bessie told her collie to move quietly and stealthily counterclockwise. In the opposite direction to Boghan, her collie circled. Saighead gently guided the remainder of the flock to tighten formation and join the animals which Boghan herded.

Bessie whistled the signal, "Stop!" Instantly, Saighead stopped.

Then, Bessie commanded, "Lay down!" Immediately, Saighead dropped. Saighead's actions mirrored Boghan's work. Herded between the collies, the sheep felt secure from predators or outsiders. The flock grazed quietly, contentedly, and closely. Saighead and Bessie established eye contact.

From the position, 'lay down', Boghan kept watch on the sheep and on David. From the collie crouch, the dog could move in any direction at instant high speed. The collie stayed alert, ready to respond to any command from David.

Or, if even one sheep should stray outside the grazing area, Boghan raced to return the animal to the security of the herd.

Likewise, Saighead kept a close eye on the sheep and Bessie. The sheep knew that Boghan and Saighead were in control.

Chapter 43 | 2019 | Tanner Family and Business

The Professors - Lecture Notes

Professor Greenwood – "In Medieval St. Andrews, tanners and shoemakers formed an inter-dependent partnership. For millennia. leather furnished a most versatile and useful raw materials. Leather could be processed into a variety of grades and colors. Supple and soft, or strong and stiff, depending on the product's purpose, leather could be formed into virtually any shape or texture. The tannery supplied shoemakers with their most important material. To form shoes and the many other items produced in a shoemaker's shoppe, required several different types of leather. Shoemakers ordered and bought substantial quantities of leather from the Tanners.

Recently discovered drawings from 14th century St. Andrews recorded the tannery. The precise location was adjacent to the North side of the Castle complex. A tannery complex required access to a dependable supply of freshwater. In the 14th century, this tannery location bordered on the outskirts of the burg."

Dr. MacGregor – "Leather's versatility served a variety of needs to improve the quality of life in medieval Europe. For thousands of years people utilized leather for many different important purposes. Leather goods enhanced the quality of life for people in St. Andrews. Properly prepared animal hides provided the raw material resources to produce high quality leather. Freshly slaugh-tered animal hides provided raw material to make leather. To transform the rawhides into valuable leather required time to process. Many steps were performed in sequential operation. Each step in the transformation of a hide into leather involved a specific treatment. To remove waste flesh from the hide, tanners invested hours of skilled work and manipulation. Whole hide soaks initiated the process. During soaks, chemical additions began the transformation. To produce valuable leather sequential baths and soaks often required several days."

Professor Greenwood – "After farmers or butchers processed sheep, cattle and pigs for food, a significant amount of animal matter remained. Local butchers harvested and dressed the farm animals. Butchers kept the trimmed meats to sell as fresh meat, smoked meat, salted meats, and sausages to their customers. Hides produced a profitable by-product for butchers and farmers. Tanners bought the hides. In addition to the hides, they also received all the remaining animal parts. Horns and hooves were attached to the hides. The remainder of the carcass included the hide, the horns, hooves, and the bones. The weight of the remaining carcass roughly equaled the hanging weight of the meat. Hides were transported to the tannery for processing."

Dr. MacGregor – "From non-edible animal parts, tanners produced glues. Horns, hooves, and other tissue contain a chemical called collagen. The Tanners boiled the horns, hooves, and tissue to break down the chemicals contained in these animal parts. When treated properly, the boiled mixture produced a very sticky substance which could be transformed into a powerful glue. For the Shoemakers, glue provided another valuable material. Glue fastened and sealed seams for many different types of leather goods. To make shoes and boots which completely enclosed and protected feet in damp, cold climates required glue. Glue, supplied by the Tanners provided an important commodity for Carpenters and Bowyers.

Tanners mastered special skills to treat the hides through the various sequence of steps to create leather. The transformation of animal hides into leather demanded hard work. Specific treatments changed hides into different customized leathers. For people who lived in a climate that could be very hot or very cold, such as St. Andrews, leather was crafted into a variety of useful products."

Professor Greenwood – "Some leather was created to be soft and supple, like the leather in fine gloves. Some could be hard and stiff, like the heel for a boot or a shoe. Other leather was stiffened to serve as protective armor. In battle, leather shields deflected blows and strokes from bladed weapons to protect soldiers. Some treatments contrived to make leather supple and tough. Belts, harnesses, even a blacksmiths' apron utilized tough, supple leather. Leather performed other important functions. It made hinges for doors on sheds or barns. Saddles, stirrups, and bridles required reliable leather in several different formats and flexibilities to ride and control horses. Strong and flexible leather bridles guided and controlled draft animals (horses and oxen) to farm the fields. Expertly crafted shoes and boots kept feet warm and dry. To carry arrows safely and efficiently, archers ordered flexible leather sheaths. Bowmen added supple leather gloves to protect fingers when they pulled powerful bowstring to bend the bow. Stiff leather arm guards protected forearms from chaffing struck by released bowstrings. Leather provided useful goods.

Many of the favorite toys for children and adolescents in medieval Scotland, were formed from leather. One prized toy was a leather covered ball. Like children everywhere and throughout the ages, Scottish children loved to play with balls made from leather in various sizes."

Chapter 44 | 1458 | Tannery Memories

Brother Tanner

Thomas the Tanner, Age 12. At the time of the story, I stood 5'3. My hair was the color of Ginger, a shade of red. However, the color of my hair did not quite match the luster of my sister's locks. Both of us possessed lightly freckled faces. Seems like some kind of freckles go with every shade of red hair in Scotland. I possess green eyes. I was almost 13. Jonathan the Shoemaker and Russell the Bowyer were my two best friends. We were the three youngest lads. We talked about anything and everything.

Margaret and I strove to learn all we could about leather. Margaret specialized in glues and lacquers. She was also interested in dyes. She loved adding color to our lives. Customers were attracted to leather in different colors.

For fine gloves, we processed super soft and supple leather. We kept track of various chemical solutions required for the vats rooms in the shoppe. To produce leather in various forms and degrees of hardness and stiffness required us to learn and master many skills. Our profession required us to stay highly organized. At our tannery we specialized in custom leather processing. Margaret maintained the inventory. She procured the chemicals required to produce superior glues, lacquers, and dyes.

In addition to fine leathers, we produced fine parchment. We served two major customers, the Shoemakers for leathers, and the other was the Augustinian canons at the Cathedral for fine parchment. I specialized in producing parchment. The Tannery and Cathedral contracted to supply parchment to the Cathedral. Father and I worked diligently to supply a sufficient quantity of top-quality parchment. It was important for the family to maintain that contract because the Cathedral paid with coin rather than a trade of goods.

I was the best artist in the town of St. Andrews.

Margaret the Tanner, Age 14 Any amount of light, whether from bright summer noonday or the glow of evening's dying embers in the hearth ignited fire within Margaret's striking copper red hair. Like a brightly polished copper mirror, her hair shone. At age 14, Margaret stood 4'10. Tiny light freckles dotted the soft pale complexion across her pert little nose and spread across her high cheeks. Eyes colored deeply like precious emeralds pleasantly complemented the structure of her cheerful face.

Since age four, Margaret worked in the tannery. Among her many skills, she knew the entire sequence of steps to process leather from a freshly skinned raw hide to super soft and supple required to make fine gloves. Margaret specialized in custom leather processing. She learned the sequence of steps to produce leather in various degrees of hardness from soft and supple to strong and stiff. Margaret was highly organized and took responsibility to keep inventory for the shoppe. She kept track of the various chemical solutions required in the shoppe and the vats rooms. She procured the raw materials required to produce our superior glues and lacquers. In addition, Margaret also set the schedule for the various stages and steps during processing.

At the time of our story, Margaret became interested in producing high quality colors. In the town, no other tannery produced color in leather. Along with Rhona, Margaret studied with the litester. Both lasses possessed a passion for producing dyes. Margaret learned of new methods and materials for dyes. She combined mordants with coloring agents which produced striking new long-lasting colors for leathers. Margaret worked most closely with the Shoemakers, our most important leather and glue customer. We produced all the custom leathers the Shoemakers required. Shoe-makers also ordered preservatives and glues. Margaret also worked closely with Carpenters and Bowyers to supply them with glues, lacquers.

To produce leather in various forms and degrees of hardness and stiffness, Margaret learned many skills. She tracked the various chemical solutions to maintain the inventory for the production of the custom leathers. In the shop her organizational skills and knowledge were prized. She also kept track of the schedule for each production stage. Timing is important to add and sequence the correct chemicals for the products from our shop. Margaret had a special affinity for the production of glues and lacquers. The families kept each other apprised of the advances in new products.

Chapter 45 | 2019 | Shoemaker Family and Business

The Professors - Lecture Notes

Dr. MacGregor – "Shoemakers were one of the two most important high value customers for the Tanners. Many of the tanned leathers produced by the Tanners were custom processed for the Shoemakers. Parts of shoes and boots required stiff, hard leather. Other parts of footwear needed supple, strong leather. Specific treatment of hides made the leather hard and stiff, or supple and flexible. In addition to purchasing a variety of processed leathers, Shoemakers bought animal glues.

Though the name Shoemaker suggests the family makes only shoes, in reality, they created many leather items to sell. Besides shoes and boots, shoemakers made products from leather armor to leather hinges, saddles, sheaths, belts, bridles, and harnesses in the shop. Shoemakers learned to cut, sew, shape, and stitch leather into new useful and desirable objects. They made and sold items to the people who lived in and visited St. Andrews. Any leather item a customer desired, Shoemakers knew how to make it."

- - - - 1458 - - - -

Brother Tanner

Marion the Shoemaker, Age 12, Height 4' 6". Marion's appearance reminded me of a little doll. She was tiny and petite. Her complexion was fair and clear. She kept her soft, shining wavy chestnut brown hair sheared to shoulder length. Below her bangs, her warm brown eyes helped her capture a speaker's attention when she practiced her powerful listening skills. Tiny flecks of gold sparkles danced in her brown irises. She smiled easily and often. Her manner charmed everyone near her. Marion's personality was invitational. We always felt she had time to share with us. She was also extremely smart. She was an excellent problem solver. Great ideas, a clear and powerful voice, and the spirit to get the things done enhanced Marion's leadership abilities. Although Marion was the youngest lass, she displayed confidence in her actions and conversation. Her confidence served her well. She helped our group to function effectively. Fortunately for me and for all the friends, we knew Marion as a complete person.

Perhaps because of Marion's diminutive size, her voice could thunder. When she talked, she expressed power. Part of that power may have enhanced the volume level she projected. There was no shyness. She spoke confidently without arrogance. Her speaking ability compelled us to listen carefully. We wanted to consider her contribution to any discussion. Her true power inhabited the ideas she shared, rather than the sheer volume. Not only did Marion want to be heard and considered, but she also wanted all to be heard. Marion always encouraged others to participate and engage in the discussion. Marion always held her frame straight and tall.

Although petite she was perfectly proportioned in every way. Marion's tiny body offered significant advantages for her to develop. Of all the lasses, Marion's hands were the smallest. Her tiny nimble fingers produced the most delicate stitches. Her ability to create tiny, nearly invisible stitchery became legendary. To tie the tiny knots, Marion did not need to see the threads. Her sensitive fingertips tied the tiny knots by 'feel'. Her knots always held. In leatherworking, the ability to create tiny tight stitches provides a highly prized asset. When the thread was drawn tight and 'finished' by a strong knot, tiny stitches sealed seams which kept fingers warm and dry.

Marion and my sister Margaret were the closest of friends. Their friendship was good fortune for both families. The Shoemaker family worked most closely with the Tanner family.

Jonathan the Shoemaker, Age 11, Height 4'7". Jonathan was the youngest member of the circle of friends, and the shortest of the lads. Jonathan possessed exceptional leather working knowledge. He developed the skills to utilize that knowledge. Though not tall, Jonathan was very strong. His hands and fingers were dexterous and skilled. He knew how to design, cut, sew, and treat leather goods. Jonathan was very smart. At age three Jonathan joined his father and Marion in the shop. He learned how to design, plan, cut, punch and stitch leather. Jonathan learned very quickly. He was quite observant. Jonathan was full of questions. It did not matter if he was asking questions of his family or his friends. Sometimes the questions seem awkward, but usually another friend had the same question. Jonathan was a precocious problem solver who possessed tenacious willpower. Once he set his mind on a problem he refused to give in until he found an effective solution. His tenacity served him well.

Jonathan loved to play all the games the group played. He led by asking pertinent and sometimes impertinent questions. Because he is short, an outsider might think he think he must be physically weak. However, working with his hands since a very young age trained him to develop tremendous strength in his arms, wrists, hands, and fingertips. Even his friends were surprised by his strength. He seemed to get stronger every day. In addition to the strength in his hands and fingers, Jonathan possessed the fingertip control of an artist.

Because Jonathan was the youngest, the others indulged his sense of humor. The best part of his sense of humor was that Jonathan could laugh at himself honestly and whole heartedly. The others sincerely admired and appreciated his honest ability to laugh at himself. Jonathan not only enjoyed laughing for himself, but he also wanted others to laugh with him.

To create new and unique products in leather, Jonathan applied knowledge, vision, and critical thinking skills. Development of the new ball necessary for the new game was just another puzzle to solve. Jonathan and Marion created many sizes and types of leather balls together.

Though the two teased each other, they were a dynamo when they worked together. To produce the highest quality leather goods the Shoemakers worked together efficiently and quickly. Jonathan enjoyed teasing. He teased everyone. We were all kept on our toes by his teasing. Usually, Jonathan's teasing resulted in a loud laugh from the group. We teased him in return. And he took it better than anyone else. The person he teased the most was his older sister Marion. Marion witnessed his teasing develop from infancy. She could always dish it right back to him. Jonathan often spoke lovingly concerning his great fortune to possess Marion for his 'big' sister. The two Shoemakers adored each other. They understood each other and appreciated the talents both possess. The way they teased each other and laughed at themselves was a manifestation of how deeply they understood and cared for each other. The two learned the leathermaking skills so well that they teased their father. He accepted their teasing with good nature.

Early in Marion's life, Father and Marion formed an exceptionally strong bond. Father loved to hold and cuddle his tiny daughter. Holding and cuddling the baby girl nurtured her to feel secure and loved. Growing amidst such love and security enabled Marion to develop a high degree of self-confidence at an early age. Marion emerged from infancy into a confident, inquisitive, curious child. Nine months after Marion's birth, the tiny girl began to speak meaningfully. At the same age, she also walked confidently balanced. Her ability to communicate at nine months old, enabled Marion and her father to connect closely. Their devoted connection empowered father and daughter to comprehend each other's feelings and concerns clearly with astonishing accuracy. From the moment Marion's father first held his daughter, he doted on her. Marion was always petite. As a toddler, Marion already achieved complete trust in her father. She felt confident that her father would protect her from any harm.

Among my earliest memories is watching Marion and her father. She was so tiny she stood confidently on her father's open palm of his hand. Watching a tiny little lass stand on a man's open palm was a magical sight for me. She performed even more magic though. When Marion first began to develop her acute sense of balance as a toddler, she and her father developed special tricks. Because of Marion's petite stature, Father could easily open his palm wide enough so that both of her wee little feet found sufficient space for her to stand with confidence. Marion's tiny feet anchored on one of Father's open and flat palms. Marion stood up straight. She posed like a tiny statue.

Marion remained completely stationary, confidently balanced for minutes at a time. She posed on father's palm as confidently as if she stood on the floor. Father slowly pushed his hand away from his body, Marion maintained her pose. Then, he pulled his hand in towards his chest, Marion stood perfectly balanced. Father raised his hand up to his shoulder, Marion kept still and straight. Father pushed his palm straight up over his head. Confidently, the tiny lass stood above the tallest man. Father lowered his hand down below his waist, Marion did not seem to even twitch. In every direction that Father shifted his hand, Marion continued to hold her statue-like pose. Her trust in Father was absolute. His faith in her the same. She was confident in her sense of balance. Marion maintained perfect posture, standing as still as a statue. Her two dainty little feet belied the amount of strength she possessed in order to stand balanced on one wide open palm.

Marion and her father loved to perform the trick they mastered. Other folk marveled at the trick Marion and her father practiced and perfected. Every time Marion and her father performed, she looked forward to hearing the comments from observers. He basked in their shared achievement. Every time folks witnessed the tiny little girl standing so still with both feet on her father's one open hand, they expressed awe and amazement. The father and daughter performance displayed strength, balance, and the total trust the two shared with each other. After Marion and Father attained mastery of the standing with perfect balance on two feet in one of Father's hands trick, the two decided to experiment with more difficult performances. Marion wanted to add movement to her statue pose. First, Marion stood on her right foot alone. She lifted her left foot, bent her left knee, and then placed her left foot on her right knee. Later, Marion learned while standing on her right foot, to extend her left foot away from and perpendicular to her body.

Marion mastered new moves. She practiced even more with Father. They both realized that she needed to become stronger. To stay balanced on one foot for several minutes, Marion and Father continued to practice. Marion learned to turn in a complete circle balanced on one foot. She also learned to hop into the air and land on Father's hand on one foot. All who watched the little girl perform on her father's hand found joy and pleasure when they viewed the acrobatic performance.

On her father's hand, Marion stood on two feet. She posed. She lifted one foot. She stood motionless on one foot. Then, she stood on her toes. She posed with such grace and confidence. I marveled at the level of trust she placed in her father. He held his open hand level and steady. She danced. She leaped. She twirled. She always landed lightly on her father's palm. I remember seeing Marion and her father at fairs and festivals. When dancing music played. Marion grabbed her father's hand. She led him outside. He opened his palm and reached down so that she could step onto his hand. Her father lifted his hand. Marion rode his hand up as he lifted. He brought his hand to waist high. Marion posed. Then she danced to the music. She executed all the steps that the lasses danced.

Chapter 46 | 1458 | Learning the Art of Leathercraft

Brother Tanner

Early in life, Marion observed Father at his workbench with deep fascination. He created many different and beautiful items. During each step of the process that Father worked, Marion learned. More and more she appreciated leather craftsmanship. Father made certain to explain every step he performed. Throughout the process, he emphasized the necessity of following separate steps in a precise sequence.

First, Father explained his vision for the project to Marion. In general terms, he described what he intended to create. Then, he explained how he planned to complete the job. Throughout the process, Father questioned Marion continually. "Can you see what I described?" Father asked her to restate how each piece would fit together.

Every day throughout the assembly process Father checked Marion for understanding. Father drew patterns for the pieces he would need to put together in order to assemble the envisioned finished product. He patiently explained to Marion why he created each pattern. Continuously, he checked with her to see if she accurately visualized the way that the pieces would fit together.

Father meticulously traced the patterns onto the leather. Marion learned to trace patterns easily. She thought tracing patterns on the leather was fun. Next, Father sharpened the knife blade. Carefully, he guided the sharp blade to cut the pieces drawn on the leather. He explained why the cuts must be made just right.

After cutting each piece, Father assembled the pieces very carefully. He showed how each piece fit with the next piece. When he placed the carefully cut pieces next to each other, Father decided where to punch holes. Father explained the purpose for precision spacing of the holes. He described how the needle would carry the thread to stitch the separate pieces snugly together. Finally, Father used the needle and thread. He skillfully stitched the leather pieces together. He tied knots which permanently sealed the stitches.

Father taught Marion about the many different types of thread used in working leather and making shoes. He pointed out the different number of 'ply's' in the linen thread. He showed her how more 'ply's' made the thread stronger. He also showed her that stronger thread required an increase in diameter.

Patiently, Father explained why he chose to match a particular size of thread for a particular purpose. He showed her how he analyzed what diameter of thread to choose. He explained why he selected how the thread had been treated for each creation. Boots, for example, required strong multi-ply, waxed linen thread. The strong waxed linen thread handled the durable, strong stitches required to protect legs and feet dry in any weather and any condition. Gloves, on the other hand, required soft supple leather. Very fine thread formed into tiny, almost invisible stitches held the flexible glove together during the entire life of the product.

Because the tiny Marion loved to watch Father work, he created a tiny seat for her. He attached her seat to his work bench. The tiny seat held Marion safely, no matter what task he performed. While he stitched the leather pieces together, Marion sat and studied. At her own pace, Marion began to place her tiny hands and fingers atop Father's skilled fingers. She gently imitated Father's finger movements. She began to learn how to follow the pattern in leather. When Marion placed her hands directly on Father's hands, he understood that she wanted to learn to perform the stitchery also. He asked, "Marion, do you want to learn how to stitch the leather together?"

Eagerly, Marion nodded her head and answered, "Aye, Father." He placed one of Marion's petite hands under the leather in order to match the punched hole. He positioned the leather pieces together for stitching. Marion looked carefully at the leather she held. Then she looked up at Father's eyes. Her look let Father know that she understood. Marion was confident that she could hold the leather. Then, Father placed the needle in her tiny right hand. Marion wrapped her fingers around the needle. She grasped the needle in exactly the same manner that she observed Father hold the needle. Without another word, Marion probed the needle in order to find the holes punched with the awl into the separate leather pieces.

Marion's hands no longer required Father's guidance. He spoke softly and reassuringly, "Now you must be very, very careful, Marion. Push the needle through the punched holes just hard enough to poke through both leather pieces. Use the pointer finger on your left hand to feel the needle point. When you feel the point, take the finger on your left hand away from the needle point. The needle point is very, very sharp. The sharp point can puncture your finger. You do not want to puncture your left finger with the needle. That will hurt. Does that make sense, child?"

"Aye, Father, I understand. I don't want to get an 'owwie' on my finger. I can feel the sharp needle point with my left pointer fingertip. When I feel the needle point, then I know the needle is through both pieces of leather. I move that fingertip away so I can push the needle all the way through the hole. After I push the needle through the holes, I can pull the thread all the way through both pieces of leather. When the thread is all the way through both leather pieces, I can make a loop with the thread. Forming the loop is necessary for me to complete the stitch. Show me what to do next, Father?"

"I think you already know what to do and how to do it, Marion." Father smiled confidently. "You have been studying what I do whenever I stitch together two pieces of leather. I think you have been learning how to stitch since before we spoke in words. Rather than show you, I will talk with you through each step to complete a stitch connecting leather pieces."

By ten years of age Marion's mastery of fine stitchery caused her father to marvel. Marion sewed the tiniest stitches in leather Father ever saw. Marion tied off the stitches with perfect wee knots. One reason Marion's stitches were so fine was due to her tiny skilled fingers. Her petite hands seemed almost 'elvin'. Strong, skilled tiny fingers provided a significant advantage to produce fine leather craftsmanship.

Marion possessed the ability to visualize a 'finished" product. She could visualize the wanted item from a customer's description. Once she saw an item she could visualize each necessary step required in the process.

Shoemakers also made Leather toys for children. Leather balls were among the favorite toys our Shoemakers produced. Father Shoemaker began teaching Marion to make leather balls when Jonathan was an infant. The Shoemakers made leather balls in a variety of sizes. They knew how to make leather balls, soft or hard. Every household in St Andrews possessed a few leather balls for children's play.

Jonathan began learning the trade at three years of age. Father Shoemaker recognized that both children possessed an aptitude to visualize and assemble leather objects. The two started working in leather by making small leather balls from discarded leather pieces. They soon made all the leather balls for the shoppe.

Inside the shoppe, Marion and Jonathan practiced their skills every day. Both learned how to select the proper leather for any specific task. They learned to plan carefully. They studied how to design each object they would fabricate. Shoemakers possessed the skill to visualize and trace the shapes they needed to cut accurately on the leather. Father believed that the skills required to make high quality leather balls provided great practice to developing Shoemakers. Skills mastered to produce high quality leather balls transferred to similar skills for fashioning high quality shoes, boots, gloves, and other leather goods. The level of craftsmanship Marion and Jonathan acquired from producing high quality leather balls pointed them on their journey to become Master Shoemakers.

In addition to development of skills, and acquisition of knowledge for young shoemakers, the production and sale of various sized leather balls provided extra income for the shop. To encourage Marion and Jonathan to work continuously on improving their leather crafting skills, Father shared the income from the sale of balls with them.

After finishing the stitches, Marion and Jonathan carefully applied glue to all seams. Glue secured tight leather seams. To the customer the ball looked and felt as if it were one solid object. In fact, Marion and Jonathan knew that each finished ball was the sum of several carefully fitted parts expertly assembled in a sequential step by step process and finally stitched tightly together.

During summer months the pilgrimages brought hundreds of people into St. Andrews. Pilgrims valued souvenirs of their journey. The most prized souvenir for a St. Andrews pilgrim to purchase was the Pilgrimage Badge showing the Saltire Cross. The next most prized souvenir from St. Andrews was a leather ball purchased from the Shoemaker Shoppe. With nearly a decade of experience, people recognized that the leather balls from the St. Andrews Shoemaker Shoppe, possessed exceptional quality. Children hoped to own their very own leather ball fashioned by Marion and Jonathan.

Margaret the Tanner brought a piece of her new blue colored leather to the Shoemaker Shoppe. The blue was a piece of sky in her hands. It was clear, deep, and pure. Jonathan and Marion were very impressed by the color. An idea formed in Jonathan's head. He persuaded Father Shoemaker to spend some of the money earned by the sale of leather balls to purchase a whole hide in the new color. Jonathan thought that blue provided a perfect color for the souvenir leather balls sold to pilgrims. Thanks to stories told by priests and illustrations on tapestries, everyone knew that Andrew the Disciple worn a robe the color of deep sky blue. A blue leather ball would be a symbol for St. Andrews. The deep sky-blue ball made a special keepsake.

Jonathan's idea proved correct. During that Pilgrimage season, the Shoemakers sold the sky-blue leather balls as fast as our Tannery could supply blue leather hides. Jonathan's idea brought a sizeable profit for the Shoemaker family. The sales also brought a tidy profit for our Tanner family.

Chapter 47 | *1399* | A Shoemaker Story

"Mother, I fear I made a crucial mistake today." Father Shoemaker confessed contritely. "I over promised several important customers. I told the customers I would guarantee that I could finish their orders by tomorrow. I believed I could finish quickly enough. But customers kept coming in. I was unable to continue working while taking the orders from the customers. I was wrong. I will not be able to finish all the jobs while providing our normal high standard of quality."

At dinner that night Father confessed to Mother Shoemaker that he did not know how he could satisfy the customers. Sadly, he realized that he would not complete the order by the deadline he promised. In order to get the work done that night, Mother offered to stay up all night and help Father.

Father appreciated mother's offer. "Even with your help, mother, there is just too much work to complete by tomorrow morning." He said that the deals were very important. If the jobs were not completed by tomorrow, he feared for the ultimate financial success of the shop for the year.

"Don't you want my help, Father?" Mother countered.

"Aye, of course I want your help, darling. Working together, we will do the best we can. We will finish the number of the jobs we can complete. Tomorrow, I will just have to explain to the customers that we did the best we could. I am sorry that I failed their expectations. I will have to make some refunds. We stand to lose a great deal of money. Nevertheless, we shall never compromise the quality of our products."

That night, Marion and Jonathan were supposed to be sleeping, but they were not. They whispered to each other. Both were thinking about the same plan. Mother and Father worked during the night. Marion and Jonathan decided to sleep. Jonathan knew Marion slept lightly. She decided to keep her ears open while she kept her eyes closed. While she rested, Marion listened for any change in activities from the workshop. Marion realized that Mother and Father had worked as long as they could work. She knew that both parents were totally exhausted. She heard them head for bed. Marion waited until she knew that both slept soundly. Both parents slept and snored. Mother snored lightly. Father's snores sounded like ten long saws cutting through ten large tree trunks all at the same time.

Marion woke her brother. "Jonathan," whispered Marion, "Don't make a sound above whispering." She motioned for Jonathan to follow. Into the shoppe the lass and lad tiptoed. "I think we can finish the rest of the work. Can you see what jobs need to be finished?"

"Aye Marion." Answered Jonathan. "Clearly there is much work remaining to complete. But not too much for us to finish before daybreak, provided we work together and work quickly." They went straight to work. They knew which orders remained to be completed. The two worked silently and efficiently. Not only did they know what work needed to be done, they knew each other very well. Both knew when Marion would need to help Jonathan on a job. Both knew when Jonathan needed to hold an implement that would enable Marion to tie off one of her famous tiny, 'invisible' knots. They worked without speaking.

Morning light arrived. Father and Mother were so tired. The efforts expended in their late-night working, forced them to continue sleeping long past dawn. Marion gratefully said their morning prayers to God for bringing the daylight. Jonathan added a morning prayer for loving parents who worked without complaint to the point of exhaustion to build a good life for their children. Lass and lad realized their parents had worked through worry and physical exhaustion. They rejoiced that their parents slept late. Though Marion and John were tired, they knew that if their parents would continue to sleep just a few more minutes, they could finish all the jobs. Silently, both prayed for their parents to sleep just a wee bit longer.

Their prayers were answered. Before Jonathan noticed sounds from their parents' room as they stirred from their long, restful slumber, it was well-nigh time to open the Shoppe. Marion heard too. Quietly, she tied off the last knot. Marion gave Jonathan a knowing look. He understood her clearly. Her look commanded, "Let's get out of here, now!"

Quick as wink, or quick as a blink, for those who cannot wink, the lad and lass slipped out the front window. They sneaked around the shoppe to the back door. Quietly, Marion and Jonathan smiled to each other, then they snuggled into their own bed.

Father and Mother walked toward the back room to check on Marion and Jonathan. Before they arrived at the sleeping area, they heard, 'Knock, knock, knock!' rapped on the shoppe door.

"Oh-oh! Customers. Well, I guess we better face the music", Father mumbled. "That will be Mr. Miller, our first customer of the day. I promised his order first thing this morning. I cannot believe we slept so long. Alas, when we fell asleep exhausted, his work was not complete. I will have to explain to him that his order is not finished. Maybe he can wait. Mother, talk to him and I will finish his job quickly." Father walked towards the front door to answer the knock and open the Shoppe for business.

"Father! Come quickly!" Mother shouted cheerily.

"What is it Mother?" quizzed Father.

"Look at your work bench!" Mother directed.

There, on the work bench, sat every order promised for the day. Each of the orders was completed and tagged. Father randomly picked up a shoe. He examined it and turned it over. He noted the excellent craftsmanship. Mother picked up the pair of gloves that she started but failed to complete before sleep claimed her last night. "Look at this, Father. The needle work is exquisite. You can barely see or feel a stitch. Yet, all the pieces are sewn together strong."

"It is a miracle!" exclaimed Father. "Mother, we will not have to give any money back to customers! We can deliver all the orders promised for today, on time. All our customers will be satisfied. We are saved!"

"What could have happened?" asked Mother. "I know we were not finished with all the work when we went to sleep."

"Aye!" Father agreed. "We were so tired. We planned to get up early and work in order to complete the jobs. We did all the work that we could do last night. We worked for as long as our fingers functioned. But we were so exhausted, we went right to sleep. Then, we woke up late. This, this is like magic. A magical miracle. This must have been the work of some magic elves." Father offered as an explanation.

"That could be." Mother answered.

Marion and Jonathan heard the entire conversation between their parents. Satisfied, they smiled at each other, and closed their exhausted eyes. Immediately, both were claimed by a deep, satisfying sleep.

While Marion and Jonathan slept, Father and Mother worked the Shoppe. To each and every customer, they told the tale of the miracle in the Shoemaker Shoppe, with great excitement. Father and Mother testified that they remembered that before they went to sleep, they knew that the work was not completed. However, when they rose the following morning, all the work was done. All the jobs completed on time. Father and Mother claimed that there must have been magic elves who worked in the Shoppe that night. Quickly, the story of the miracle in the Shoemaker Shoppe spread all over St. Andrews.

When the lads and lasses met to play that day, Robert the Carpenter asked the question ten other friends wanted answered. "Marion, Jonathan, what can you tell us about the miracle in your family Shoemaker Shoppe last night?"

Marion and Jonathan smiled at each other. Then they looked around the Circle of friends. "I guess miracles really happen." Jonathan responded slyly. "What do you believe, Marion?"

"I truly believe in miracles, Jonathan." Marion grinned.

And that was all Marion and Jonathan ever told us about the St. Andrews Shoemaker Shoppe miracle. Nevertheless, we always knew only Marion and Jonathan could make better leathercraft than their parents, our own St. Andrews Shoemakers.

Chapter 48 | *2019* | Carpenter Family And Business

The Professors - Lecture Notes

Dr. MacGregor – "In the year 1378, a massive fire seriously damaged the Great Cathedral in St. Andrews. Bishop William de Landallis launched a massive repair and reconstruction project immediately. The repair project continued until the year 1440. Bishop Walter Trail succeeded Bishop Landallis in 1385. Bishop Trail continued the building repair until his death in 1401. Succeeding bishops continued the repair and reconstruction project. The bishops promised to restore full glory to Scotland's greatest Cathedral. The reconstruction required decades to complete.

Professor Greenwood – "Representing all building trades skilled workmen arrived to complete the massive repair and reconstruction project. Restoring the largest building in Scotland comprised an enormous undertaking. Hammermen (metal workers) repaired roof, drainage pipes, and worn out metal. Stone masons inspected, removed, and replaced damaged mortar and stone. The arrival of many skilled workers spurred a building boom for the town. Prior to the arrival of the workmen, other than the Cathedral and the Castle, most buildings in St. Andrews were timber construction. As a result of the influx of workers the town began to evolve. Stone buildings gradually replaced the previous early medieval wooden structures."

Dr. MacGregor – "Master carpenters brought journeymen, apprentices and laborers. Master carpenters combined skills with knowledge. In Medieval St. Andrews those skills were in high demand. The young aspirants increased income for the master carpenter team. Skilled carpenters removed, repaired, and replaced wooden framing. Various parts of the structure were envisioned, recreated, constructed, modified, re-envisioned, and maintained by carpenters.

The list of master carpenter skills included how to; cut, shape, bend, splint, attach, sand, lacquer and finish wooden objects. They constructed everything from building frames to furniture. They created buildings to function for human beings. Carpenters built many useful, necessary, and important items. Some items were large. Some were small.

From forests surrounding St. Andrews, a variety of trees grew. Carpenters possessed knowledge concerning advantages and disadvantages with all types of lumber. That knowledge guided their process. Carpenters selected woods which worked best for each purpose. Some woods were soft and pliable. Soft wood is easy to saw and to sand. Softwoods worked well for framing. Some woods were light in weight and easy to shape. Some woods were flexible. Other woods were strong and stiff. To craft fine furniture carpenters chose hardwoods."

Professor Greenwood – "To perform a variety of tasks, carpenters mastered many tools. Carpenters required saws, drills, lathes, files, rasps, and planes. They made square shapes and round shapes. Carpenters shaped wood to connect right angles. They carefully crafted and smoothed curves in wood.

Skilled craftsman used the tools of the trade to join wooden pieces to other pieces securely. Carpenters created several different types of joints to connect wooden pieces securely. Drills made precise circular holes. Dowel rods fit tightly in the holes. To build cabinets and tables, chairs, and gables, carpenters applied knowledge and skill to their labor. Master carpenters created fine quality furniture for the nobility and the church. For shops and ordinary cottages other carpenters built rough but substantial furniture. Carpenters sometimes worked together with weavers to custom build looms and spinning wheels.

In ancient Egypt, people discovered that animal parts could make strong, long-lasting glues more than 6,000 years ago. Egyptian carpenters used glue to make strong, durable, and graceful furniture. Carpenters and Bowyers used glue extensively. Both trades share important business connections.

Even though the final products produced by Carpenters differ markedly from the Bowyers' final products, both families endeavor to form useful objects from wood. They shared many tools and materials to make to craft wood into highly prized useful products.

Some woods were more suitable for fuel than for construction. Scrap wood from carpenters and bowyers was never wasted. Wood fires warmed the cold winter air inside the cottage. Nourishing foods cooked over wood fires in the open hearth.

- - - - - - - - - - 1458 - - - - - - - - - -

Brother Tanner

Heather The Carpenter – Heather's rich burnished golden hair captured the deep color of the first quarter hour or the last quarter hour of the day's sunshine in tight waves. The texture of her hair emulated the queen's gold crown. No one could ever recall when even the wisp of a single hair fell out of place. Frequently, she wove her favorite color, bright yellow yarn, or ribbon into her hair.

At age 13, Heather stood an even five feet. Her smooth white gold complexion glowed. We all basked in Heather's company. Part of her charm stemmed from the fact that she never seemed to recognize her beauty. Heather's deep, luminous brown eyes invited friends to come near. She listened with her eyes. Heather valued each of us. I knew that when we talked Heather was pleased. Her personality was supportive. We knew Heather believed in us. We never wanted to disappoint her in any way. Heather's quiet demeanor made everyone feel comfortable to be near her. We all wanted to be close to her.

Every time I spoke with Heather, her eyes captured me. I experienced a magical feeling. In the rich dark brown pools, I observed my own reflection. I felt like I was seeing myself the very way that she saw me. I wanted to live up to what she saw in me. She made me feel that I was her best friend. Others in the group spoke of experiencing the same feeling.

Like all carpenters everywhere, Heather possessed strong hands. The carpenter's craft developed very skilled hands. For Heather, combining skills and strength resulted in a feeling of confidence in her abilities. Heather quickly grasped any situation. She possessed vision to solve difficult problems by employing carpentry. To the family shoppe, she brought creativity and art to complement the engineering solutions of construction.

The Carpenters worked closely with the Bowyers. They also maintained a close professional relationship with the Tanners. The Tanners supplied glues, stains, lacquers, and wood preservatives. Carpenters also worked closely with the Weavers on loom repair and construction.

Robert The Carpenter – Robert's hair piled into sandy blonde curls that framed a confident, friendly face. A ready smile highlighted his ruddy complexion. At age 14, Robert stood 5'4. The carpenter's daily repetitive motions included swinging a hammer and sawing through wood. Those repetitive movements developed bulging powerful forearms. All of the friends possessed strong hands. However, Robert's arms and hands were the strongest. To efficiently guide their tools, carpenters employ specific grips. Proper grips enable carpenters to perform repetitive movement work throughout a full day of labor.

In addition to muscle labor, carpenters use their brains. They transform raw lumber into useful articles. Robert possessed superior analytical knowledge to problem solve. Father Carpenter taught Robert and Heather how carpenters approach problem solving from an early age. Carpenters take pride knowing that Jesus worked as a carpenter.

Robert was naturally quiet. When he did speak, others paid close attention. Frequently Robert's insight required explanation because of the sheer volume of technical knowledge he understood. Robert enjoyed making clear explanations to the others so that they can understand his vision. His opinions were highly valued. To solve problems and make quality products, carpenters learn and master specific skills. Those skills include wood shaping, precision measurements, accurate tracing, saw, plane, sanding, joinery, finish, lacquer, preserve, glue. Hands are skilled and accurate with a touch or a feel. He could translate his knowledge through his hands when he worked in shaping and joining wood. He possessed superior knowledge of wooden joinery, glues, lacquers, and finishes.

Father Carpenter and father Bowyer decided it would be advantageous to build their shoppes adjacent to each other. So, Russell and Barbara, the Bowyers, often walked to and from destinations together with Robert and Heather, the Carpenters.

Chapter 49 | 2019 | Bowyer Family and Business

The Professors - Lecture Notes

Dr. McGregor – "During Late Medieval time in Scotland, few children received formal schooling. To believe that children were not skilled problem-solvers however, would be a grave mistake. Early in their lives, children of craftsmen began to learn the skills required to create any products offered from the family shoppe. Medieval craftsmen possessed an extensive knowledge base in scope and sequence. They learned how to identify acceptable raw materials. They oversaw the processing of materials. They learned to craft raw materials through to beautifully finished products displayed in the shoppe. Bowyers are excellent examples of craftsmen."

Professor Greenwood – "The Yew tree (Taxus baccata) occupies an important position in Scottish history. Fossil records of trees similar to yews date to the Permian Age, 200 million years ago. During that time, our present-day continents were still conjoined into one supercontinent, which scientists call Pangea. To survive for such a long time, the yew evolved a remarkable set of advantages.

For several thousand years, yew trees connected with sacred places in Scotland. Often, yews are found near churches and church cemeteries. Celts and Druids held rituals in yew groves. On instructions from higher authority, Christians built their churches in places the pagans held sacred when the Christian religion arrived in the British Isles. Many times, the sacred places were yew groves. Often the yew trees are far more ancient than the churches next to them.

The village of Fortingall, Perthshire lies some 74 miles distant from St. Andrews. In the village churchyard, The Fortingall Yew continues to flourish. The age of the tree has been estimated to be between 2,000 and 6,000 years. Modern estimates place the age between 2,000 and 3,000. A local legend claims that Pontius Pilate was born beneath the Fortingall Yew. Interestingly, there is a possibility that Pilate may have been born to a Roman soldier and a local woman. However, the years of Roman occupation and Pilate's lifespan do not quite match confirmation."

Dr. McGregor – "Sometimes, yew trees were planted after the church was built. Yew is poisonous. Virtually every part of the tree is toxic. When working with yew wood, including the sawdust, people should apply great caution. They should be very careful to avoid inhaling or ingesting the dust. Historians speculate that toxicity is among the major reasons that yew trees were planted in church cemetery yards. Farmers made certain their livestock avoided the poison trees. In turn, graves in the church yard cemeteries remained undisturbed by animals for centuries.

For some three centuries during the Middle Ages, bowyers in Great Britain crafted the finest bows in the world. Staves, which are long pieces of wood that looked like sticks, were quartered from logs. Yew staves furnished the preferred raw material to craft the high-performance longbow. The toxicity of the yew made the wood extremely resistant to insects and rot."

Professor Greenwood – "Accomplished master bowyers passed the knowledge from generation to generation. The list included how; to harvest, to cure, to cut and to shape the staves into the high-performance weapon. The long bow design depended on staves which deliver a remarkable combination of strength, flexibility, and durability. To win battles, archers counted on the inherent reliability within yew longbows. The Bowyers in St. Andrews produced the longbow.

Yew staves provided the most sought-after wood stock to craft the 14th Century world's most effective weapon, the longbow. For longbows, yew was harvested in logs over six feet long, approximately 8-12 inches in diameter. Following harvest, each log was carefully inspected to detect flaws in the grain. Logs which passed inspection were aged and dried. Bowyers split sawed the logs into quarters. Each quarter measured approximately 4 inches across. One sawn quarter yielded one raw yew stave. At this point during the process, Bowyers the bark remained on the stave. To begin the process of transforming a stave into a prized weapon bowyers selected only the very best staves."

Dr. McGregor – "To fashion the raw stave into an elegant longbow required precision workmanship throughout a several step process. During the first step, bowyers carefully removed bark from the stave. Removal of bark revealed the sapwood. Sapwood is that part of the tree which conducts fluids through the trunk and to the leaves. It is the living part of the wood protected by the bark. In yews, the sapwood is light, almost white in color. Sapwood possesses a uniquely important property which makes yew the best wood for a long bow. Sapwood provides flexibility to the stave. While performing the careful bark removal, bowyers retained as much sapwood on the stave as possible. The inside part of the stave is a deep, rich red in color. That is the heartwood. In a yew stave, the heartwood is strong and powerful.

The combination of flexible white sapwood, on the side facing away from the archer, together with the power contained in the heartwood, which lies in the palm of the archer's hand, is the reason why yew makes the best longbows. To transform the stave into the rounded 'D' shape of the long bow, bowyers used knives of different shapes and sizes. The thickest part of the bow was in the middle. At each end, the bow tapered to a diameter of less than half an inch."

Professor Greenwood – "To indicate the proper line for an arrow to rest, the bowyer carefully marked the middle of the stave. The index finger marked the position for the arrow. The other three fingers marked the amount of extra heartwood to fashion for the archer's grip. The thick heartwood in the middle of the bow added increased power. The bend matched the length of the draw weight. When drawn to full length by the archer's pull of the bowstring, the bow stored power in the form of potential energy.

On each tip, bowyers carefully carved a v shaped notch. The notches held the bowstring loops securely in place to string the bow. A master artisan custom crafted each long bow. Each bow was designed to fit the body size and match the strength for the individual archer. Bowyers adjusted length and draw weight to custom fit the bow to the individual archer."

Dr. MacGregor – "Bowstrings constituted a critical component of the English longbow weapon system. A strong bowstring harnessed the power of the yew longbow. Multi-ply strands made from flax and silk threads provided the raw materials. To craft an effective bowstring, bowyers twisted the threads together. Permanent loops were braided into each end. The loops fit into the v-notches to string the bow. Effective, reliable bowstrings formed a necessary component of the powerful longbow weapons system.

Bowyers often glued a leather handle onto the bow. The leather handle aided the archer to achieve consistency and accuracy. It guided the archer to grip the bow in exactly the same place every time he picked up his bow. He never needed to refocus his eyes by taking his vision away from the target. Like the carpenters, the bowyers obtained glue(s) from the tanners."

Professor Greenwood – "The ability to 'feel' the exact center of the bow string without refocusing the archer's eyes away from the target enabled a skilled archer to launch arrows at a high rate with astonishing accuracy. The archer needed to nock and affix the arrow to the bow string quickly and efficiently. The rapid rate of arrow flights delivered a deadly advantage of speed to the combination of accuracy and power. A protective 'serving' was wrapped around the waxed bowstring. To mark the center of the bowstring, bowyers installed an arrow nock on the serving. The wrap and knock made it easy for the archer to identify the center spot on the bowstring by touch. Without a glance at the bowstring, archers nocked each arrow perfectly and quickly.

The wrapped serving aided the archer to develop a smooth consistent release of the arrow into flight. Material in the horizontally wrapped serving felt different from the vertical twists in the plies bowstring. The archer confidently placed the arrow in the nock. The 'feel' of the bow grip, the centered nock, and the serving, enabled the archer to keep his eyes focused on the target.

Loops braided into each end connected the bow string to the tips of the bow. The loops comprised a high stress part of the bow string. The loops were also wrapped and waxed. Wrappings on the bowstring loops to fit into the bow end notches also helped extend the bow string life. Wrapping the serving also lengthened the life of the bowstring. The center of a bowstring was the most susceptible to tear apart and wear. Wrapping the serving protected that most vulnerable spot."

Dr. McGregor – "In timed rhythm, the archer reached for an arrow and placed the arrow on the arrow rest at the bow handle. Then, he 'nocked' (securely connected in order to place) the arrow on the center of the bow string. By 'nocking' the arrow at the exact spot, the archer knew the arrow had been properly placed. The archer felt confident that the arrow aligned with both the bow and the bow string by his sense of 'touch'.

The center serving on the bow string enabled experienced, well-trained archers to reload the bow rapidly. Rapid reloading provided a dramatic advantage during battle. The ability to deliver deadly flights of arrows at a rapid rate provided archers armed with longbows a dramatic advantage versus those armed with crossbows."

Professor Greenwood – "Europeans possessed a powerful accurate weapon in the crossbow. However, during the heat of battle, the crossbow suffered one significant weakness compared to the longbow. The crossbow required a significant amount of time to reload. To reload a bolt (projectile) into the crossbow required the archer to crank the string for as long as a minute. In contrast, archers using longbows, loaded, launched, re-loaded, and launched flight after flight of hundreds of arrows in mere seconds. During combat the rapid delivery of flights of deadly arrows stormed the enemy as incessantly as ocean waves crashed on a beach. Flight after flight of hundreds of iron-tipped arrows delayed, pinned down and stopped an entire army in its tracks.

In addition to crafting longbows, the Bowyer family created arrows of both military grade and target grade. Longbows propelled the military grade arrows for great distances. The military grade arrow was capable of astonishing accuracy at 300 plus yards. The weapon system which combined longbow, military grade arrows and skilled lethal archers struck fear into European adversaries until the advent of gunpowder and cannon."

Dr. McGregor – "To make arrows, Bowyers employed woods far different from the yew. Sturdy bows required hardwood. Though the preferred wood for bows, yew failed as a good choice to make arrows. To be accurate at long range, arrow shafts required wood that was straight grained, smooth, and free of knots. Arrows needed softwoods. Ash, spruce and poplar provided the favored woods for straight arrow shafts. Softwoods are straight grained and knot free shafts. If the soft-wood shafts happened to become bent or curved, they could be easily straightened using a quick, simple, and efficient technique. Arrow makers, armorers and archers simply rolled heated, soaked, soft wood shafts on a smooth surface until the arrow shafts straightened.

The lightweight of ash, spruce, and poplar provided another significant advantage to the longbow and arrow weapons system. The light weight of the straight shaft permitted installation of a larger payload at the tip of the arrow. More weight could be loaded into the metal arrowhead."

Professor Greenwood – "Most often the military grade arrows were tapered. A thick bulbous nock, rather than a simple slit at the end of the arrow tapered to the thinner end. The thinner end of the arrow shaft was inserted into the metal arrowhead. The design of the thicker nock for the bowstring was critically important. A fully drawn bowstring placed tremendous pressure on the integrity of the arrow shaft. Average draw weights on the longbows ranged from 90 pounds to an incredible 160 pounds. When the archer pulled the bowstring to maximum draw length, the nock was subjected to the tremendous amount of stored energy. Such tremendous pressure on simple split softwood nocks often broke straight grained arrow shafts apart. For the archer to pull the bowstring to bend the powerful longbow required great strength and precise control. The thicker, bulbous arrow nock prevented the bowstring from splitting the arrow shaft while the archer held the bow at draw.

Feathers were trimmed into uniform fletches approximately 5" long. Trimmed fletches maintained stability for the arrow in flight. Feathers for fletching came from geese and swan, though goose feathers were preferred. To attach fletching, bowyers glued the spine of the feathers onto the arrow shaft. They wrapped the fletching to hold it in place until the glue set.

For an arrow, all fletches came from the same wing side, either right wing or left wing. Feathers on an arrow were never mixed. The cock fletch is perpendicular to the nock for the bowstring. The other two fletchings, the hen fletchings are set at equal angles to the cock fletching. When loading the arrow onto the bow and nocking the arrow to the bow string, the archer placed the 'cock' fletch up, facing him. Correct application of the fletchings from flight feathers, either wing or tail feathers dramatically improved the stability of the arrow during flight. A stable flight improved accuracy."

Dr. McGregor – "For military use, arrow shaft lengths were standardized. Military grade arrows were produced in three lengths. Lengths of 27", 29" and 31" were identified as the standard. Arrow shafts came in different weights. To make long distance shots, archers chose light arrow shafts. Archers selected heavyweight arrow shafts for close distances and for maximum penetration of armor. Military archers received standardized sheaves. Sheaves were wooden boxes containing twenty-four arrows. Each standard sheaf consisted of two dozen arrows of the same length, as ammunition to launch into flight.

Another feature of the military arrows was the military grade heavy iron, double bladed tip. The heavy tip provided the capability for the arrow to penetrate chain armor. The heavy arrowheads were attached to the shaft with wax. Wax attachment of warhead to arrow shaft provided an important advantage to the archers. The advantage was important to other allied soldiers, those in the infantry and the cavalry. Soldiers did not want their own military grade arrows to be retrieved by the enemy to be shot back at them.

To make certain that soldiers were not shot by their own arrows picked up by the enemy, military arrows incorporated a unique design. When the arrow hit the target, the wax connection meant that the arrowhead detached from the shaft. When the enemy attempted to retrieve an arrow stuck in a body the arrowhead remained stuck in the victim. The enemy could only retrieve the arrow shaft."

Professor Greenwood – "Technology for weapons changed. When gunpowder and cannons emerged the effectiveness of the longbow fell. Artillery rendered the longbow obsolete.

Bowyers searched for new products. They wanted products to draw upon centuries of study and knowledge of wood. How could hardwoods processed and shaped with the skill bowyers practiced be transferred from making a custom fitted bowstave to other products? What products could they be?"

Chapter 50 | 1458 | Remembering The Bowyers

Brother Tanner

Barbara The Bowyer. When I remember Barbara, I see her shining ash blond hair. The color captured the luster of moonglow filtered through the veil of a moving translucent cloud layer. Barbara implored Bessie to precision shear and shape her hair to a length just a few inches above shoulder. At almost 15, Barbara was the second oldest lass. She stood 4'9. Her posture was always erect and proud. Her favorite color was blue. Barbara's bright silver blue eyes sparkled a hint of the energy barely contained in her heart. Sometimes on the Links Barbara launched herself to cartwheel ten times in a row. The next day she might perform ten consecutive back walk overs. We just watched and marveled. She was also a wonderful dancer. She combined fitness and flexibility. Barbara's spirit resounded with cheer. She infected us with her 'can do' approach. To Barbara, no problem was unsolvable. She was tenacious. She would find a way.

When Barbara took leadership, she voiced enthusiasm. We knew that she believed each of would bring our best to any situation. At the same time, Barbara displayed faith in each of us. Barbara was a confidence builder and supportive.

If Barbara wanted to best us in a race when it was her turn, she chose acrobatic stunts. None of the lads could challenge her acrobatic abilities. Marion wanted to learn acrobatics, and Barbara taught her. The two lasses loved to perform the stunts in unison.

Barbara's approach to problem-solving was analytical. After considering her analysis she opened her mind to new possible solutions. She listened wholly. She showed the speaker her understanding by repeating the speaker's words. Each of us knew that we were valued. She understood the importance of quiet calm. She studied problems with resolve. Barbara was always poised and balanced. Her demeanor exuded confidence in herself.

Barbara possessed very strong hands. To make the powerful longbow she worked with yew, the strongest wood. Such work using both hands developed strong fingers. To fashion arrows she developed highly skilled finger control and touch. Performing such work enabled Barbara to develop a high level of confidence in both her physical skill and strength. To produce the longbow required her to master skills including making precision measurements, tracing, sawing, cutting, shaping, smoothing, preserving wood, shaping horn to fit bow shaft.

To make arrows, Barbara selected, cut, and shaped the cedar shafts. Barbara selected and trimmed goose and swan wing feathers to making fletching. She installed the fletching to the shaft by expertly applying glues and wraps. The arrow shafts must be accurately centered and knocked. Arrows and arrowheads must be effectively joined and precisely balanced.

To make bowstrings, the family grew flax plants. After harvesting flax plants, they separated the stems into long fibers. The fibers were braided together to form a string that was strong enough to pull and bend a long bow.

I remember a moment with the entire group of friends. I shared an early memory about Marion dancing on her father's hand as a tiny girl during Festival. William interrupted me. 'Thomas, you are too young to remember, but Barbara and her father performed a similar trick. I grant you that Marion is a superb dancer. Barbara also danced beautifully. But Barbara added acrobatics to the performance. She performed cartwheels and back walkovers on her father's open palm. To end her performance, Barbara made a signature move. When her father held his hand steady at waist height, she leaped into a double back flip. She landed and her feet stilled. She stuck that landing like the point of a knife into dirt. Barbara always received an ovation from her audience."

Barbara was a great listener. She was courageous. I think she was a natural leader. Barbara accurately grasped any situation quickly. She asked excellent questions which clarified our thinking whenever we confronted a problem. Barbara often showed us how to see and accept new and different viewpoints.

Russell The Bowyer. Russell's light brown hair grew thick and straight. His smooth fair complexion framed a friendly inviting smile. Russell stood 5'5. Over that summer, in the midst of a growth spurt, he added 3 inches. At twelve and a half, Russell was the second youngest lad. Russell counted Jonathan and me, together the three youngest lads, as best friends. Because of the relationship of their family businesses, Russell was also very close with Robert the Carpenter.

Russell's hazel eyes harbored astonishing powerful vision. At long distances, Russell saw objects clearly the rest of us didn't see. None of us were able to identify an object, which Russell described perfectly. We respected his clear vision. Often when unsure of a target, we asked Russell to tell us what he saw. Russell was the best archer. He launched arrows with astonishing accuracy. At ranges up to 50 yards, Russell consistently placed a three-arrow shot group measured within the span of half a hand. To launch arrows at long range, Russell matched the pace and distance of the top men archers. Russell possessed supreme confident in his skill. He knew he could make any shot. Then he performed the shot just the way he visualized the outcome. Archers in Scotland functioned as a team. Russell modeled the role of a team player.

Bowyers took pride in providing archers with the complete longbow weapons system to perform at peak level. Building a bow to fit an individual archer was a critical commitment to improve teamwork. To build a proper fitting, high performance longbow, Russell solved several problems. Russell was an excellent listener. Longbow production required several crucial decisions. Russell applied process to solve issues involved in the craft. Russell's ability to focus served him well in all aspects. He focused on targets. He focused on shots.

Russell focused on fitting an archer. He focused on producing a custom fit, high quality, durable, reliable longbow. Russell made precision measurements. He accurately traced, sawed, cut, shaped, smoothed, and preserve wood, particularly yew. Yew was a poisonous wood. It required careful handling to keep the bowyer safe.

The Bowyers worked most closely with the Carpenter family. They also worked closely with the Tanners.

Chapter 51 | 1399 | The Shoemakers' Idea

Marion and Jonathan, the Shoemakers walked leisurely home together. After the team shared the joy of hitting the ball on the Links, the Shoemakers talked with each other. They agreed that hitting the ball with the L-shaped crook provided great fun.

Talking invited the sister and brother to explore thoughts about hitting the little hard leather ball. Thinking leads to ideas. In this case, Marion wished to share a new idea. She believed that her idea would make hitting the ball more satisfying and more fun. She decided to test the idea with her brother first. Marion proposed, "Jonathan, I am quite certain we can make a better ball than the one we hit with David, Bessie, and our friends. Do you agree with me?"

"Of course I do, Marion. Father taught us how to make great leather balls by the time we turned four. Between us, you and I have years of experience in making leather balls. The leather balls we produce are the highest quality. All the people in St. Andrew say that. Pilgrims come to our shoppe. They often say that they were told before you return home be sure to buy a leather ball from the Shoemaker Shoppe.

When you talk to me like this, Marion, I know you already formed a plan in your head. You always like to check out your ideas by talking with me. I appreciate the trust you have in my judgment. I recognize when my big sister gets an idea. And I know when she has a good idea. So Marion, what is your idea? What is your really good idea?"

"Ha! Actually, two ideas came to me, Jonathan. I thought about the new game. I am excited about the activity we practiced. Hitting the ball with the stick on the Links was so much fun. My first idea is this. I think for our new game, each player should possess his or her own ball. If we each possess a ball, we can take more turns. If each person has a ball, we will still take turns. However, we can hit the ball far more often during the time we play the game. Sharing just one ball between all twelve of us requires a dreadful amount of time. Whatever game we develop, the more often we get to hit the ball, the more fun we will have while we play.

Instead of spending so much time waiting for all the others to complete their turn, a ball for each person means we will spend more of our time playing the new game. In fact, with each of us having our own ball, we can hit back and forth to each other most of the time. Do you agree with me? Do you think that the idea of having each person possess a ball, sounds like more fun than twelve people sharing just one ball between them?"

"Marion, that is a splendid idea! You are right. We will get to hit the ball far more often than we do now. Hitting the ball is definitely the most fun part of the game. I am afraid I complained many times about waiting for so long to get another turn to hit. When each friend possesses a ball many more possibilities for the new game open. I am sure that all our friends will agree with us.

Now that the first idea is taken care of, what is your second idea?"

"Jonathan, do you remember when the whole group participated in the first brainstorming process? Remember when we began to formulate ideas to create our new game on the Links? We all insisted that it was very important to make the new game fair for all participants. My thoughts continue to dwell on that concept. What can we do to construct a game that is fair for everyone?"

"Aye. Designing the game to be fair for everyone is crucial. As the two youngest, and the two smallest, both of us appreciate when we recognize an opportunity for fair competition. We want a fair chance to succeed. I am gratified that all of our friends think fairness is a very important part of the new game on the Links. I am excited that all of our friends want to make a game where everyone, including the youngest and smallest, have an opportunity to succeed." Jonathan replied.

"Okay Jonathan, when I remembered how each of us wanted the game to be fair for everyone, that thought brought to mind my second idea to improve the new game. In the spirit of incorporating fairness into our new game, I propose that all the balls should be the same size."

"Interesting. Do you have a rationale to present to our friends? Do you think you can convince them?"

"I think I can. Consider with me. One, all of us have been hitting the same very small ball already. Two, the ball is small in volume. Three, the ball is also small in weight. Four, we have already seen that the distance the ball flies is most connected to how squarely the ball is struck. Five, we know the distance the ball flies is not a function of how hard the player swings the stick. Instead, distance results from the solid contact between stick and ball. In order to be fair for lasses and lads to achieve distance, the size of the ball we hit, for example, is not as critical as the different size of a shot putt, or discus, or hammer for men and women to throw." Marion enumerated.

"Aye, Marion. From what we experienced when we took our turns to strike the small ball, the critical element is not strength. To launch a successful and accurate flight, striking the right part of the ball with the right part of the club is the critical element. What are you thinking?"

"In croquet, the other game we saw that involves a player striking a ball with a club, all the balls are equal size. The equal size of the balls helps to make croquet a fair game of skill rather than a game that relies on brute strength. I think for our new game we ought to consider making all the balls the same size for each person. If we make each ball the same size, we will reinforce one of our goals for the new game. That is the idea concerning the importance of total fairness for each player."

"You have been thinking Marion. I agree with you. All the balls should be the same size. When we play the new game on the Links, a ball of small size that we strike with a club offers an equal challenge to each participant. We learned that to strike the small ball solidly and cleanly is a function of skill rather than brute strength. Even though the stick is larger than the ball, in order to hit the ball correctly, it is critical to contact the correct spot on the ball. On a small ball, the correct spot on the ball is tiny. To strike the tiny spot is demanding. You and I are the two smallest and the two youngest. Yet when we strike the ball at the correct spot, the ball flies as far as when anyone else hits it."

"When we do decide on a proper target, say a target similar to one of the kinds of targets involved in croquet, having each person hit the same size ball will be essential to establish fair play and competition. How do you think we should present our idea about that every ball should be the same size?" Marion asked.

"I think we need to make a plan to share your two ideas with our friends, Marion. I have two suggestions. First, let's assure our friends that you and I agree that we can make a high quality, durable hard ball for each person. Second, we will tell our friends that we believe that we should make all the balls the same size for the new game. Then, we can ask for their thoughts."

"A straightforward typical Shoemaker approach. I like those suggestions, Jonathan."

"Aye. No doubt we can create a high quality, durable hard ball for each friend. We could begin by producing one ball. Then show that ball to our friends to inspect and evaluate. Then, we can test the ball to see if everybody agrees that that is the ball we should produce for our game. We want everyone to agree that we have the right size ball, made from the right materials using the right procedure. When everyone agrees then that ball will provide us with the pattern to copy. Copying the exact pattern will ensure that all of the other balls we produce will be exactly the same size." Agreed Jonathan. "However, I do have a question."

"I bet I can guess this question, brother Jonathan."

"Oh. you think you know me so well. Do you really think you can read my mind, Marion?"

"Of course, I know you so well. Who else could know you as well as your sister, Jonathan?"

"Certainly, 'tis true. No one knows what I think as well as my sister knows. Go on then, Marion, tell me, what do you think my question is about the ball for each player?"

"Very well, Jonathan, your question is this, what size should the ball be? Am I correct?"

"Aye. Tis true, Marion. That is precisely the question I had in mind. Since you knew my question, I believe you have already put some thought into the size of the ball for every player. Am I right about that, sister?"

Marion chuckled. "Aye, you are right, John. I suppose since the way sisters know brothers better than anyone else is true, that the opposite is also true. Brothers also know sisters better than anybody else. Definitely, that idea works out both ways for us, doesn't it, Jonathan? Since I know you so well, you must know me…almost as well as I know you."

"Ha! Indeed, I was thinking about what size the ball should be. I remember so many of our games we played with all our friends when we were younger. Do you remember when we competed with games which involved throwing? To be fair for everyone, the older friends deliberately chose objects that all of us could handle and throw also. Many, many times the object that was chosen to throw was about the size of a chicken's egg. Do you remember that we threw that size object, too?"

"Aye, I recall that chicken egg size object, most often a stone. We favored that size for nearly every throwing contest." Jonathan recalled.

"Before we begin to make new balls for everyone, I would like to share these ideas with our friends. I want to see what they think about both ideas, too." Marion cautioned.

"I agree." Jonathan continued. "Before we invest much more time in design and production of a separate ball for each of our friends to play our new game, we do need to talk with them. We need to know what our friends think about our ideas. Let's see what the other friends in the Circle of Twelve have to say about both ideas after we tell them what we think about the ball in the new game on the Links."

"Alright. Tomorrow, when we go to the Links, we will ask our friends what they think. Whenever we can get all twelve of us to agree on an idea, I believe, we seem to have hit on a pretty good idea to pursue." Marion closed.

Chapter 52 | 1399 | Bowyers' and Carpenters' Idea

The Bowyers and Carpenters walked home. Russell the Bowyer wondered aloud, "I am thinking about the joy of hitting the small hard leather ball with a stick. The shape of the shepherd's crook keeps interrupting my thoughts. I want to share with you to see what you have to say. In my opinion, the shepherd's crooks provided by David and Bessie, do not provide the best design to strike a small hard leather ball and launch it into controlled flight effectively, or repeatedly."

Robert the Carpenter responded enthusiastically, "I agree. I believe you are correct, Russell. Similar thoughts struck me. I think about our daily work as carpenters. Many, many times every day we strike small objects with force. In fact, we strike objects that are far smaller than the ball. When we strike an object that is far smaller than a ball Father Carpenter taught us to use a special shape tool. When carpenters need to strike a small object with force, we must control accuracy and we must deliver a precise amount of power. We employ a tool with a shape completely different from the long cylinder shape of the shepherds' crook.

We strike small objects consistently and accurately several times a day with a tool designed for that job. The shape of that tool enables us to perform the job efficiently."

"What tool does a carpenter use for striking a small object with accuracy and power?" asked Russell.

Heather responded. "That's easy. The first tool every carpenter ever learns to master. We first use the hammer. Carpenters utilize the hammer to strike nails with power and control. We drive nails into wood. The nail head is way, way smaller than the ball that we have been striking on the Links. When we were wee small children, we learned to strike a small nail with a hammer, didn't we, Robert? We also struck the end of dowel rods with a hammer. For the hammer head to deliver a firm, accurate blow to the tiny nail head every single time, the flat striking surface provides a perfectly designed shape."

"Heather, I had a strong feeling that you and Robert probably were talking about how carpenters employ a hammer to strike a nail. Like Robert, I wanted to be positive. I certainly agree. To deliver a firm accurate strike, the flat shape of the hammer head provides a superior striking surface. To hit a tiny object, the flat striking face delivers much greater consistency. The flat surface is the shape we want. When we strike a small ball, we want a club that will combine accuracy with power. When compared to the cylindrical shape of a shepherds' crook, the flat striking surface offers a dramatic improvement!" Barbara the Bowyer continued.

"I knew we could envision a better striking stick to hit a small hard leather ball than the shepherds' crook. By working together, I believe that we can create a new design to improve accuracy. At the same time, a new design will allow us to provide more power when we hit the ball." Robert added.

"Do you believe you can create a flat striking surface face made of a hardwood, Robert and Heather?" asked Russell.

"Aye!" Robert answered. "No doubt. Do you want Heather and I to concentrate on producing a club head with a flat striking surface, Russell?"

"Aye, Robert. If you and Heather are able to produce the clubhead with a flat striking face, I am certain that Barbara and I can find plenty of acceptable sticks to produce the stick shafts."

Barbara continued, "Yew is my choice for the shaft. To produce longbows, yew is the best wood to use because it is quite strong. In addition to strength, yew is a durable wood. For those same reasons, strength, and durability, I think our first choice when we begin making sticks for the club head should be yew. I believe that we will easily find a sufficient number of sticks which will work sufficiently well. I believe we should start by sorting through the rejected yew staves."

"I know that by working as a team, Barbara and I will design and build a better stick than the shepherd's crook. We craft bow staves to be flexible, strong, and durable. The shepherds' crook is strong and durable, but not flexible. The combination of strong, durable, stiffness makes the crook a great tool in order to move, to prod, to guide or even to lift an animal that needs assistance, or to be guided out of danger. In addition, the crook provides balance to a shepherd when she or he must negotiate rough terrain while walking." Noted Russell.

Barbara added, "Those characteristics help define a great shepherd's crook. However, for a stick to strike a ball consistently, to send the ball flying at high speed with accuracy, the characteristics for a shepherd's crook do not provide the best combination. Perhaps there are other characteristics to consider if we wish to produce the ball striking stick that we desire."

Robert the Carpenter agreed with Barbara's assessment. "I believe there are several ideas we might examine regarding the best wood to choose for the task of hitting a ball at high speed. You know yew!" Robert smiled. "You two Bowyers know yew better than anyone in St. Andrews. Maybe as well as anyone in England or Scotland. Heather and I trust you two to choose the best staves to craft into the shafts we need to design the new hitting sticks in our game."

Then, Barbara asked, "Heather and Robert, if we find staves to build a better striking stick for the game do you think that you could design and build a consistent striking surface to attach to the stick? If we combine a better fitting stave with a flat striking surface, I know our ability to hit the ball will improve. Our club will possess more power and more accuracy than the rounded surface of the crook!"

"Aye, without a doubt," Robert answered. "A smooth, flat surface will be far better suited to deliver a high-speed blow to a small hard leather ball. I am sure we can design and craft a more effective ball striking surface. The design will feature a more efficient shape to strike a small ball. Our stick will permit us to deliver force with accuracy."

"Making a flattened face on the club head is a fairly routine task for skilled carpenters," Heather acknowledged. "We store a variety of different hardwoods in the shoppe from which we can choose. Elm, walnut, oak, maple, for example, are hardwoods for us to consider. I thought of those hardwoods as possibilities to shape into the club face because they are strong, stiff, and durable. We possess plenty of those woods."

Robert added, "We can cut the block of hardwood to any size. Cutting to size is not really an issue. It will be important to decide the best size. After we determine the size we want, we can form the block to any shape."

"There will be another significant challenge, though." Barbara noted.

"What would that challenge be?" Heather asked.

"The challenge will be to find a way to attach the club head to the stave." Barbara stated.

"Aye. Suppose you produce a better club face, and we produce a better stave, do you think can solve the attachment problem? Can we find an effective method to attach the improved club head to the improved stave? We will require a connection strong enough to withstand the force of hitting the ball hard, over and over, again and again."

Heather responded, "The joinery we create must combine two separate pieces, the stick and the club head permanently into a single tool, a striking stick. We want to create a tool like the scythe, a tool that combines a handle with the blade. Or the hammer, which combines an iron head with a wooden handle. Or the steel axe head that is attached to the wooden handle. All those tools combine two pieces to act as one striking tool. To strike a hard leather ball using a powerful swing requires a strong, durable joinery. We have a design and engineering problem to solve."

"Solving this connection problem will be different from making a joint connection for a chair or a table. The design for the stick shaft attached to a club with a striking surface will also require a design far different from the standard design of a shepherd's crook." Robert explained.

"Let's talk about that challenge. What is the best way to connect the shaft to the club head? Robert, I was just thinking about how we can attach the club head to the stave." Heather interjected. "Father just received some new permanent glue from the Tanners last week. I think we should consider that glue."

"I agree. The new glue is an option. However, in order to create the permanent connection, I think we need to design more strength than that provided by even the strongest glue alone. We need a strong design structure for the attachment. I think we might begin with a tenon and mortise joinery." Robert offered.

"Robert, a tenon and mortise joint is a splendid idea!" Heather exclaimed. "The tenon and mortise joinery will make a strong connection between the stave and the club head. Tenon and mortise joinery is both strong and durable. We insert the shaped end of the stave into a hole. To shape the hole to fit nearly the same size as the nub of the stave is a classic carpenter design. We have a great amount of experience in making tenon and mortise joineries. We take pride in making joineries that fit together tightly and securely."

"When you bring some staves, we will decide what size hole we need in the clubhead. If you make the end of the stave as small as possible without sacrificing any strength, it will be helpful when we fashion the club head." Robert ordered.

"Do you have a size in mind for the width of the tenon? We don't want to exert too much pressure on the wood block for the club head. If we make the mortise too big, there could be a problem. If the hole is too big, there is a danger that the shaft might cause the block to split." Heather mused.

"An excellent question, Heather." Robert agreed. "A hole about the diameter of my pointer finger, will be safe I think. With that size, there will be no danger that the hardwood will split. It will not matter which hardwood we select. Do you think you can shape the nub of the yew stave to that size?"

Russell responded, "Absolutely, we can make the nub of the yew the size of your pinkie…heh! Or mine. The yew stave will lose no strength when we shape it to that size diameter. Of that, I am certain. We often shape bow staves to about the diameter of a man's pinkie. Even smaller sometimes."

"Okay, to connect the stave to the club head, we begin with a mortise and tenon joinery. We can generate a tight fit. The tight fit will be strong and durable. But we can do more to strengthen the joinery than just fabricate a tight fit."

Robert visualized. "After we fashion a tight fit between the stick and the club head, we apply the new glue. I think we should apply glue both inside the mortise and on the outside of the tenon. When we insert the tenon into the mortise, we will double the amount of glue. We allow the glue to thoroughly dry overnight. When the glue dries, the tight fit of the stave and the hole will form a solid and permanent connecting bond. The combination design connecting a tenon glued into a mortise will produce a bond that will strong and durable."

"I like the design, Heather. I agree. That connection will be extremely strong and feel solid."

"Russell, since you agree with that design, I wish to offer another idea." Barbara Bowyer stated. "I believe there is a very good way to add strength without adding much weight. Remember how Father Bowyer experimented with wrapping? We wrapped strong, thin, linen cord at the connection points on that last order of long bows."

"Aye, I do, sis. The customers were very excited. They were pleased with the addition of the linen cord. To a man, all thought the cord wrap would improve strength and durability of their new weapons." Russell commented.

Barbara continued, "I think I could use the same cord and apply the same concept that we used on the bows to our clubs. Wrapping the mortise and tendon joinery, will provide strength to the connection. It will act like a brace. In addition, the cord wrap will protect the joinery from the elements. I propose that we wrap linen cord around the joinery.

I still want to do more to the club. I think we can strengthen and protect the joinery. After wrapping, I want to apply a coat of the new lacquer to protect the wrap. The lacquer will bond with the cord. The lacquer will also serve to coat and protect the cord wrapping. The lacquer will shield the wrapping from abrasion caused by the sand. The lacquer will keep the cord protected under wet conditions.

To summarize, the combination of a double dose of glue will connect the tight fit of tenon and mortise joinery. After the glue dries, we wrap linen cord around the joint of stave to club head. Finally, the application of lacquer will provide more protection for the wrapping from abrasion caused by sand and water on the wet environment on the Links."

"Aye, Barbara, I think we have an excellent design concept. The club head and the stave will feel and function as one piece." Heather concurred.

"I do have one more idea," added Russell. "I am thinking. If all four of us work together, I think we can make twelve clubs fairly quickly. We can make a club for each one of the friends. Do you agree?"

"Russell, that's a great idea!" Barbara exclaimed.

"I am absolutely sure that all the friends will want their own clubs. Already I know I do. I think that concept is very exciting." Heather agreed.

"I think my club should be longer and heavier than Heather's club." Robert stated.

"I agree, Robert." Heather nodded. "A club that fits you, Robert or Russell, will be far too long for me. That extra length will also make the club much too heavy for me to control and swing."

Barbara added. "Just like Father says when he builds a bow for a customer. 'I need to fit the bow to the archer. I cannot fit the archer to the bow.' When we make the new club, I believe we shall make the club fit the player, not expect the player fit the club."

"Certainly, Thomas the Tanner will want a club that is fitted to playing with only one hand." Robert added.

"Thomas never asks for anything different or special." Barbara noted.

"Aye. No matter what we are doing he wants to join us. Thomas always does his best. It doesn't matter if we are playing a game, or Thomas prepares a hide for leather or parchment. If ever there was a drawing contest, we all know Thomas would win." Russell explained.

"No one can draw like Thomas." Barbara observed.

"I never even think about Thomas as different from us anymore." Heather stated.

"Aye. Even though Thomas hits the ball using only his right hand, he produces plenty of power. It is as if his right hand possesses the strength of two hands in one." Robert pointed out. "When we design and craft the stick for Thomas, we shall take extra care.

The Carpenters and the Bowyers skipped home. The ideas bounced in their heads. All four felt the excitement of creating something new. They could hardly wait to present the new club design to the other friends. The four also looked forward to the reaction they would receive from the other eight friends the next time they all met on the Links.

Chapter 53 | 1399 | Friends Share Ideas

Straight along Market Gait, ten friends dashed through town. Pumping arms and stretching legs as fast as they could, each runner breathed hard. Out to the Links, they sprinted.

David and Bessie faced each other while they leaned on opposite sides of the Old Stone Bridge. Anxiously, they awaited the arrival of ten friends. The two Shepherds smiled. The smiles broke into joyous laughter. Both especially enjoyed this moment of their day. They loved that instant when they recognized that the friends raced in their direction.

Bessie and David stepped up to the far end of the Old Stone Bridge. The two held their Shepherd's crooks parallel to the ground. All the way across the end of the bridge, they faced towards each other and lightly touched ends. The touching crooks formed the finish line for the friends' daily race across the Old Stone Bridge.

As the exhilarated runners approached the finish line, each extended an arm in order to grip a crook. As soon as a crook was grabbed, David and Bessie released their hold. Whichever friend held a crook in hand was declared the winner of the race for that day.

This race resulted in a unique ending, an unprecedented tie. During their daily races, ties did frequently occur. But for the first time ever, this race ended in a new and different type of tie. All ten runners held onto the two crooks at the same time. Before David and Bessie could even announce the daily race results, ten out of breath friends shouted in unison, "I have an idea about our game!"

Laughter erupted. Hearing ten breathless companions shout the same words in unison struck the entire group as hilarious. "Okay. Who wants to speak first?" Bessie questioned, "How about you Marion?"

"Aye, Bessie. Thank you, I am happy to be first. Actually, my brother Jonathan and I bring the same idea to the circle. Together, we invested a great deal of time into thinking about the hard leather ball. We talked at length about the characteristics. We want to share some of what we consider to be our better ideas about how a new leather ball may benefit the new game.

First, Jonathan and I agree that our new game will be much more fun if every person retains his or her own individual ball. When each person possesses a ball, there will be less time we waste before we can hit again. While we wait for a turn to hit the only ball, we experienced feelings of frustration. Since we will not waste time by waiting for our turn to hit the only ball, that means we will play far more. Plus, we will experience more opportunities to savor the best part of the game, when we get our turn to strike the ball. We are tired of waiting to hit the only ball."

Jonathan the Shoemaker followed his sister, "Second, with our idea, when each participant plays his or her own ball, we will save steps. After we hit, each of us will walk to our ball, instead of all players walking to the same ball every time. By saving both time and steps, we know there will be way more time to enjoy the game."

The friends murmured approval. Finally, Russell the Bowyer asked, "Those are two convincing reasons, Shoemakers. The idea that each player should possess his or her own ball opens many new possibilities for the game. Thank you for presenting your ideas, Marion and Jonathan. I believe we are all in agreement. However, we seem to have a problem."

"What is the problem, Russell?"

"The problem seems quite clear to me. The problem is, how are we going to get a dozen balls? Finding just this one ball was sheer fortune. Well, to be sure, there was some good work by David. We certainly enjoy hitting this ball. For each friend to possess his or her own ball to hit, we need twelve balls."

"Aha!" Jonathan answered, "Marion and I anticipated that question. I believe we have a satisfactory answer for you, Russell. Last night we talked about that very issue. We believe there is a way that we can all carry our own ball. Marion and I feel certain we can assemble a ball that is superior in quality and durability to the ball David brought to us."

"Jonathan and I already make all the leather balls that are sold in our Shoemaker shoppe here in St. Andrews." Marion continued. "Both of us have been cutting, drilling, and stitching leather to make balls since before we were 4 years old. Father Shoemaker believes that producing leather balls provides great training to become a master Shoemaker. He taught us how to make leather balls long ago. We construct leather balls of any size. We mastered the production of leather balls employing several different patterns. We make high quality leather balls of all sizes."

The other ten friends unanimously agreed. In their opinion, the Shoemakers of St. Andrews crafted the finest quality leather balls in all Scotland. Everyone in St. Andrews knew that the Shoemakers produced superior leather goods. Many travelers to St. Andrews pronounced those same sentiments. During pilgrimage, most travelers bought a leather ball. To commemorate their successful journey, the faithful first desired to obtain a pewter badge featuring St. Andrew and the saltire cross, which declared that a pilgrim completed St. Andrews Way. The next most popular souvenir purchased by the visitors to take home from the pilgrimage experience, was a leather ball. The pilgrims especially prized the exquisite leather balls produced by the Shoemakers of St. Andrews.

Marion continued, "Thank you for accepting our idea, friends. Also, we do have one more idea to share with you."

"What is that idea?" asked Rhona the Weaver.

"We think the balls should all be the same size." Jonathan blurted.

"Aye!" David the Shepherd interjected. "Making all the balls the same size responds to our concern for fairness. Remember, we wanted our new game to be scrupulously fair. At the very beginning, when we decided that we needed a new game, we all agreed our new game must be completely equitable for all competitors. For each player to carry a ball that is uniform in size provides an important step to achieve equality. I think the possession of balls equal in size is a crucial to consider while we construct a game that is fair. I agree with Jonathan and Marion. Every player should possess a ball that is the same size that every other player uses."

"If all the balls are exactly the same size, that will help to make one important part of the new game to be equal. In my opinion, whatever we decide the game will become, every way we can find to make the game equal. offers us the best choice to consider." Rhona concurred.

Marion continued. "This ball is small. We already discovered that each of us enjoys hitting a ball of this size. Unlike a heavy hammer to throw, or a solid steel shot to put, or a large caber for the men to toss, not one of which is fair to each player, the small ball offers no advantage regarding one's strength and power. Those objects from the Games are way too heavy, too large, too unwieldy for even the strongest woman to be able to compete fairly against a strong man."

"Hitting the small ball solidly, as we already discovered, requires skill. The player must employ eye contact, rhythm and control to strike the ball squarely." Jonathan pointed out. "Skill, eye contact, rhythm and control are far more important to drive the ball a reasonable distance, than brute strength. To hit the ball high and far requires skill and timing. Although there is ample reward for being a physically strong player, brute strength alone fails to overcome a poorly struck small ball, to achieve distance."

Again, all the friends agreed. For the new game, all balls will be the same size and weight. The balls will be constructed as close to identical as possible. The decision about the same size of all the small leather balls achieved unanimity. The friends unanimously reaffirmed their commitment to a scrupulously fair game.

"Okay," continued Jonathan, "we have another item for discussion. The next question Marion and I talked about is, what size ball should we build? We thought about creating a ball the size of a chicken egg."

David thought aloud. "Well, this ball is the size of a chicken egg. This size is pretty good. But I wonder. After hitting, I wonder if this ball, this chicken egg size may be just a wee bit too big. I was thinking about a ball more similar to the size of a walnut. What do you think? Jonathan, do you think that you and Marion could make the ball smaller than this one?"

"David, I am sure that Marion and I can develop a leather ball as small as you want," bragged Jonathan. "I have watched Marion stitch leather balls that were way smaller than a walnut. She produces incredibly dainty needlework in leather. After Marion stitches the pieces together, we plan to coat the seams with lacquer. The lacquer will protect a very strong, very hard ball. We plan to design and produce a ball that will be impervious to water. The new leather ball we build will also have a harder shell than the old one we used."

Thomas the Tanner spoke, "Shoemakers, you brought some great ideas to the new game. I am very impressed at the way you thought about the ball. You brought details to consider in order to solve problems. Thinking about the ball produces some very important ideas for us to talk about. Having all the balls the same size truly does help make the game fair. A smaller ball that is hard and impervious to water will offer rewards for good contact. In a similar manner, when the contact from the stroke is poor the smaller ball will punish the player."

Chapter 54 | *1399* | Replacing The Shepherd's Crook

"Bowyers and Carpenters! Last time all the friends met, the four of you told us you had been very busy thinking and talking about the new game. Are you ready to share your thoughts with us? What ideas did you bring to discuss and consider?" Asked Bessie the Shepherd.

Barbara the Bowyer looked at her brother, Russell. Then, she looked at both Carpenters. Russell looked at Heather. Heather looked to her brother. Politely, the four silently looked to Robert indicating that the four decided Robert would speak to the entire circle first.

Robert began, "Aye, Bessie. Last night, we gathered to discuss your two Shepherds' crooks. As a result of our conference, we concluded unanimously that we believe that we can construct a stick to improve the new game significantly.

The first idea is that each player shall possess his or her own stick for striking the ball. We were unhappy that all the lads shared just one stick, and all the lasses shared another stick. We decided to recommend that each player possess his or her own personal stick."

Immediately, the friends agreed with the Robert's recommendation. All could see several advantages to possess one's own stick. Controlling one's stick would save time. Time would be better used when all players possessed an individual stick combined with all players possessing their own leather ball. We can use the time we now spend waiting for a turn more effectively and hit the ball more often.

Jonathan the Shoemaker judged, "Bowyers and Carpenters, the proposal that each individual player possess a stick received unanimous approval."

"Do you bring any other ideas for the circle to discuss and consider?" asked Margaret the Tanner.

"Aye, Margaret. The four of us wish to offer another idea for discussion and consideration by the whole group." Robert resumed. "To make this idea come to fruition will require that we combine skills and products using both the Bowyers' and the Carpenters' workshops and skills. It is our unanimous opinion that we can dramatically improve the design of the hitting stick. We envision a new and improved club designed to improve the player's success rate."

Heather continued, "The striking stick we envision will make playing the game far more enjoyable. Compared to using a shepherd's crook to hit the ball, the new design will improve performance. We envision a heavier club head containing a flattened striking face attached to the shaft. Players will experience more consistent contact when striking the ball."

"By producing a more consistent strike of club face to ball, players will realize an important advantage for the new design. Compared to using the Shepherds' crook, the more consistent strike from the new stick will dramatically improve a players ability to control the ball with accuracy." Barbara explained.

Russell added, "In addition to improved accuracy, our unanimous opinion is that our new stick design will enable the player to significantly increase power. Increased power at the strike of club to ball translates to longer distance and greater accuracy. Because the new flattened face design will allow the player to make consistent and reliable contact with the ball more often, the player will increase confidence. Players ability to control the flight of the ball will improve."

"Our hypothesis is that when the player develops confidence in the ability to achieve consistent contact between club and ball, then she or he will also learn to increase power to the stroke." Heather stated.

"Compared to the shepherd's crooks, our new hitting stick will offer a dramatic improvement. On our new striking stick, the club face is specifically designed to hit the ball accurately. The increase in accuracy will also lead to a significant distance improvement." added Barbara the Bowyer.

"You present convincing arguments for your new design. Can you explain how you plan to design and produce a superior stick? What can you tell us about why the design you envision to hit the ball will improve our ability to strike and drive the ball when compared to the design of our crooks?" asked Bessie, incredulously.

"Bessie, you asked the set of questions we asked ourselves during our discussion. First," Barbara continued, "for the shaft of our new hitting sticks we propose to use rejected yew staves for the long bow shafts from Father's shoppe. More than enough staves which have previously been rejected as acceptable for a longbow, will function perfectly as the shaft for the hitting stick. The majority of those staves were rejected because the sticks were simply too short to serve as a quality man's longbow."

"However," Russell continued, "even though a rejected stave is too short for a longbow, nothing is inherently wrong with either the strength or the durability of the stave. The shorter yew stave retains all its strength and durability. In addition, yew possesses just a wee bit of flexibility.

Most important, when we make a shaft for the striking club length of the stave will not be an issue for us. No one wants a stick as long as a longbow to strike the ball in our game. We envision the length of the new sticks to be approximately half the length of the longbow."

Barbara the Bowyer added, "We think that just a wee bit of flex in the stick can be an advantage. A wee bit of flex should add to the distance during of the ball flight. After all, the distance that an arrow flies is a direct function of the powerful flex contained in the yew stave. By pulling the bowstring, the archer bends the bow. The power results from the bowstring bending the bow. When the archer releases the bow string it launches the arrow at an extremely high velocity. We believe that when we strike the ball, that wee bit of flex from the shaft added to the speed developed by the swing will increase the distance the ball flies.

The Carpenters provided some very interesting ideas. Russell and I fully agree with the Carpenters. We share confidence, that compared to a shepherd's crook, by working together the four of us can build a far better striking stick."

Robert took control of the presentation, "Aye, we have some ideas we do think you all will find compelling. We believed that when we improve our ability to strike the ball we will improve accuracy. Thank you, Russell, and Barbara. We should begin with an examination of the shepherd's crook as a tool to strike a ball.

Note that the shepherds' crook is rounded on all sides. When David and Bessie must touch, must control, or must move an animal, they want to avoid any damage to the animal. The crook's rounded shape helps to control the animal safely. Because of that smooth rounded shape, no serious damage occurs to either the animal's skin or muscle. Even when Bessie and David must apply considerable force to guide an animal, there is little danger from the rounded crook to injure the animal. For example, sometimes David and Bess are required to completely lift the sheep out of a potential trap to save it. The crook is strong enough for David and Bess to control the sheep completely. The shepherd can safely maneuver the animal with no worries that the crook may break or bend. Using crooks, shepherds can turn an animal's direction. Shepherds can bring the animal to a complete stop. Or shepherds can prod the animal to move. The Shepherd's crook is perfectly designed and produced for Bessie and David to manage the job of controlling sheep."

"However, it is our opinion, even though perfect for the Shepherd's job, as an adequate design to deliver a controlled strike on a small, hard, leather sphere, the cylindrical shape fails. In fact, we think the rounded shape of the crook creates a significant problem to strike the ball." Barbara added.

Chapter 55 | *1399* | Improved Striking Club

"Aye!" Heather expounded excitedly, "Instead of using a stick with a rounded surface, there is a far better surface to launch a ball into controlled flight! When carpenters strike a small object, we never use a rounded surface. To strike objects as small as a nail head, or a dowel rod we use a hammer head. The flat striking surface allows a carpenter to deliver controlled power to a tiny nail head. The power transferred through the flattened face drives the nail. Nail heads and dowel rods both are considerably smaller than our leather ball. Each workday carpenters drive thousands of nails accurately. The power delivered by the hammer surface drives a nail through the hardest wood."

Robert added, "Rather than driving nails into wood, our new flattened face club head design will allow us to drive the ball with consistency. To drive the ball, the flat face of the wood block will function in the same manner as the smooth face of the hammer. The flattened face will make it easier to drive the ball into the air, or bounce and roll the ball across the ground. Improved striking accuracy will grant us the ability to choose to strike from a range of controlled power."

"We envision a new design that connects a flattened striking surface shaped into a wooden block fastened securely to the shaft. The Bowyers are responsible to produce and fit staves, now called shafts. To fit the shaft directly into the club head, we will work together. We plan to connect the two pieces, the club head to the stave employing tenon and mortise joinery. The tenon and mortise join the two pieces together to form one club. For the new game the club will create a superior striking tool." Heather proposed.

"To connect the shaft to our flat faced wood block requires a strong, durable connection. Our design will combine skills, knowledge, and tools used by carpenters and bowyers." Barbara stated.

"Once the block is complete and finished, we carve a hole at one end." Robert explained. "We will carve the hole to the same diameter as the width of the shaft end. By using equal width for the hole and the tip of the shaft, we will insure a tight fit. The tight fit will be the first step for us to assemble a strong connection."

"We reinforce the connection between shaft and club head by constructing permanent joinery. We will thoroughly coat both the inside of the hole and the outside peg, with the new powerful glue that the Tanners recently invented." Heather noted.

"When the hole in the club head and the tip of the shaft are thoroughly and completely coated with glue, we will insert the tip of the stave into the hole in the block. The glue forms an effective, strong bond. At this point, after the connection is fitted and glued, we will return the manufacturing process to the Bowyers". Robert concluded.

Barbara began, "In order to make the connection between the stave and the block even stronger, we will add this step. We wrap the connection of the stave and the wooden block with strong linen cord. To finish the club connection, we will apply a coating of lacquer to the wrapping. The lacquer coating will permanently seal the wrapping around the connection."

"In addition, the lacquer will provide advanced protection for the wrapping thread." Russell continued. "The lacquer will coat the wrapping thread. Because of the lacquer coating, neither water nor sand will break the wrapping. The complete procedure consists of four steps. We will form a permanent connection between the stave and the block that will remain strong and powerful.

To review, the process begins with a tight fit of the stave into the hole. Next step is the application and hardening of glue. After the glue hardened, we will wrap thread cord around the connection. The thread wrapping will serve to protect the joinery from water and sand. Finally, to protect the thread wrapping we will apply a coating of lacquer on the thread, the stave, and the club face. The lacquer will provide even more protection."

"When we used David's crook, or Bessie's crook, we were all forced between only two sizes. We had only one size stave for the lads, and only one size for the lasses. Using only two sizes of crooks seriously inhibits the ability of nearly every player to stroke the ball with maximum effectiveness. Should we expect to make only one or two lengths of shaft?" Robert asked.

"One more saying from Father Bowyer guides our work as Bowyers," Barbara replied. "Father loves to remind us, 'I cannot fit the archer to the bow. My job as a bowyer is to fit the bow to the archer'. We shall follow Father's admonition. We propose to make an individual shaft to fit each player."

"We argue against all players being forced to choose the same size hitting stick. Just because we all use the same length and diameter shaft does not make the game fair. However, we think there is an argument for a similar sized club head. In fact, we already agreed that if all of us play the game using the same length shaft it will be seriously detrimental to our ability to compete. During the Scottish games, as we noted previously, for example, women throw a smaller, lighter shot put, and a smaller, lighter hammer, than men throw. It would neither be fair, nor would it be competitive in events like the shot put and the hammer throw for women to throw equipment the same size that men throw. Almost all women are significantly smaller than almost all men. Therefore, the people agreed that women should throw smaller shots and hammers." Russell argued.

"When we frame a scythe for reapers, we very carefully measure the reaper's arm length, height, and hand grip size. For example, we measure height of shoulders, length of arms, the exact point at which the arms reach the legs, and the width of shoulders. All of those measurements are necessary in order to custom fit the tool to the user. Those measurements help guide us as we construct a scythe that will custom fit the reaper. With a properly fitted scythe the reaper is able to work for the entire day. A proper fit allows the reaper to move and work employing an effective rhythm to maintain a consistent pace. We can custom fit the length of the shaft. Remember, in our new game we want fair competition between men and women." Barbara explained.

"We will also fit the diameter of the grip to the player's hand. Each player will possess a club that fits comfortably." Russell added.

"So, for our new game, we decided, that all players will have their own individual ball. The hitting stick fits the player." David summarized

"In addition," Barbara continued, "all players will possess their own individual hitting sticks. The stick will be designed to fit each individual player by measuring length, weight, and handle diameter. Each custom hitting stick will fit the player."

"We decided that in the new game, there should be no advantage for a large player versus a small player. We agreed that we wanted no advantage to a fast competitor versus a slow competitor in our game. We wanted fair competition between male players and female players in our game. Therefore, the hitting sticks will differ in size. The size of the stick will differ because the size of the player should match the ability to control the stick. A custom fitted stick will be advantageous for each player to practice and perform." Heather explained.

"In fact, because the stick will fit the player, there will also be no advantage for a two-hand player versus a one hand player." Russell added.

"Nor will there be an advantage for a one hand player to compete against the two-handed players." Chuckled Thomas.

"What do you think of those ideas, Bessie?" asked David.

"I am very impressed. Never would I have thought about redesigning our shepherds' crooks. I believe the Bowyers and Carpenter brought a grand idea to help players enjoy our new game. I am very excited to see how they will make a custom fitted stick especially designed to hit a ball. At the same time, I can't wait to get my hands on my very own custom fitted stick!"

"Sister, I agree. I would never have considered designing a stick different from our crooks either." David added. "I am so happy to have friends who possess a variety of skills and knowledge. The variety of skills and knowledge provides different ways to envision possibilities. Different viewpoints help us enrich our own experience. We can share a vision. Close friends, people we trust completely, who possess a variety of skills and knowledge provides a great advantage to a group. I am most anxious to see, hold and try the new clubs. Especially, the club made just for me."

Bess concluded. "We came a long way towards achieving our mission to design a game fair to every player, today. I feel proud of all of you, my friends."

Chapter 56 | 1399 | Dissecting The Old Ball

"How much time do you think you will require to make a new ball for each friend, Marion?" Bessie the Shepherd asked anxiously. Other group members nodded in agreement. That was the question several others wanted to ask. Expectantly, ten sets of eyes focused on Marion. All anxiously awaited her response.

"Let's think about that question together, Bessie. Jonathan and I want all of you to consider the process required to make a leather ball. I need to make a pattern for a test ball first." Marion the Shoemaker, responded. "From the pattern, I will make one ball for all of us to try. When we try out the test ball, we need to decide to come to an agreement as an entire group. We need to determine the proper size and proper weight.

After we all try hitting that test ball, I will be able to provide you with a better answer for how much time I will need to make a ball for each of us. Normally, Jonathan and I can make about four balls in a day's work. I don't see why making our new ball should require any different amount of time to produce. My best guess is that Jonathan and I are capable of making the new balls at a rate of four balls in a day."

"Well," David the Shepherd, continued, "the ball we have been hitting is pretty raggedy. That ball seems almost unusable now. No matter how well the ball is struck, it no longer flies anywhere near as far as we used to see it fly."

Bessie added, "Remember when we first acquired that old ball. At that time, the ball was hard and resilient. Now, our old ball is pretty much used up. The ball is considerably softer now than when we first used it. The old ball no longer performs the way it did when we first began to hit it. The shape of the ball changed from a nearly perfect sphere into a shape more similar to a hen's egg.

Instead of the hard, smooth leather, covering the resilient ball, like when we first found it, the ball is different now. Each time we hit the ball now, we see accumulation of the wear and tear on the leather surface. The cover of the ball transformed. It became softer and suede like. You can see many small tears and cracks in the leather covering. We all realized that the inside of the ball softened and turned mushy."

"Aye. That's true, Bess." David agreed. "So, the sooner we can each get our own new extremely hard leather covered ball completed, the sooner we will get started to design and experiment with our new game."

"Can I see the ball?" Jonathan the Shoemaker asked.

"Sure." replied Bessie.

"If we all agree that the condition of the old ball is too dilapidated to use, maybe Marion and I could go ahead and take the ball with us today. If we can take the old ball apart, we might find answers to help us make the new balls better than the old ball. When we dissect the old ball, we can discover the specific materials used to construct the ball.

In addition, we will be able to identify specific techniques and stitches used by the ball maker. Dissecting the ball is a critical procedure to help us understand how the ball was constructed. For example, we need to know exactly what materials make up the inside of the ball." Jonathan explained.

David acknowledged Jonathan. "Jonathan, your argument, to dissect the old ball, is logical and clearly explained. I am convinced that the dissection offers the best opportunity to enhance our understanding regarding how the old ball was constructed. I agree with you. Dissecting the old ball is important."

"David, do you think we could take the old ball with us? That way we can cut it apart tonight?" Jonathan asked.

"Also, we need to perform a close examination upon the outside of the ball. I think the pieces we examine can help us design a good pattern for our new and smaller ball." Marion requested.

"Certainly, take the old ball with you", answered David. "The sooner we get a new ball into each player's hands, the sooner we get each player back to practice hitting. The sooner we resume practice hitting, the sooner we resume working on designing and experimenting with our new game."

Marion scooped up the precious battered ball. Jonathan joined her. Excited, the two briskly began to walk toward the shoppe.

Margaret the Tanner asked, "Marion and Jonathan, do you think Thomas and I can come with you? If you agree, I think we may be able to provide some expertise. I believe, by tapping into our knowledge concerning leather, we may be able to offer some insight. We know how to identify several types of leather, including the animal the skin came from. In addition to identifying the animal used for the leather, we can help to determine what part of the hide is used for the leather covering the ball."

Thomas the Tanner continued, "If, as I believe there is some glue used in the process to seal the seams, we can help. To preserve and protect the leather cover, I think lacquer may also have been applied to the ball. If we are able to examine the glue remnants, we may determine what glue was applied. In addition, we may be able to tell the kind of lacquer. That information could help determine what glue and lacquer to recommend for our new game balls."

Marion replied, "Certainly, Tanners. I know Jonathan agrees with me that we would love to have your eyes join ours. We will need to dissect the old ball. Many people think, 'oh that's just leather'. However, you know, and we know, a particular job requires leather which offers a special set of characteristics. We have a pretty good idea about how we want our new ball to perform.

If any of the friends can tell us something about the leather, it will be you two. We should have thought to invite you at the beginning. I apologize for my short sightedness. Thank you for speaking up and asking to join us."

Then, Rhona the Weaver spoke. Rhona also asked to accompany the Shoemakers and the Tanners. "I think my brother and I could offer some insight if we were able to come with you to witness the dissection, as well.

Many times, the filling for small balls is comprised from some type of wool fabric scraps. Other times the filling is made from animal hair. Our knowledge of thread, yarn and fabric will help to identify the filling used inside the old ball. We could learn how to stuff the right filling for the ball. Stuffing the ball with the right filling will be crucial to produce an effective hard ball. We want a ball that will deliver consistent performance and fly!"

Jonathan observed, "You are right about that, Rhona. When we make hard leather balls, we often use scrap wool as a filler substance. In addition to filling with wool scrap, we have successfully stuffed hair to fill small hard balls. I never thought about combining the two before, though. Combining wool scraps and hair offers an interesting concept to consider. Such a combination might make a resilient and durable filling for a hard leather covered ball. We want to deliver consistent flight and rolling performance in the ball."

The Tanners and the Weavers joined the Shoemakers on their way. Together, six friends jogged to the Shoemaker shoppe. Questions remained about construction of the ball for the new game. Ball dissection might provide important information to answer questions. To create superior new balls information would serve as a guide. Answers from the dissection offered a good start.

To make better new balls required the friends to access information, share their knowledge and combine their skills. All felt confident that their friends possessed expert training from their fathers and mothers. The friends respected the skills each one possessed. Also, the friends recognized the need to depend on each other. To analyze accurately, and to interpret clearly, what they found during the dissection of the ball could be crucial. To complete the mission to create twelve balls, they needed to share information.

The two Shoemaker apprentices spoke to the critical importance to check the thickness of the leather. Leather required a certain thickness to possess enough strength to hold permanent stitches. On the other hand, the leather needed to be thin enough to flex into a curved surface. Having the Tanners available to share insight during examination of the leather expanded the knowledge base. In addition, sharing information with friends who possessed a high level of expertise increased their level of confidence about leather covering the old ball. Valuable information would help guide the friends' decisions.

Similarly, the Weavers' brought expert knowledge. Knowing what filled the inside of the old ball would help determine what stuffing to use. Stuffing the ball with the right filling, in the right way, enabled them to construct the core that would maintain the spherical integrity for the new balls.

At the shoppe, Jonathan announced, "All right. Let's get going."

To examine during the dissection process, the lads and lasses needed to spread the separate pieces. First, the friends wished to learn how separate leather pieces were stitched together to cover the ball. In addition, they needed to determine the thread diameter and material.

Shoemakers understood the various characteristics of different threads. They rated thread for strength, diameter, material, and durability. Based on critical characteristics the function of the crafted object determined thread selection. They wanted a small, hard leather ball to produce consistent performance. The ball would collide numerous times with a wooden club in a sandy, often wet outdoor environment. The ball must be durable.

The friends knew that they would need to stitch pieces of leather together to form a cover a permanent durable leather cover. To achieve that performance objective, required strong thread. In order to pull the leather pieces tightly together strong thread was necessary. Using strong thread, the right stitches would lock the pieces permanently.

At the same time, thread needed to be as thin in diameter as possible. In order to pierce the leather near the edge without tearing, leather required tiny holes drilled at precise intervals along the leather edges. The finest shoes used strong thread with a thin diameter. The thread required sufficient strength to bind the leather together tightly. Strong thin thread also must be durable. Elements, such as snow, ice, mud, freshwater, and saltwater would challenge the hard leather outer surface throughout the life of the ball.

However, an even bigger mystery than the type of leather, the type and size of thread needed solution. The Shoemakers wanted to know the number of pieces to make the ball. The number of pieces utilized to make a small, hard leather ball was a vital concern. The Shoemakers were interested in determining the kind of thread. To perform specific tasks Shoemakers and Weavers worked with specific threads.

Weavers expert advice would help in the decision for the filling. What constituted a filling to maintain a spherical shape even after the ball had been smashed with a stick many times?

At the shoppe, Jonathan reached for his favorite knife.

"No, Jonathan, not that knife. I know that is your favorite knife, but that knife is way too large for this dissection." Marion guided. "Get the smallest knife in the tray. Before we cut anything else, I want to cut the stitches. Let's see if we can get these leather pieces separated. After we separate the pieces, then we can flatten the pieces of leather out. To soften the leather enough to flatten the pieces we may need to soak it. We may be able to use the flat leather pieces as a guide to pattern for the new balls."

The Shoemakers knew the options available to select a pattern to craft a small hard leather ball. A two-piece pattern, a three-piece pattern, or even a four-piece pattern could be fashioned and stitched into a leather ball. For this small hard ball, which pattern offered the best choice for a durable ball?

The task was to produce a ball capable of maintaining its spherical shape following a high-speed collision initiated by a block of wood, several times the size of the ball. To fly through the air for a hundred yards or more, then descend to the ground, maintain a spherical shape in order to perform with the truest bounce and roll, what shapes of leather pieces would best form into a tight, solid sphere?

Together, the Shoemakers, the Tanners and the Weavers regarded questions they needed. The friends knew that the new game required a well-designed ball. The new ball must be high in quality and durable in construction.

The friends would need to select the right leather in order to produce a stiff, hard round ball that would last. They would need to decide the best diameter for thread to provide a combination of size and strength to stitch the leather pieces. Then, Marion would need to decide on the best stitches to complete the small hard leather sphere. Finally, Marion and Jonathan needed to determine the number of stitches to finish each ball.

Together, Marion and Jonathan, the Shoemakers, Margaret and Thomas, the Tanners, and William and Rhona, the Weavers examined the precious, battered ball. To find out the secrets already held in the that sphere required the dissection of the only ball.

The leather cutting knife held a sharp edge. Cutting leather required finely honed skill. Father Shoemaker taught the two siblings how to cut leather safely and effectively years before. Both mastered the skill of cutting leather. When the family shoppe repaired shoes, the Shoemakers learned how to remove old stitches. Removal of old stitches determined the decision process to either repair or replace old worn-out thread. Since a cobbler moved into town, the Shoemakers sent shoe repairs to his shoppe and the Shoemaker Shoppe concentrated their business only on new made shoes, boots, and leather goods.

Marion needed to combine her acquired knowledge with her considerable skill to discover what thread kept the old ball together. Such information would guide Marion and Jonathan Shoemaker as they determined diameter and thread material as the best choice to use in the new balls.

"All those balls will be as close to identical in weight and size as we can make them. I propose that we place an identifying mark, or brand on the ball. That way we can tell our "identical" balls apart. We want to make sure each player is playing the correct ball." Jonathan added.

Chapter 57 | 1399 | The Ball Pattern

Carefully, Marion cut through the stitches. Then, she passed the ball to her brother. Three pieces of leather constructed the old beaten leather shell of the ball.

Jonathan carefully applied strong, skilled fingers to the surface of the ball. He worked diligently. He found a spot to begin to peel the leather pieces of the shell from the interior of the ball. Two identical leather pieces cut in circular shapes fashioned opposite parts. Two circles functioned as caps for the ball. The middle piece of leather, a long rectangle connected the two caps.

"After we took the ball apart I thought we would find a three-piece cover." Marion commented. "I am not surprised. In fact, Jonathan, I am pleased to verify that the ball is made from a three-piece pattern. A three-piece pattern to make a leather ball offers a simple design. In this pattern, there are two identical, circular 'caps'. Each cap covered approximately one third of the surface area of the ball. To make a three-piece ball pattern, we only need to cut the leather into two different shapes. The top and the bottom, also known as 'the caps', will be identical in size and shape. The third piece is a rectangle. Cutting a rectangle is even easier than cutting the two identical circles."

Jonathan continued, "Good, we only need to cut two different shapes. For every rectangle we cut, we will cut two circles."

"When we start, the leather will need to be very pliable. We need to start with dry leather. At first, we will flatten the leather. We will trace and cut the two circle shapes, the 'caps', and the rectangle shape. Later, we will form the leather into the shape of the ball." Marion explained.

"We need to figure out the size of the circles and the rectangle. Once we know the sizes, we can measure the pattern pieces. The pattern pieces must be in exact proportion to each other. After we stitch the leather pieces together, we can begin treatment to make a hard ball. We will need to repeat the treatment sequence precisely. To produce many identical hard balls similar to the walnut size ball we need to repeat the treatment sequence with precision."

"Let's examine the leather pieces. We need to determine the kind of leather cover for the ball." Thomas the Tanner spoke.

"The leather pieces look like cowhide to me." Margaret the Tanner observed.

"If you look closely, you can see tiny holes left on the smooth side of the leather. The smooth side leather is the side where the hair was scraped and removed from the hides. I agree, Margaret. That leather does look like cowhide to me, too." Thomas concurred.

Margaret nodded, "Friends, Thomas and I are certain. The leather used for the outside is definitely cowhide. The fact that this leather is cowhide is good news for us. We can secure plenty of scrap cowhide in large quantities. At the tannery, there is always a sufficient amount of high-quality cowhide scrap available. A sufficient supply of cowhide to produce a large number of smooth, hard, small leather balls will not present a problem."

"Jonathan, we also need a piece of the thread to examine. Can you get a length, say of an inch, of thread for me?" asked Marion.

"Getting an inch of thread will be tricky. I will do my best. What will you be looking for?" Jonathan questioned.

"Good question. You asked the right question at the right time. I am all but certain that the thread is made of linen. We know that to stand up to the abuse this ball endured woolen thread is too weak. What I wish to know concerns the linen thread. I am also sure that the linen thread was treated with beeswax. When we make shoes with the cordovan leather, we use waxed linen thread almost exclusively. Remember, when we purchased that full cordovan leather hide, Thomas and Marion."

"Aye. The Cordovan was a rich reddish color of high-quality leather. You asked Father if he would be able to manufacture such a hide. Margaret, you remember?" Thomas recalled.

"Certainly, Thomas. Father greatly admired the quality of that piece of Cordovan leather. He went to work immediately to determine how we could duplicate the color and quality of the hide. On the third try, Father was satisfied with the product. We brought the third hide to your father, Marion."

"Aye, that is correct. Father was delighted with the Cordovan leather, both the color and quality of the hide. He made a point to tell us that you Tanners exceeded the quality of the imported hide. When he showed us the hide you brought to the Shoppe, he compared it to the imported hide. Right then, Father vowed to only use Cordovan leather produced by the St. Andrews Tanners. Father immediately ordered a two-year supply of Cordovan leather from your tannery."

"Aye, Marion and John. Your father's order for a two-year supply of our cordovan leather hides was important to the financial success of the tannery. Because of the generous order, Father was able to invest in the construction of two more new vats. In addition, Father increased his own order for supplies. He made certain we kept enough supplies to make the dyes to create the cordovan color."

"Interesting memory, Marion. But what does this have to do with me finding a piece of thread from the old ball?"

"Ha! This is my brother. His ability to concentrate and focus on solving a problem is wonderful. That quality will serve him well, I believe."

"Knowing the quality of goods produced in your shoppe, I agree." Rhona observed. "What is your answer to Jonathan about the length of thread? I still want to know that."

"We know that the thread must contain a combination of strength and durability. Linen thread is the strongest thread we possess. But some linen thread is stronger than others. To make the thread stronger, we increase the number of linen yarns that we spin together. We call the number of yarns, "ply's". The strongest thread we use is 8-ply. If we are to use 8-ply thread, it will make putting the stitches in more difficult.

To use 8-ply thread we will need to make bigger holes in the leather. Bigger holes will be more difficult to seal when we pull the thread tight than smaller holes. For the size ball we plan to make, I would prefer to work with 5 ply waxed linen thread. The 5-ply waxed linen thread is strong. Importantly, the holes we punch will be significantly smaller, as well. Smaller holes help maintain the integrity of the cover. I need to learn what is the best size thread to make our leather ball hard and durable. Does it make sense why I want to look at an inch of thread?"

"Aye. You make perfect sense. That was a clear explanation. I will do my best to get an inch length. I know what to do now. When I obtain the thread, I will attempt to unwind it. Then, I will be able to count the number of 'ply's.'"

"Jonathan, I understand exactly what Marion explained. I work with linen yarn and linen thread, often. I have a pretty good touch. As a practicing weaver, I possess a familiarity with the qualities of both yarns and threads. When you procure that inch of thread, would you like my assistance?" Rhona offered.

"Rhona, how kind of you to offer your expertise. You were so right to ask to join us to learn all we could about the construction of the ball by dissection. I will feel most comfortable if I can just give you the thread. Then, you can perform the unravelling. Are you okay with that?"

"For certain. I am glad to help."

"Can you stitch the three-piece ball, Marion? It looks like a lot of stitches." Jonathan asked.

"Sure, I can stitch a three-piece leather ball. It will take some time. I don't want to rush through the stitching. I want to get the shape properly smoothed. Then, I need to work carefully. Tightening the stitches and tightly tying the knots will require full concentration. I am confident I can do a good job stitching the pieces together to form a spherical leather shell.

Do you think you can make identical cuts from the pattern, Jonathan? What do you think of the leather choice for making a ball we can hit with a stick, so that it will fly more than a hundred yards in the air?"

"In your opinion, what makes the stuffing? What forms the inside of this ball?" Margaret questioned.

Jonathan answered, "I need to slice through the stuffing so we can take this hard core apart. To hold the ball we will need to use Father's wooden vise. Let me secure the ball. To start the cut I will use the small saw. I will slowly and carefully draw the blade across the ball surface to make a groove."

Carefully, Jonathan placed the ball in the vice. When it was properly positioned, he turned the crank until the jaws caught. The wooden vice held the ball securely. Then, Jonathan exerted all his strength to tighten the vice so the ball was locked stationary. Satisfied that he could tighten the vice no further, and that the ball would not move, Jonathan selected the smallest saw blade available.

Jonathan marked a line to circle the ball. He placed the blade in the middle of the marked line. Slowly and carefully, he pulled a stroke with the saw blade through the center of the line. The extremely fine sharp teeth on the saw blade caught the well-worn exterior of the ball. The stroke of the saw blade marked a shallow cut into the ball. The controlled movement of the teeth deepened a thin pathway along the marked line. With each stroke, the teeth of the blade cut the groove deeper.

After only ten strokes the blade finished the cut completely through. The inside of the old ball separated into two halves. Jonathan loosened the vice. He removed the two halves of the ball. Jonathan handed one half to William to examine. The other half he gave to Rhona.

"William! This material looks like scrap wool cloth mixed with wool yarn pieces. What do you think?" Rhona inquired.

"Aye. I agree, Rhona. Scrap wool cloth and yarn pieces tightly packed inside the leather shell is the material which enables the ball to maintain its round shape. I think the ball makers probably packed the wool scraps, first. Then, they used the yarn to fill in the smallest spaces. I am also sure that when they packed the wool scrap and yarn pieces in, that all the pieces were wet."

Chapter 58 | 1399 | Recipe To Make A Dozen Balls

"Why are you so certain they packed the yarn and fabric pieces in wet, William?" asked Marion.

"Marion, when dry, wool and wool yarn contain lots of space between the fibers. Sometimes, in order to create a tight weave, we moisten the yarn. Really, that space in the yarn is air. When we wet wool and woolen yarn, the pieces seem to shrink. In fact, the fibers do not shrink. By wetting the wool and yarn, we removed the air from between the fibers. No space remains between the fibers in the wool. When we pack the wool and yarn pieces wet, squeezing the air out of the wool allows us to pack the inside of the ball tight enough to form a hard, solid spherical shape. A sufficient quantity of wool pieces packed into the core forms a sphere strong enough to maintain the shape." William theorized.

"We know when the maker stitched the leather covering it was wet." Marion observed. "Wetting the leather kept it malleable. It is important for me to stitch soft leather. With soft leather, I can finish stitching and tying the knots for the ball after it is stuffed."

Jonathan added, "After the ball makers pulled the stitches tight, they tied the thread off into knots. Knotted stitches hold the leather pieces in place permanently. At that point the ball was thoroughly wet both inside and outside."

"To dry and finish the ball we can tell that the ball makers cooked the wet ball in the fire to dry. Heat dries the inside of the ball all the way through. The heat cooks the ball inside and outside. Cooking also makes the outside leather shell very hard. In addition, the hard leather shell will be durable. The shell should be durable enough to withstand thousands of hard strikes from a wooden club." Marion related.

Jonathan continued, "The tricky part will be to get all the balls exactly the same size when they are dry. Cooking the balls will cause the water to swell out of the wet wool scrap pieces and yarn on the inside. At the same time, the wet leather covering will cook dry. When the water cooks out of the filling and the leather shell covering the ball at the same time, it will cause the entire ball to shrink in size and weight."

"You know what that means, don't you?" questioned Marion.

Jonathan answered, "Aye, Marion. Treating the balls with heat, or cooking, means that one of us will need to keep careful watch while balls cook dry. When the balls are dried to the desired size, we need to remove the balls away from the fire. If the balls cook too long, they will shrink to a size smaller than the size we want the balls to be."

"Is there a solution to the problem of the same time for cooking and drying?"

Thomas answered. "How about this? If we put all twelve balls into the boiling water at the same time, we know they are all cooking at the same temperature."

"Aye! That's true." Jonathan agreed. "And that means if we remove all twelve balls from the boil at the same time, that all twelve balls cooked an equal time. Thomas that is the solution."

"To dry the balls the same amount of time, we place them the same distance from the fire. Each time we turn one ball to dry, we turn all the others the same time and in the same direction." Thomas continued.

"Since all balls were prepared from the same pattern, and stuffed with the same material, when wet, we produce twelve identical balls." Margaret summarized.

"At our Weaver shoppe, we always have plenty of scrap cloth pieces. Also, there are scraps of yarn too small to be used in the loom. We will collect and store scrap cloth and scrap yarn. That way we will stockpile plenty of material for the filling inside of the balls. I guessed, and you might say, I hoped, that woolen cloth and yarn would comprise the filling. But we needed to be sure. Now we have our answers." Rhona observed.

"Dissecting the ball together as Tanners, Shoemakers and Weavers provided valuable information. We discovered answers to several questions about how to make a good ball for our game. We know what materials were used to make the ball. We learned how the materials were processed to make the ball. For our new game, we know we can obtain all the required materials right here in St. Andrews. But most important of all, we know that we have the skills and possess the knowledge to make balls that are identical." Jonathan summarized.

Marion spoke, "Aye, Jonathan and I will start by making a three-piece pattern. Then we will share the plan for all of our friends to possess their own individual balls. We can show the friends that each individual ball is exactly the same as every other ball."

Thomas handled a piece of cowhide leather. "Let's try the smooth side of the cowhide on the outside of leather ball, first. The rough side, or suede side, is the inside of the ball next to the filling."

Jonathan handed the waxed linen thread piece to Rhona. Rhona held the thread almost as if she was going to thread a needle. She observed the direction of the braid. With astonishing dexterity, Rhona rolled the waxed thread in the opposite direction of the braid. She also removed some of the wax to the thread fibers to aid in separating the spun yarns.

Rhona's delicate fingers trained to work with the finest threads on the Weaver's looms separated and counted. "1, 2, 3, 4, 5. Well, well! Marion, it looks like your wish came true. You wanted five ply linen thread to work with in order to stitch the leather shell of the ball. Five ply linen thread is precisely what is used in this old ball. Five ply linen thread waxed with beeswax is exactly what to use."

Marion nodded agreement, "To stitch the pieces together, I need strong five ply waxed linen thread. I will stitch the pieces together first with the smooth side in. I can set almost all of the stitches before we turn the ball inside out. Then, I believe it will be good for us to turn the shell inside out. Turning the ball inside out will place the suede side inside the ball. When we turn the suede to the inside, I think we should thoroughly soak the leather covering in water. Wetting the leather covering will enable us to stretch the leather as much as we need. The suede side will retain far more water than the smooth side. The suede side will definitely keep the stuffing, the scrap wool and yarn on the inside wet longer, too?"

"Aye. That is an excellent plan, Marion." Jonathan continued, "We can soak the wool and hair in water. Soaking we will allow more wet wool scraps and hair into the shell. The more fully we can stuff the wool yarn into the leather shell, the closer we achieve the spherical shape we desire."

"Our hard leather ball is also durable. The ball requires as much filling as we can possibly stuff into the shell. When we completely stuff the filling into the ball, I will tie the final stitches on the outside of the ball with knots. A soaked leather shell covering a ball full of wet filling, will allow us to pull the stitches extremely tight. The wet ball will be ready to cook." Marion recapped.

Chapter 59 | *1399* | The Ball Bee'n

"Knock, knock, knock!"

Knuckles thumped the Shoemakers' locked Shoppe door. The unexpected knocking interrupted Marion and Jonathan from their work. The two Shoemakers looked at each other quizzically. The Shoppe was closed. Who could that be?

"Did you hang the sign to show the Shoppe is closed, before you locked the door, Jonathan?"

"Aye. I did put up the sign. Don't worry, Marion. I will tell whoever is knocking that the Shoppe is closed for the day. I will ask them to please come back tomorrow." Jonathan offered.

Jonathan rose. He walked to the door and pushed it open.

"Beg pardon, for disturbing you at such a late hour. I made this pilgrimage all the way from Skye. I bought my shoes new at home. The journey to see the bones of the Saint was more arduous than I anticipated. The soles of my shoes are worn completely thru. I noticed the sign above your door with a shoe. Can you help me? Can you replace the soles? Can you repair my shoes?"

"Thank you for coming to our Shoppe. Our Shoppe is the Shoemaker Shoppe. We do not repair shoes. I am sorry we cannot be of service to you. As Shoemakers, we make only new shoes. We do not perform repairs.

There is no need to worry though. When you continue to walk down the street in the direction toward the ocean, you will see another sign. That sign will display a worn shoe combined with a needle and thread. The sign is eight doors away. The sign bearing the worn shoe designates the shoppe for our village cobbler. Cobblers repair shoes and boots. Shoemakers only make new shoes, boots, and leather goods.

Our St. Andrews cobbler performs excellent work. Please go to the cobbler shoppe. Be sure to tell our cobbler that the Shoemakers sent you to his Shoppe. Our cobbler will treat you honestly and fairly. More importantly, he will repair your shoes so that they are exactly the way you want them to look and feel. If you require new shoes, please come back tomorrow, and we will gladly serve you."

"Thank you, sir. I will do as you suggest. Your information surely saved my feet for the trip back home. I bid you good night. I wish blessings and good fortune to you, as an honest businessman."

"Good night, pilgrim." Jonathan closed the door. He returned to Marion so they could hark back to work on the ball patterns.

"Knock! Knock! Knock!"

"Oh! Good grief. Can we never get our work started? Much less completed? We really need to get started." Jonathan whined.

"Take it easy, Jonathan. You just did a wonderful, professional job when you took care of the pilgrim. Your recommendation definitely saved that pilgrim's feet. In addition, you helped him save money. I am equally certain our cobbler will be thankful for the paying business you sent his way, also.

Now Jonathan, please, see who is knocking on our door before Father and Mother awake. They put in long hours for the Festival Days. They need their sleep so they can get an early start in the market stall tomorrow."

Jonathan rose, walked purposely to the door, and pushed it open. He was prepared to say the Shoppe is closed for the day. However, a big surprise greeted Jonathan.

At the door, stood Barbara the Bowyer, Heather the Carpenter, Margaret the Tanner, Bessie the Shepherd and Rhona the Weaver. "We came to help!" the five lasses chorused in unison.

"Shh! Not so loud, please. Mother and Father are resting." Jonathan whispered.

"When Marion said it would take a day to make four new balls, we were a wee bit upset. And we were quite worried." Rhona explained. "We began to feel that we were asking way too much from our Shoemakers. We agreed unanimously, that expecting one family to make all the balls was not a fair request."

Bessie continued, "All of us learned to sew and stitch early in our lives. From the time we were little lasses, we practiced sewing. We learned to master many stitchery skills. True, we learned and practiced sewing on cloth, but we can learn to help with stitching leather."

"All of us realize that if we can learn to stitch leather, we will acquire an important skill." Rhona continued. "Learning to master leather stitching will be an advantage for the rest of our lives."

"We already know how to trace patterns carefully. We have all practiced tracing patterns to get the pieces exactly right. Whether we trace a pattern on cloth, or on leather, tracing a pattern will be the same skill." Heather added.

"Cutting patterns in leather will be different than cutting on cloth, we know." Margaret observed. "All of us have cut many patterns on cloth, but like you Shoemakers, I learned to cut leather at an early age from patterns. I can help the lasses learn how to cut patterns in leather. Or Jonathan and I can work together to cut the leather pieces from the tracings."

"Before Marion stitches the pieces together, we also need to punch holes around the edges of the leather pieces. I measured how far apart the holes were for the stitches in the ball we dissected. To drill holes on the circle pieces I use an awl. I make the holes on the suede side. The holes match the same distance from each other for the holes drilled in the circle piece. After I make the first circle piece, we can use it as a pattern to punch the awl through for all the circle pieces. We could prepare all of them at the same time, or one by one. Then Margaret and I will do the same for the rectangular piece." Jonathan explained.

"Do you have more than one awl of the correct size?" Margaret asked.

"Aye. That's the appropriate question, Margaret. Here in the Shoemaker shoppe, each family member possesses his or her own set of tools. You may use Marion's awl."

"Marion, I promise to take good care of your awl. When I finish punching the holes in the leather, I will return your awl to its proper place on your workbench."

"Thank you, Margaret. I trust you. I appreciate that you took especially good care of my tools. If you have any questions, Jonathan can answer them for you."

"Tracing the patterns in the leather and making the holes in each piece will require an invest-ment in time. Stitching will demand even more time." Jonathan replied. "Margaret, I think when the two of us work together we can trace the pattern onto the leather fairly quickly. Cutting will take far longer than tracing. I know that when you use the correct tools, that all of you are good at cutting. Margaret, you can help me trace. Then we will cut and sort all the leather pieces."

Marion directed, "We can start punching holes in the two circles and the rectangle strip. The circles and the rectangle will be stitched together by the rest of the lasses."

"We can each learn a separate step in the process to make the new balls. To make a new ball for every friend, we need to work together." Barbara the Bowyer observed. "We can all sit together while we perform each step."

"To make one ball for each friend, we need to complete at least twelve balls. So, each time we get together, we need to make several balls." Bessie stated.

"On Wednesday morning of every week, our mothers, aunts and grandmothers gather at the Cathedral to make quilts. The ladies call it a 'Quilting Bee'n'. There is one element of the Quilting Bee'n which they treasure. While they work on making new quilts, the ladies love to sing." Rhona offered.

"Also, while the ladies work, they make sure to pray. Often, the church Fathers stop by. The church Fathers lead the ladies in prayer when they begin the Quilting Bee'n." Bessie pointed out.

"Whenever the whole community participates in any type of Bee'n, our parents always sing and pray." Barbara concluded.

Over the course of their young lives, St. Andrews lads and lasses participated in many Bee'ns. They expected to participate in many more. A Bee'n, defined a gathering of the people in order to work together to accomplish a very big task. The people divided and shared the work.

Working together in a group allows us to break the big task into smaller steps. We will greatly reduce the amount of time to complete the big job. The large group will complete the big task more effectively than what one man, one woman, one couple or even what one family, could ever hope to accomplish. For example, the women often gathered to work together to make quilts. They called the gathering a quilting Bee'n. Some of the St. Andrews women who were skilled in needlepoint, gath-ered for another type of Bee'n. They met to create needlework for the sacred fabrics housed in the Cathedral. The sacred fabric included vestments, prieau deu cushions for the people to kneel when they pray to God, and seat cushions for the church sanctuaries.

When a family needed a new structure, a house, or a barn, all the men and women in the community worked together. They met together on a designated day to help build the new house or the new barn for their neighbors. When all worked together, the folks finished a big job in one or two days. While the men and women worked in community, they enjoyed an added benefit. House raisings, barn raising and bee'ns were prominent social events. Gatherings invited neighbors to share and catch up on newsworthy events in the community. In and around the town, folks learned what happened with their neighbors. For example, important news included: to find out which people in the community were sick or injured, who was feeling down, who needed some help, who was courting whom, or who was expecting a baby.

At a bee'n, the members of the community talked with their neighbors and friends. While they worked, there was time to enjoy hearing news about each member of a family. Men and women wondered and talked about new ways that the community of St. Andrews might generate wealth. Accumulating new wealth would help to improve the lives of the people who resided in St. Andrews. The folk talked about the local market. The local market included many available items: salt, fish, and wool, for example. Men and women shared talk about their dreams and desires. Of prime interest in St. Andrews, folk shared how they might continue to serve the many travelers who trekked to make pilgrimage to the Great Cathedral.

"Jonathan, Rhona, Margaret and I talked about the process and the separate steps involved to form each ball," Marion began. "We agreed that the leather pieces and the wool pieces must be wet while we work with them. First, we will turn the suede side out to stitch the pieces into a loosely fitting pouch. When we stitch the three pieces together loosely, we will turn the pouch suede side in.

"The next step is to stuff the pouch. We want to stuff as much wet wool scrap, loose yarn and hair into the leather pouch as we can fit." Jonathan instructed.

"Instead of needles, we will use hog bristles to stitch the five-ply waxed linen thread into the wet soft leather shell. Hog bristles are strong, durable and we can cut a sharp end. The bristles are small enough in diameter so that they will fit through the drilled holes. Most importantly, when we begin to close the cover of the ball, after we stuffed the wet yarn and scrap, the hog bristles are flexible. Flexible bristles allow us to curve the stitches. To be able to create curved stitches is important to finish off the shape of the ball."

"After we finish tightly packing each of the wet balls, Marion will put the final stitches in the leather shell." Jonathan continued. "I can pull the last stitch quite tight. Marion can then finish the stitching. When Marion completes the final stitch, she does so in such a way that almost no knot remains visible."

All the friends agreed with Jonathan. The group planned their work so that Jonathan and Marion could concentrate on completion of the final stitches for each ball. Marion's skill in finishing leather piece work set the standard of the highest quality. Everyone celebrated Marion's remarkable skill and dexterity to complete the leather balls.

Marion explained, "The wet wool and wet leather, will allow us to use the Coir Boilon process. We think the Coir Boilon process will enable us to make the leather ball both hard and durable."

Jonathan prepared a small brick oven. "In this oven, we will "boil" the leather balls. We need to count how much time it will take to boil the leather covering until the ball shrinks to about 7/8ths of the original size, with which we began."

Marion explained, "While the water boils, both the wet stuffing inside the wet leather shell and the leather shell will cook and shrink at the same time. The inside of the ball will expand due to the water on the inside of the ball also boiling.

Working in combination the technique will cause the leather shell to shrink, while the wet wool and yarn filling expands. The heat will cause a dual action. Heat will shrink the leather shell while simultaneously expanding the wool and yarn filling. That dual action caused by the heat explains how we plan to make leather balls that are hard and resilient all the way through with a durable hard shell on the outside. Boiling the leather balls will enable us to form balls that are hard, round, strong and durable. Application of the Coir Boilon process, will allow us to generate exactly the degree of hardness for the kind of leather ball we require to hit as we play our new game."

Bess evaluated, "Marion and Jonathan, you two have thought the process through completely. You explain what materials are required to manufacture a hard, durable, round leather ball. Because of your thorough explanation, I believe all of us totally understand the task we need to accomplish. Does anyone have any questions about what we need to do?"

The lasses looked at each other. No one raised a question. The looks on the faces of the lasses communicated to each other, 'I am ready to get to work.'

"Okay, lasses, let's get to work. We need to make a ball for each friend to use. I can't wait until we can hand a ball to each person in our Circle of friends to play." Marion declared.

Singing and praying brought great joy to all the folks of St. Andrews. Singing helped the workers to keep focused on their tasks. Many important tasks the people needed to accomplish were tedious and repetitive. Nevertheless, those repetitive tasks created the quality of life enjoyed by the citizens of St. Andrews. Singing brought an added benefit to repetitive work. Singing relieved the tedium of repetition. Music incorporates rhythm. Rhythm helped the workers to set and maintain an effective pace. Keeping pace helped to keep the dedicated workers on task. The friends were astonished to see how quickly they accomplished the amount of work they set for their daily goal.

Chapter 60 | *1399* | Driving for Distance: New Balls, New Clubs

"I have a good idea!" Russell the Bowyer crowed.

In two lines, thirty yards apart, the lads and lasses stood and faced each other. Whenever the team practiced hitting, they enjoyed this formation. One by one, each took a turn. For the first time the friends swung their custom fitted sticks to strike new balls on the Links.

Each friend aimed the ball to stop close to a friend in the opposite line. No longer did they need to wait for all eleven others to share hitting one ball, before getting another turn. Taking turns in formation, plus each friend owning a custom fitted club, hitting twelve identical balls, meant they hit balls often. Each friend hit more balls than ever in this one day.

New equipment changed the way the friends thought about the game. Now that each person owned a ball, new ideas abounded. All agreed several possibilities opened up more action for the friends to consider as they designed the new game. More action promised more fun.

When the friends saw the new sticks, they smiled. When they held the new sticks, they felt overjoyed. The Carpenters and Bowyers design dramatically improved the players' ability to make consistent solid contact. Each player reveled in how the fitted, balanced stick felt. They prized their new sticks. The new clubs greatly improved the ability to strike the ball solidly. The Carpenters were correct. The larger flat surface increased the striking area.

The larger striking area meant the players experienced solid contact far more often. Even when they failed to achieve a perfect strike, the contact still produced good ball flight. Improved accuracy plus increased distance prompted a higher level of confidence for every player. The more confident they felt, the more fun they experienced. When the friends saw how far the new balls flew, they felt joy. Each time the friends swung the clubs, the more they strove to execute a solid strike. The Shoemakers and the Bowyers delivered wonderful striking sticks.

Each player owned a new bright white ball identical in size, shape, and weight to every other ball. The new hard ball was a dramatic improvement. For quick identification, each owner marked the new ball.

Most important, the combination of new ball and new stick provided an opportunity for the friends to experience an immediate performance improvement. Friends noticed improved accuracy immediately. The club helped players guide the ball close to the desired line of flight with noticeably improved consistency.

"Russell, I can't wait to hear your idea!" answered Rhona.

"I think this will be fun." Russell continued. "Let's have a contest."

"I love contests! What do you have in mind?" Rhona asked.

"Now that we each possess our own stick, plus our own new ball, I think it is important to explore some new ways to compete. What do you think of this idea? Let's see which lad, and which lass, can drive the new ball the farthest. How does that sound?" Russell posed.

"Aye, Russell, contests always seem to start our thinking about new ways to compete fairly. Your idea for a contest to drive the ball for distance does sound fun." agreed Robert the Carpenter. "Now that all of us have our own clubs, I have been itching to see how much more we can accomplish. With our own ball and our own stick, we know there will be much more action. Besides getting more hits, I just want to see how far the new balls will fly when we really connect. How much difference in distance can we expect when we achieve good solid contact using a full swing with the new custom fitted sticks to strike the new hard leather ball?"

Marion the Carpenter asked, "Do the rest of you want to participate in the driving for distance contest? I know I do. I already feel like I hit the new ball far more solidly. Also, I believe that compared to when I struck the old ball with Bessie's shepherd's crook, my swing is far more consistent. I could feel more power in my swing. I am anxious to make a full swing with my new stick, too."

"I agree." Bessie the Shepherd affirmed. "Hitting the ball with my crook was fun. However, to achieve a solid strike on the ball consistently was tricky. Already I am convinced that hitting our new balls with our own new clubs is way more fun than before. I am also happy with the performance of the new ball. It is far better than striking the old mushy ball.

David the Shepherd added, "The new stick far surpasses the performance of my crook. I love the feel of solid contact with my new club. When I use my custom crafted club, I know I hit the ball better. My swing feels natural. When I hit the old ball with my shepherd's crook, my swing never felt this good."

Jonathan the Shoemaker, the smallest and youngest of the lads added. "Of course, let's have a contest! I really want to see how far I can make the ball fly. I think hitting the ball to see just how far it can go is a great idea. It will be fun. What do you think, Thomas?"

Eleven sets of eyes focused on Thomas the Tanner. "Absolutely", Thomas concurred. "I want to participate in a driving for distance contest. In all of our contests we expect each friend will always give her or his best effort. Knowing that we give our best effort in our contests creates the most enjoyable competitions. Count me in for a contest to see how far we can drive a ball."

At that point, the lads and lasses reached unanimous agreement. They decided to hold a driving contest for distance as Russell suggested. All were excited to use their new clubs to drive a ball for distance.

David asked, "Russell, have you thought about what we should do to make certain that this contest is fair and fun?"

"I have. As I said, I think one way to compete is to pit lads against the other lads and lasses versus the other lasses. We will need to take turns. When the lasses hit, the lads will keep track of each ball. That will make it easy for us to take our turns. Let's take turns the way we do when we practice driving the balls with the lads in one line facing the lasses. If we share the balls between brothers and sisters at first, each lass can strike two balls during each turn.

When the lads get a turn, each will also strike two balls. We could measure halfway between the distance for the two balls. Or we could take the longest of the two balls. There are advantages either way that I can see. The simplest way is to just take the longest ball. I did not decide on that part of the contest. I thought I would offer choices to the entire Circle. Do you wish to discuss and make that decision now?"

"There is no reason we can't try both types of measurements on different days. But since we all want to give it a go, why don't we just use the longest ball today? I think that would be the easiest and quickest way to measure." William the Weaver asked. "Anybody object?"

"I just want to hit! I want to whack a couple of new balls with my new stick!" John the Shoemaker shouted impatiently. "Sometimes I think we do way too much talking and not nearly enough hitting!"

"This time I totally agree with Jonathon." David laughed. "Let's go hit! I can't wait to try the new club to hit the new balls, also."

The twelve friends split into the two groups. The lasses remained on the normal practice line. The lads trotted thirty yards. The lasses and lads stretched and warmed up. Each one made several dry practice swings with the new clubs. During practice swings, each player felt a surge of power in the swing. Finally, the lasses decided to hit in order, from youngest to oldest. Marion the Shoemaker, the youngest lass poured a cone of sand. She poured the cone higher than she normally did. Carefully, Marion placed her ball on top of the cone. She followed her pre-shot routine. When she was ready, she stepped up to address the ball and take her swing.

"THWOCK!"

The ball leaped off the face of Marion's club! It flew higher and higher. At thirty yards, where the lads stood, the ball just began to descend. Laughing, the lads raced back while eyeing the descending ball. The ball landed on the ground 45 yards from the striking point. The amazed lads shouted the distance the ball traveled! 45 yards! The lasses congratulated Marion. Her face beamed with joy.

"What a difference!" She exclaimed. "That is farther than I ever hit a ball! Taking a full swing with my new club is a great feeling. I felt the solid strike of a new ball helped to produce a remarkable improvement in performance for me. This is a great combination! I know I did not gain so much strength since the last time we hit the mushy old ball that I could hit my new ball that much farther."

"Aye! I arrived at the same conclusion, Marion." Bessie concurred. "I know none of us gained that much physical strength since the last time we hit. The new club and the new ball make a difference. Using a fitted club specially designed for striking a ball looks like great fun."

"Oh, aye! It is great fun!" Marion took her second turn. She attempted to swing a little bit harder on the second attempt. However, the second time Marion took a swing, she did not connect with the ball cleanly as she did the first time. Even though Marion swung the club harder, the sound of the contact between club and ball indicated that the connection was clearly not as solid. Her ball landed twenty yards closer than the first stroke. She realized that she failed to make solid contact. Marion looked a wee bit sheepish.

"25 yards!" The lads shouted back to the lasses.

"Hmmm. I knew I did not hit the second shot quite as good as I hit the first one. Still, 25 yards beat the distance I used to drive the old ball. When I used Bessie's crook to drive the old ball, I felt limits to my distance. I am quite happy with both these hits. Who is the next lass up? I want to see if any of the rest of you can make the lads run back by hitting the ball over their heads like I did." Marion chuckled.

Each lass took her turn. They swung their new clubs to hit two new balls each. Every lass improved her personal best distance by more than 10 yards. However, one lass blasted both balls considerably farther than any other lass. Both of her balls landed more than 15 yards farther than any of the other lasses. The lass who hit the ball so much farther than any of the other lasses, was not Bessie. Prior to acquiring the new balls and clubs, Bessie routinely hit the ball much longer than the other lasses. Because of her experience, some might have predicted that Bess would continue to hit the longest drives. It was not Bess. Some might have predicted that longest drives would be struck by the tallest lass, Rhona the Weaver. But it was not Rhona.

After all the lasses took their turns to hit, the lads possessed all the balls. Each lad possessed two balls. The lads took their turns. The lasses were surprised! When the lads swung, the balls soared way, way over their heads. The lasses turned and chased the balls. As they ran to retrieve the new balls the lasses laughed joyfully. Every lad increased distance at least 20 yards more than his previous personal best long drives. After each lad crushed the new ball for a personal best distance, the lad pumped up his bicep muscles.

One lad outdrove all the other lads by more than 30 yards. I remember thinking, "If anyone asked me, 'Who will drive the ball farther than any of the other lads? Which lad will outdrive all of us by 30 yards?' At first, I thought that the answer must be David. Employing the same line of reasoning, if there was one lass who would drive a ball farther than the other lasses, that would be Bessie. David and Bessie were our teachers. During the whole time that we enjoyed hitting the old ball by swinging the shepherds' crooks, the two Shepherds easily drove the balls farther than any of us. I remember how surprised I was. The winner out drove the rest of us by at least 30 yards. Both balls landed within five yards of each other. The winner was not David. It was not William. The lass and the lad who drove the balls farther than any others shared the same last name.

Chapter 61 | 1399 | The Hammer Grip

Questions formed in my mind. The two people who hit the longest balls were a brother and a sister. Was it coincidence that the lad and the lass who hit the ball the farthest shared the name Carpenter? Were the Carpenters the strongest of all the lads and lasses?

I knew the answer to that question. No. The Carpenters were physically strong. The other lads and lasses were also strong.

We all struck virtually identical balls. Balls made from the same leather. Leather pieces traced from the same pattern. The same person cut the pieces. Using the same thread the same person stitched the leather together. All the stitchery was identical. All balls cooked the same temperature and time.

Each person possessed a club designed and crafted for the ideal fit. The diameter of the shaft fit each person's hand size. The length of the shaft matched the combination measurements for the player's arm length and height ratios. Therefore, I must conclude equipment does not account for the difference in the performance exhibited by the Carpenters.

The realization that the Carpenters hit the longest balls by a significant distance set me to wondering. I realized I needed to do some rethinking about how to swing the new club to strike the new ball. What then, made such a difference in distance for the Carpenters? Did the Carpenters know something that the rest of the friends did not know? Was there some technique they knew and shared?

That seemed to be a logical conclusion.

Quickly, I formed questions. Were the Carpenters doing something special when they hit the ball? I think that is a possibility. What did the Carpenters do as part of the swing differently from the rest of us? Answering those questions might provide some insight to why they so easily outdistanced all the other contestants. I wanted to find answers.

To find the answers, I knew I needed first, to observe. Second, I needed to ask questions. The next time the Carpenters took turns to strike the ball, I observed each Carpenter carefully and purposefully. I noticed a difference between the way the Carpenters made a swing compared to the others. It looked to me like the Carpenters used a grip which differed from the way the rest of us gripped the club.

When David and Bessie first introduced us to the joy of striking the ball all of us copied the way that they held the stick. Both Shepherds employed a grip similar to the way one would grip a club as a weapon. From the time we began to hit the leather ball with the crook, we continued to use the same grip. All of us gripped the stick like a club weapon. No one ever questioned that grip. The club grip seemed to work fine. When we took our turn to strike the ball, we all had fun. When each lass and each lad drove the ball, we knew the farthest distance the ball would travel. Until we began the contest using our new sticks and balls, the Shepherds, who acted as our teachers always hit balls farther than anyone else. However, the more we practiced hitting balls, the more we closed in on hitting the ball the same distance as the Shepherds. We were all delighted with the new equipment. We relished the performance improvement. We were all excited. We were so pleasantly surprised. We all hit the ball farther than ever before.

Right away, I noticed that both Carpenters gripped the new stick in an identical manner to each other. Both gripped the stick in a different way from the way everyone else held the stick. The rest of us continued to grip our new sticks the same way we gripped the Shepherd's crook. That observation prompted my first question for the Carpenters.

"Heather and Robert, I notice that you do not grip the new stick the same way the rest of us do. It appears to me, that the two of you are using the same grip as each other. Everyone else, including me, continues to grip the stick the same way we gripped the crook. Am I correct that you are using a different grip?

"Aye. You are quite observant, Thomas." Heather answered. "You are correct. We both are using a grip different from the grip we used with the shepherds' crook. We both use the same grip. "

"Alright then. I have another question. Can you tell me why you grip the new stick differently from the way you gripped the crook before?"

"Aye. That is the essential question. We are happy to explain why we decided to change grip. Let me ask you a question. The question is an important starting point to understand the explanation to change our grip. Do you recall the rationale we presented to redesign the hitting area on the new club?"

"Aye, I do recall the reason. You persuaded us that a flat hitting surface, like the flat face of a hammer, would provide a larger and far more effective surface to strike a small hard ball than the cylindrical shape of the crook."

"Aye. We argued our case to produce a different shape to the group. We presented a rationale that we could build a better surface design to strike a sphere, than the cylindrical shape of the crook. We believed that a new design would provide superior control. Because of the increased control, the new design would allow the hitter to increase force when striking the ball. You remember the argument we presented very well, Thomas." Robert added.

I responded. "You suggested that we change to a flat surface to strike the ball. I believe you argued that fashioning the club with a flat surface design would provide a far more effective design to strike a spherical ball with power. I believe you compared the concept of the flat striking area to using a hammer. You made the point that the flat surface on the hammer head can drive a tiny nail head more accurately and more efficiently than a cylinder shape. Have I remembered correctly?"

"Aye. Very good, Thomas. You stated the reason precisely. The flat striking surface provides for delivery of a very accurate strike. The flat surface allows us to harness that increased accuracy to apply more consistent force when we contact the ball." Heather recalled.

Robert explained. "When we changed from striking the ball with a cylinder shape to a flat striking surface, we made the club striking surface similar to the familiar flat striking surface of a hammer."

"You convinced us about the flat surface. We all hit the ball better with the flat surface than we did with the crook. I completely agree with you. But what does the flat striking surface have to do with the grip that the two of you are now using?"

"Thomas, you asked the right question. Because we changed the striking surface on the club to make it similar to a hammer, Heather and I thought differently about the new club. We began to think about how we gripped a hammer. Even when we still used the crook, we talked about changing our grip. However, when we started talking about how to improve the design the new hitting stick we became so excited we forgot about our talks concerning the grip."

"Once we assembled the new club and held the finished product in our own hands our thoughts returned to the grip. We concentrated our thinking about striking a small object with a hammer. We discussed the way we gripped the club. We decided to apply the grip which we use to hold a hammer when we strike a small nail, when we swung the stick to strike the small ball."

"Ever since we were first old enough to hold a hammer, father trained us how to form the proper grip. Every time we use a hammer, we use the Carpenter's hammer grip. Carpenters strike a small nail head with a hammer several hundred times, sometimes several thousand times each day. Most days experienced carpenters never miss a solid strike on the tiniest nail head.

Because carpenters use a hammer so often, they discovered the most efficient rhythms to the hammer stroke, including the way to hold the tool for maximum effectiveness. To make maximum effective use of a hammer to drive a nail requires two elements, accuracy and power. The proper technique substantially improves both accuracy and power.

There are different ways to grip a stick. Father taught us the proper grip for the hammer. We call it the 'hammer grip'. The way we gripped the Shepherd's crook, we call the 'club grip'. When we hit the ball with the shepherd's crook, we used the same grip that everyone else used. That grip, the 'club grip' identifies the way a man grips a club when going into battle. The 'club grip' felt odd to us.

As we said earlier, Heather and I talked about using the 'hammer grip' instead of the club grip. But we never did use the 'hammer grip' to swing the shepherd's crook. The 'hammer grip' offers two distinct advantages over using the 'club grip' which we used before. First, the 'hammer grip', allows us to align the striking surface of the hammer with, for example, the nail head or the end of a dowel rod. To strike the ball, we align the flat side of the clubhead with the ball. The 'hammer grip' dramatically increased our ability to strike the exact part of the ball we target.

In the club grip, we first placed the stave in the palm of the hand and then roll our fingers around the shaft. The club grip uses the palm of the hand for strength and control. With the hammer grip, we depend on our fingers more than when we used the club grip. To begin the hammer grip, we use the opposite sequence. We start the grip by using our fingers to grasp the stick. Our palms never touch the shaft. Controlling the shaft relies upon accurate finger control with the proper 'hammer grip'.

When we hammer nails, or when we drive dowel rods through drilled holes, the carpenter's hammer grip dramatically improves accuracy. When we work as carpenters, we always use the 'hammer grip'. Precision accuracy provides an advantage when we wish to deliver a power strike.

Compared to the 'club grip' we add significant power at the point of contact with confidence. The resulting increase in efficiency and accuracy saves the expense incurred by a significant number of bent nails and broken dowel rods. When we employed the hammer grip with our club, we noticed that the carpenter's grip helped us align the striking surface with the precise spot we wished to strike on the ball. By aligning the striking surface, we increased our accuracy to strike a precise spot on the ball with the exact desired spot on the club.

In other words, Thomas, we felt and heard 'THWOCK!' far more often." Robert smiled.

"Second, the hammer grip allowed us to apply a dramatic increase in the amount of force or power to strike a precise point. Correct application of the hammer grip allows us to make a far more powerful accurate strike. More importantly, we add that power without overswinging." Heather joined in.

"When we swing the hammer, we learned, 'never start the swing by applying all the force we can muster'. Carpenters know that if we start the stroke by swinging the hammer as hard as we can, it is a recipe for disaster. If we miss the exact spot of the nail, we might bend nails. Nails are expensive. Or if we miss the exact spot on the dowel rod, we might break dowel rods. Dowel rods are expensive. Or if we swing hard and miss the nail or the dowel rod, we severely damage expensive wood. We have to control the strike precisely.

Therefore, to start the stroke under control carpenters developed a successful technique. Starting the stroke slowly enables us to see when the hammer face aligns along the precision pathway. If the hammer is not on the proper pathway, we see it. Then we stop the stroke.

The hammer grip guides us to start the stroke slowly. The stroke with the hammer grip offers a completely opposite feeling from starting the stroke with a club grip. The club grip invites us to apply full force as we begin the stroke. Starting the controlled stroke slowly with the hammer grip enables us to accelerate the hammer head without increasing arm speed.

To increase the speed of the head of the hammer head there is a secret technique. The secret is to perform a wee flick of the wrist. Right before striking the nail, or the dowel rod, a wee wrist flick generates a dramatic acceleration of the hammer head. The acceleration of the hammer head causes a dramatic increase in power.

Most important, that increase in power we direct precisely on the target using the well-controlled stroke of the hammer head. To increase power and accuracy in the stroke, the wrist flick is the secret of the 'hammer grip'.

Think about when you split wood into kindling with an axe. It is a tiresome chore. You want to get the work done efficiently without overtiring yourself. You learned to strike the blade at a precise spot right along the grain of the wood. You learned the importance of adding power to accuracy on that downward stroke by flicking the wrists.

In summary, the carpenters' 'hammer grip' provides two distinct advantages. First, the 'hammer grip' provides improved accuracy. We can contact the precise point on the club face to the exact spot on the ball. Which means we connect two 'sweet spots.' We connect the 'sweet spot' on the club face to the 'sweet spot' on the ball far more often.

Second, the 'hammer grip' incorporates the 'wee wrist flick'. The 'wee wrist flick' increases controlled power. Use of the wrist flick provides the most accurate stroke to drive the small hard ball. To apply controlled accurate power to drive the small leather ball for distance, the 'wee wrist flick' is our secret technique.

Chapter 62 | *1399* | Lesson: Hammer Grip Plus Wrist Flick

"Does our explanation about the hammer grip and the wrist flick make sense to you, Thomas? Heather questioned. "Do you feel that we responded adequately to your question?"

"Aye. I believe your response offers an excellent explanation. Your explanation makes perfect sense to me, Robert and Heather. Now, will you help me learn to apply this information to change my grip? Can you show me the hammer grip up close? Can you demonstrate the application of the wrist flick during the stroke that you just explained?"

"Aye. Either of us can demonstrate, Thomas. Robert, why don't you show Thomas the 'hammer grip' first. I will stand beside you Thomas. That way I can guide your hand so that you can experience the feel of the 'hammer grip'. After you feel the grip you can more accurately follow Robert's model of the 'hammer grip.'"

Robert stood so that I could see the difference in the way he held the grip. I found the 'V' shape between thumb and forefinger where I placed the stick. The sensation was new. I noticed immediately a change in the way I clutched the stick. The palm of my hand made no contact with the stick. Instead, I noted how my fingers, far more sensitive than the palm, controlled the stick. I could feel the difference.

Before, when I gripped the stick, I held my hand differently. I employed the same grip on my stick that I used when I cleaned the skin and hair from the hide before we processed the hide into tanned leather or parchment. I punched wet skins tightened on a stretcher by holding a knife like a club.

For me, this 'hammer grip' was new. I needed help to understand whether I correctly copied Robert's 'hammer grip' or not. Heather helped. She adjusted my fingers. Finally, Heather was satisfied that I controlled the stick in the same manner that Robert demonstrated.

"That's it, Thomas. You are using the 'hammer grip' to hold the shaft correctly." Heather coached.

"Aye. You have gripped the shaft correctly, Thomas. Thank you, Heather, for adjusting Thomas' fingers. Now Thomas, I am going to move my stick slowly along the pathway to strike the ball. I want you to watch the slow movement of the stick carefully. I can share with you how the 'hammer grip' allows you to add power with the wee flick of your wrist. To understand you need to see how the wee wrist flick works.

Let's continue. But this time, Heather will demonstrate the movement with her stick. I will switch over to check your movement to introduce the wrist flick to you. I want you to feel the moment when to apply the 'wee wrist flick' during the swing pathway."

Heather picked up her stick. She gripped her stick the same way that Robert did. I mimicked her grip, modified of course, for my singular hand. Robert checked and approved.

Before Heather drew her shaft back, she placed the club face very near the ball. "I place the club very near to the ball for a very good reason, Thomas. In my mind's eye, I place the club face near the ball in order to 'measure' the precise spot on the club I want to contact when I strike the ball. In addition, I want to see the spot on the club face, where I want to concentrate, to strike my target spot on the ball. That exact spot on the ball is what I want to strike with that precise part of the club face. My eyes will focus on the exact target spot on the ball.

Carpenters focus their eyes on the object they wish to strike. You may have noticed that carpenters place the hammer face on the nail or dowel rod, first. When carpenters use a hammer, they feel the hammer. After they measure the spot on the nail or dowel rod that they want the hammer to strike, carpenters do not look at the hammer. They may tap the nail or dowel, once or twice softly, for a start.

So, there is a spot on the nail that we want to connect to the spot on the hammer head. There is a precise spot on the end of the dowel rod we want to connect with the precise spot on the hammer face. In the same way, there is a precise spot on the ball that we want to connect with the precise spot on the club face. While we cannot tap the ball, the way we start a nail or a dowel rod, we can take an imaginary practice 'tap'.

We can choose a spot very, very close to a spot behind, or to the side of the ball. Then we can waggle the club and focus on that spot on the ball. Taking the imaginary tap helps me to align the pathway for the club face during my swing. I will no longer look at the club face, just as the carpenter no longer looks at the hammer. Instead, I will 'feel' the location of the club face in the same way that the carpenter feels the location of the face of the hammer. I will focus on the precise spot on the ball I want the club face to contact."

Heather drew her club back. She prepared to strike the ball. "Use the same motions that Heather used, Thomas." Robert directed.

"Now Heather, slowly drop the stick into the pathway which you visualized to strike the ball squarely. Watch her closely, Thomas. Notice that as her club moves down toward the ball, she will flick her wrist. When the club head descends to a spot about a yard in length prior to the strike of the ball with the club face, she flicks the wrists."

In slow motion, Heather modelled the movement of her hands during the down stroke. About a yard prior to the ball strike, Heather flicked her wrists. Even in slowed motion I noticed how that wee flick of the wrist affected the speed of the club head. To see how much faster the club head accelerated in slow motion clearly illustrated the function of the hammer grip to perform the wrist flick.

My new knowledge felt like a magical revelation. Without overswinging the club, the speed of the club head, accelerated substantially. The increase in speed, especially when Heather demonstrated swinging the club slowly, was easy to see. That moment marked an epiphany to my understanding of how the stroke works. I understood clearly the concepts involved by combining the 'hammer grip' in tandem with the 'wee bit of wrist flick'.

"I see it! The 'hammer grip' combined with the wee wrist flick is an amazing technique. Heather, please take a swing so that I may study the way your wrists move."

"Aye, Thomas. This time I want you to focus on Heather's wrists. Even though you are using one wrist, you will be able to control the action of the wrist flick required to strike the ball with precision and power. You will experience the same combination of accuracy and power with one wrist that we experience with two. Most of the time carpenters use only one wrist when we hammer nails and dowel rods. We swing the exact way that you will when you use the hammer grip to strike the ball." Robert instructed.

With Robert carefully watching over me, I took a few practice swings. Robert wanted to make sure I gripped the stick in the 'hammer grip' correctly. Heather also checked my 'hammer grip'. I felt fortunate to have two trusted friends coach me in this technique. When they were both satisfied with my grip, Robert instructed me to make a slow-motion swing.

I took a stance. I took a backswing. Then started a slow swing. As I dropped the club into the down swing, Robert surprised me. He stepped in and caught my stick. Robert caught my stick in order to show me the exact moment in the path of the swing that I should apply a wee flick with my wrist.

"Thomas, it is true that you understand the concepts of both the 'hammer grip' and a wee bit of wrist flick. You even explained your understanding how the grip and the wrist flick combination works. We want you to realize that Heather and I have practiced the combination of the 'hammer grip' and 'wee wrist flick' every day for several years. For you to feel the way the combination actually works, you will need to practice using the grip and the wee flick, often.

When you practice the right way, you will begin to feel when you perform the stroke correctly. When you do it right remember how it feels. You will also feel when it is not right. When it does not feel right forget that feeling immediately. The more often that you practice the wrist flick in combination with the 'hammer grip', the more often you will feel when you get it right. Daily practice will help you to develop the best rhythm to your swing."

I practiced a few more slow swings under supervision from Heather and Robert. Then, Robert coached, "Go ahead Thomas, swing the club a bit faster. Keep swinging. Continue to increase the speed until you feel a good rhythm through your body that combines with a controlled powerful swing. That speed will be the speed you wish to replicate for a full swing.

Remember, full speed doesn't mean swing as hard as you can swing. Full speed means use a swing speed that permits you to feel in complete control of the club face. You want to control the combination of accuracy, balance, rhythm and power."

I took five full swings. With each swing, I felt my confidence grow. I began to experience a feel for the natural flow of the swing to develop. I recognized that I possessed more control of the path for the clubhead to travel during the swing. My new full swing felt quite different from the way I felt when I made a full swing previously.

I could not wait to hit some balls. I looked forward to incorporating the use of my new 'hammer' grip. I wanted to make certain that I included the 'wee flick of the wrist' on the downswing.

Between Heather, Robert, and I, we owned three balls. Heather offered, "Why don't you two hit some balls. I will run out about 50 yards. I will 'shag' (chase and gather) the balls you hit, then I will hit the balls back to you. Robert, you stay here and continue to coach Thomas."

"Ha! Sister, I see what you are doing! You are going to get some extra hitting practice while I offer instruction to Thomas. That's a good idea, Heather."

"Aye. You saw right through my plan to 'shag' balls, brother." Heather laughed.

Heather jogged out to the landing site. Upon arrival she turned back toward us and waved. Heather indicated that she was ready for us to hit.

"Thomas, go ahead and tee your ball up on a cone of sand. Go through your normal routine. Then hit one ball. I will watch you."

I bent down and formed a sand cone. I placed the ball on top of the cone.

"Step back and take a practice swing first. I want to observe your grip. I will check to see that you apply the wee wrist flick during the practice swing."

I took the practice swing. Robert indicated satisfaction with my application of the wrist flick. I was excited and anxious. I wanted to hit a ball using the wrist flick. Then, I set up to hit the ball. I first gripped the stick in my brand new 'hammer' grip. Armed with my new knowledge about the Carpenters' hammer grip combined with the wee wrist flick, I took a swing.

"THWOCK!"

Soon I began to hit the ball much farther than any of my best previous hits. I hit the ball significantly harder, even though I never did swing harder again. I felt in total control of my swings. My body moved in comfortable rhythm throughout the entire stroke. Throughout my new swing I maintained balance.

Chapter 63 | 1399 | The Target Landing-Area

Twelve lads and lasses gathered at the Old Stone Bridge. Some leaned on the bridge. Some sat on the soft carpet of bent grass. Others stood and talked. The purpose of their meeting was to discuss two items. First, they would review progress in the quest to invent a new game. Second, the group would discuss the next steps to pursue.

"It is fun to hit the ball far," William the Weaver observed, "but I am not persuaded that hitting the ball for distance is the best challenge we can offer. To invent a game which will be fair for all participants, I think we need something more than hitting only for distance. For example, I think we might consider a game which combines the pleasure of hitting for distance with the skill required to direct the ball towards a target. As we know in the Highland Games, it is quite a challenge to throw the caber end over end. However, to win the contest, 'tis not enough to throw the caber end over end."

"Aye, to win the caber toss contest one must toss the bottom end of the caper to flip over the top end. Then the caber that lands in the straightest line from the launch point is the winning toss." Thomas the Tanner explained. "Caber is a contest of strength and accuracy!"

"We all know the tremendous amount of skill in archery." Russell the Bowyer remarked. "Yet, merely to launch the arrow into the air offers no challenge. When we first learned to launch an arrow, we thought it great fun to pull the bowstring back as far as we could. Do you remember how we just loved to watch the arrow fly high and fly far? Shooting an arrow high and far just to see it fly became rather tiresome very rapidly. We enjoyed the feeling of power that accompanied shooting the arrow high and far. However, all of us soon realized that we wanted to do more than simply apply power to shoot an arrow. Right away we wanted more challenge. Hitting the sky with our arrows was way too easy." Russell laughed out loud.

"Aye, Russell. We also learned that sticking the ground with an arrow was way too easy." Jonathan added, eliciting chuckles from the rest.

"Aye," continued Russell, "We realized that what we really wanted to do was learn how to control the power in the bow. The purpose of archery is to propel the arrow with power and accuracy. We wanted the arrow to hit a specific target. And we wanted to deliver arrows on target consistently and frequently. After we hit the target consistently, then we wanted to stick the arrow right in the bull's eye of the target. We wanted to improve our skills. We wanted our aim to be so accurate that we would stick the arrow right in the middle of the bull's eye."

"Aye, arrows are effective only when they strike the target. The real challenge in archery is to hit the target every time. Meeting the challenge by hitting the target brings a good feeling to the successful archer. To hone their craft, we know that the archers invest hours and hours of diligent practice. We observe archers engage in individual practice following a routine schedule." Russell the Bowyer explained.

"When the individual archer achieves the required level of mastery, he joins the company of the King's archers. The King's archers meet regularly to practice. During practice they work together. They become a team.

The company of the King's Archers works to organize their abilities. The team of archers practice so that they respond to communicated commands quickly. For example, the King's Archers practice to launch an entire flight of arrows at the same time. The precision launch of a flight of arrows which arrives at a specific target at the same instant devastates the enemy." William the Weaver noted.

"Since we all agree that in archery hitting the target from a distance provides a challenge to an archer's skills, I wonder, what do you think about making the object of our game that we aim the ball to hit a target?" asked Russell.

"Aye Russell! I agree. To aim the ball at a target is a grand idea for the game!" Jonathan seconded.

David concurred, "We do need a target for the game! Aiming to hit the ball to a target is an excellent idea!"

"So far our targets have been to make the ball come to a stop close to a friend. I think we need a more specific target. We need to invent a better target than merely stopping the ball at a friend's feet." Robert stated.

The friends agreed unanimously. Targets would provide the right challenge for the new game.

Russell questioned, "What kind of target should we create? What makes a fair target for the little leather ball to acquire? The first thing that comes to my mind is that the target must be something that either sticks in the ground or lies on the ground. To hit a ball that will reach a certain exact spot will challenge us. When we hit the ball into the air, the ball lands, and rolls. Hard leather balls don't stick in one spot in the manner that a sharp pointed arrow sticks in a target."

"Or sticks in the ground." Jonathan giggled.

"Aye. Or sticks in the ground." Russell chuckled. "When an arrow flies, eventually it either sticks in the target, or it sticks in the earth. I think, perhaps, we can mark a target area on the Links. We can aim the ball to land and stop inside the target area. What say you, friends?"

"True. I agree." Offered William. "We need to aim the ball to hit a target. Simply hitting the ball into the air, will not be challenging or fun, for long. While it has been fun to attempt to stop the ball near our friend's foot, that does not seem to offer the fair target. I think that there are other more inviting targets to consider for the game. If we aim the ball at a specific target each time it is our turn to strike the ball, we will be forced to concentrate."

"I think we should seek a somewhat level place on the Links for a landing target," observed Barbara. "We want to find, or else create somewhat level places. The target ought to be where the ball can land, bounce, roll and come to a complete stop."

Bess added, "I wonder about the challenge required to land the ball on the target. During our hitting practice sessions, we learned that getting the ball to come to a stop near our friends' feet provided a test. To stop the ball from rolling at a specific distance while the ball remains in line toward the target, created a test of skill required to control the flight of the ball. A somewhat level target would offer a fair test of that skill. I would like us to keep that concept. I say that to stop the ball from rolling and remain on a level target provides a fair challenge of skill."

"We might consider making the landing target surface as uniform as possible. Will a uniform level landing target surface offer a fair challenge? I can see some real advantages that such surfaces would provide. A uniform surface will reward players who select and execute different types of strokes as they work the ball to the target." Russell said.

David offered, "I agree. I think it will be advantageous to create a target area with a surface of sand. A sandy surface will be disturbed by animals and weather. However, a sand surface is simple to maintain. We can easily smooth the sand on the target area. For example, we can rake sand to smooth the target area. After the reapers rake the cut fat grass and spread it to dry, they leave the wooden rakes on the Links."

The friends agreed that the abundance of sand on the Links could work well for the target landing areas. They knew they could easily rake sand into a smooth level surface. Sand surfaces would be easy to design, easy to develop and easy to maintain as smooth level targets.

"What if we stand a stick in the center of the target area. The standing stick could serve as the target on the landing area." Robert noted. "After all players hit the ball onto the sand target area, we take turns to roll the ball to touch the stick. We can easily measure distance from the target to each ball."

"For example, we could begin with the ball farthest from the target stick. That player will rake a pathway from his/her ball straight to the target stick. The player will start the raked path by beginning to rake just behind the mark for the ball. The pathway should be raked level and smooth. It should also be raked smooth to extend two club lengths beyond the target stick."

William concurred, "The first player will then take a turn to roll the ball to contact the stick. The first player should continue to stroke the ball until it hits the target. To measure distance the ball lies from the stick, all we need is a twine string attached to the bottom of the target stick. Pull the twine to touch the ball. Pick the ball up, stretch the string from the stick to the same distance and place the ball on the raked path. The second farthest, then should mark the length of the ball away from the target with the string. Following anyone's turn, should some spot smoothing with the rake be needed, we will allow that."

"Well, this is all very interesting." Thomas noted. "You have done some important thinking. Permit me to offer an idea. We could make the game so that we just hit at one target. Sometimes, archers just aim at one target for practice. But I think we might enjoy more fun if we shoot at several different targets. After we shoot at the first target, I think we should then take aim at a second different target."

Rhona said, "Aye, Thomas. I like your idea very much. To help make our game interesting and fun, we should perform several different types of strokes. In order to develop a skill, practice is necessary. Once we develop skills, we will want to test and improve our skills by playing the game. The more possible outcomes available in a game, the more the game will provide different challenges. A variety of different challenges and obstacles will ultimately enable us to make a game that is interesting and compelling. I agree with Thomas. I think we should look for several available sites to serve as targets for our new game.”

“What do you have in mind, Rhona?” asked Heather.

“Excellent question, Heather,” Rhona responded. “I think we should consider designing many different target zones. Several different target zones will invite us to enjoy our walk around the Links. Remember, when we first talked about what we wanted in a new game. We treasured the opportunity to walk and talk with our friends while we experience the unique beauty of the Links.”

“That is true. A stroll around the Links is enjoyable. All who live in and around St. Andrews enjoy this special place between the town and the Sea.” Barbara reminded the friends, “One of our original goals for the ‘New Game’, was to enjoy and experience the beauty of being outside on the Links.”

“When I walk on the creeping bent grass covering the sandy land it makes me think of what it feels like to walk on a plush carpet. The feel of the grass on the Links is even more plush than the carpet in the Cathedral.” Rhona expanded.

“True, when we weave a carpet or a tapestry, we strive to make fabric that achieves that same plush feel we enjoy when walking on bent grass. We treasure the feeling of a walk on the bent grass.” agreed William.

Marion added. “I remember when we began thinking about the new game. We all agreed that we wanted to enjoy walking outside while playing our game on the Links. Also, we wanted to walk at a pace which would invite us to talk so that we could visit with our friends. To enjoy a walk and talk with friends was so important we made it one of our goals.”

“By playing our new game on the Links, we can enjoy the breezes off the Ocean.” smiled David.

There was no more discussion on that topic that day. The arguments persuaded all twelve friends to agree. They resolved that they would meet on the Links the following day. The purpose of that meeting would be to find and prepare several targets for the new game on the Links.

Chapter 64 | *1399* | Laying the Course 'Out'

"Friends, shall we stroll around the Links,?" inquired David. "I think it is important that all of us walk the Links together. While we walk, let's talk. Our purpose is to find prospective landing target areas for the new game."

"Aye, I agree. It is time for us to walk the Links. We can talk about the game while we walk. We need to agree on acceptable target locations." Bess seconded. "I think where we stand is a good spot to begin the game. We could strike the first ball from here. Do you all agree that this is a good starting point?"

Barbara answered, "Bessie, there can be no doubt. You have chosen wisely. I love this panorama of the Links. We face straight north. The sea fills the vision on the right."

"Aye, it is a lovely spot, Bess." Rhona agreed.

No one dissented. The friends agreed. Together, they began walking the Links. They walked with purpose, to find suitable landing targets. They walked away from town. Of course, the friends began talking immediately.

The twelve aimed to stroll out to where the North Point of the Links punctures the water. All sets of eyes searched the landscape. They looked for targets within the natural features of the Links. All agreed on the ideal target. They wanted nearly level spots approximately twenty-five yards across. A target of such size presented a fair challenge for players to land and stop balls.

On the way out to the North Point the friends found eight level sandy areas. All agreed that the eight level areas made an acceptable number of targets. Finding suitable targets was fairly easy on the way to the North Point.

"We can easily rake the level areas into sand targets." William suggested.

The friends stood on the peninsula's North point. Looking North, the Eden estuary flowed on their left. On the right they enjoyed a view of the German Ocean. At that spot the friends stood as far from town as one could and remain on the Links. The friends agreed. This spot should become target landing area number eight. The last landing area provided a beautiful place. The lasses and lads turned around. The view of town took their breath away.

The twelve paused. They found acceptable target areas which all agreed were challenging, yet fair. They felt satisfied. The friends believed that they had accomplished their goal. They located and marked eight targets. Eight targets seemed a fair number to play the game. They smiled. They congratulated each other. Then they took a moment to celebrate.

The Course

	Eight Target Zones	Distance in yards
TARGET ZONE	1	339
TARGET ZONE	2	375
TARGET ZONE	3	321
TARGET ZONE	4	401
TARGET ZONE	5	325
TARGET ZONE	6	335
TARGET ZONE	7	145
TARGET ZONE	8	261
OUT TOTAL		2,502

Silently, the friends gazed toward the spot near the Swilcan Bridge, where they began their search. In their minds they recalled the exact spot where they began the long walk out to the North Point of the Links. Far in the distance, the friends' eyes feasted on the grand view of their town. On the left, the tall tower of the Castle framed the view. Against the line of the southern horizon to the right, the two taller towers of the Great Cathedral silhouetted.

"Wait!" David shouted.

Chapter 65 | 1399 | Walking The Course 'In'

"Why do you want us to wait?" Bess questioned.

"Because" David stated. "We should never end 'The Game' out here!"

"Why not?" Asked William the Weaver.

"Look where we are!" David commanded.

"Aye. We are standing at the North Point. The end of the Links." Rhona replied.

"Exactly right, Rhona. We walked 'out' as far on the Links as we can walk. Look! Here we are standing at the edge of the water." David continued. "We cannot remain here. We still need to go home. The sea is not our destination. After we complete our game, we don't want to be way out here. We must return to town anyway. To arrive here, we walked 'out'. I think we should find a way to play the game on our way back. We should play the game as we walk back 'in', to town."

"That is a very interesting observation. You make an excellent point, David." Bess added. "I agree with my brother. Definitely, we do not want to end our game out here away from town. Alright, so far, we found eight level landing targets. Let's walk back into town. Let's look for more landing targets for the game while we walk and talk on the way back in. We need to return home. It just makes sense to play our way home."

"So, Bessie, you are saying, when we reach the water, we need to make 'The Game' turn around! We will play the Game on the way 'out'. Then we turn around and play the game while we go back 'in'." Jonathan clarified.

"Aye," said Marion, "We play 'out' to the Point. Then we make a turn. We turn around. And then, we play our way back home. After we make the turn, we will complete 'The Game' when we play back to town. We complete our new game by going back home. We play the first part of The Game 'out'. To finish, we play the Game back 'in'."

"You have it, Marion. That is exactly what David and I mean by playing 'out' and playing back 'in'." Bess approved.

By unanimous consent the friends agreed to the Shepherds' proposal. Then, the team responded to Bessie's challenge. Find more landing areas. This time find landing areas on the way home, on the way 'in'. The friends accepted their next mission. This time they searched for suitable landing areas to play in the opposite direction. Finding the fair and level target areas which all agreed were suitable level landing targets proved to be a far more formidable task than finding landing targets on the way 'out'.

The friends mapped out an additional six landing targets. The friends realized that two target landing areas on the way 'out' were exceptionally large. They could be played on the way 'in'. They decided to use those two natural landing targets that they originally used on the way 'out' on the way 'in', also. On the large landing targets, the group decided they could place a target near each end of the target zone. They agreed that newly created target on the way 'in' provided no interference with those who were playing the opposite direction, on the way 'out'.

Finally, the friends completed the mission. The last landing area they found was large. It was located immediately west from the place where the friends started the game. The players finished close to town. The friends shared their enthusiasm. They completed an important task for the new game. They felt so excited. On that day they laid out a full course for the new game they envisioned.

IN

	Hole Number		Distance in Yards
Target Zone	9	-	296
Target Zone	10	-	150
Target Zone	11	-	304
Target Zone	12	-	377
Target Zone	13	-	326
Target Zone	14	-	342
IN TOTAL		-	1,795
ALL TOTAL		-	4,297

Working together, the team completed three tasks. First, they located the fourteen landing areas. Second, they established the sequence to play each target area. Finally, they mapped out the route for the landing areas for 'The Game'. On the way 'out' to the turn, stopped by the Sea, the friends marked eight landing areas.

They turned around. The friends marked an additional six landing areas on the way 'in', or on the way home. Altogether, the original course possessed fourteen separate target zones.

The friends thought about distances from one target zone to the next target zone in line. None of the distances from target area to target area were the same. Some of the distances were short. One good, strong well-placed stroke could land the ball on the target area on the short distances. Some distances were long. To reach the longest distanced Landing Targets required three full, well struck strokes. Most distances from Target area were in between the one stroke distance and the three strokes distance required to reach the Landing Target. On the remaining Target areas two well struck hits would put the ball on the Landing Target.

On St Andrews Olde Course the holes were in a line and thus could only be playein a given order, which eliminated confusion and interference.

Scottish Golf History

Chapter 66 | 1399 | The Flag

"I know the location for each of the target zones. Yet, from where we now stand, I am unable to see even one. Can you see the target zones?" Marion the Shoemaker asked earnestly. She was the youngest lass and the shortest member of the team. The twelve stood at the starting point. They gazed out over the Links.

Standing on the southern edge of the Links, the part closest to town, three friends answered that they could the first target. The two tallest lads, David the Shepherd and William the Weaver, plus the tallest lass, Rhona the Weaver affirmed that they saw the first target zone. The remainder agreed with Marion. They were unable to see the target zone.

When one player is able to see the target and another is unable to see the target, the one who can see the target holds a significant advantage. The lads and lasses agreed. The friends revisited their original discussion. They recalled agreement on the need for a new game. They reaffirmed their commitment to create a game fair for all players. A game which offered no advantage to size, to height, to strength or to agility. Fairness remained a critical element for the game.

All the friends agreed. They had a problem. Some players could see the target, other players could not see it. When players aimed their shot, those unable to see the target clearly experienced a disadvantage. All agreed. No player ought to be disadvantaged due to how tall they happened to stand. Fairness remained the goal.

"What can we do to make the target zones visible for each and every player?" Marion asked. "I want to be able to see the target. When I see the target I see the line for aiming my ball."

"Even if players do not play the game on the Links often, each player should be able to know the location for each target zone." stated Bess.

"The ability to see the target is crucially important. In order to aim, a player needs to see the target." Russell agreed. "Somehow, some way, we must create a way for the target zones to be visible to every player. Each player requires a fair view of the target."

"If we are unable to resolve this issue, tall players will be able to see the target, while shorter players are unable to see it. The tallest players will hold a distinct advantage." Robert stated the problem.

The friends puzzled over the clearly stated problem. How could they resolve the issue of unequal visibility? They wondered.

Thomas the Tanner posed the problem in a question, "The question before us is, 'What is in our control that we can change in order to insure equal visibility of the target for all players?'"

"We know we need to make the target easy for each player to recognize." observed Jonathan the Shoemaker, the youngest of all the friends and the shortest lad.

"All the target zones are located on relatively flat level ground. We selected target zones because of their relatively flat slope." Barbara recalled. "The combination of fair visibility for a flat target, located at ground level, does create a difficult problem to resolve. We want to provide equal and fair target visibility for each player. However, we cannot change the heights God gave to each of us."

Eleven friends fixed their gaze on the Links. Heather turned to face the opposite direction. She stared towards the street named North Gait, in town. Heather looked down the street. Her mind fixated on the problem before the team. She thought, "What can we do to make a flat target area at ground level equally visible to each player, regardless of how tall the player stands?"

Something sparked! Suddenly, Heather's eyes focused sharply. In front of each shop, above each front entrance, Heather noticed a hanging sign. She blinked and refocused her eyes. Each sign clearly displayed a distinctive shape. The shape on the sign accentuated an easily recognizable symbol garbed in attention-grabbing, contrasting color. The attention-grabbing colors combined with the distinctive shapes, represented recognizable symbols.

The recognizable symbols illustrated important information to potential customers. The symbol illustrated the goods or services offered in the shop. When potential customers recognized the symbol, they knew where to find the shop which could fulfill their needs. Shop owners wanted customers, so they wanted to make the shop easy for every potential customer to find.

"We need signs!" Heather exclaimed.

"What do you mean?" queried Barbara the Bowyer. She turned to look into Heather's eyes.

But Heather was not looking at the Links. She was not looking at the problem in the same way as the rest of the friends while they pondered the problem. Heather looked in a different direction. Heather looked at the town.

"We need a sign! For each target zone, we need a sign!" explained Heather. She turned to make eye contact with her friends. She looked at each one.

"Everyone, look down the street! Do you see sign in the shape of the shoe? We all know what a shoe symbolizes. That's the Shoemaker Shoppe. Do you see the sign that shows a chair? That's the Carpenter Shoppe. The sign with the bow and drawn arrow is the display for the Bowyer's shop. Businesses erect signs to target prospective customers. Everyone can easily see the sign. Signs help customers find where they want to go. For the customer, the target is marked clearly by the sign. But notice, not one sign rests on the ground. If the signs lay flat on the street, no customers would notice the signs when they looked down the street. To increase visibility the signs are displayed high above the ground.

Every single one of us can see every single sign. It does not matter if you are the tallest person or if you are the shortest person, we can all see every single sign. Putting signs up high makes it easy for the shortest person to see."

"That's an interesting observation, Heather." William the Weaver stated. "I think I see where you are going with this. I like your idea very much. Please continue."

"Aye, William. In our game, we know the object is for the player to get the ball to stop on the target zone. Even though we are unable to see the flat level target zone, if we place a sign that stands high enough for all the players to see, then we would create a fair target. Everyone can see the sign. Everyone can know where the target zone is located.

We can place a sign on each target zone. Do you agree that a sign above the ground level would resolve our dilemma? There would be fair and equal visibility for all players when they took their turn. All players could use the sign to help them aim the ball towards the target zone."

A murmur of recognition buzzed through the teammates. Enthusiastically, the friends assented approval. Heather's insight occurred when she looked at the problem in a different direction from everyone else. Heather's thinking led to finding a workable solution for the problem of equal target visibility for every friend.

All the friends agreed that a sign on each landing area would indeed provide a solution to their problem. The friends understood that for the signs to be effective, they should stand high enough above the ground to be visible for every player from the previous target zone. Signs enabled all the players to aim at the target.

The group also decided that play toward the next target zone would begin from the previous target zone. Therefore, the signs needed to be visible from one target zone to the next target zone. A sign visible to every player to indicate the location for the next target zone resolved the visibility issue, fairly. The friends agreed to create and erect a sign on every target zone.

"What sort of sign do you have in mind, Heather?" asked Robert. "Shoppe signs can be expensive to purchase. Installation of new signs can also be very challenging to finish."

"Robert, you ask a good question. I did think about signs for the game. Considering our limited resources, we do not want to purchase expensive signs, like Shoppe signs." explained Heather. "We require a total of 14 signs. Expensive signs are out of the question.

The requirement for the signs is that they be highly visible to every player. We want signs that are simple to make. The signs should be easy to maintain and replace. Our signs are going to remain outside. The signs must function in the rain, the wind, the bright sun, and the fog on the Links. In addition to being highly visible, our signs must be durable. The signs must stand tall. They must function in the strong winds on the Links. Our signs probably need to bend with the wind, as trees bend.

We want a sign design that is simple to put in place. To accomplish our goal, we could start with a stick tall enough for each of us to see. To make the stick highly visible to every person, perhaps we attach a piece of brightly colored cloth, maybe twelve inches by twelve inches in size. The bright colored cloth attached to the stick, fluttering in the wind, will look like a flag.

We need to fasten the cloth, or flag securely onto the stick. It will be simple to place that little flagstick on the target zone. I think we might fashion a cloth flag from bright contrasting colors. When the wind causes the flag to flutter, the flag will increase visibility significantly. All of us can then see the target. What do you think? Do you think the tall stick with an attached brightly colored flag offers a solution which will resolve the visibility problem? Do you think that we can make a stick and flag?"

"We have plenty of bow staves that are either slightly damaged or cracked. Flawed staves never become longbows. Some staves possess knots in the grain. Other staves may suffer cracks, or they are just too brittle to be used for a bow. I believe that we can find plenty of rejected bow staves. We can re-purpose the discarded staves into flag sticks. We can fasten and display the high visibility flags onto those sticks. I mean, right now, we just burn the rejected staves. The rejected staves are not much good for firewood. Barbara, do you not think we can collect 14 rejects to serve as flagsticks?" Russell, the Bowyer offered.

"Aye, Russell. We do have many rejected bow staves. They will work well as shafts for the flags. I think all the shafts should be of equal height. If the shafts are all the same height, the flag will aid us to judge our distance to the target zone. We can measure and cut the staves so that all will be the same height." Barbara continued.

"I think it is simple to attach a piece of cloth. Probably, it will be even easier to secure a cloth to the shaft than it is to attach a bow string to a bow stave." Rhona stated. "For flags, I believe we can find scrap cloth that is twelve inches by twelve inches. Bright colors would produce highly visible flags. I do not see any problem for us to make flags the same equal size and shape. We can produce all flags in the same bright colors. Or we can make flags with different colors. Which do you think is a better idea?"

"That's a good question for us to think about as a whole group. Let's talk about the flag colors together. Perhaps if we share ideas, we will find the best solution. Even if we do not find the best, we might reach a solution acceptable for everyone. If someone is willing to look at the question from a completely different direction, we might find something completely new." Marion posed.

"If we choose to make flags of all the same colors, we can map a specific pathway for players to follow while playing the Game." Rhona offered.

"On the other hand, if we choose different colors, we can use the colors to determine which target we play." William interjected. "For example, we can identify the red target, the yellow target, the orange target and the pink target. I can see advantages to both ways of selecting the colors on the flags. Maybe we can try a few different colors. That way we can test to see which colors are the easiest to see."

Robert spoke. "How about this idea for flag colors? Let's consider that we play the course 'out'. We make the turn, and we play the course 'in'. There are two large target zones. We agreed to put two target sticks on those so that we would have six target zones to play on the way 'in'. Suppose we play flags of one color as we play 'out'. Then, when we play 'in', we play flags of a different color. Does anyone like that idea?"

Margaret agreed. "Robert, I think that is the best idea for the flag colors. We only need two colors. The different colors will be helpful as we play. They will be especially helpful on the two large holes."

The Bowyers volunteered to produce the sticks. The Weavers fashioned the flags. "I think we can have the fourteen different sticks and with securely attached flags ready to install in two days." Rhona promised.

"Alright, once the sticks and flags are finished, we can place the sticks. We will plant flagsticks in the middle of the target zones. By sticking the flagstick in the middle of the target zone we will create a specific target. The stick will function similarly to a bull's eye in an archery target. We will know to aim the ball at the precise spot where the flagstick stands." Thomas said.

"Before we go back home, let's hit some balls." cracked Jonathan.

"Yeah! Let's do it. I have been thinking how to hit that ball. I want to show you what I have been thinking about." Marion exclaimed.

"Who wants to aim for a couple of target zones?" asked Bess.

All the lads and lassies answered, "Aye!"

Chapter 67 | 1399 | The Tee

Before taking a turn to hit the ball, each player carefully shaped a small sand cone. The player placed the ball atop the cone to raise the ball above the surface. Raising the ball improved the lie. The improved lie provided easier access to strike the precise spot on the ball.

The more times the players hit balls, the more they learned. They learned how to launch balls into the air. The hitters discovered that the longest drives occurred when they struck the ball on the down stroke of the club face.

At first, the players reasoned that to launch the ball into the air they should hit when the club began to move up on the swing path. It seemed that if the contact with the club face occurred as the club path was on the way up, the ball would easily fly into the air.

The friends discovered that balls hit with the clubface on the way up disappointed them. Balls contacted on the upswing often flew very high. The ball did fly into the air, but it simply failed to travel very far. In contrast, when the club face hit the ball on the down stroke, the ball launched into a beautiful flight. Balls hit on the downstroke flew the ball much longer distances.

The friends asked, "Why does contact of club face on the down stroke result in a more beautiful and longer flight?" They wished to resolve the puzzlement.

David and Bess worked on the issue. They wanted to understand why the downstroke worked so much better. The two determined to make a close-up observation. They wanted to observe the moment that the club struck the ball. Sister and brother decided to take turns.

The task for the two players:

1. Observer focus on the ball closely while the other strikes the ball using a full swing.
2. Observer to provide immediate feedback about the observation results to the hitter.
3. Hitter and observer discussed their observations. Both posed questions regarding what they observed and what they felt.

"Bess, would you hit the balls first? I want to get my eyes as close to the ball as I possibly can. I want to see the instant the club face actually strikes the ball. I wonder if I will be able to see the actual moment of contact between club face and ball surface."

"Is that what you are looking for, David? That moment of connection between club face and ball?"

"I don't know for sure what I am looking for, Bess. I know I want to observe the club and ball closely as possible. Perhaps I will discover something. Who knows? I do believe it is very important for us to talk together, ask questions about what we see, and what we feel."

"We are very good at talking. And we are very good at asking questions of each other." Bess laughed.

"Aye. That's true. I am going to sit here across from where you stand. I want you to take the stance you use when you set up to hit the ball. Will I bother you by sitting here? Or will I inhibit your concentration in any way?"

"No David, not all. Let me ask you something. Even though you are not sure about what you are looking for, I wonder, do you have any questions you would like to ask me before I make my first swing?"

"Aye, Bess. I do have a question. Picture the ball atop the cone of sand. Can you tell me if there is a precise part of the ball that you want to contact? Or do you just look at the entire ball? If there is a spot on the ball that is your target, what part of the ball do you wish to contact on the downswing?"

"David, I believe that is a most perceptive question. We learned that merely hitting the ball failed to provide a consistent launch. We also learned that when we hit the ball on the upswing, we could get the ball to launch into the air, however, that contact failed to drive the ball for distance. When I began to deliver consistent solid contact to launch the ball into flight, I realized that I did aim at a precise spot. I aim to strike a spot just a wee bit below the widest part of the ball at rest."

"That is most interesting."

"David, why did you say that?"

"I aim to strike the ball just a wee bit below the widest part of the ball, too."

"Okay, then. We have a guess. We think we know what we want the observer to look for. We have a hypothesis to test. Put yourself in what you believe is the best position to observe."

David knelt at approximately a club length across from Bess. She carefully teed the ball. Bess took her stance. She made a practice swing. Carefully, Bess measured the club face to the ball. Then, she lined up her club. Bess took a full back swing, then she dropped her club into an accelerating downswing.

"THWOCK!"

Bess and David lifted their eyes to find the ball she had launched into the air. The ball flew up, up, reached the apex, then floated and fell. The ball sailed down to bounce, bounce and roll on the bent grass.

"Bess, I could see it!" David exclaimed enthusiastically. "The club face struck the ball just a wee bit below the widest part. After contacting the ball, the club face continued the stroke down just a mite longer. Then, the arc of the swing resumed. The club face carried on through the upward portion of the arc. I want to watch again. I want to see if I can confirm my observation. Here, hit my ball."

Bess and David repeated the experiment. The results were nearly identical.

The second ball came to a rest less than five yards away from the first ball. Bess and David walked towards the two balls. While they walked, they talked about striking the two balls. Bess and David shared their observations.

"I am very happy with those two strikes." Bess evaluated. "I wanted to make both balls stop close to each other. Remember when we first hit the ball to each other? We did our best to make the ball stop at the other's feet. I attempted to hit both balls with the same force and along the same line of direction. Look David, see how near the two balls are to each other! That indicates to me that I hit both balls along a similar line. I feel satisfied."

"Bess, I think you should be very happy with those results. You stopped the two balls so close together. The position of the two balls shows that you executed your plan with excellent control. When you consider how far the two balls traveled, the degree of control you achieved is especially impressive. From watching the fathers during archery practice, we know that when measuring the combination of distance and accuracy for an object launched into flight, the ability to consistently repeat the flight is critical. You achieved remarkably consistent results. Now, I will attempt to stop the ball as close to the target as the two balls you hit."

They walked to the two balls, Bess said, "Alright David. It is my turn to observe now. Because of our discussion, I know what I want to look for. I want to observe the actual strike of the club face to the ball. I already know the point on the ball you want to make contact."

"Aye Bess. I will use roughly three-fourths of maximum power on my swing to strike the ball. I am going to aim for the ball to land in line with the next target zone."

Bess took a position across from David similar to the position David adopted when he observed her stroke to make her observation.

David placed the ball atop the sand cone. He took his practice swing. He measured the club face to the ball. David waggled the club. He made his back swing. Then, David released the club into the accelerating downswing.

"THWOCK!"

The ball launched into the air. David and Bess turned their eyes to find the soaring sphere. Up, up it climbed. Then down, down, bounced and splatted on the sandy landing zone.

"Wow! David that shot was so beautiful. Just the way you planned. Your club face contacted the ball just a wee bit below the fattest part of the ball. The results were spectacular. The ball you hit rolled very close to the stick on the landing zone."

"Aye. Thank you, Bessie. That shot felt great. I felt like the club face contacted the exact spot on the ball I aimed to strike."

"Well then David, let's see you hit the second ball. After you execute one good shot, your challenge is to do it again. Can you repeat the results? Can you swing the club in the same manner? Can you make the same contact between club face and the ball again?

"Aye. That is the challenge, isn't it, Bessie? Hitting an excellent shot once is great. However, truly, the next challenge for me is this, 'can I achieve the same excellence again the next time I strike the ball?' Are you ready to observe, Bess?"

"Aye, David. Hit the ball!"

Bessie and David continued to talk about their observations. They shared what they hypothesized. They compared what they experienced. Then they stated what they theorized.

Sister and brother shared a feeling of excitement. They were eager to share their observations with the friends.

The flight of each well struck ball 'painted the sky with beauty'. Bess and David never tired of watching the ball inscribe its arc in the sky. The ball soared up, up, up, and away into the air. Then, the ball descended back to the earth. The descending ball drew a mirrored arc in the sky. Scots loved to see things sail high through the air and then return to Earth along the opposing pathway.

Chapter 68 | *1399* | The Grass

"Summertime will present an extremely difficult season for playing the game on the Links." David the Shepherd declared to the friends. "In fact, I think during late spring and the first half of summer may be well-nigh impossible to play the game on the Links."

"Why do you say that David?" asked Jonathan the Shoemaker. "Late spring and early summer are lovely times. To enjoy the outdoors I think summer is the best season. Everyone loves to walk with friends and family on the St. Andrews Links in that summertime."

"Aye, your comment reflects an accurate observation, Jonathan. Summer is a lovely time to enjoy the Links. Allow me to respond. There is one important reason that I believe late spring and early summer will be difficult to play our game on the Links. Bessie and I know what happens then. From late spring to midsummer, the fat grass grows fast. During the long hours of sunshine on the Links, fat grass grows tall and thick. Nutritious grass invites people to graze dairy cattle on the Links during late Spring early Summer." David explained.

Bess continued, "But, at Lammas, after the middle of summer, the grass changes. From Lammas throughout Fall, Winter, and until late Spring, no one pastures dairy cattle here. Following the hay harvest, then until late Spring, the fat grass growth time is finished for the year. During the rest of the year the grass that grows on the Links does not contain sufficient nutritional value to feed the dairy cows adequately. After Lammas, cowherds move the dairy cattle to feed on greener pastures in richer soil. In winter, even those dried pasture grasses must be supplemented. Winter is when the hay harvested by Lammas day are fed to the dairy cattle."

"During the months from midsummer until late Spring, only sheep and goats graze on the Links. Bessie and I direct our collies to move the sheep and goats into selected grazing patterns.

Each day, we check wind, soil moisture, sunlight, and temperature. Each day we select several different spots for the flock to graze. So that the flock does not overgraze in only one place, we work the collies to move the sheep around several times each day. Moving the flock keeps the height of the grass level and even. Managing the flock by moving the animals into selected feeding zones enables us to maintain a healthy pasture. Tending the pasture to maintain a uniform height, limits the spread of noxious weeds. We work hard to control the health of the grass all over the Links." David explained.

Bess continued, "When we play the new game, we want to be sure that we don't hit the ball into the flock. While the sheep graze, we do not wish them to be disturbed. Therefore, when we play the game, we will move the sheep to different grazing areas. We think we should plan to design, and develop the course to play the New Game throughout the nine-month period when the flock keeps the grass on the Links closely cropped."

"The way we manage the flock will control the height of the grass. Level grass mowed to a low height will allow us to find our balls easily. We will direct the sheep to mow pathways from where we hit the tee shot to the target zone. In fact, when we selected the target zones, we noted pathways through where the fat grass grows. Those naturally occurring pathways are comprised of creeping bent grass."

When we play the target zones 'out', Bessie and I will direct the collies to move the sheep to the 'in' target zones. We will move the sheep to a safe area while we play the 'going out target zones'. Then, when we turn around to play 'in', we will switch the herd over to be safe. We will direct the collies to herd the sheep to graze on the other side, the 'going out target zones', when we play the 'coming in target zones' David added.

"By moving the flock from one side to the other side, we will maintain the height of the grass level also." Bess chuckled, "I look forward to playing our game at the same time, I get some work done."

"The grazing sheep will mow the creeping bent grass to a uniform height." David explained. "All we have to do is schedule the feeding patterns. Three hundred managed sheep will munch a lot of creeping bent grass. They will keep the creeping bent grass at a perfectly manicured height on the Links."

"Three hundred sheep will keep the creeping bent grass well fertilized, too!" Jonathan interjected. The friends enjoyed Jonathan's contribution.

Bess continued, "We will outline a fair pathway with manicured creeping bent grass. We can easily see a fair way to the next target zone. Players can use the fair pathway of bent grass all the way to the target zone. David and I talked about how to maintain the grass on the Links for the game. We decided to call the pathway of creeping bent grass, Fair Ways."

"Our collies are responsible and reliable. The dogs will gently guide the flock right where Bess and I tell them in a safe efficient manner. The collies also guard the feeding sheep. The sheep will graze securely under the watchful eyes of the herders. We already employ the collies' ability to direct and control the movement of the flock to exactly the place where we want them, at the time when we want them there. The collies keep the flock right where we want them to graze.

All we have to do is whistle loudly. The dogs locate the source of the sound. Then they connect by making eye contact. When we make eye contact with the collies, we know that they await our commands. The collies follow our commands to put the sheep right where we want. The collies maintain control of the flock."

Chapter 69 | *1399* | The Way Fair

fairway (n.)
1580s, "navigational channel of a river," from fair (adj.) + way (n.). Golfing sense is by 1898.

Dr. McGregor – "From the invention of golf until the mid-19th century, shepherds managed sheep to maintain the fairways on golf courses. Sheep appetites mowed the creeping bent grass. Sheep manure fertilized the soil. The manure supplied rich nutrients in just the right form and amount. To manage a flock of three hundred sheep presented significant daily challenges. Bessie and David faced quickly changing, often perilous weather conditions on the Links. Shepherds planned and controlled grazing rotation patterns on the pasture. They maintained vigilance to protect the flock from predators. Shepherds guarded the safety of the vulnerable lambs. The shepherd team directed the flock's daily trek from barnyard to pasture and back."

Professor Greenwood – "Critical to precise control of the flock is the well-trained, highly intelligent, responsive collie. 'Collie' is an old Scottish word meaning 'useful dog'. The breed of collie living in the border counties of Scotland and England is thought to trace to the time of the Roman occupation. Romans brought their own dogs to herd sheep. Later, descendants of the Roman dogs cross bred with native Spitz type dogs of the Viking tribes to produce ancestors of modern collies.

The carefully bred instincts and intensely trained collies, enabled the shepherd team to function. Shepherds sought dogs who possessed a combination of traits. They looked for highly intelligent disciplined dogs. They required dogs who communicated and responded instantaneously to shepherds. Those dogs developed into working collies."

Dr. McGregor–"Working collies respond to commands instantaneously. To deliver commands, handlers employ three different modalities. In order to communicate a command clearly and quickly the handler selects the modality based on distance. When the handler is close enough for collies to hear the handler speaking a moderate conversational volume, handlers employed voice commands. Collies respond best to voice commands delivered in conversational manner. Voice commands utilized the collies' large vocabulary. For example, (whoa, lie down, come by, away to me, move counterclock wise to me, move counterclockwise to me, back, walk up, in here, look back, get back, stay, steady, there, that'll do)."

Professor Greenwood – "Collies' directional ears create ultra-sensitivity to sound. Because of their sensitivity to sharp loud sounds, collies hate to hear people yell. When their handlers increase voice volume, collies interpret that as the handler being upset with the collie. Loud voices cause collies to react immediately. The reaction indicates how they feel. Collies strive to please their humans. Often, a loud human voice is interpreted by the dog as displeasure from the human. They feel the handler is yelling at them, and they don't like it. Whenever collies think people yell at them, the sensitive dogs react as if they failed, as if they did something wrong. When collies fear that they failed or made a mistake, they show disappointment. Sometimes the disappointed dogs shut down. They may even depart the working area, briefly.

Collies share traits often attributed to perfectionists. Sometimes, rather than risk failure, perfectionists fail to take action. Often, they pout. Fortunately, collies love to work. Their desire to work is powerful. Desire usually overcomes any wish to pout. When collies receive clearly communicated commands from their handlers, the disciplined, driven dogs immediately carry out the work to completion."

Dr. McGregor – "When distance from collie to handler exceeds the effective range of a comfortable conversational tone and volume, handlers select a different command delivery system. Still, the dogs refuse to tolerate yelled commands. The shepherd must explicitly communicate the commands. Effective flock management demands that the collies immediately understand and instantaneously respond to the orders. To deliver clear communication to the collie two other options are available for the handler to select.

At medium distances, shepherds employ the whistle. Whistles transmit messages to a collie over a far greater distance than the human voice. A combination of pitch and duration of blast from a whistle, delivers the messages. Shrill, crisp whistle bursts deliver clear tones. Each separate tone, each precise duration of the whistle blast, conveyed a special message to a specific collie. Due to the dogs' superb sense of hearing, they clearly understand the meaning of each whistle command."

Professor Greenwood – "Brutally strong winds scouring the Links often obscure sounds. Howling winds impede the clear delivery of whistle blasts to collies' ears. Those are times the whistle commands fail to communicate clearly and quickly. Shepherds still utilize the whistle to perform one additional crucial task. The shepherd transmits a long blast at maximum volume. A full volume long whistle blast garners the collie's immediate attention. Upon recognition of the full whistle blast, the collie promptly stills. The collie faces the handler. Stance and eye contact send a clear message to the shepherd. The collie signaled that readiness to switch from whistle blasts to hand signals. When the handler sees the collie stand at attention, the shepherd makes the switch from whistle commands to a combination modality. The shepherd employs whistle blasts combined with hand commands. The shepherd assumes a posture so that hands are highly visible to the collie. Hands and arms function to signal the command to the collies."

- - - - - - - - - - - - 1399 - - - - - - - - -

Bessie began, "David, I think between you, me, and the collies, we can manage the flock to keep a fair pathway from tee to target zone. We can command the collies to herd the flock so that the sheep will mow the grass just where we want. They will clip the grass to a uniform height. Keeping the grass mowed will permit us to extend play of the game into the summer season also."

"That would be fun. Our friends want to play the game in the late Spring and early summer, too. How do you think we can extend playing the new game into the summer season, Bessie?"

"I am glad you asked that question. I have been applying considerable thought to how we can play in late Spring and early Summer. Right now, only a few of the target zones we set up can be reached in one stroke. Think with me. What steps can we take to improve the Links for the new game? We can choose the grazing area. We will guide the flock to graze in a distinct pattern. The grazing pattern will mow a pathway, or a lane of creeping bent grass. Players can use the lane as a pathway to get the ball to the next target zone safely. That closely mown grass pathway will provide a fair lane to the target zone.

The player will aim the ball to stop on the lane of closely mown creeping bent grass. We will maintain a lane of closely mown grass all along the way from one sand target zone to the next target zone. A player who lands the ball in the closely mown grass will be rewarded. The ball that lies in the short grass will provide the player players with an excellent opportunity to execute a fair shot. The execution of those shots from the fair lane will constitute an important part of the game. Players must make strategic decisions. They choose from options where to land the first shot. Successful players will plan for the next stroke. Players may even strategize the next two strokes."

"Three kinds of grass grow well on the Links. Sheep's Fescue, rye, and bent grass continue to flourish even during the Winter. To survive and grow well on the Links requires grass that:
1. has a high tolerance for salinity, and
2. grass that can grow during the cold season.
Bent grass meets those two requirements. In addition, bent grass forms into a mat", David responded.

"Right, David. Bent grass offers important advantages to the new game. Bent grass will survive during the summer season. We can continue to allow long grass to remain on the course. During the game, when the players fail to execute an accurate shot, they may miss the fair lane and land in the fat grass. Landing the ball in the long fat grass will penalize an errant shot. The next shot will be difficult to execute. An accurate shot lands on the bent grass. That ball rolls and comes to a stop on the bent grass. That ball is ready for the next shot." Bess intoned.

David added, "Just as the caber must be accurately thrown in line with the target, or the thrower receives a deduction. Just as our arrows require accurate launching to reach the target. If the arrow fails to hit the target, there must be a penalty. When the arrows fail to hit their targets, the penalty is costly to all the soldiers in the King's Army."

"Aye. I see what you are proposing. In our game, the ball that is struck well and lands on the fair way will receive the reward of a good, long roll. The roll will add considerable distance to the shot. On the short, bent grass the ball will be easy to find. The player can tee the ball up for the next shot from a position much closer to the landing zone. All those reasons will encourage the player to strive to execute an accurate controlled swing to achieve solid contact. When the player strikes the ball square and true, the ball stops on the fairway. When balls are not struck well and true, there should be a penalty to the player.

David, you and I will carefully manage the sheep. The controlled grazing by the flock will mow the grass. The mown grass will mark a fair lane that will inscribe a line for launching and landing the ball. The closely mown short grass will form a fair, playable pathway. The fairway shall extend all the way from one landing area to the next landing area. With our collies we can easily control our sheep to keep the fairways in a state for fair play." Bessie informed the friends.

David agreed. "During late Spring and early Summer, we position the dairy cattle and the sheep each day. We will position the cows to graze on the long, fat grass. To control grazing cows in the fat grass is relatively easy work for the collies. Collies can move the cows in any direction. Once the cattle are in position where we want them to graze, then the collies will keep the cattle where we want them to stay. The cattle will continue to graze in the rich fat grass until the grass in that spot is hayed for midsummer stacks."

"The cows will stay out of the short mown or cropped grass when there is tender, long, rich fescue and rye available. Dairy cattle will not graze on the closely mown creeping bent grass, anyway." Bess explained. "Heather will continue to grow along the boundaries to the target zone. In fact, two fairways will be bordered by heather. Keeping bare sand available is important to maintain healthy links. We need to keep bare sand on the Links for the mining bees. The mining bees visit all the flowers, including the sweet clover the dairy cattle love."

"The bare sand serves the game." David added. "It is the site to launch the ball to begin play. And the next target zone is comprised of bare sand. All the target zones will be bare sand. The Links is also potted with sand bunkers. On the Links, grazing animals endure severe weather. When severe weather arrives, the animals herd or flock together for shelter. The hooves of a herd or a flock dig and soften sand. The wind blows over the herd and forms a bunker with a sand floor. Each time a storm occurs, the flock returns to the safety of the bunker. Some sand bunkers are deep. Some are large. A few are large and deep."

Chapter 70 | *1399* | The Target Problem

The Norman game of croquet arrived in Britain during the 11th century. The conquerors brought croquet from France. To win the point in croquet, the ball contacts the vertical target stick. When the friends first thought about a target for their new game, they chose a vertical stick. They added a flag to the stick.

As in croquet, the friends pictured a ball touching the vertical stick as the goal. Since play consisted of a ball propelled by the strike with a wooden club, as in croquet, the vertical stick seemed like a natural idea for a target. However, while the friends played an entirely unforeseen problem with the stick target occurred. Compared to croquet, there were significant differences in the new game. The vertical stick target for their "new game" created an issue for a much smaller leather ball.

To determine a game winner, the friends decided to count the numbers of strokes used to reach the target. They counted strokes from the tee shot on the target zone until the ball contacted the stick target on the next target zone. Hitting the stick in the lowest number of strokes to determine who won the hole sounded like a good idea.

To begin play, the friends chose to group players by fours, consisting of two lads and two lasses to a group. That seemed a fair way to team all members of the group. The friends also thought it fun to split up the families.

Group 1. Bessie the Shepherd with William the Weaver, and Margaret the Tanner with Robert the Carpenter.

Group 2. Barbara the Bowyer with David the Shepherd, and Rhona the Weaver with Jonathan the Shoemaker.

Group 3. Heather the Carpenter with Russell the Bowyer, and Marion the Shoemaker with Thomas the Tanner.

Since the friends began play with three groups, they did not think of an important reason to wait for all the people to start play at the first striking area. They decided that Group 1 would walk to Landing Target 2 and begin play by teeing off from Landing Target 2 and playing to Landing Target 3. Group 2 walk to Landing Target 1 and begin play by aiming to Landing Target 2. Group 3 stayed at the beginning tee and aimed at Landing Target 1.

All agreed that each person would play all fourteen target zones. Starting in this sequence, allowed all groups of four players to start play at the same time and play all the landing zones. Then all three foursomes should finish playing at nearly the same time. The twelve friends all agreed that this format was fair. In addition to a fair opportunity to excel in the game, the format provided an equal experience on the Links.

Croquet is played in close quarters compared to the wide-open distances in the "new game". Because the players are close to the stick in croquet, when the wooden ball hits the target stick, it is easy to see. Usually, it is easy to hear the larger wooden ball strike the wooden stake. All croquet players agree when the point was scored. With the "new game", however, the twelve soon realized a significant difference between croquet and the new game. When the players stood distant from the flag, it might be difficult for all the players to know whether the leather ball struck the stick or not.

"THWOCK!"

Russell the Bowyer struck his second shot solidly. It felt good! Russell looked up. His eyes found the ball flying through the sky. He knew the ball was on line. From Russell's perspective, the flight of the ball lined directly towards the stick at the center of the target zone.

"The ball is going right at the target! That ball is going to hit the stick, I know it is!" Thomas exclaimed.

"Russell, that's a great shot!" confirmed Heather.

"Looks like your ball is going to hit the stick, Russell! Your ball is going to be very, very close for sure!" Marion agreed.

Thomas the Tanner cheered. "That is a wonderful shot, Russell! I know the ball is close! However, I do not believe the ball touched the stick. Though it is very close to the stick for certain!"

"What do you mean, the ball did not touch the stick? That ball was hit perfectly. I am sure the ball hit the stick." Russell claimed.

"Well, Russell, did you hear the ball hit the stick? In croquet, we hear the ball when it hits the stick. You know it hit the stick because we hear it. Did you hear the ball hit the stick? Do you know for certain in the way we planned for the game, that the ball touched the stick?" Thomas doubted.

"No Thomas. I could not be sure that I heard the ball hit the stick. Marion, Heather, could either of you hear the ball hit the stick? I am sure the ball hit the stick from the line it was on. Yet, I must confess, I did not hear the ball actually strike the stick."

"For one thing, how can anyone hear a ball hitting a stick from this distance?" asked Heather. "Out here, on the Links, the constant wind roars. Often, unless we stand extremely close to the stick, to hear the little leather ball contact the stick will be nigh impossible."

"I thought the ball was on an accurate line to hit the stick. But from way out here, I cannot be certain that the ball struck the target stick." Thomas added.

Marion agreed. "Heather, I thought the ball was going to hit the stick from my vantage, too. I was counting on hearing the ball strike the stick, the way we planned in order to determine that the target was achieved. But other than the wind rustling the shrubs and whipping the flag on the Links, I heard no sound."

Russell found himself feeling quite upset, even a bit angry. He reacted defensively in his disappointment. "You all saw the ball. Even though we did not hear the ball hit the stick, I am sure the ball struck the stick. I hope when we get to the target zone, I can prove to you that the ball did contact the stick."

"Sincerely, I hope there is ample evidence to support your belief, Russell. Evidence enough to convince me that your ball hit the stick will work for me. Even though none of us heard the ball and the stick connect, evidence can persuade me." Thomas counselled.

"What kind of evidence would conclusively show that the ball contacted the stick?" Wondered Russell.

"Hmm, that is an interesting question, Russell. Well, I confess, I don't know for sure what would provide convincing evidence." Thomas responded. "Perhaps there will be a mark showing where the ball landed. Or perhaps, we will find a trail left by the rolling ball on the sand. A trail like tracks from a crab or a bird walking across the sandy beach. I don't know for sure. Russell, what kind of evidence do you think would be totally convincing to someone who did not hear the ball strike the stick?"

Heather intervened, "This is a problem. We definitely want the game to be completely fair. The last thing we want for our new game, is either a disagreement or an argument. Disagreements and arguments are not fun in any game. In fact, disagreements and arguments make the game no fun to play."

"Personally, I don't want to see Russell so upset. He just struck a marvelous shot." Marion stated. "He should be reveling with joy! The fact that he hit a great shot ought to be a cause for celebration. Instead, Russell is upset. He is upset because none of us can prove that the ball did, in fact, hit the stick. Even if the ball did not strike the stick, that was still one terrific shot. I think it is really important that we can all celebrate when one of us hits the ball like Russell did."

"Aye," continued Thomas. "Whether the ball struck the stick or not, does not detract from how well Russell hit that ball. That remains a quality shot. I can tell you; I do not wish to be a part of an argument with my friend. We need to think carefully and clearly about how this situation affects our new game. How can we redesign the game so that there is no disagreement about when the target has been acquired? This issue raises a crucial question. We must find a way to resolve this issue. Right now, I feel this issue brings into question the whole point of enjoying our fair game."

The four players brought the problem to the entire twelve. Unless players stood on the target zone, the friends discovered there could be honest disagreements concerning whether or not the ball contacted the stick. The players realized they needed a better way to know when the target was successfully acquired. Sound failed to provide proof to determine that a leather ball touched a vertical stick when the players stood at a distance. The friends wanted to find a way to achieve complete agreement about when the ball reached the target.

The twelve friends realized that they needed a different kind of target for the leather ball. The small hard leather ball differed markedly from the larger wooden croquet ball. The players wanted a target that everyone would agree had been acquired. When the friends found the right target for the small, hard leather ball, there would be no doubt when the ball hit the target.

The lads and lasses continued to ponder over the puzzle, what would be the best possible target for their game? Out over "the Links" at the landing areas, the twelve friends gazed.

Chapter 71 | 1399 | The Hole Solution

Hares darted and played. The small creatures nibbled the late summer grasses that covered the Links. The friends delighted in watching the soft, gentle, furry animals haphazardly lope along.

A looming shadow glided and darkened the grass where the hares gamboled. The shadow terrified the playful unsuspecting hares! Panicky animals darted helter-skelter.

The friends gasped. They bore witness to the marked behavior change in the terror filled creatures. Scurrying hares zig-zagged frantic dashes. To escape the looming streak every hare committed to evasive tactics. The diving shadow bracketed a solitary hare. With deadly aim the dark shadow sharpened focus.

The frightened, scampering hare refused to surrender. Rather, than rely on straight line speed, just as the shadow sharped to life size, the hare cut one last desperate high-speed zag!

Bam!

The diving hawk missed the hare!

Tumbling and rolling, the unsuccessful raptor recovered from the diving crash. The great bird regained balance. Strengthening both legs, the hawk proudly stood upright, tall, and fearless. Quickly, the bird ruffled its feathers and shook out the grit. He blinked his eyes. He surveyed the scene of the escape.

The great bird scanned the Links for another rabbit meal, and then refocused. The hawk spread powerful wings, flapped down, and lifted off the surface of the Links. Flapped the wings again and rose, the flight carved beauty in the sky, before the hawk soared into a circling glide.

The hare, the hawk's target, simply disappeared from the sight of the observing play. The hare escaped. The hare found safety.

Sometimes a swooping, diving hawk successfully plucked and harvested an unsuspecting hare. Sometimes a zigging, zagging, dashing hare simply disappeared from view and evaded capture. The serious struggle, the life and death contest between the hawk and the hare repeated itself often on the Links.

By disappearing from view, the hare found safety. A disappearing rabbit may seem like magic. For centuries, magicians fooled audiences using the illusion of a disappearing rabbit. To the hares on the Links, the ability to disappear represented the goal and marked the difference between life and death. But how did the rabbits on the Links magically disappear? The friends realized there was no magician. There was no magic.

The friends discovered the answer to the illusion. They learned the secret to the disappearance as a result of careful observations. On the Links, the hare found safety when it acquired its target. The hare's goal was to disappear into its target, better known as the rabbit hole.

After witnessing this race for life between the hawk and the hare, the silent friends gazed upon each other's astonished faces. It was crucially important for the hawk to find food. However, if the hare failed to find safety, the price for the hare was an immediate capital mistake. The struggle between the two was not merely a game. Between hawk and hare, the struggle formed a competitive contest resulting in life or death. Yet, many aspects of the struggle between hawk and rabbit resembled the intense competition inherent in a great game. In great games, intense competition created a feeling similar to the reaction contained in an element of danger. That feeling of being in danger was a powerful emotional feeling. The excitement accompanied by that feeling of danger transformed a good friendly game into an exhilarating, thrilling great game.

The friends possessed no desire to create a truly dangerous game. They remembered. They definitely knew that they did not want a game where a competitor faced injury or death. Perhaps though, they thought, there were ways that they could create a 'feeling of danger' in the new game. Maybe they could find a way to create an intense feeling in the game.

A question formed. Could the team constitute some element of the hawk and hare struggle which would provide feelings as exhilarating and exciting as when one experiences an encounter with danger? If they were able to create the feeling of impending danger, that would enhance a high level of excitement while playing the game. The friends agreed that confronting a feeling of danger offered exciting possibilities to build challenge into the new game.

"When we watched that life and death struggle between the hawk and the hare, I was thrilled. I felt exhilarated while we watched the contest. I am thinking about that feeling of intense excitement I experienced!" pronounced Bessie the Shepherd. "I am thinking about an idea for what our target should be!"

"Go on Bessie!" Smiled Mary. "I want to hear what you are thinking after we watched the disappearing rabbit. I want to see if you think the same that I am thinking,."

"Aye, we all saw the hare disappear. The hare found a hole. When the hare entered the hole, it achieved safety. The hare in the hole knew it was safe from the hawk. Even the hawk knew that the hare was in a safe place when it disappeared into a hole. There was no disagreement between the hawk and the hare. That particular hare was safe. There was no danger to that hare from that particular hawk at that particular time.

When the hare drops into the hole, the hare is safe. When the hare is outside of the hole, the hare remains in danger, and the hare knows he is in danger.

Nevertheless, the hare that reaches safety must venture out of the hole again eventually, else it will die. In order to live, the hare must leave the safe hole. It must leave to find food, water, and others of its kind." Bessie explained.

"When the hawk sees the hare outside the hole, the hawk knows the hare is in danger. But when the hawk cannot see the hare because the hare is in the hole, the hawk knows that the hare is safe." Mary continued. "I think I see where you are going with this idea, Bessie."

"The hole! That's it! The solution to the target problem for our game is the hole!" Bessie exclaimed.

"Suppose the target in our game is simply, a hole. In our game, when the ball is in the hole, the ball reached safety. When the ball is in the hole, the target has been acquired. Or to the contrary, as long as the ball is outside the hole, the ball has not yet hit the target. When the ball is outside the hole, the ball remains in danger. The ball cannot be both inside the hole and outside the hole at the same time. It is either in the hole and safe, or it is not in the hole and still in danger."

"Bessie, I really like your idea for the target!" exclaimed Marion.

"What a great idea!" shouted William.

Russell announced, "A hole! A hole is the perfect target for our game!"

"Putting the ball into the hole will test skill and strategy!" added Thomas.

Jonathan stated, "There will be many different pathways to put the ball into the hole. On the journey from tee to hole, the ball will travel at many different speeds. In order to guide the ball into the hole it will be necessary to control the strike of the ball."

"Bessie, everyone agrees with your idea." Heather said.

"I do have one question though, Bessie." David posed.

Chapter 72 | *1399* | An Important Question

"What is your question?" Bessie asked.

"My question. I wonder, 'how big should the hole be?'" David asked.

Bessie responded, "Team, let's talk about David's question. Finding the right size for the hole will be crucial. The right size hole will help us establish the feeling of being in danger we want in our game. But before we consider David's question, perhaps we might think about other questions. For example, should all the holes be the same size?

We must get the hole the exact right size. Obviously, we don't want to make the hole too big. For the hare, if the hole is too big, the hare is not safe. The hawk can still reach the hare.

If the hole is too big for our game, it will be too easy for the player to put the ball into the target. We already decided that for our game to be fun that the game needs challenges. If the target is too big it fails to provide the feeling of being in danger which tests a player's control of emotions and skills."

"Aye, Bessie, I believe your concerns about a hole that is too large, are right. If it is too easy to put the ball into the hole, the game fails to provide a sufficient challenge. The point of the game is to put the ball into the hole. We definitely must get the size of the hole right." William the Weaver spoke.

"On the other hand, if we make the hole too small," Rhona the Weaver continued, "the task will be too difficult. If it is too difficult, the game will frustrate the players too much. To put the ball in a wee tiny hole a player may take too many strokes to maintain a good pace of play. A hole too small fails to provide a fair test of a player's skill as well."

"We could experiment." offered Russell the Bowyer. "We could dig holes of different sizes on different target zones."

"Aye. You make a good point, Russell. Instead of guessing, we need to aim toward different size holes. Otherwise, we are merely guessing about the best size of the hole. Whereas, if we take some strokes at different size holes, we produce solid data to consider. We can apply solid data to guide us toward an informed judgment regarding hole size. We will learn what size is too big. We will know what size hole is too small. Then, we will decide what size hole. A hole that will be neither too big, nor too small. We will find the size of hole that is just right!" Robert responded.

"To perform our experiment what different size holes do you think we should consider?" questioned Barbara.

"I say we try the smallest hole at five inches across. The five-inch diameter hole will be just a wee bit more than two times the size of the ball." Robert answered.

"Aye, I agree that five inches is the smallest hole we should try. The fact that the five-inch hole is roughly twice the size of the ball makes an interesting point to try the smallest hole. I can see no reason to consider a hole smaller than five inches.

I suggest we experiment with another hole at eight inches across. I would offer a reason for the eight-inch hole. The eight-inch size is just a wee bit more than three times the diameter of the ball."

"Alright, then why don't we also try the largest hole at 12 inches across? Though I do think that size is too large, we may as well gather data in order to evaluate our decision."

"Three sizes are plenty to begin the evaluation of hole size experiment. Five inches, eight inches and twelve inches offers a reasonable range of sizes to begin our experiment," Thomas Tanner observed. "Can we close discussion on hole size, now?"

"Why Thomas? Do you want to move the discussion?" Margaret queried.

"I do. I wish to offer an idea about the shape of the hole. We could make square, or triangle or rectangle, for example." Thomas stated. "We could make the hole any shape we want, but animals usually make their safe holes, the holes for nests and shelter, in one shape. Animals almost always create holes in a circular shape. Because the ball is round, I think a circular hole offers a fair shape for the Game. I like using a shape often found in nature as the most natural shape for our game. I propose that we agree to make the target hole, a circular hole."

"Does anyone disagree with my brother's proposal of a circle for the shape of our target hole?" Margaret the Tanner asked.

All the lads and lasses indicated agreement. Thomas Tanner's suggestion for a circular hole was approved.

Margaret continued, "Now that we agreed on shape of the hole, plus three diameters for our experiment, I think we should consider how deep the hole should be."

"Good grief! Why do you believe that the depth of the hole is important for the game?" Jonathan questioned.

"Thank you for the question, Jonathan." Margaret smirked. "I think there is a valid reason for choosing adequate depth. Our concept for the hole as target, centered on the rabbit's ability to disappear from danger. To disappear from danger meant that the rabbit found safety. In order to be considered home and safe, I think the ball has to stay in the hole until it comes to rest."

"Alright, sister. I concede." Jonathan admitted. "The depth of the hole is relevant."

Margaret looked at all the friends. She found no disagreement.

"How about a depth of about four inches?" offered Marion. "Four inches is a bit less than two times the diameter of the ball. I do not believe we want the hole to be too deep. If the hole is too deep, ball retrieval might be difficult. A four-inch hole provides sufficient depth for the ball to come to rest. Yet, four inches is also shallow enough so that the ball remains in reach for us to retrieve the ball out of the hole. The object of play is to put the ball in the bottom of the hole."

"Once the ball rests safely in the bottom of the hole, we can pick it up. The goal is achieved." Heather stated. "After every player picks up her or his ball, we compare the number of strokes used to put the ball in the bottom of the hole."

"Then, we can get ready to tee off to play to the next Landing Area." Thomas observed.

"Let's play!" shouted Jonathan.

"Let's experiment!" Rhona chimed.

Chapter 73 | *1399* | Putting in The Holes

"After we hit the balls onto the target zones, we can dig a hole in the center. We will only need one spade." David suggested. "Can someone please bring a hand spade?"

"I have the hand spade with me." Bessie responded.

All the friends took a turn to tee off from the first spot. Each player hit her or his own ball. Each friend used her or his own club. Each player took careful aim at the flag signaling the first target zone. All players took note of where each ball landed. Together, the friends walked to the balls. While they walked along the fair way, the friends chatted happily.

"What a delightful way to enjoy the company of friends while playing the game!" Marion reminded the friends. All enjoyed the walk and the talk.

The friends arrived at the first ball which belonged to Bessie. Bessie looked carefully at the flag in the center of target zone one. She took a step behind her ball. She visualized a line between her ball and the flag. She judged the line and the distance in much the same way that her father and the other archers judged the angle and distance to the target during archery practice.

Bessie stood back to take a practice swing. She stood a little away from where she would stand to strike the ball. Employing a practice swing enabled Bessie to consider whether she felt she selected the proper line to the target. In addition, she estimated the right speed needed for her ball to reach the target. After completing her practice swing to her satisfaction, Bessie felt that she was ready to strike the ball. Only then did Bessie place the club head behind the ball at the same angle she visualized for the flight of her ball.

Confidently, Bessie coached herself, "I got this." Bessie pulled the club back of her right shoulder. She wanted to make a full down swing to hit through the ball. Then, she released her swing. She accelerated the club face down the path and through the ball.

"THWOCK!"

Bessie's swing connected the club to the ball cleanly and powerfully. Up, up, up! To its apex, the ball soared in a beautiful trajectory. Then down, down, down. Bounce and roll. The ball seemed to inscribe a direct line to the stick standing in the center of the target zone.

"Hooray, Bessie!" cheered Margaret.

"That is a great shot!" exclaimed William.

"Well done, Bessie!" congratulated Jonathan.

All teammates congratulated Bessie. They moved to the next ball.

"Here is my ball," claimed Russell. Like Bessie, Russell moved to stand two steps behind his ball. He aligned the ball to the pole and thought about the amount of force he required to land his ball on the target zone. Then, he positioned for a practice swing. He wanted to warm his muscles for a free and easy swing. Russell set his club in a precise angle on-line to the pole. His swing was free and easy.

"THWOCK!!"

The ball rose in a beautiful arc and descended on-line. It landed a few feet in front, bounced onto the target zone then rolled toward the flagpole.

"Wow!" exclaimed Marion.

"That was a beautiful shot, Russell!" complimented Margaret. The friends praised his shot. They marveled at how near the ball came to the flag.

The friends walked towards the next ball. They talked while they walked. Friends love to talk. They shared observations. They asked questions. Time invested with friends brings joy and fun to people everywhere. The game provided a wonderful opportunity to join together.

While the players practiced physical skills, they considered mental challenges. To control powerful emotions, the players practiced self-discipline. The emotions they encountered included a fear of failure, or self-doubt. The friends found that while playing the game, talking with friends helped them face doubts and fears. In addition to talk about the game, they also found time within the leisurely pace, to talk about other aspects of their lives.

The next ball belonged to Heather. Excitedly, she approached her ball. Heather made a splendid stroke. "This is the longest ball I ever hit," she celebrated.

"I thought you found the best rhythm for your swing," her brother Robert agreed. "Now that you found your rhythm, I know you can do it again. When you can repeat the rhythm in your swing every time, your confidence will grow.

When the fathers practice archery, once they find the right pull, the right stroke, the right release and hold rhythm, they want to practice over and over again. Archers practice to build confident about where the arrow will strike. The right rhythm enables the archers to achieve consistency even when performing a difficult physical skill."

"Thank you, brother," replied Heather. "I believe practice and repetition are critically important. To help me want to improve, I know that positive observations such as you just shared with me, let me know when I am doing the right things in the right way. Hmmm, that's kind of funny. I know when I am on the right track. Like hunters know they are on the right track of the animal when they pursue game in the forest. Hunters know the different tracks of each animal. To find the quarry they pursue, hunters talk about when they are on the right track."

"Take your time. Think about the pathway you want for the next shot. When you stand behind the ball, you can see the line you want the ball to follow." Rhona instructed.

Each teammate took a second shot. All landed the ball on the target zone in two shots. When the friends arrived at the target zone, they noted the position of each ball. The flag stick stood at the center of the target zone. Bessie brought the spade. Thomas pulled the target stick out of the ground. Bessie dug a twelve-inch diameter hole, four inches deep in the hard sand. Each player took the opportunity to refill their sand pouches. They spread the remainder of the sand from the twelve-inch diameter hole onto the target zone.

The freshly dug hole, served as the target. The friends decided that the farthest ball from the hole should take the first turn.

Russell noted, "My ball is farthest from the hole. So, I go first."

The target zone was a circle, some 40 yards in diameter. Soft gray sand covered the zone. Following the hay harvest several wooden rakes were left on the Links. The friends placed a rake on each target zone. Using a wooden rake, players smoothed the sand.

To measure the distance from his ball to the hole, Russell stretched a length of twine connected to the flag stick bottom. Next, Russell raked a smooth lane. He began to rake from one club length behind his ball mark. He dragged a pathway through the soft gray sand to a point approximately two club lengths beyond the hole.

After Russell created a smooth path for his ball. He stretched the twine so that the length of twine measured a distance equal to the distance his ball lay from the hole. Russell picked up his ball. He placed the ball on the spot measured by the twine.

Russell stood behind his ball. He looked towards the hole. Russell visualized a pathway that he intended for his ball to roll right into the hole. Next, he eyeballed the distance from the ball to the hole. He processed the data. His sighting informed him about the distance plus the intended pathway. Processing specific data guided Russell's decision. He estimated the speed needed for the ball to travel the distance to the hole. He selected the amount of force to move the ball at that speed. He chose the direction to start the ball rolling towards the hole. After compiling data on distance, direction, and necessary force, Russell took a stance near the ball. He made a practice stroke. During the practice stroke, Russell envisioned the stroke he would take. He made two more practice strokes to feel the force.

Satisfied with the practice strokes, Russell stood over the ball. He took one more look at the pathway. He sighted the alignment of club, ball, and hole. Finally, Russell made a small backswing. He allowed the club to swing forward and stroke the ball. To impart the right speed to deliver the ball to rest at the bottom of the hole, he applied the force he practiced. He stroked the ball along what he believed to be the correct line.

The ball rolled, then slowed slightly. Slower, slower, until it almost stopped. Still barely rolling. Stopping, stopping almost stopped, the ball turned one more revolution and plop! Right into the hole it dropped.

"Wow! That was an impressive shot!" noted Marion.

"Well done!" cheered Heather.

"Step it off! Let's step off the distance from where you struck the ball to put the ball in the hole." Bessie exclaimed.

"That's a good idea!" Russell agreed.

"One, two, three … nineteen, twenty plus two feet. That makes 62 feet! I wonder though, was it a good shot? Or is the hole too large? We need to see how all of the rest of us do when we take our turn to put the ball in the hole." Heather questioned.

"Who is the next farthest away from the hole?" Bessie asked.

Two balls seemed to be the same distance away from the flag.

The balls belonged to Marion and Jonathan.

Bessie offered, "Why don't you each stretch the twine the distance from your ball to the hole? Then we will know who should be next to put the ball in the hole."

Marion picked up the twine and stretched it to her ball. To mark her distance, she tied a small slip knot.

Jonathan then picked up the line and walked to his ball. It was clear that Marion's ball was closer than Jonathan's ball.

"It's your turn, Jonathan." Marion stated.

Jonathan raked a path from his ball to two club lengths beyond the hole. He employed a routine similar to Russell's. Jonathan placed his ball equal to the distance his ball rested from the hole on the path he raked. Next, he stood behind the ball. In his mind he visualized a pathway to the hole. Jonathan thought about the speed for the ball. He made a practice stroke. Then, stood over the ball. Jonathan aligned club, ball, and path to the hole. He stroked the ball.

The ball started towards the target. It approached the hole. The ball began to curve away from the hole. But at the last second, it barely caught the edge of the hole and dropped in.

"Well done, Jonathan!" His sister Marion congratulated.

"I wonder," Jonathan thought aloud. "I am happy I put the ball in the hole. However, I didn't think putting the ball in that hole offered much of a challenge. I know I failed to send the ball along the directional line I envisioned. I did apply the force I thought I needed in order to move the ball at the speed I intended. I wonder. Perhaps a twelve-inch hole fails to present a sufficient challenge for our game. After you each take your turn to put the ball into the hole, let's see what the rest of you think."

Marion took her turn. First, she raked a similar pathway to the hole. She mimicked the same routine as Russell and Jonathan. She took a good practice stroke. Marion moved to stand over the ball. She stroked the ball. Marion's ball rolled rapidly. Then lost speed. The rolling ball began to swerve away from the line Marion envisioned. The rolling ball found the right edge of the hole. Momentarily the ball rested on the edge before dropping into the hole. Success!

The remaining players took their turns, raking sand and taking shots to put the ball in the hole. All players successfully put the ball in the hole. All used only one stroke to put the ball into the 12-inch hole.

The players aimed for the second target zone. Each friend poured a sand cone on the target zone to serve as a tee. Each one hit the ball. Target zone two was short, only some 45 yards from target number one. All reached target zone number two in one stroke.

While the friends walked to landing zone number two, they talked. All enjoyed the satisfaction of reaching landing zone two in one stroke. They arrived at landing zone two. Bessie said, "Let's dig this hole 8 inches in diameter. I want to see how we do with the medium sized hole."

Russell took the spade. He drew a circle eight inches in diameter. He dug the circle four inches deep.

Jonathan was the first to attempt to put the ball in the hole. His attempt was from 42 feet. He stood behind the ball to select the pathway. Then he stood near the ball. He practiced the stroke he believed would deliver the proper speed. He carefully drew back his club. Then he allowed the club to fall forward and start the ball toward the hole. The attempt looked like a good shot. However, Jonathan did not provide quite enough force to deliver the ball all the way to the hole.

Heather was next. Since Jonathan's ball was so close to the hole, she asked Jonathan to go ahead and put his ball in the hole. That way his ball would not interfere with the pathway she envisioned for her attempt. The other players agreed that Jonathan should take his time. Jonathan stepped up to his ball, took a deep breath, then tapped his ball into the hole.

Heather followed her routine. She stood behind her ball to see the pathway. She moved over her ball and took a practice stroke. Then stroked the ball to put it into the hole. The ball rolled toward the hole, but with 3 feet to go, the ball veered left away from the hole.

Robert was next. He asked Heather, "Please go ahead and put your ball in the hole? Take your time. Do not worry about my ball. I am happy to wait for you to complete the hole."

"Thank you," Heather answered. Confidently, she stepped to the ball. She gave the ball a smooth tap. She easily put her ball in the hole.

Robert walked to stand behind his ball. He examined possible pathways to put the ball in the hole. He selected a pathway. Robert stood over the ball. He made two practice swings to judge the right speed for the stroke to put the ball in the hole. Robert placed his club directly behind the ball. He brought the club back and let it go forward to strike the ball. He propelled the ball with the correct speed and line to put the ball in the hole. The ball rolled dropped into the hole. Robert enjoyed a feeling of satisfaction.

After all the friends completed their turn, they compared their scores. Four had completed in one stroke. Three had finished in two strokes. One required three strokes to put the ball in the hole.

"You know," Jonathan began, "Getting the ball in eight-inch hole was more challenging than the 12-inch hole. When I put the ball in this hole in one stroke, I felt a thrill. When I put the ball in the 12-inch hole, it just seemed way too easy. I feel this size hole is both challenging and fair. This hole offers a fair chance to put the ball into the hole. At the same time putting the ball in this hole is a very challenging goal. I believe we should abandon the twelve-inch hole."

David agreed. "When you put the ball in this hole, I saw you felt joy and happiness. We want that kind of feeling in our game."

Bess added, "Putting the ball in the hole once we are on the sandy landing area offers a fair test. It means nothing for a player to be physically strong, or large, or a fast runner, or lithe and acrobatic to put the ball in the hole. The only thing that matters is using the least number of strokes to put the ball in the hole. To do that successfully, requires mental judgment, creating an accurate vision, and employing the physical skill to execute the stroke."

Mary wondered. "Putting the ball in the hole tests emotional control, as well as a physical skill. I noticed that before I swung the club, I felt fearful that I would fail to hit the ball in the right manner. I had to consider accuracy. Will I hit the ball along the path that I believe is correct? If I hit the ball in the path I see, did I choose the right path? Even if I hit the ball on the path I chose, and assuming I had, in fact, chosen the right path, there remained a question.

Next, I must select the correct speed to stroke the ball. If I don't hit the ball hard enough, the ball does not even get to the hole. If I hit the ball too hard, the ball rolls on past the hole. All those decisions require me to make accurate observations of the target zone.

When I added in, make the correct physical motion to hit the ball squarely, I noticed that I began to worry. I felt very concerned about my success. I was afraid that I would not put the ball in the hole. True, there are mental questions. What is the right path to choose to put the ball in the hole on this stroke? What is the right speed to put the ball in the hole? I want to choose a stroke that is not too soft, and the ball doesn't get to the hole. Or not so hard that puts the ball past the hole, but to stroke the ball with a speed that is just right?"

"You know like the three beds when the old maid, 'Silverlocks' found the cabin in the forest. You remember what she said. 'This bed is too soft. This bed is too hard.'"

"But this one is 'Just right!'" All the friends repeated in unison the line from the story their parents used to tell them long ago before bedtime.

"Last, the most important part is to execute the physical task correctly. To execute a smooth stroke correctly requires moving the body in sequence. Taking a practice stroke to tell your body to hit the ball just like this. Measure off the distance to stand from the ball. Then, step up to the ball. Finally, actually make the stroke to put the ball in the hole." Mary concluded.

Chapter 74 | 1399 | A Putting Contest

"I have an idea!" Heather announced. "What if we make a contest that takes place completely on the sandy target zone? Would anybody want to compete in such a contest?"

"I want to. That's a great idea! A contest which takes place completely on the target zone will be fun. We can concentrate just on one part of the game. In this case we concentrate on the stroke to put the ball in the hole. We designed our game, so that there is no advantage to being tall or small. There is no advantage to being big and strong." Jonathan the Shoemaker recalled the original vision to construct a new game and furthered the discussion.

William stated, "A contest on the sand target zone to see who can put the ball in the hole in the fewest number of strokes is a terrific idea, Heather. To succeed in this contest players need to observe the problem accurately. We need to judge distance, slope, and select the pathway to roll the ball.

To solve the problem we formulate a plan. Select the correct line from the ball to the hole. Decide how much force required to put the ball in the hole. Finally, execute the plan, hit the ball. Then, evaluate the results. Immediately we know if we were successful. If the ball is in the hole, success! When the ball is not in the hole, we still have work to do to find success. Like the end of the 'Tug of war' contest, everyone knows the result immediately."

"For this contest, we all start from the same place. Each player takes a stroke to put the ball in the hole. The one who puts the ball in the hole in the fewest strokes from each distance is the winner. What do you think?" Marion asked.

"I like that idea." affirmed Robert.

"So do I." agreed Margaret. "Let's enjoy this contest. Let's see who is better at putting the ball in the hole when each of us strokes the ball from the same distance."

"Remember, at the Scottish games how much we enjoyed the 'Tug o' War' because the contest was a total team effort?" William reminded the group.

"Aye! I remember." Added Russell. "We enjoyed 'Tug o' War' because everyone knew who won and who lost! There was no need to wait for judges to say who won. In the same way for this contest, there is no need for a judge. Everybody will know the ball is in the hole."

"Do you remember when we began to think about a new game, we wanted to make a game for team play? I think we could compete as teams in this contest. In fact, I like a team of lasses competing against the lads." Rhona continued, "What about it, lasses? Do you believe we can beat the lads in this contest?"

"Well," Bess added, "I, for one, am up for any fair opportunity, make that any opportunity, to compete with the lads. I know the lads are all good players. I appreciate that all our brothers are strong, young men who grow stronger every day. However, in the portion of the game played on the sand target areas, success depends far more on judgment, planning, and execution of the plan. Play on the sand target areas make brute strength, which, I grant, our brothers possess in greater quantity than we lasses, a moot point. So, count me in for a lasses versus lads contest to put the ball in the hole."

When Bess mentioned that the lads possess brute strength, each lad smiled. They curled their arms and flexed their biceps. Lads love compliments. Lads especially love compliments on their manly strength. They proudly accepted Bess's comment as a compliment to their developing manly stature.

Barbara teased, "When I think of these six lads, I believe they are all very smart. For their age these are the smartest lads in St. Andrews. I believe they might be the smartest lads for their age in all of Scotland.

And then, my dear lassies. I see a clear difference in the level of intelligence between the lads and the lasses. I think that the word, 'judgment' is a critical trait which our gender possesses at the highest level. I am pretty sure that we lasses possess a superior level of judgment over you lads."

"Careful there, Barbara," cautioned David. "I do not deny the good judgment that you and the lasses exhibit on a daily basis. I think in an undeniably fair contest competition will be fun with you lasses. What say you, lads? Are you with me? Shall we accept our sisters' challenge?"

"Count me in, David," smiled Robert. "A game of lads versus lassies always brings out the best in our competitive spirits, especially when the game is fair. As I see it, putting the ball into the hole is about as fair a skills contest as there is. It will be fun to win!"

"Oh, now who's talking big? And look who is bragging?" Rhona responded good-naturedly. "I do believe the lasses are ready for the contest. It's time to stop talking! It is time to put up or shut up! Let's play this game! Let's do this!"

"Alright. I will mark an X in the sand. Each lad and each lass will place your ball on the X. Then, you will take one stroke. To count, the ball must go in the hole and stay in the hole. We will not count the balls that are close. Remember when we observed the rabbit attempting to evade and escape from the hawk? Close to the hole, the ball remains in danger. The ball is safe only when it rests in the bottom of the hole. Even if the ball hangs on the edge of the hole, that will count as a miss. To put the ball in the hole the player must take another stroke. For the stroke to count as good, the ball must go in the hole and remain in the hole." Bess clarified the rules.

Jonathan formally proposed the format for the contest. "Each team decides which player will take the first, second, third and last stroke for the team. After each player takes a stroke, we count which team has put the most balls in the hole. If the result of the round of shots is a tie, I mark X in a different spot. We repeat the process until the game ends when either the lasses' team or the lads' team wins. Everyone agree?"

The team of lasses and the team of lads separated. Each team huddled together. They decided the order their team would use for the contest.

"Jonathan!" Marion called to her brother. "Here, catch!" Already Marion's club softly flew towards him. Jonathan reacted swiftly. He reached out with one hand. Confidently, he grabbed her club in mid-air.

Marion and Jonathan looked at each other. Jonathan held the club handle straight up perpendicular. Marion grabbed the club with her right hand so that the skin of her hand touched just the top of Jonathan's hand. Jonathan grabbed the club and placed his left hand in the same way, so that the skin of his hand touched Marion's hand, just above her right hand. Then, Jonathan released his bottom hand from the club. Marion released her bottom hand in order to repeat the alternating process with one hand just above Jonathan's hand. The sister and brother repeated the one hand over the other process until the hand holding the top of the club belonged to Marion. Marion won the 'hands up" game. They used that process to determine which team went first to put the ball into the hole.

"Lads, since we won the right to select who should go first in our contest fairly, we think you should have the opportunity to make the first try." Marion and the lasses graciously deferred the first opportunity to put the ball into the hole to their brothers.

"All right then", Russell crowed. "I will show you how to put the ball in the hole in one stroke!" He bent over to place his ball atop the X. Then, Russell walked six steps behind the ball. From behind and above the ball, Russell looked for the proper pathway to choose the route he wished to put the ball in order for the ball to roll right into the hole. In his mind, Russell visualized the pathway. He selected the speed he believed would bring success.

Russell stood over the ball. Then, he stepped back. He took two practice strokes. He judged how much force to apply to the ball. He placed the club directly behind the ball aligned with the pathway. Russell lifted the club, then brought the club back. He tapped the club to the ball softly. The ball rolled along the pathway. The ball looked like it was going straight to the middle of the hole. However, right before it reached the hole, the ball stopped.

"Oh no!" Groaned the lads in unison.

Then, all the other lads and lasses congratulated Russell for a great attempt.

"Alright, who is the first lass to try?" asked Russell, as he tapped the ball in for a count of two strokes.

"Well, brother, that would be me!" Barbara exclaimed.

"All right, Barbara!" Cheered her team of lasses. "You can do this!"

The show of vocal support surprised the lads. They were slightly amused.

Everyone watched as Barbara stepped behind the ball. She moved confidently. She chose the pathway. Barbara took her place next to the ball. She took two practice strokes. She placed her club behind the ball. Barbara made a controlled backswing. She allowed the club to swing forward. The soft contact sent the ball towards the hole. The rolling ball mirrored Barbara's air of confidence. The ball rolled towards the center of the hole and dropped in.

"Yea!"

"Well done, Barbara!"

"You had it all the way." Congratulated her teammates.

"Amazing shot, sister!" Added brother Russell.

"You put that ball right in the center of the hole." Remarked David.

"That makes the score, Lasses one. Lads nil." Announced Barbara.

"Aye." Jonathan answered. "And I am next for the lads."

Jonathan placed his ball on the X. "Jonathan, you got this." David cheered.

"Aye," agreed Russell.

"Yes, you can." Added Robert.

Basking in his teammates enthusiastic support, Jonathan followed the same pre-shot routine as the Bowyer siblings. First, he stood behind the ball to find a pathway to the hole. He mentally chose the speed he wanted. He practiced a stroke for the chosen speed. Then, with an air of confidence similar to Barbara's, Jonathan addressed the ball. He took two more practice strokes to simulate how much force he needed in order to make the ball roll for the speed he wanted. He placed the club behind the ball, then confidently stroked the club forward to propel the ball with the proper speed. Along the pathway Jonathan selected, the ball rolled true. He felt he stroked the ball with a perfect speed. The ball dropped right in the middle of the hole.

Eleven players clapped and cheered. The friends enjoyed the feeling when they celebrated a friend's success. All enjoyed watching a perfect stroke put the ball in the hole. Jonathan lifted his ball from the hole. He looked at his friends. A brightness illuminated his face.

"I just had an idea for our game. Especially with this part of the game. The part when we aim towards the hole."

"What are you thinking, Jonathan?" queried Marion.

"I was thinking about the special strokes we use on the landing zone. And I was thinking about what we attempt to do with the ball when we use this stroke. I think we need a specific name for the kind of stroke we use when we have landed the ball on the landing area and aim to put the ball in the hole. Since we aim to put the ball in the hole with one single stroke, I propose that we call that stroke a "putt". What do you think, friends?"

"Jonathan", Marion spoke gleefully, "That is a positively brilliant idea. Though I may be a little prejudiced because you are my smart brother. How about that, friends? Do you agree with my brother to call this stroke a putt?"

Looking around, the friends nodded in agreement. First, they agreed that their friend, Jonathan was brilliant. Second, the friends agreed that the name of this stroke would be a "putt".

"Well then," Bessie continued, "let's call this contest, a "putting" contest. So, let's resume the match. Marion, I believe you are up next for our team. Let's see you make this "putt". A made putt will keep the lasses in the lead."

"Yea! Marion!"

"You can do this", encouraged the other lasses.

And Marion repeated the success for the lasses' team. She putted the ball solidly. "That felt really good!" Marion observed. The ball rolled at the perfect speed right down the middle of the pathway she intended. And rolled right into the hole.

After the first two putts for each team, the score stood, Lads 1, Lasses 2.

The next three lads made their putts. The next three lasses made their putts. The score: Lads 4, Lasses 5.

Time for the sixth and final putt for each team. David Shepherd was the final putter for the lads, and his sister Bessie would take the final putt for the lasses.

David made his putt easily. Lads cheered. Lasses congratulated.

Bess followed her routine to putt the ball. She stood behind the ball and eyed a pathway to the hole. The 'fear of failure' emotion flashed through her brain. To combat the emotion, she knew she should control everything she could control. Following her routine would help her focus on positive feelings. Once she chose the pathway, Bess stood even with the ball and made two practice putt strokes. Satisfied that she practiced the right speed, Bessie placed her club head behind the ball and took her putt.

"Hooray!" Celebrated her lassie teammates.

"Well done, Bessie! I am very proud of you sister. It is not an easy task to be the last one. While you took your turn all the other players on both teams stared at you. So many thoughts race through your head. I could see that you definitely felt pressure on your emotions.

But you knew just what to do. Even more important, you knew just how to do it. You knew you practiced striking the ball successfully when you used a routine. You went through every step of a successful putt in your head. Find the right pathway. Find the right speed. Loosen your shoulders, loosen your arms, relax your hands, finally, loosen your fingers. Take your time and two practice strokes.

Then, step up to the ball. Place the club head in the right position. Then, just stroke the ball the way you planned.

Lasses, I salute your excellence on the putting competition. You won fair and square…today. I think we ought to continue this competition every week. Give us a chance to win another day. What do you say, lasses?"

Bess spoke. "You are absolutely right, David. We should continue putting competition. I think when we putt in front of all our friends it will help us to handle pressure and develop confidence in our ability to putt accurately. Lasses, do you agree that we ought to continue this putting competition with our brothers at least once each week?"

The lasses looked at each other and their brothers. "Competition made the contest thrilling and fun." Marion seconded. "I agree."

The other lasses smiled, "Sure. Let's do a putting competition every week. Of course, we could make things even more interesting with a little wager on it." Rhona suggested.

"What would be a fair wager for winning a putting contest, Rhona?" Asked Margaret.

"I was thinking since we all share the milking chore. You know, the lasses milk every other day, and the lads milk on the opposite days. I propose that the losers do the milking chore for the winners on the next day of the winners' milking turn." Rhona offered.

David looked at the lads and spoke, "Rhona, we accept the wager. The lads will certainly look forward to the next time we have a putting contest. With a wager on the line, I think we just might earn that extra day off from milking."

Jonathan spoke. "Only one player missed the putt at the eight-inch hole. I think we answered the question about the size of the hole. The eight-inch hole does not provide enough challenge. The answer to our original question about the size of the hole is the five-inch hole."

Heather responded, "I agree with Jonathan. Can we make that a unanimous decision?"

A chorus of ayes agreed with Jonathan's proposal. The decision was clear.

Bess laughed, "Yes, David, we will see how it goes next time. You lads will probably need to invest some practice time in putting, if you are going to want to get that day off from milking."

Arm in arm, the winners high stepped all the way to the Swilkan Bridge. When they reached the bridge, they changed their gait. No longer did the lasses step. Triumphantly, the lasses skipped over the bridge and across the final leg of the Links. Not to be outdone, the lads followed. Also arm in arm, the lads matched their sisters' steps at the same pace. Had any of their parents been looking out over the Links at that moment, they would have wondered at what they saw. The parents might have thought they witnessed their sons and daughters practicing a new dance. Maybe, they invented a new dance for the next Festival competition to share with the other communities in the kingdom of Fife.

putt (n.) c. 1300, "a putting, pushing, shoving, thrusting," special use and pronunciation of put (n.). Golfing sense is from 1743.

Chapter 75 | *1399* | Discussion: Fear of Failure

"Last night Robert and I talked. Both of us enjoyed the putting contest. We talked about how we felt during the putting contest. Watching each of you take a turn to putt in front of all of us was fun. I saw that all of you were excited to take your turn.

My turn to putt arrived. I knew how you felt when you putted in front of everyone. The best way I can describe it was feeling pressure to succeed. When it was my turn to putt the ball in front of everyone, I wanted to perform well.

I felt the 'fear of failure'. I was afraid to miss putting the ball into the hole. I feared I might fail in front of you. I wonder if each of you felt the same pressure in the same way when you took your turn." Heather opened the dialogue for the friends.

"Oh, my goodness, Heather!" exclaimed Rhona. "You put into words the same feeling I experienced. When it was my turn to putt I experienced that same pressure to succeed. I felt that same fear of failure."

"Aye. Well said, Heather." Russell. "I felt so much pressure, I could actually feel my hands shaking."

Jonathan the Shoemaker added. "It certainly felt different to take a putting stroke when I knew that others are watching me. When my friends watch me, I felt immense pressure to succeed. When I practice my putting stroke alone, I feel confident. In the putting contest I felt the pressure you identified, Heather."

"At any rate, I enjoyed the competition during the putting competition." Added Robert.

"Of course, I enjoyed the outcome of the contest just a wee bit more than Robert did." sassed the smiling Heather. "Since we lasses were the winners."

Happy lads and lasses crossed over the Swilcan bridge. Robert and Heather, the Carpenters, addressed the friends.

"Ahh, it is true that you lasses played the putting game very well. You were also quite fortunate. Luck smiled upon you. We lads wish to claim another chance to compete as a team against you. Not only do we ask for a new chance to compete, we lads also want to offer a new wager." Russell the Bowyer put forward.

"Russell, thank you for that statement. Robert and I enjoyed the putting contest so much that we wanted to create other contests. We thought that, like the putting contest, we might isolate other parts of our new game. In fact, we want to isolate another short part of the game. We want to make another part of the short game into a contest." Heather offered.

Robert continued, "The intentional design of our game always promises a new opportunity for a player to succeed on the next shot. We already learned that to hit the ball onto the sandy target zone, or what we could now call the putting zone, provided a compelling challenge. Each new opportunity offered a problem for the player to solve with the next shot. New challenges keep players focused on the game at a high level of interest. When the ball rests on the target zone, we can still salvage a good score. If the player sinks the putt on the next shot, she or he succeeds.

The next shot always promises an opportunity to succeed. When we hit an accurately placed second shot, we put ourselves in a good position to achieve success. A well-placed short stroke stops the ball close to the hole. When we use short strokes, we realize how important it is to guide the club precisely. Control of short strokes enables players to pitch the ball accurately towards the target. Execution of effective short strokes demands finesse and control.

Even though the long power strokes and short strokes differ, many crucial aspects of the stroke remain the same. The short stroke differs from the long stroke in subtle ways. When players hit the ball they strive to deliver an effective strike. Creating a good stroke begins with visualization. We want to see the precise pathway to the target. When we apply the right amount of force to the ball and guide it along the proper pathway, the ball will travel just the way we want. The ball will travel the pathway and roll right to the hole."

"Ha! We all get it. That is what we all want to do. We want to do that every time. It sounds so easy when you describe it that way." Jonathan smirked.

"But it is not easy. It is so hard to accomplish." Heather observed.

Barbara added, "Aye. When we do put the ball in the hole, the feeling is so satisfying, so special."

"I think the fact that it is so difficult to put the ball into the hole, is the reason that we feel so good when we succeed." Bessie stated.

"If it were easy to make a good short stroke, if it were easy to put the ball into the hole, we would not experience the intense feeling that accompanies a successful stroke." William explained.

"Are you saying that the difficulty of putting the ball into the hole is the reason that success feels so good in our game?" Marion asked.

"Aye." William answered.

"We have created a game that is very difficult." Bessie said.

"We are also going to experience frustration because the game is difficult." David added.

"True. There will be frustration for every player." Rhona continued.

Robert explained. "Frustration will be the great test of our game."

"In our game, success will come to players who learn to handle frustration." David promised.

Chapter 76 | 1399 | A Pitching Contest

"So, friends", Heather added, "Robert and I propose another contest. In this contest, instead of teeing off on the landing zone, we begin with short strokes. Instead of a drive, we will pitch the ball onto the putting zone. To make the contest fair, each player will pitch the ball from the same spot. After each participant pitches onto the putting zone, we complete the contest by putting the ball into the hole."

"We propose to begin play with the ball some 20-30 yards distant from the putting zone." Robert instructed.

"Does everyone understand the contest?" Heather questioned.

Robert followed up, "Is everyone interested in competing in this contest? If you like the idea, we can perform this contest in the same manner that we played the putting match. We could compete in the contest as teams of six, as teams of four, or as two person teams. Or we could compete as individuals. But, to tell the truth, I want some revenge. I want us to consider continuing competition as the team of the lads versus the team of the lasses. Perhaps, the lads can even up the number of victories. Heather and I think the pitching game will provide a fair challenge of skill."

Heather laughed. "I agree with my brother. Contests pitting the lasses versus the lads provides intense competition between well matched teams. Speaking for myself, I look forward to winning another contest against the lads. Since we agreed to wager our cow milking chores on our putting contest, I think we ought to consider a similar wager on the result of this new pitching contest. The contest sounds like a perfect opportunity to create a very interesting wager. Lasses, I believe sincerely, that my hands could use a rest from milking for a couple of days," teased Heather.

"Oooo, yes!" Chorused the other lasses.

The lads smiled at each other. "Robert, I think our sisters just made another friendly wager with us." Russell acknowledged. "What say you, my lads? Shall we put our sisters to work? Shall we assign the extra milking chores to them by winning this contest?"

"Aye!" Chorused the lads.

"All right! Enough talk. Let's play! I can't wait to start the pitching game." Jonathan challenged the others.

"Wait! Let's be clear." Bessie questioned. "Is the object of the pitching contest to stop the ball closest to the hole? Or is the object of the pitching game to put the ball safely in the hole using the least number of strokes?"

"Argh!" Grumbled Jonathan.

"Aye. Bessie is correct!" proclaimed David. "We do need to agree. What is the object of the pitching game? Before we begin play, we need to understand the rules for the pitching contest. To compete fairly, we must agree to the object and the rules for the contest."

Marion offered her opinion. "I think we need to play this contest as if it is within the larger context of our game. Our putting contest definitely targeted a part of the game. I think the pitching contest should target the short stroke part. I can see an argument for pitching the ball to stop closest to the hole. I can also see the contest as the combination of pitching and putting to get the ball into the hole."

"In the putting contest, we wanted to compete in an isolated part of the game. We agreed that the intent of the putting contest was to put the ball safely into the hole using the least number of strokes. We already agreed that the object of our game, is to putt the ball safely into the hole by taking the fewest number of strokes, so I believe it is only logical that we ought to continue to measure success in this pitching game by putting the ball into the hole." Thomas argued.

"That is quite a persuasive argument in my opinion. I don't think any of us can disagree with your premise, Thomas." answered Barbara. "Does anybody disagree?"

By consensus, the friends reached agreement. The game began from a distance 30 yards away from target zone. David stepped off the distance and marked the spot with a small stick. Each player would first pitch a shot from that same spot. Then, if necessary, each player would putt the ball, until the ball resided safely in the hole.

"However," Bessie countered, "We still have another decision to make for this contest."

"What's that, Bessie?" Barbara asked.

"We agreed to compete by team," Bessie provoked. "But does each person play only her/his own ball? Or do we play by team? By playing as a team, I mean that the team will select the ball closest to the hole, struck by a member of our team. Then all the members will receive a chance to take the next shot. That means, together as a team, we select the best pitch made by any member of our team. All team members then can putt the ball from the same distance unless someone sinks a ball into the hole."

"Oh, I see what you are asking, Bessie." Jonathan interjected. "If we each play our own ball, it is almost as if we are playing the game as an individual, rather than playing as members of a team. I can see playing a contest, even a team contest the first way. On the other hand, if we choose which ball to putt, I think we put an even bigger premium on more teamwork."

"Today, why don't we play the contest by allowing the team to choose the ball they want to putt. Then, everyone will putt the ball from that same exact spot until the first ball is safely in the hole. The team will certainly select the ball closest to the hole today?" Barbara proposed.

Both teams agreed. Bessie was satisfied. Everyone knew and understood the rules of the contest clearly.

The friends walked towards the first putting zone.

Heather stepped to the designated spot 30 yards from the center of the target zone. There she poured the cone of sand to tee up the ball. Since the lads took the first stroke to start the putting contest, the friends decided the lasses ought to take the first stroke to start the pitching contest.

First, Heather took a position behind the ball. There she aligned the direction of her stroke. Without moving her feet, Heather took a practice swing while staring directly at the flagstick. During the practice swing, Heather estimated the amount of energy she would need to generate with her swing. She decided how much force to employ to transfer power from her club to the ball. Heather chose the force that she believed would propel the ball right to the hole, but not send the ball far beyond the stick.

Then, Heather approached the ball. She aligned her feet precisely in the direction she wanted the ball to travel. Heather took two more practice swings to gauge the right speed. She placed her club just behind the ball. She waggled her club. She took a measured backswing. Heather kept her head still. She locked her eyes on the part of the ball she wished to strike. Heather let the club swing down and through the ball. Heather took a short stroke. She stopped her swing short of a full follow through.

The ball leapt from contact with the club. Up and towards the hole the ball flew towards the stick. The ball stopped about five feet short. It was a good stroke, a good shot, and a good result.

"Yea!" The lasses cheered.

"Heather, a shot well placed!" William congratulated their friend.

"That's a great shot, sister!" Robert bragged.

"Heather, I think your ball is perfectly in line with the hole. Why don't you mark where your ball rests? Pick up your ball so that my ball does not collide with it. If I hit my ball as straight as I intend to hit it, and as straight as you hit your ball, I could dislodge your ball."

"All right, Robert. That is a good idea. I will place a mark and remove my ball from your line."

Robert took the first stroke for the lads. He lined his shot between the ball and the flag stick. Robert used a similar routine to the one Heather used. Robert approached the ball, took his practice swings. Then, placed his club behind the ball, and waggled the club. Robert took a carefully measured back swing. Then he swung his club down and through the ball. He stopped his swing about halfway between the point of contact and a full follow through.

At contact, the ball separated from the club. The ball flew directly on-line with the flag stick. The ball just missed the stick. It flew past the hole before coming to a stop about 7 feet beyond the hole.

"All right, Robert!" Roared the lads.

"Surely, we can sink a putt from where that ball lies." David observed.

All the lasses gathered round Robert. Immediately, congratulations poured out.

"A wonderful shot, brother!" Heather complimented. "Between us, we have the target bracketed, Robert. Like our fathers say at archery practice. You know, when one of the archers shoots the arrow perfectly on-line, but it falls short. And the next archer also shoots the arrow on a perfect line, but it flies too far. If we could have put our shots together, we would have put the ball into the hole. That is what our fathers mean, when they say the target is bracketed. At that point they know the range with extreme accuracy. Well now, let's see how well our teammates handle the pitch after they observed how our attempts bracketed the target. Will our teammates get the distance perfect? Who will get the precise range?"

The next lass, Barbara took her turn. She too, followed her routine. Her shot landed off-line. The ball traveled a near perfect distance, but it was about 8 feet to the right of the hole. So far, Heather's shot looked like a better chance to putt the ball in on the next stroke. The lasses decided that Barbara should pick up her ball.

No ball struck by the lasses' stopped closer to the hole than Heather's shot. None of the lads' shots stopped closer to the hole than Robert's. The players picked up the remaining balls.

Finally, it was time for the last lass and the last lad.

"Come on Bessie! You got this!" Encouraged the lasses.

Bessie stepped behind her ball to choose alignment. She recalled the different swing speeds each player used. Bessie had a good idea of how hard she wanted to hit the ball. She thought. "It's not how hard I swing. It's how hard I hit the ball."

Following Bessie's pre-shot routine, she stepped up to the ball. She waggled her club. She made a short backswing. Then, she swung the club down.

Only one question remained. Did Bess choose to hit the ball with the right speed? With unflinching focus on the exact spot of the ball she wanted the sweet spot of the club to contact, Bess kept her eyes fixed until she felt the stroke produce sweet contact between club and ball. The club travelled on a pathway right through the center of the ball. Instantaneously, the ball launched toward the flag stick. On a perfect line toward the flag stick, the ball flew. After she felt the contact, Bess allowed her eyes to look up. She found the ascending ball. Bess saw the ball arc to the apex then descend. The ball continued directly on the perfect line towards the hole. Questions came into her mind: Was the contact too hard? Was the contact too soft? Both thoughts raced through Bessie's mind. Bess believed she hit the ball perfectly.

Bessie knew the ball was going to stop close to the hole. She wanted to keep her feet anchored to the ground. She kept watching the fly toward the hole. Would the ball go in the hole? Or would the ball stop in a placement that would offer a better shot for the team than the placement that Heather accomplished.

"Looking good, Bessie!" The lasses cheered. The ball bounced, rolled, and slowed, and slowed and slowed, until…the ball almost stopped. The ball travelled to the edge of the hole. Then it made one more revolution and dropped into the hole.

"Hooray!" yelled the lasses.

"You did it! That shot was perfect."

Bessie felt great about her shot. However, at the same time, Bess felt a wee bit humbled by such attention from her friends.

The lads cheered Bessie's shot also. "A perfect shot, Bessie." David offered heartfelt congratulations. "So proud. I am so proud of you!" Her brother exclaimed and hugged.

"This contest is not over yet!" Russell shouted. "Our last player is David. I know how good David is at this game. If any lad can match Bessie's shot and knock the ball in on one shot, it is David."

"Come on David!" Erupted the lads.

"You got this!"

And David followed the same pre-shot routine he always did prior to hitting the ball.

David swung the club half speed. The club face traveled down and through the ball. He held his eyes on the spot on the ball he aimed until the last possible moment.

Then, David looked up. He saw the ball travel on a perfect line to the flag stick. Had David repeated Bessie's shot? Had he hit the ball, like Bessie, right into the hole? Would David's shot tie the score for the lads with the lasses? Or would his ball fail to find the hole?

The ball continued to roll on-line. It rolled towards the hole. Rolling, rolling, rolling. Until it stopped. The ball rested one inch short of the hole.

The contest was, oh, so close. Nevertheless, David's ball stayed outside the safety of the hole. The lasses won another contest.

From thirty yards away from the landing zone today, the lasses won!

"I believe I told you, I could enjoy another day without milking." Heather chortled.

"I know you did. Don't worry, I will take care of the milking for you." Robert smiled.

The lasses complimented David for a superb shot.

David thanked the lasses.

The lads complimented the lasses upon winning the short stroke pitching contest. All the lads acknowledged they would gladly pay off the milking chore wager for the victorious lasses that evening. All in all, the lasses and lads rejoiced in the experience of yet another glorious day outside. Across the Links, the twelve friends interlocked arms and danced. Over the old stone bridge they skipped. Joyfully, they laughed and danced their way back home.

Happy and satisfied, the friends rejoiced in the recognition that their new game continued to develop each day. The game offered a pleasing way to experience the wonder of the outdoors. They appreciated their activity alongside the neighboring ocean. Just as the twelve hoped, they savored the joy their new game delivered when played with close friends whom they treasured. Now, it was time to go home, to finish the day's chores, to enjoy family fellowship with a nourishing meal and to get some healthy sleep.

"See you tomorrow!" Friendly happy echoes bounced off the stone walled buildings. Each brother and sister walked home as darkness descended on the town of St. Andrews.

pitch (n.1) 1520s, "something that is pitched," from pitch (v.1). Meaning "act of throwing" is attested from 1833. Meaning "act of plunging headfirst" is from 1762; sense of "slope, degree, inclination" is from 1540s; musical sense is from 1590s; but the connection of these is obscure.

Chapter 77 | 1399 | The Putting Path

"Friends, let's talk about the putting surface. Have you noticed how much time we spend raking sand? Even if it only takes a minute to rake a level pathway for a player on the sandy putting surface that means with four players we spend four to five minutes raking. To obtain a good roll when we putt the ball, we do need a smooth surface, a smooth pathway. Is there a way to eliminate some of that raking time?" William opened the conversation for the friends.

"Aye, William, I agree. Consider how much time and effort is invested every time we get ready to putt. When we rake a new path for each person to putt that takes too much time. Raking sand takes time away from playing. Instead of squandering time by raking up to four different pathways to the hole, I would much rather enjoy our time playing." Margaret reinforced William's point.

"Aye, what both of you say is true. However, a smooth pathway on the landing zone is necessary for fair play. For a ball to roll, a smooth pathway is necessary." Jonathan stated.

"The sand in the target area is way too rough, too choppy and too soft to expect the ball to roll. Without a smooth surface, putting the ball into the hole fails to be a test of skill. It would just be a matter of luck. Each player deserves a smooth putting surface. When a player putts there simply must be a smooth pathway." Heather agreed with Jonathan.

"There is only one rake per landing area. We even wait to take turns to use the one rake." Barbara added.

William responded. "I hear you, Heather, Barbara and Jonathan. We require a smooth pathway for a fair putt. However, I believe there is a way each player can have a fair smooth pathway, without raking a pathway for every player."

"How would you do that, William?" Jonathan asked.

"Thank you, Jonathan. You asked a good question. Let me ask, what would you think if we could rake only one pathway to the hole on the sand and still play fairly? In order to ensure a smooth pathway on the landing area to putt, I wish to propose a different approach for our consideration."

"What are you getting at, William?" asked Barbara.

"Aye, Barbara. I will get right to the point. I think we should rake just one path. When it is their turn to putt the ball each player then uses the same path." William explained. "The idea came to me after we used the same raked path for the putting contest."

Rhona posed a follow up question to William's explanation, "William, how would we get the correct distance for each ball from the hole? Almost certainly all the balls will not land on the same pathway to the hole. For fairness each ball is putted from the correct distance."

"An excellent point, Rhona. To resolve your question, the first step is to measure the distance from the hole for each ball. We are all quite expert at 'stepping off' distances. Since we were toddlers, we stepped off distances with our fathers at archery practice." Russell answered.

"Stepping off the distance is a good approximation for how far away the ball is from the hole. We can accurately use a step off method." William agreed. "However, I think there is far more accurate method to measure the distance for each ball."

"That sounds interesting, William. How would we do that?" asked Robert.

"I propose that we fasten a length of twine long enough to reach from the center of the hole to the outer edge of the landing zone. We attach the twine to the bottom of the flag stick. To measure the distance from the ball to the center of the hole we stretch the twine from the flag stick to the ball. That is how we mark the distance on the twine. Then we simply pick up the ball walk to the putting path and place the ball at the measured distance on the putting path. We will not need to place the ball on the raked path until it is our turn to putt. The distance from ball to hole will be accurate. Stretching the twine to the location of the ball will also be faster than counting off steps."

"Why do we want to measure the accurate distance for every ball from the hole?" Marion queried.

"When we know how far each ball is from the hole, we place each ball alongside the already raked putting path. We place the ball at the exact distance that the ball was from the hole. Does that make sense, Marion?" Russell explained.

Bessie continued, "The player whose ball is the longest distance from the hole is the player responsible to rake a smooth pathway in the sand. The player will rake a smooth, level path from the ball to a distance two steps beyond the hole.

"Why do we rake a path beyond the hole? Asked Jonathan.

"Good question. It is important to rake the pathway beyond the hole so that if a player misses the hole, there will already be a smooth, level area on which the ball continues to roll. The player has a pathway for the following putt."

"Aye. Then, the person who has the longest putt, takes the first putt." Marion understood.

"If the ball goes in, that stroke is counted. If the ball misses and requires another short putt, let the first player complete taking strokes until the ball rests safely in the hole. To get the score, count the number of strokes to putt the ball in the hole." William added.

"Then, the person next farthest away, takes a turn to putt and so on." Heather said.

"When all players putt on a single path, we will reduce the total amount of time spent in raking. What a great idea, William!" Rhona concluded.

Jonathan continued, "Sharing a single putting path solves that problem. We will really enjoy more time to play our new game."

"More of our time in playing our game means more fun for all of us. We will have more fun in the same amount of time we spend in playing the game." smiled Marion.

"And more time for us to enjoy the company of all our friends." Heather laughed.

"Does anyone want to hear my poem?" Bessie asked.

Chapter 78 | *1399* | Bessie Gets an Idea

Shepherds performed their lonely task every day. Bessie and David loved the company of the two working collies. Even though the sister and brother received satisfaction from managing the flock, days on the Links could grow long. When each animal grazed peacefully under the careful watch of the collies, the two often noticed that their concentration wandered. They also realized when they felt freed from intense concentration, their imaginations flowered.

Often Bessie and David granted permission to the other to escape the daily tedium. When granted free time, both often indulged their passion for the game. They invested much of their free time in practice. While one Shepherd managed the task of watching over the flock, the other practiced the strokes in the game.

The Shepherd freed from flock management responsibilities packed stick and ball then headed out to the course. They practiced. Practice was a time to experiment. Both believed that practice offered the best way to develop and to master the many different strokes the game required. Experimenting with different strokes, led to new discoveries.

One might choose to practice the 'driving stroke'. The driving stroke offered great fun. Every time the players watched a ball soar high into the air and paint the sky with beauty, they reveled in the joyful feeling. There was a major drawback to practice the 'driving stroke'. When they practiced the driving stroke, it took a long time to retrieve the ball. Because it took more time to retrieve each long driving stroke, they did not hit the ball nearly as many times as when they practiced shorter strokes.

To work on the 'pitching stroke', the player selected various distances to practice. Pitching the ball with a short stroke was fun. A player could execute several short strokes in the same amount of time compared to hit just one long drive.

Most often, players worked on putting. A player practiced more strokes on the putting zone than any other stroke. They realized the importance of practicing the putting stroke. To improve the putting skill, it was important to develop confidence.

Every single day Bessie and David committed time to develop a smooth 'putting stroke'. Putting on the target zone allowed each player to practice many strokes. Putting practice limited the amount of walking to retrieve the ball. After each putt, it took only a few steps to retrieve the ball. Whether the ball went in the hole or missed, the walk was minimal. Of course, whenever the ball missed, the player took another putt, or enough additional putts to put the ball in the hole. Each time the ball dropped in the hole the player enjoyed a feeling of success. They practiced putting from various distances, and various speeds. The more the 'players' practiced putting, the more confident they grew each time they faced a putt. The more confidence they gained, the less fear of failure they experienced.

Bess and David learned to control the speed of the ball. They studied how to control the direction. Players learned how to control the club to start the ball rolling. More practice meant more success. A high success rate developed a soaring level of confidence. Players realized that success resulted from specific practice. Work to improve putting enabled each player to gain in confidence when they competed during contests.

The putting stroke became a favorite skill to practice for several reasons. First, it was not necessary to practice the putting stroke on ALL the different target zones. All the target zones were of similar size. Except for the two large, shared target zones, each one was circular in shape with a diameter of 25 yards. The similarity of each target zone encouraged players to practice putting the ball in the hole every day. To practice putting strokes, the freed Shepherd usually chose the closest target zone to where the flock grazed.

By practicing on the closest landing zone to where the sheep grazed, the Shepherd remained near the flock in case a problem occurred. Whenever the 'on duty' Shepherd needed immediate help, a pre-arranged blast of the whistle served as a signal. The 'player' quickly returned to sheep herding duty. To secure the flock both Shepherds worked together.

Today, David was 'off duty'. Bessie remained on watch. David practiced making putts from various distances on the target zone nearest the flock.

Comfortably and quietly the sheep grazed. Peaceful solitude invited Bessie to free her mind to wonder. Over the Links her eyes wandered. Bessie always loved birds. Gulls and ravens abounded on the Links. During the many hours she invested observing gulls and ravens, Bessie uncovered much about their various interesting behaviors.

Birds glided in the gusting winds. Gulls and ravens dove and landed on the tidal flats. There, the shorebirds strutted and hunted for shellfish. Neither gulls nor ravens possessed beaks capable of forcing open the shellfish they captured. Nor could gulls or ravens force open the shells with their feet. Even the application of a combination of beaks and feet failed to unlock the shells.

Only by breaking open the shells could the birds harvest the succulent nourishment locked inside. Over the course of numerous observations, Bessie determined that both the gulls and the ravens contrived an ingenious method to break open the hard, thick shells. At a strategic point between the flock and the tidal flats, Bessie situated herself. From there, she observed the busy birds trotting around the wet zone. Whenever a bird located a mussel or a cockle, the trot halted. The birds hunted shellfish that they could dislodge, then grasp in their beaks. Each time a gull captured such a treasure, the bird immediately took flight.

Carrying the shellfish in the beak, each fortunate gull, and each successful raven, flew to its very own special designated place on the Links. But the bird did not immediately alight at that designated spot. Instead, the bird fluttered to attain a predetermined altitude directly above the designated target. The bird knew that the stipulated spot functioned capably for the next step to open the shell. In a stationary hover directly above the target, the fluttering bird released the precious cargo.

The dropped shellfish fell and collided with the hard surface. When the shellfish successfully hit the target, the crash broke the hard shell apart. The bird landed. The broken shell exposed the succulent meat. The successful bird picked out the best parts and devoured the nutritious feast.

Bessie observed gulls and ravens closely over many days. She acquired sufficient data to differentiate and identify individual birds. She noted such characteristics as body markings, vocalizations, and unique behaviors which allowed her to identify individual birds.

Every day Bessie observed animals directly. From commanding the collies to manage the flock of three hundred sheep combined with her observations of the wild animals on the Links she learned much. Bessie determined that most animal behaviors were instinctual. However, she also realized that in addition to instinctual behaviors, some animal behaviors were learned. Bessie was sure that the behavior of gulls and ravens she witnessed to feed successfully on shellfish, was a learned behavior.

Bessie knew enough about gulls and ravens to realize that both species ravenously stole food. They even stole food from other birds of the same species. The robber behavior led Bess to examine the behavior of identified young gulls more closely than before.

Along the rich waters of the Eden Estuary, shellfish abounded. To find the shellfish in its natural habitat, however, was clearly not the same as finding food. Bessie noted that the young gulls who carried shellfish in their beaks watched the mature birds, whenever they carried a shellfish. Each mature gull immediately flew away to its own spot. At the designated target, the gull released the shellfish. The shellfish crashed and broke apart. Opened shellfish became food. Young gulls watched and learned the lessons from the elders.

Bessie observed young gulls imitate the adults' successful feeding behavior. In order to learn to execute the procedure successfully, the young gulls employed trial and error as a process. For the young bird the first task was to find a target rock to break the shell open. After finding a suitable target, young birds learned to hover above it to make an accurate drop. Then, the young gulls experimented to discover the right altitude. If the drop was too low, the shellfish failed to break. On the other hand, if the altitude was too high, other gulls easily swooped down to eat the fresh shellfish before the young gull could get there. The first bird to arrive at the open shellfish, ate the food. The birds learned the "Silverlocks" altitude, the 'just right' height to break the shell and swoop down to consume the meat before other birds could steal the food.

Bessie realized that gulls and ravens acquired learned behaviors as a supplement to their instinctual behaviors. From watching gulls and ravens, she made another observation. When the bird carried a cockle or mussel while flying alone, and no other birds hovered in the nearby vicinity, the bird fluttered about two meters (6 feet) higher than it hovered when potential robber birds flew in the area. The added two meters altitude assured that the shellfish broke open on the first drop.

On the periphery of Bessie's vision, a bright yellow quickening movement caught her eye. The yellow flash flitted around, up, and down. Then, down, and up and through the bushes. She focused on the bright flash. The color did not identify a butterfly, although the flash of color floated almost as ethereally.

Bessie recognized the flash of flitting color as a brilliantly attired goldfinch. Identifying the various birds who shared the Links with the other denizens of St. Andrews brought joy to the lass.

In addition to the bright yellow of the goldfinch, she was familiar with red breasted robins and pink breasted redpolls.

Highly colored feathers adorned the songbirds. Bright colors in motion painted the sky. The tiny birds enhanced the close surroundings with beauty. Bessie paused to ingest the wonder in the moment. She murmured a thankful prayer for sharing moments with such glorious creatures. While engaged in the reverie shared with the flittering songbirds, a flash of insight struck Bessie.

Bessie's moment of wonder, spawned by the appearance of the goldfinch, the robin, and their colors, connected her to a different question. This time she formed questions about birds. Bessie thought, "This bird is about the same size as a field mouse."

Her thought transformed into questions. "Why could the bird fly? Why could the mouse not fly? Between the mouse and the bird, what were the similarities and what were the differences?" Bessie asked herself.

Then, she listed in her mind. "Mice and birds both have tails. Mice and birds both have eyes. Mice and birds both have mouths." Finding similarities came easily, if elementary. However, her responses failed to lead her to either, form a conclusion, or pose a question of real importance.

So, Bessie turned her question around. This time she thought about the differences between the field mouse and the gold finch. She listed the differences. "The tails on the mice and birds are different. The mouse tail was long and narrow. The bird tail was covered with feathers. The feathers could be controlled. The feathers were strong. Feathers folded into different shapes. They prescribed a variety of angles. When flying, the tail feathers aided the bird."

At least Bessie's list of differences contained far more interesting information than the list of similarities. Feathers folded the wings and tail when the bird rested or walked. Feathers spread into various shapes when birds powered into flight or glided. The birds' eyes were on the sides of the face, but the mouse's eyes were located on the front of the head."

Bessie resumed her thinking exercise. She recalled her observations. "The mouse possessed back legs and so did the bird. But the forelegs on the mouse functioned as running legs for speed and balance when the mouse moved. In addition, the forelegs could serve as graspers when the mouse was not moving. The grasping action was very important for the mouse to find food and eat, or build a nest, or even groom another mouse."

"Hmmm, I wonder." Bessie continued to compare and contrast the two animals. "The bird on the other hand, had no forelegs. Instead, two powerful wings were located near where the forelegs would be." Bessie realized one important difference between the flying bird and the non-flying mouse. Then, she thought of another animal similar to a mouse that could fly but was not a bird. These animals came out only as the day darkened into night to fly. They were bats. Bessie knew that bats flew at night because she had heard their sounds later when the night was quite dark.

That was when Bessie realized another difference the bird and the mouse. In fact, it was a similarity for the bat and the mouse. But also, it marked an important difference between the bird and the bat. Different coatings covered each animal species. Hair, or fur covered the mouse and the bat. Feathers covered the bird. Even the tail of the bird was covered with feathers, totally unlike the tail on the mouse. And totally unlike the covering on the bats' wings. But she dismissed the idea about the bats for several reasons. Bats were not nearly as numerous as birds. Even if she could capture the bats, obtaining an appreciable amount of hair or fur from bats would be impossible.

Bessie thought about the hair, the fur covering. She thought about the feathers. And that was when a new idea captured Bessie. This time though, this one time, Bessie decided NOT to share her idea with her brother, David. Instead, Bessie thought it might be fun to share this new idea with the other lasses, and only the other lasses. Bessie treasured secrets. She knew that the other lasses thought secrets were precious, also. In addition, Bessie knew that all of the lasses could keep a secret. She was certain that the lasses would especially enjoy keeping a secret from their dear brothers. Bessie chuckled.

At that moment Bessie reached a decision. Her new idea would be the lasses' secret.

Chapter 79 | *1399* | The Lasses' Secret

"Alright Bessie, pray tell us. Why do you want all the lasses to meet in our shoppe today? Asked Marion.

"And why do you want to meet lasses only, with no lads present?" queried Rhona.

"Good questions, Marion and Rhona. I am excited to share my response with you. Yesterday, on the Links I observed a sight that set my mind to wondering. David and I often cover for each other. I watch all the sheep sometimes. Sometimes he watches all the sheep. By covering for each other, it allows each of us to enjoy a delightful spell of free time. So, yesterday as I covered for David, I watched over the flock alone.

David walked out on the Links away from town. He didn't go very far. I knew David was close enough to hear me signal him with a whistle if I should need him quickly. You all know David loves to hit the ball for our new game. He walked over to a place where he could safely practice his drive strokes.

Really, I watch the collies as much as I watch the sheep. The collies control the flock. It's a fair trade. David and I both enjoy our free time. So, we provide the free time in equal amounts to each other. And I like to hit the ball at the Landing targets also."

"That's very interesting. We know that to manage the livestock you two practice great teamwork. But Bess, what is your point? Why did you wish to bring all the lasses together?" Asked Barbara.

"I am getting to that, lasses. While watching over the flock, my mind wandered. I found myself thinking about our new game. I know I am not the only lass who is fascinated by the game. I think about our new game often. We are all interested in the construction of the new game." Bess explained.

"True!" Echoed the others.

"I especially love winning wagers from our brothers." Emphasized Rhona.

"Even though the wager is only winning relief from a daily chore, the real fun is winning. Especially when we beat our brothers in a contest." Heather agreed.

"If my new idea works as I think it might, I believe that we just may win a few more wagers from our brothers. We can test the new idea without our brothers' knowledge." Bessie continued. "Do you all agree with me, that winning a few more wagers from our brothers, sounds like a good reason to bring the lasses together, with no lads present?

"Aye, Bessie. I think all the lasses are ready for you to share the idea with us." Barbara observed.

"Meanwhile, back on the Links," Bessie crinkled a smile, "My eyes were drawn to a flash of bright yellow. The yellow flitted around the bushes. I thought about the game. Something about the flash of bright yellow challenged me to connect my thoughts with the game. When I focused my eyes on the color, I realized immediately that it was a lovely little goldfinch. My thought became a question; 'Why can the goldfinch fly so beautifully? Why does some other animal, roughly the same size as the bird, not fly at all, beautifully or not?'

There are many different sizes of birds. And there are comparable sizes of other animals to each size of the birds. But the birds fly and flit, dive, and soar through the air. While the other animals, even the same sizes of animals move on the land. At the most, even the swiftest and most graceful can only remain in the air for an instant. Following those brief few seconds of sailing through the air, all the other animals must come back, must return down to the earth." Bessie put forth.

"That is a very interesting observation, Bessie. Your question also raises curiosity. However, I continue to be a bit confused. How did this observation lead to an idea about the game? I still don't understand what you are connecting." Margaret the Tanner redirected.

"I am getting there Margaret, trust me, my friend." Bessie continued. "When a lass shares a new idea with her friends, she wants to explain the birth of that idea. We all know that to be true. I believe that if I can share with you in a way that you understand how the idea arrived, it will help you, my friends, understand the pathway the idea traversed.

Obvious differences exist between the birds and the other animals. In place of forelimbs, or arms, the birds are blessed with wings. And that was where my thinking paused. I thought I was stuck on the wings, as the critical difference between birds and other animals. I didn't give up on the wings as the only important difference, though. I made myself continue to think about the birds.

At that point, I asked myself another question about the differences between the birds and the other animals. I think the answer to that question may have proved pivotal. The other important difference between birds and other animals which I noted, is the material covering the body. Other animals are covered with hair or fur or scales. But birds are different. Birds are the only animals covered with feathers. That difference was key." Bessie smiled and asked. "Does anyone see where I am going at this point, when we think about The New Game?"

Puzzled, the lasses looked from face to face.

"Feathers or fur? Hmmm, the difference between the two coverings does offer some interesting questions. Especially questions about the ball, doesn't it?" Margaret wondered aloud.

"I want you all to think about one more object, which we all see fly, at least once per week, that also has feathers on it. Think of an object with feathers, rather than birds." Bessie offered.

"You must be talking about archery practice. You must be talking about arrows. The arrows that fly straight and true to their marks. We know there is one reason that our arrows fly straight and true. They fly straight and true over a long distance due to the three feathers fletched carefully onto the arrow shafts. Feathers are carefully shaped, then matched to install on the shafts. Three feathers come from one side of the wing. If they don't come from the same wing the arrow fails to fly straight and true. We place one feather perpendicular to the bow string and bow. We call that one, the cock feather. The other two feathers are placed equally distant from the cock feathers, we call those the hen feathers. Instead of spinning, the combination of two hen feathers and one cock feather, perfectly sized, perfectly shaped, and perfectly matched, enables the arrow to fly straight and glide true to hit the target." Barbara the Bowyer spoke. "The feathers are attached to the shaft of the arrow by strong glue."

"Feathers make flying possible for birds. As you stated, feathers increase the accuracy and the flight of the arrows to hit the target. Feather fletchings attached to the shaft enable the arrow to fly and glide smoothly through the air. So, I wondered, can feathers make a difference in the new game?" Bessie asked.

"Are you, perchance thinking about the ball, Bessie?" Asked Marion.

"Indeed, I am, Marion!" Bessie chuckled.

"There is absolutely no way we can put feather fletching on the outside of the ball." Barbara stated.

"Aye, Barbara. I agree." Bessie replied.

"Are you thinking about something new for the inside of the ball? Like maybe, instead of wool scraps and animal hair inside the ball, we stuff feathers inside of the ball?" Rhona asked.

"Aye. That is exactly my thought. Feathers are meant for flight. Hair and wool are not. I think that if we stuffed feathers as the filling, we might produce a better ball. Feathers inside the ball just might make a ball that would fly higher, that would glide farther, than the ball filled with wool and hair. I thought I would rather ask five lasses to see what you thought, than attempt to persuade twelve people at the same time. What do you think, lasses? Do you think we can make balls for the new game in the same size, with the same leather coverings, but instead of filling with wool scraps, we will fill the balls with feathers?" Bessie offered.

Bessie's idea was on the floor for discussion.

"Can we produce a leather ball stuffed with feathers, rather than a ball that is stuffed with wool scraps and hair?" Marion responded. "Of course, we can. I am already convinced. I want to give it a try. I want to do this. I want to make some new balls stuffed with feathers."

"Can we obtain enough feathers for two balls for each of us?" Bessie added.

"And can we obtain a sufficient quantity of feathers to produce twelve new balls, without arousing suspicion among our brothers?" Rhona asked.

Margaret stated, "Sure. Getting the feathers in secret will be fairly easy. While we work on our chores, our brothers pay absolutely no attention to what we do. I think a more important question to consider might be, 'Would there be a safe place we can store the supply of feathers in your shop, Marion?'"

"Aye, there is a secure spot to store a more than sufficient quantity of feathers, Margaret. I have my own space right over here. During chore time, just come over. Bring all the feathers you can gather when you sweep and tidy up. You can place the feathers behind my bench. No one ever looks under my workbench. Then, I will put the feathers in a safe place. This empty wool bag will serve nicely to securely store all the feathers we require." Marion offered.

"Shall we schedule another ball bee'n? However, this time the ball bee'n will be just for the lasses to make new balls. If the lads do ask, we will tell them we are making some new balls for the game. That is a true enough statement." Margaret asked.

"I think we ought to make two new balls for each lad, and two new balls for each lass. The lads' balls will be identical to the other balls we use to play the game. Those balls are of exceptionally high quality. Each lad will receive two new balls. The lads will continue to play with the same balls we already use. Already we know the balls we made are far superior to the original ball. The ball we used when we first began to strike a ball with a shepherd's crook. What do you say that we name the ball the lads continue to use, the 'Hairies'?" Barbara proposed.

"I think the lasses should each receive two new balls. But our balls will not be stuffed with wool and hair. Our new balls will be stuffed with feathers. We agreed to call the balls used by the lads, 'Hairies'. We need a name to differentiate our new balls from the 'Hairies'. What do you think about naming our new balls the 'Featheries'?" Rhona asked.

The other lasses agreed. 'Featheries', sounded like a terrific and descriptive name for the new ball the lasses created.

Margaret agreed enthusiastically. There was another idea forming in her head about the new ball. In that very instant a new thought about the 'featheries' grabbed her mind.

The Feathery
"Golf as we know it was first played with a leather-covered ball stuffed with goose or chicken feathers." ("The Feathery — The Evolution of the Golf Ball") Several pieces of substantial leather were tightly stitched, leaving a small opening. The casing was then turned inside out, and feathers — a "gentleman's top hat full" by measure — were boiled and softened, then tediously stuffed into the casing before the final stitches were made.
The resulting surprisingly hard feather ball was hammered into roundness and finally coated with several layers of paint. Because of the difficulty and time involved in making Featheries, they were relatively expensive. This fragile missile was used for almost four centuries.

Chapter 80 | *1399* | Margaret's Idea

Margaret looked to the faces of the other lasses. She examined the new leather which they prepared in order to make the new balls. She thought about the new balls. She wondered about the balls they would stuff with feathers inside. The feathery inside interested her. However, Margaret's expertise and knowledge centered on the leather shell of the new balls.

At the tannery, Father often experimented with surprising ideas. He searched for ideas so that the Shoppe could meet the customers' wants and attract customers to new product. What could they do to make leather more attractive to their customers? That idea required thinking about their customer's customers, also. He committed the tannery to supply the customers.

Margaret thought about the leather hides in the Tannery. Specifically, Margaret thought about process. Mentally, she went through how the Tanners prepare new hides. Recently, the Tanner shoppe experimented in the development of several new dyes.

The Tanners realized that their customers' customers were comprised of two large groups, those who lived in St. Andrews and the pilgrims who visited. Often the customers possessed considerable wealth. Pilgrims were nearly always eager to spend money in the shoppes.

Pilgrims found the new colors of leather to be quite attractive. The Tannery showed a rainbow of leather colors. The Shoemakers often sent customers to select a specific color for a product or an ensemble of dyed leather at the Tannery. To those customers, paying the higher prices for specific leather colors simply was never an issue.

Margaret believed the other lasses might also enjoy some new leather colors. "Lasses, may I have your attention for a moment? I have a question for you." Margaret proclaimed. "So far, we have only used white leather scraps to create the balls for the game. We treated the leather on the outside of the balls with alum. Alum helps to make the leather balls bright white, and highly visible for the new game.

Recently, in our Tanner Shoppe, we experimented with colors. Our experiments were quite successful. We produced a few new light colors for our leather goods. The Shoemakers bought some leather hides we produced in yellow and light blue, already. Did you get to see those colored hides, Marion?"

"Aye. The new colors are quite striking. We found them extraordinarily attractive, Margaret. We plan to fashion some dainty gloves using the yellow and light blue leathers. We are immensely satisfied with the new colors in leather." Marion acknowledged.

"We successfully produced leathers in a light pink, and a light orange also. When we started the process, we desired to make leathers that were also a bright yellow, in addition to a light-yellow colored leather." Margaret continued. "What I want to know is this, if I can find enough scrap leather available in some of these new colors, would anyone want to possess new balls in those colors?"

"Oh my! Of course. I would much rather have a ball with color, instead of a boring old white ball. The light color leathers drew my attention the first time I ever saw them. I think light yellow is just what I want. That is, if you can find enough scrap for us to make a ball that is light yellow." exclaimed Marion.

"Since Marion showed us how to make the balls for the game, I think she should have first choice for colors. I know I would like a colored ball rather than a white ball, as well. However, I am not picky about which color. I really like all the colors you exhibit in the Shoppe." said Barbara the Bowyer.

"Does anyone have a favorite color? Maybe we have leather of your favorite color in stock already, that is, if you want your balls to be in your favorite color." asked Margaret.

"I do. My favorite color is light pink. At the Lammas Festival, I saw a lady pilgrim wearing a light pink belt. I asked where she found it. She said she bought the beautiful belt at the Shoemakers, while the pilgrims made their way through St Andrews. The light pink belt was so pretty. The color was bright enough to stand out in any crowd. The light pink accentuated her dark blue dress." stated Rhona.

"Alright. Light pink for you, Rhona. Light yellow for Marion. Barbara, thank you for going last. I think we can find six different colors. I would like bright yellow. So that means that already three colors are chosen." explained Margaret.

"Ooooo! May I get bright blue? Blue is my all-time favorite color. I think the bright blue will be easy to see on the Links." asked Heather.

"You surely may, Heather." responded Margaret. "Two lasses left."

"Why don't you pick, Bessie? Really, I do like all colors. So, any color is good with me." Barbara emphasized.

"Thank you, Barbara. Going last and taking whatever color remains is magnanimous of you." stated Bessie. "I truly love the light orange leather. The light orange color reminds me of the robins when they return to the Links, announcing that Springtime returned."

"Okay then," Barbara concluded. "That leaves the bright orange leather for me. Bright orange will standout boldly on the sand and grass of the Links. As it so happens, I do love bold bright colors."

"The colored leathers will certainly help us to keep track of the feather balls." Bess stated.

"Yes, the lads will continue to use white balls." Rhona added.

"I think this experiment is going to be fun." Heather offered.

Barbara blurted, "I can't wait to play with our new balls!"

"Alright then. The sooner we get to work on making these new balls, the sooner we will get to hit them. The sooner we get to play our new game on the Links." Margaret urged.

"And the sooner we can begin the experiment. Let's get to work, lasses." chimed Rhona.

"Aye, I can't wait to find out how the 'featheries' fly!" Bess exclaimed.

Chapter 81 | 1399 | The Lasses' Surprise

All the lads stood on the final putting zone. They raked a putting path to mark the entire diameter of the putting zone. Three lads stood on each side of the hole along the putting path. They took turns putting every third ball from the same spot.

"Hey David!" shouted Rhona, as David lined up his putt.

The lads looked up to see all six lasses headed their way.

"Hey yourself, Rhona!" David responded.

"We brought a surprise for you lads!" Barbara announced.

"I love surprises!" Thomas exclaimed. "We wondered where all our lasses disappeared to. Jonathan told us you were at the Shoemakers with Marion."

"I love surprises also!" agreed Jonathan. "The lasses were very busy. As soon as they all arrived, they told me that they had 'woman's work to do'. They shooed me out of the Shoppe."

"Surprises from smiling lasses are the best!" William agreed. "Especially surprises from sisters!"

"We truly believe that all of you will enjoy the surprises we brought." Margaret stated.

"As Jonathan told you, for the better part of two days we have all worked together. Every moment we could find, we worked together on this surprise." Heather declared.

"Did you lads even notice that your sisters were not around? I bet not. Probably all six of you were out here on the Links, selfishly playing the game. Not even one of you gave a second thought to the whereabouts of your sisters." Marion teased.

Russell responded. "Marion, that's hardly fair to us. Whenever I asked Barbara why we were not seeing the lasses on the Links, she shooshed me away. Barbara always said, 'Go on with ye, brother. Don't bother any of the other lasses or me. We have some important women's work to do together.' Isn't that true, Barbara?"

"Aye, Russell, that I said. Brother, could you not tell that Marion and I were merely teasing you and Jonathan a wee bit?" Barbara smiled.

"Aye. Barbara has been known to tease me a wee bit now and then. So," Russell smiled, "what is the surprise that caused you to keep yourselves hidden from your brothers for a full week?"

"Anyone want to guess?" Rhona asked.

"I will take a shot. Does your surprise have anything to do with the new Game?" David questioned.

"That is a great guess." Rhona answered. "And the answer is, aye!"

"Alright lads, if you want a surprise, close your eyes!" Marion commanded.

Jonathan said, "Marion loves that rhyme. And whenever she says it, she gives me a delightful surprise."

All the lads closed their eyes.

"Keep your eyes closed. Good! And hold out your hand!" Bessie added.

The lasses enjoyed the sight of their brothers standing with eyes closed. Each one held out a hand. The lasses smiled at each other. In unison each advanced to her own brother. Each lass plucked two brand new shiny white balls from her pouch. Each lass held her brother's hand open.

"No peeking!"

"Keep your eyes closed!"

"Don't spoil the surprise!"

"Wait! Wait!"

"We want you to all get the surprise at the same time."

"This is fun!" Thomas exclaimed while keeping his eyes tight shut.

"Aye. It is fun for us too." Margaret responded to her brother. "Keep your eyes closed tight. We are going to put the surprise in your hand. Then, we are going to close your fingers. Wait until we say, 'Open your eyes, alright?"

"Aye!" the brothers answered in unison.

Each lass placed the balls into her brother's hand and closed his fingers. Each lass stepped back. At a nod from Marion, the lasses sang out, "Open your eyes!"

When the lads looked at the shiny new white balls their eyes opened in wonder.

"Wow!"

"What a wonderful surprise!"

"This is great!"

"Thank you, so much."

"I can't wait to hit these balls. They are so white they sparkle!" Thomas exclaimed.

"But you lasses don't have new balls. Is that fair?" William worried.

"Ha! You are wrong about that, William. We have another surprise!" Marion proclaimed.

Each lass reached into her pouch. Each lass pulled out her own two brand-new balls. The lads also noticed the difference right away.

"Why are your balls not white?" William asked.

"We did not see any reason why all the balls should be white." Bess proclaimed.

Barbara added, "You lads all know that bonnie Scottish lasses love color. You surely know that we appreciate adding color to our lives in every way possible."

"There were enough different colors including in the leather scraps, that we were each able to choose our own favorite color. Don't you think the covers for our balls display beautiful colors." Margaret explained.

"The colored balls are a grand idea, lasses." Russell judged. "However, I am happier with my bright white ball than if you gave me a yellow, or pink, or orange ball. So, thank you for the surprise. And thank you for making two new white balls for me."

"I must agree with Russell." David said. "The colors of the balls the lasses chose are lovely. However, I believe I still prefer the sparkle generated by the bright white ball. If it makes you lasses happy to play with the balls of different colors, then I am happy also."

"Hey!" shouted Jonathan. "Doesn't anybody want to play with our new balls?"
"Aye! Jonathan. I agree. Let's go play!" David exclaimed.

Chapter 82 | *1399* | The Lasses' Request

"These new balls possess truly high quality workmanship. They are exquisitely crafted." David restated his appreciation for the surprise gift. "The seams are almost invisible. I can barely feel any stitches. The shape is as near to a perfect sphere as I can imagine. The leather covers look hard and durable. When I compare the quality of these balls to the first ball we hit, the new balls rate far superior. Possessing these balls makes a difference as we design our new game. The new balls make playing the game far more enjoyable."

"Aye!" agreed William. "The balls you surprised us with are so much better than the original leather ball. Indeed, in my opinion these new balls appear to be better made than the single new ball you and Jonathan made for each of us. I look forward to playing with these new balls. I am amazed that you could make so many balls."

Heather acknowledged, "We worked very hard. We worked secretly because we love to surprise our brothers. We wanted to surprise you. Stitching is the trickiest part of assembling the balls. We felt with each ball we produced we improved the quality. Special thanks go to Marion. She showed us how to improve our leather stitching techniques. She even shared secrets on how to tie tiny knots."

Jonathan proudly stated, "Remember when we first talked about making a ball for each player. I told you then, Marion is an artist in stitching leather. My sister is a leather stitching genius."

"Aye, Jonathan. You were right about that. You must agree that these surprise balls are magnificent." Thomas stated.

Bessie interjected, "It is true that Marion taught us how to improve our own stitching techniques. However, you lads should know, Marion still does the most crucial and the most difficult stitching. To finish each ball, Marion completed the final stitches. After we carefully stuffed as much wet filling into the wet leather shells as we could manage, Marion tied the final knot."

"Watching Marion finish the stitches amazed all of us. She expertly applied hog bristles to guide the thread into and through the tiny holes. Hog bristles are strong and flexible. Then she secured the final stitches. To complete a quality job rapidly, we practiced teamwork. All of us worked on stitching and stuffing the leather shell. That way we freed Marion so she could concentrate on completing the final stitches. We accomplished our goal as a team! We produced two more new balls for each friend. In two days, We completed a total of twenty-four new balls. To make two dozen balls in only two days required us to commit to teamwork." Rhona concluded.

Robert stated, "Wow! I am impressed. What an awesome job you accomplished!"

"On behalf of the lasses, I say 'Thank you!' Barbara answered. "But as hard as we worked, the task depended on Marion's skill. Her leadership drove us to finish the job in only two days!"

Russell shouted, "Three cheers for Marion! Hip, hip!"

"Hooray!"

"Hip, hip!"

"Hooray!"

"Hip, hip!"

"Hooray!"

"Friends, please. There is no need for such flattery!" Marion blushed. "Your kind comments embarrass me. All of the lasses brought their diverse talents, their special skills, their creative ideas, and discipline to work to our Circle. In order to solve problems as we strive to develop our concept of a new, fair, game we collaborate willingly. I am honored to contribute my talents. When I contribute, I feel like I do my part. To invent our new game requires that we combine the skills, the talents, the ideas and the discipline to work that each of us possess. Our duty to each other demands us to speak up and offer our ideas to the group. You all know that what I say is true."

"I thought we were ready to go hit our new balls to play the game," complained the ever impatient, Jonathan.

Bessie laughed, "You are right Jonathan. We are ready to play. However, before we play, we lasses have a request."

"Come on…" Jonathan whined.

William ignored Jonathan and questioned. "What is your request? I am certain that all the lads will gladly wish to honor whatever you ask."

"All right, then. The lasses request that we play this first game using the new balls as foursomes. We want two lads and two lasses in each foursome." Answered Bess.

"That's not a problem, Bessie." David replied.

"Thank you, brother. But that's not all we are asking. We wish to add a wee bit more to our request. We want to group the foursomes by age. So, that would mean foursome one contains the four oldest friends. Margaret and I are the oldest lasses. William and Robert, the oldest lads." Bessie stated.

"Heather and I are the youngest lasses. Jonathan and Russell, the youngest lads." Marion announced.

"That leaves, Rhona and me. We will play with Thomas and David." Barbara added.

"Okay. We assigned our foursomes. I hope everybody is happy. Finally. Now are we ready to play?" complained Jonathan.

"Aye. Jonathan. I believe we are now ready. Let's go play." Rhona said.

"At the end of the round, we want to get the whole circle to meet after the final hole. We would like to have a large group discussion. Does anyone object to that?" Bessie concluded.

"Hmmm, that request sounds ominous!" Robert replied. "And fun!"

No one objected.

The friends headed to the first tee. Group one led off. As soon as they teed off for the second hole, Group two followed. Finally, Group three teed off.

Chapter 83 | *1399* | Debriefing After The Round

Following the round, all twelve friends circled around the final hole. They sat in an arrangement that allowed each friend to make eye contact with whichever friend spoke. Eye contact with each speaker demonstrated how the friends valued opinions and observations from each person. Polite behavior was one way of sharing respect for each other. Listening to the speaker without interrupting was polite behavior. Making eye contact and actively listening to the speaker was even more important than polite behavior. The friends knew that when they listened and made eye contact with the speaker, they also sent a powerful message to the speaker. The combination of good posture, eye contact with the speaker and no side talking told the speaker, "I value your opinion. I want to understand you clearly and accurately. You are important to me. What you say is important to me."

Bessie opened the Group Discussion. "Lads, thank you so much for respecting our request. It was important to us to play in the age grouped foursomes for the first time that we all played the game with brand new balls."

William responded, "That was no problem Bessie. Any time we can meet your requests brings joy to the lads. To enjoy playing the game in foursomes with you, it will not be necessary for you to bribe us with new balls. Nevertheless, playing our game with the new balls was a truly delightful experience. Thank you again for this wonderful surprise gift of two new balls apiece."

"Actually, there is still a wee bit more to our request, William."

"What might that be?"

"We have a question. We want your honest observations and response. We want to ask if during the round of play with your foursome you noticed something." Bess began.

David responded. "The high-quality workmanship came through in performance. The balls fly straight. When we putt on the sand pathway the balls roll true. The new balls are a pleasure to play."

"Have you observed anything different during this round of our game from any other rounds we played the game?" Bess specified.

"Playing a round with the brand new balls was different. I did notice a difference while the lasses played with the colored balls compared to the lads play with the bright white balls." Observed Jonathan.

Russell agreed with Jonathan, "Speaking of differences, the lasses in our group crushed some extremely long drives. When the lasses struck the colored balls, the balls seemed to climb, to soar and to fly through the air so beautifully. The colored balls seemed to just hang in the air for the longest time."

"In fact, as I recall, in our foursome, the lasses outdrove the lads on every hole today. I know you lasses are all strong drivers. Certainly, you lasses are at worst equal in striking the ball for distance skills to each of us lads. On other days, it is not unusual for a lass to drive the ball farther than a lad. However, before today, most days that we played the game, the lads usually drive the ball a wee bit farther than a lass of equal age." Thomas added.

"Was there a reason you wanted the players in the foursomes to be of equal ages?" Robert questioned.

"Aye, there was an important reason." Bess responded.

"Did the reason the lasses consistently drove the ball farther than the lads, today, have anything to do with the new balls? Russell continued.

"Aye, that was a reason." Margaret replied.

"In our foursome, the lasses drove their new colored balls farther than the lads drove their new white balls on every hole but two." William noted.

"What was the experience in your foursome?" asked Bessie.

"As I recall, the lads drove their balls farther than the lasses on only four holes." Jonathan answered.

"That is very interesting information. We all received new balls to play at the same time. We built foursomes that contained players of the same age. So, when we played the game today, we eliminated age as a variable." Barbara explained.

"The lasses' balls and the lads' balls measured identical in circumference size. The lads' balls were white. But the lasses' balls were different colors of leather. Today, the lasses' balls travelled farther than the lads' balls, almost every time. Yet, whenever we played the game before, most of the time the distances are quite similar, the lads hit the ball farther than the lasses a wee bit more often. Except, of course when Heather hits the ball compared to any of the lads." Robert surmised.

"Lasses, did you, per chance, perform an experiment without telling us?" David asked.

Bessie answered, "Aye. We did perform an experiment with you."

"Were you attempting to determine if there was a significant difference in distance between colored balls, hit by lasses, versus white balls, hit by lads?" Inquired Russell.

"That is a good question." Rhona chuckled.

"I have a request." William stated.

"What is your request?" Barbara snickered.

"Do you think we could hit the colored balls?" William finished.

"I think that is an even better question. Lasses, what do you think? Are you willing?" Bess grinned.

"Only if we lasses hit the new white balls." Barbara smiled.

"Aye. Let's do it." Marion commanded.

Each brother and sister traded balls. Each lad hit two colored balls. Each lass hit two white balls.

After we switched new balls with the lasses, I remember asking, "What were the results?"

The lasses wanted to know the answer to that question. The lads wanted to know the answer, also.

The answer to that question was that there was a significant difference in the results. Every lad but Jonathan drove the ball much farther than his sister. Jonathan's drive was only a yard shorter than Marion's.

"Hmm," mused William. "Does this data mean that colored leather balls travel farther than white leather balls?"

Bessie smiled. She looked each lass in the eye. Each lass returned Bess's smile.

"Aye. Your conclusion seems valid, William. The colored balls do indeed travel farther than the white balls."

"Who would have thought that colored leathers would have produced such a difference?" David asked.

"Just a minute! Wait a minute!" Russell exclaimed. "Let me see the balls. I want to compare my white balls to your colored leather balls, Barbara."

Barbara tossed Russell's white ball to him. Russell held one white ball and one of Barbara's light orange balls. "The two balls feel very similar. To my eye, the two balls look the same. To my fingers the diameter of the two balls, colored leather, and white leather, feels identical. But hmm. I believe I detect a difference. I feel a slight difference in weight. I believe the white ball is a wee bit heavier than the colored ball." Russell stated.

Each lad asked his sister to allow him to judge for himself. Was there indeed a difference in the weight of his new white leather ball, compared to the weight of his sister's new colored leather ball? From each lad, Russell received confirmation of his observation. Each white ball did seem to be a wee bit heavier than each of the colored balls.

"Is that the difference, Bessie?" Russell asked. "Is that why you wanted to observe the oldest play versus each other?"

"Russell, your observations are correct. We did want to see if there was an observable difference in the performance of the colored balls versus the white balls. Besides the color of the leather coverings, you discovered another difference. You observed there was a wee bit of difference between the weights of the white balls and colored leather. However, we can assure you that the weight difference is not caused by the color of the leather."

William understood, "Okay. There is a slight weight difference. The difference is not the weight of the leather coverings. The balls are identical in outside measurement. The thread is identical. That only leaves one conclusion."

"What is your conclusion, William?" Bessie queried.

"The inside of the colored leather ball is different from the inside of the white leather ball." William responded.

"Aye. You have it, William." Barbara stated enthusiastically.

"All right then," Thomas asked, "Our new white balls feel the same as our old balls. What is different about the white balls and the colored balls? The old balls were stuffed with wool scrap and hair. What else would you use to stuff inside a leather ball, besides wool scrap and hair?"

Bessie looked at the five other lasses. Each one of the lasses returned Bessie's look. She winked at the lasses. Then, the six lasses counted out loud, "One, two, three!"

"Feathers!" Six lasses sang in unison.

Chapter 84 | *1399* | Keeping Score

"How can we intensify the player's interest? What can we do to make every shot important throughout our game?"

"What do you have in mind, David?" questioned Rhona.

"Think with me," David responded. "When we participated in our putting and pitching contests, we were intensely engaged. We all talked about feeling the pressure to succeed. We named that pressure 'a fear of failure.'"

"The intensity brought great excitement to the strokes we took. A pitching stroke or a putting stroke, it didn't really matter what stroke we performed in front of our friends, our feelings were important." Rhona added.

"While hitting the ball is fun, when we faced possible failure in front of our friends, our hearts beat faster."

"Robert, I could feel the blood pumping through my veins right down to my fingertips." Barbara agreed.

"I became aware of my breathing rate. I felt out of breath. I took a deep breath to calm myself."

"Russell, I did too." Marion said.

"I held my breath." Jonathan confessed.

"All of us felt the intense excitement." Rhona summarized.

"Right. That is it. What I want us to consider is how can we pack that kind of intensity into every stroke for our players?" David brought the discussion back. intense, we need to find a means of making every shot feel as important as we felt the 'fear of failure' in when we hit the ball in front of our friends."

"I think you may have already said what we need to do, Heather."

"What do you mean? What did I say?"

"David, you asked, 'How can we make every shot important?' Another way to ask that question and capture the same meaning, is to ask, 'How can we make every shot count?'" William explained.

"I like that."

"I like it, too. Bessie!" Barbara agreed.

"Oh, I see what you mean. Let's COUNT every stroke!" David understood.

"We all know how to count!" Jonathan exclaimed.

Chapter 85 | 1399 | Match Play

"For example, as we play each hole, we count the number of strokes each player requires to get the ball in the hole. We start counting from the tee shot. Then we continue to count strokes until the ball rests safely in the hole."

"We could explore several ways to keep a score as a team."

"I like playing in groups of four. With four people we don't seem to wait so long for our turn. Playing with three friends allows plenty of time to walk and talk. We also enjoy a teammate. A teammate can offer support and pep during the game. All of us have seen and felt how helpful cheerful support and belief lifts our game."

"If we play in a format of one person against one other we do play very fast. That is an advantage. However, then we play versus one opponent. We only have one friend to talk with. That is a disadvantage."

Bessie continued, "When we keep score with the hole scoring method, we realize that three outcomes are possible. The first possibility is that a player 1 or a team 1 sinks the ball in the hole in a fewer number of strokes than player 2, or team 2. When team 1 uses fewer strokes to putt the ball into the hole then team 1 wins the hole."

"The second possible outcome occurs when Team 2 sinks the ball in fewer strokes than Team 1. Then team 1 loses the hole to Team 2.

The third outcome is when Team 1 and Team 2 require the same number of strokes to complete. With the hole scoring method that means that neither Team 1 nor Team 2 won the hole. When we count the number of strokes for each player to put the ball into the hole, and at least one player from each team produces the same score as a player on the opposing team, there is a tie. Because there is a tie score for the hole, no team wins the hole. When no team, wins the hole, then we say that the score for the hole is nil. Or we can say that the hole is shared or halved." David expounded.

"Each time a player, or a team, wins a hole, they count one whole number for their score. For example, when a team wins the first hole, we say that means the team is 'one up'. When the same team wins the second hole, we say that team is then 'two up'. And so on." Robert stated.

"If Team 2 wins the next hole. Then, the score for Team 1 is subtracted by one whole number. Team 1, which was two up, is only one up again. If Team 2 wins the next hole, then the score is tied, or "all square." Heather explained.

"We have 8 holes going out and 6 holes coming home. That makes a total of 14 holes to play. In hole scoring, we will keep count of which team wins the most holes. Whichever team is one or more up at the end of 14 holes, that team is the winning team." David noted.

"Keeping track of scores by hole works when we play one person against another person. It also works when we play one team versus another team. All we have to do is keep track of the number of holes each player or team wins." Jonathan agreed.

"Who wants to play by teams?" asked Marion.

Chapter 86 | 1399 | Team Best Ball Scoring

"I have a question!" Heather exclaimed. "I love to play the game by competing as part of a team. I really want to keep the idea of playing the game as members of a team. I know it is fun to play the game alone. I agree. Keeping score of one's own accomplishments is fun, too. Whenever one of us is free, we can always play the game alone. In fact, we have already invented two ways of scoring for individual play. For keeping track of all the strokes for an entire round we have stroke scoring. We designed the hole scoring method in order to keep track of which player won the most holes. What if we consider how we might set up another method to keep a team score?"

"At the very beginning we wanted to create our game so that we would enjoy fun time with our friends. I do not recall that we intended to design our game to require individual competition all the time." Margaret commented. "Do you already have an idea in mind to fashion a team score, Heather?"

"Aye. Heather, like Margaret, I am interested in how we incorporate teamwork into the game." Barbara interjected. "Every time we worked to solve a problem for our game together as a team, rather than as an individual, I noticed something. I noticed that I experienced a good feeling when we shared our ideas. We shared smiles. We shared in the experience of those same good feelings. I wonder, do you think there may be another way to design a score keeping method? Can we design a method which leads us to work together towards winning as a team? Is there a way to compete that would help us experience those same good feelings when we succeeded in overcoming obstacles and problems?"

"Barbara, thank you. You clearly articulated the exact issue that concerned me. I want the team to work on a scoring method which would incorporate true teamwork." Heather clarified.

"You mentioned you have an idea, Heather?"

"I did and I do, Rhona."

"Lass don't be shy. Please, tell us, what is your idea?"

"Barbara, let's consider the method we devised to score the contest by counting the number of holes each player won."

"Heather, I think you are referring to the method we called, "hole scoring"."

"Aye, Margaret. My idea is to keep score of each hole as a team, the hole scoring method. To do that, we keep track of the lowest score earned by a member of each team. The player who puts the ball into the hole in the lowest number of strokes wins the hole for her/his team."

"So, to help us understand, Heather, can you give us an example of how this idea works?"

"Hypothetically, we all play Hole Number One. One person on the team puts the ball in the hole in four strokes. No one else on either team matches that four stroke score. She wins Hole Number One for her team. Her team is now, 'One Up'."

"But what happens if another person on the other team makes a four also?"

"Just the question I wanted, Barbara. Your question helps me to continue the explanation, thank you. If even one person on the other team matches the four, then neither team wins the hole.

We can say that for that hole, the score is nil. Or we could say the score is halved. We might say that the score for that hole remains even."

"Sure, Heather. We can select the name for the terminology, later. Right now, we want to understand the concept."

"That's right, Margaret! So, in this team scoring, at least one person from the team must score lower than anyone else on the opposing team to win the hole."

"Yes, Margaret!" Heather brightened. "If two, or three, or even all four members of the first team score lower than any one person on the opponents' team, then the first team wins the hole."

"I think I see. I like the idea, Heather. I believe the idea you explained is a fair method to keep score. I think keeping score by hole as a team will strengthen our appreciation to work together." Margaret added.

"Not only do I agree that you offered a fair way to keep score. I think this sounds like a fun way for teams to keep score." Rhona offered.

"I see this method as an extension of our hole scoring method." Barbara said. "The lads already agreed that the hole scoring method is fair and equal. I don't see how they can disagree with this manner of hole scoring the game for teams. Who wants to explain this score keeping method to the lads?"

"Bess, would you make the explanation to the lads?"

"I certainly can, but I believe Heather will do a great job. She explained the concept to us. How about it, Heather? Would you like to present the scoring system to the lads?"

"Aye. I think it will be an honor. But if I stumble, will you step in and help me?"

"Certainly. We will all be right there with you. We have your back!"

"How shall we select teams?" Rhona asked.

"Will it matter how the teams are selected?" Barbara wondered. "I don't really think the method used to select teams will matter too much. However, it will be important that at least one of the better players is a member of each team."

"Let's go find the lads. We will explain Heather's idea. Then, we will see if the lads are up for a fun match playing the game." Margaret stated.

"What shall we name Heather's idea for keeping score when playing the game as a team?" Rhona asked.

"How about we name this method, 'Heather's idea'?"

Rhona looked at Barbara. Barbara looked back at Rhona. Then, Barbara looked at Margaret. Then, Barbara and Rhona looked at Margaret.

Then, Barbara, Rhona and Margaret simultaneously looked at Heather.

"No!" All three lasses responded in unison.

Heather countered, "How about we call this scoring system, 'Team Best Ball'?"

"Team scoring sounds like a great way to have fun. In Best Ball scoring, each player plays his or her own ball from tee to the hole. Each player keeps track of the number of strokes she or he took to put the ball into the hole.

At the end of the round, players report the number of strokes for putting the ball in the hole.

Each team determines the lowest score for their team. Then, the team identifies the player with the lowest score. The best score on the hole for each team is compared to the best score for the opposing team(s). When one team reports a lower score than all of the other teams, that team wins the hole. That team goes one up. If no team wins the hole, the score is nil."

Chapter 87 | 1399 | Scramble Scoring

Following completion of daily chores, all six lads met at the Weavers' Shoppe. The lads called a meeting to talk about more ideas for the game. Specifically, the lads wished to discuss new ways to score team play.

Russell, Jonathan and Thomas, the three youngest lads and best friends brought an exciting new concept for team scoring to the meeting. Originally, the idea ruminated and rumbled about in Russell's head for a few days. Russell decided to share the idea with Thomas and Jonathan. By sharing with the two younger lads initially, he could comfortably test their reaction to the idea. Thomas immediately thought Russell's idea worthwhile. Thomas encouraged Russell to present the idea in the meeting with all six lads. Jonathan agreed with Thomas. Presenting Russell's idea to all the lads to examine and discuss offered exciting possibilities for the game.

"Lads," David signaled to all the lads. He informed William and Robert that the youngest three wished to offer an idea to the group for discussion. "What have you brought us?"

Thomas spoke first. "Russell thought about ways to score the new game for team play. He puzzled over what we can do to make the game interesting and fun. He shared an interesting idea with Jonathan and me. Jonathan and I really like Russell's idea. We agree that scoring the game in the way Russell designed offers a way to play the game as a team that will be exciting and fun."

Jonathan added. "Thomas and I believe that Russell's idea for scoring the game will reinforce teamwork. We also think that Russell's idea will add a level of excitement by rewarding team play."

"The way we score the game offers a true opportunity to reinforce and enhance team play. Russell, please tell the whole group what you shared with Jonathan and me?" Thomas directed.

Russell thanked Thomas and David for introducing him. "To begin play each member of the team takes a regular tee shot. After every player on the team finishes the tee shot, team members observe where each ball lies. After looking at all four balls, the members of the team decide which ball offers the best possibility for the next shot for the team. Then, all team members hit a second shot from within a club length of where that ball lies."

"Following the second shot, team members repeat the same process. During the game, following each successive shot, team members continue to choose the best shot. Because team members always hit from the lie of the best ball, we should produce very low team scores."

"In fact," David observed, "Russell, I feel sure that you are correct. By playing and scoring this way, compared with any other way, teams will produce much lower scores."

Robert added, "I agree with your conclusion David. Russell, you have done well. This idea of yours does sound like a fun way to keep score. In addition, we will highlight the joy depending on each other and playing as a team."

William looked at the other five lads, who returned his questioning stare. Then, his face broke into a smile. "The idea of selecting the best lie to hit for the next shot offers a great idea. Getting really low scores will add to the fun. I already envision differing strategies to this game."

"So can I," agreed Robert. "On the one hand, we can take chances, because we know our teammates can help us recover from a mistake."

"On the other hand," William continued, "I think there is room for strategic play. Someone on the team may need to make a safe shot for the team."

"When should a player go for the safe shot?" David asked.

"When should other players take a high risk shot?" Asked Robert.

"We still must choose whether to make a safe play or take a high risk shot when we play alone to go for a low score. When we decide as a team when to take a high risk shot, or a safe shot the importance of making choices will be magnified." Thomas added.

Russell continued. "While I was thinking about designing a team scoring method, I realized that I wanted the questions of play safe or high risk to remain. I know that decision making is an important mental aspect. Shot selection is something to think about and talk about as teammates. In addition, I wanted us to feel exhilaration when our team makes a really low score."

"Really, by keeping score Russell's way when we play as a four-person team, the team receives four opportunities to make a good shot." Jonathan added.

"Even if three players hit bad shots, one player can 'save' the team from three bad shots, with one good shot. The team only needs one good short each time." Thomas shared.

"I think playing the ball with the best lie will really add to the fun of this scoring method."

Chapter 88 | *1399* | Team Alternating Shot Scoring

"Bessie, why aren't you sleeping?" David whispered.

Bessie giggled, "David," she echoed, "why aren't you sleeping?"

Neither David nor Bessie could catch sleep. Thoughts about the Game raced haphazardly through both minds. Each felt challenged to find an idea to improve the Game. They focused on how to invent another way to keep score for team competition.

Despite Father's slight snores, Mother and Father slept comfortably.

"Because I can't stop thinking about the game."

"I know. I feel the same way. I know we talked about different ways to score the game. However, I believe other ideas still remain for us in our quest to develop the game. Building challenge and intensifying interest added to the enjoyment of the game. I wonder, can you and I invent a different way to keep score for the game?" Added Bessie.

"The game is fun when I play alone. When I practice parts of the game I enjoy myself. However, for me, playing the game with friends is way more fun than when I practice parts of it by myself. I especially like talking with friends while we play. Complimenting friends when they execute a good shot feels like a great way to share the fun."

"Aye, I agree with you. Complimenting friends on a successful shot shares the satisfaction. In addition, I find that talking during the game also offers an opportunity to tease friends, good naturedly. Especially when a player mishits the ball. Whenever, I hit a '*thunk*', instead of a "THWOCK!", I can rely on Jonathan or Robert to needle me with a zinger. When I don't get teased after such a flub, I feel like my friends let me down."

"Needling and teasing can offer good lessons for us. When a trusted friend teases us, we know that such comments are meant to help us. For instance, it is important to remember that while our game is fraught with "danger", in reality there is no real danger to the safety of the player. The danger is only to a good score in the game. When our friends tease us while we play the game, they help us maintain a proper perspective."

"I am sure you noticed that all of our friends do not share the same skill levels for the game."

"True. I noticed something else about skill level. Skill level does not seem dependent on how strong, how big, how tall, or how small the player is."

"Some friends excel in certain parts of the game. In other parts of the game those same players lack skill proficiency."

"Aye. While the remaining friends excel in precisely the parts of the game that are so difficult for others."

"What if...?"

"Whenever you start with those two words, I think you already formed an idea in your head. Is that true at this time?"

"Aye, 'tis true. However, just because I formed an idea, it does not mean my idea is a good one. That's one reason why I value talking with you so much. You challenge me to communicate my idea clearly. I want my explanation to be clear enough that you can truly grasp the idea as well as I understand it."

"Sometimes to understand what idea to bring, presents a big challenge to me. But then, when I do comprehend your idea, it's like I see the candle burn brighter. You share ideas that are so compelling. So, what is this idea you conjured? Do you think this idea will compel our friends to become more intensely involved and enjoy the challenges the game offers?"

"I am thinking about these questions: What might happen if, rather than each person plays his or her own shot each time, what if we assign two players to a team? Especially, what are the possibilities if we were to pair players who excel at different strokes in the game? And then, consider how we might form a scoring system where the players take alternating shots? What would be the strengths and weaknesses involved in playing and scoring the game when the players alternate shots? One advantage is that players contribute the strongest parts of their game to the team. On the other hand, while playing with teammates, players confront the most challenging parts in their game."

"Ha! Now who would have thought of such a strange, convoluted way to score the game? How did you conjure the idea of using alternating shots between team members? Only you could have thought of a method as unique as this concept to score the game. I am really intrigued by this approach to scoring the game."

"Quite often, you think my ideas are crazy as a loon, David. But you always wait until I explain the logic. Usually, you continue to listen beyond that first reaction. That is one of the most important reasons I look forward to sharing my ideas with you."

"True. Yet, after you explain what you want to accomplish, Bess, you often convince me that the idea can work well. Not only will the idea work well, but it will be fun. So, convince me. Why will alternating shots be a fun way to play the game as a team?"

"Alright. Here we go. We need some time together to think about this scoring method. Let's think about a team consisting of two players. Player one hits the ball long and straight from the tee. Near the landing area however, that same person doesn't play so well. Player one could improve her/his overall game by developing finesse and accuracy.

Player two does not hit the ball from the tee nearly so long as player one. However, when player two hits from within 50 yards of the hole, he or she is almost always in the hole in three strokes or less. At first thought, it would seem the best team strategy should be to have the person who is best at hitting the ball longest always hit the ball first."

"That seems quite simple then. Doesn't seem like much strategy involved. The 'big hitter' takes the long shots and the 'skilled short game player' takes the close in shot."

"That was what I was thinking, at first. But playing alternate shots does not mean that every hole will work out that way. Remember the players must alternate shots. That means the strategy of having the big hitter hit the tee shot will not be available each time. The strategy you describe will work only for the first two strokes. After that, who knows?"

"Unless the skilled short game player hits the ball in the hole on the second shot. In that case, the strategy is over."

"Sure. And almost no one will hit the ball in the hole on the second shot. For a short hole, even our best players think three shots is a good score. Putting the ball in the hole in three shots remains the target for a good score. Four shots for a medium length hole marks a good score. For the long holes, we agree that five shots makes a good score."

"Well, since the strategy is over after shot number two, unless the second shot goes in the hole, why would we want to play with alternating shots?"

"I am so grateful when you ask the very question that bedevils me. That was my puzzle. But I think I can offer a persuasive reason to play with alternate shot scoring. In fact, I think the reason affords even more challenge to both players on the team."

"Now I am curious. You just agreed that when the 'Big hitter' tees off first, and the skilled short game player takes the second shot, the strategy for alternating shots was over, following the second shot. At that point, the strategy ended."

"Do you agree that the purpose of the game is to have fun?"

"Of course. The game is designed for all players to have fun. Finding ways to challenge the players to adjust strategy and execute shots, will make the game even more fun."

"Do you agree that playing the game with our friends is an important part of playing the game?"

"Absolutely. We designed the game to be played with our best friends. We placed the game on a course in the out of doors. We designed a specific pace to play the game. We designed a pace of play for participants to enjoy a good walk, during which they could talk, joke and tease with each other. During the walk up to the ball, there is time to pause, time to think, time to talk, and time to share strategy for a particular hole."

"So, think about what can happen when players who possess different levels of ability use "alternating shots" scoring. Players do get to hit shots which they hit the best, sometimes. And then at other times, players face shots that offer the biggest challenges to their individual game."

"I am not yet convinced. I still don't see why you think hitting shots that are the most challenging for a player is an advantage to 'alternate shot' scoring?"

"The chance to pause, to think, and to talk about a shot with a teammate is important. We are all competitive. We all play to win.

A teammate offers support. A teammate shares in analyzing the situation. Such support and analysis help the player develop and strengthen skills. The more skilled player can coach the less skilled player. She can advise the less skilled player how to approach the shot and the hole. Teammates are invested in helping each other because, they must play the result of their teammate's next shot."

"Ah! I get that. Coaching a player to pause, and to think, by talking about hitting shots on the course, provides an excellent opportunity for players to learn. Two players discuss the choices for a shot. Discussion about how to make decisions about shots, helps both players strengthen the mental aspect to the game. While I like this about alternate scoring, I still don't understand why the skilled player would enjoy 'alternate scoring.'"

"For the more skilled player to enjoy 'alternate scoring' other advantages exist. I will begin with this reason. Suppose we tee off for a long hole, one shot long enough that a good score is five strokes. To enable our discussion, let's suppose that on the preceding hole, the long hitting player made the putt. Because of alternate scoring, the skilled short game player is required to tee off."

"A scenario like this sounds as if that alternate shot scoring would be a disadvantage to me."

"I agree. It is a disadvantage, for that particular hole. However, when we play and use other methods of scoring, the skilled short game player is facing the same shot she or he always faces. So, the 'big hitter' must think ahead. Players want to envision the specific shot faced at the moment. Both players must see the problems presented by that hole. They think about the best place on the fairway for the partner to land the next shot. After making that visualization, the two players need to share information. They arrive at a decision for the landing spot by reaching agreement together."

"Well, if the short hitter partner hits the tee shot, the ball will not land where the 'Big Hitter' normally hits a second shot when playing on the long five stroke hole."

"Exactly the point I want to make. The 'Big Hitter' will receive a different look, a new look, at the hole. Instead of the ball resting from the normal shot played, the ball will be much shorter in length than the normal shot on the fairway. Therefore, the next shot will require a new strategy. After the two players see the position of the lie, they talk about the new problem. To create a strategy to achieve a successful score, they work together. For the skilled short game player, the teammates need to visualize where they want the next shot to land. The two players come to agreement about their landing target.

"On the other hand…."

"Well, what else are you thinking about? Whenever I hear that phrase, I know you have another idea. I know you have been thinking about something else."

"I was thinking that we could add more strategy. We could add more strategy by allowing the teams to pick which player would hit the first shot at each hole."

"If that is the case, would not the long hitting player hit every first shot?"

"At first, I thought it might seem that it is always best to allow the more skilled player to hit first. Then, I thought more about the different holes we play. For example, when we play some short holes, the accurate short stroker might give the best shot for a low score."

"How would that occur?"

"Consider that if the accurate short game player is able to hit the ball onto the landing target in one stroke, that player may land the ball closer to the hole. Then the long hitter player gets the opportunity to make an easy putt. The team puts the ball into the hole on the very next stroke for a score of two."

"True. On some of the short holes, the short accurate hitters never miss the Landing Area. If the short hitters can reach the landing area in one stroke, they could give the team the best shot at scoring a two. I agree with that strategy, because they get the ball so close to the hole at the center of the Landing Area."

"And on those holes which we think that a five makes a good score, the short accurate hitters can get the ball to a good place for a second shot. The accurate player could conceivably drive the ball to a great spot on the fairway. A good lie for the second shot would allow the big hitter to take a chance, by using a big swing for distance. In fact, it is possible that on a couple of those holes, the "Big Hitter" obtains a good opportunity to reach the Landing Area on the second shot.

Or at least land the second shot very close to the target zone. That would also make the third shot right into the accurate players strength to place the ball on the target zone."

"Who would have thought that the invention of an 'Alternating Shot' scoring system would offer so many possibilities to design team strategy and demand teamwork?" David asked.

"Duh! Of course, your magical sister would have thought about that!" Bess crowed.

"Aye. Why did I ever ask such a question? Especially with my magical sister next to me?"

"At the same time, whenever two players invest time, share thoughts by talking about each stroke, and select a target, both players benefit. Investing the time to think about and learn more about the game rewards both players. To improve in the game, players commit to develop new individual skills continuously. To maintain their ability to execute strokes effectively, players must practice skills as part of a daily routine." Bess explained.

"I look forward to presenting the concepts for the 'Alternating shot' scoring system with the team. I predict that once team hears about the ideas they will be interested. When we explain the strategic options, I think they will agree that this approach to team scoring will offer a lot of fun to play the game."

Chapter 89 | *1399* | The Importance of Being Honest

"Let's recall our original thoughts when we agreed to create a new game. Let's revisit our purpose." Bessie opened the discussion.

"We wanted a game to provide us with time to enjoy the company of our friends. Do you remember how we valued our fellowship connection?"

"Aye, that's true, Heather. We placed a high priority on fashioning a game where we could enjoy time with our friends. We incorporated time with friends as a goal. We paced the game to invite talking and enjoying companionship." Rhona remarked.

"Having friends whom we can trust, is a treasure with no price," William pronounced. "We realize that friendship contains a commitment. In the same ways that we connected to this point, our connections will continue to grow and mature throughout our lives."

"I believe we succeeded in achieving that goal. Our game gave life to our dream. We created several ways to compete. When we participate in our game, we play and compete as teammates and as friends. Would you all agree?" David mused.

"Aye, David." Answered Jonathan. "We have fun each time we head out on the Links to play the game!

"No two times does the ball land at the same place," Russell observed. "Every shot, each stroke is different. Sometimes the difference is just 'a wee bit'. Each time we take a stroke, we encounter a new challenge. We confront a new problem to solve. We assess each problem. We decide how we want to strike the ball. After taking a swing we know immediately if we made the solid contact we envisioned or not."

"The game provides an exciting experience every time." Margaret added.

Thomas agreed. "Each round we play we encounter the course in a new and different manner."

"Bessie and I think about our new game often. Recently, we came up with a different way to think about our new game. The two of us share ideas several times every day."

"Sometimes," Bessie continued, "we cannot play the Game with friends. You are busy working in town. We shepherd on the Links every day. During those days, either David or I can sometimes play the course alone. We encountered a new situation. We asked, 'Can we devise a scoring system which will allow us to compete with the same intensity, even if our friends are not with us? In other words when we play alone on the course, can we compete?"

"That is a thorough explanation. I look forward to learning the scoring system you explain." Heather stated.

Robert asked, "Is there a way to share the results of our round with other friends and competitors at a later time?"

"In this scoring system, Bessie and I wanted to maintain the idea of the game as a contest."

"That is the reason why we wanted to devise a different approach to score the game." Bessie continued.

"That's very interesting. I am intrigued by this scoring concept. There may be opportunities for us to get away and play when no one else may join." Barbara added.

"Aye, Barbara. We hope all of you will access the course as often as you want to play. Even if no other friend can join you. We want to increase opportunities for each one to get to the course as often as possible. And we want the play to be meaningful."

"True. We could each practice and play around the course alone. Practice on the course is important." Jonathan observed.

"But we feel the urge to compete. This game encourages us to compete and to improve." Russell continued.

Barbara explained. "Even when we walk the course alone, we want to compete. We want to experience the thrill, the spirit, even 'the fear of failure' that we constructed into the game."

"The game is exciting!" Marion exclaimed.

"Keeping score, nay, sharing score adds intensity." Heather expounded.

"When we play together, we know that keeping score enhances the feeling of competition." Bessie continued.

"Our parents taught us the advantages of being honest with each other." David began.

William spoke, "They are all honest with each other."

"In our parents' business dealings, honesty, trust, and fairness go together."

"True, Rhona. When merchants and tradesmen establish reputations based on honesty and fairness with each other, and with customers they find success."

"I agree, Barbara. As Shoemakers, we trust the Tanners to supply us with quality leather and glue, at a fair price, delivered on time. If we cannot depend on them to deliver, we could not stay in business. We trust the Tanners with our livelihood."

"Marion, I believe we have proven that we trust each other. Without trust at a high level, we would not have created this game. For the scoring method we propose that high level of trust and integrity is paramount. There is nothing more sacred to a Scotsman than his honor, his word and his promise".

"David and I believe that complete honesty and trust is necessary for this scoring method when you play alone. We trust you completely." Bess concluded.

Chapter 90 | *1399* | Stroke Scoring: Par for The Course

"When one plays the game alone, we view the competition as a contest between the player and the course."

"How can you have a contest with the course when you play the game by yourself, David?" Barbara asked.

"That is the appropriate question, Barbara. Often, Bessie and I work on the Links with sheep and collies for our only company. Even with no friends available to join us on the course, we still want to play the game.

We began by asking, 'How can we play the game alone and have a contest?' We think we found an answer. We invented a way to keep score for the individual player. Before we did that though, we came to a realization. We realized we already assigned a score to the course."

"I don't get it. How does the course score?" Jonathan wondered aloud.

"Excellent question, Jonathan. Bessie and I discussed that very question. From the time a player tees off, until the stroke that putts the ball into the hole, count how many strokes were taken. Each time we play a hole, we add the strokes to our score. So we keep an accumulated score as we play.

Jonathan, I want you to recall an earlier discussion. Do you remember when we reached agreement as a group concerning how many strokes made a good score for each hole?"

"Aye, David. I remember. We discussed that question thoroughly. I remember the concerns. Eventually, we all agreed upon a fair and reasonable number of strokes to reach from tee to each landing area. We also changed the name from landing area to target zone. Then, we checked the comfort level from each person. All agreed on the fair score."

"Well stated, Jonathan. That is the way we remembered that discussion as well. Bess and I decided to put that information to use. To each hole, we assigned the agreed upon fair score. That was how we determined the score for each hole on the course." David continued.

"Keep in mind the set number of strokes on a given hole. That number is the score for our opponent, the course.

For example, let's look at all fourteen target zones for the Links. Bessie and I want to share with you what we believe is the fair number of strokes for each hole. On our course, there are 14 holes."

OUT		Yards	Par
	HOLE 1 -	339	4
	HOLE 2 -	375	5
	HOLE 3 -	321	4
	HOLE 4 -	401	5
	HOLE 5 -	325	4
	HOLE 6 -	335	4
	HOLE 7 -	145	3
	HOLE 8 -	261	4
	OUT TOTAL -	2,502	33

IN		Yards	Par
	HOLE 9 -	296	4
	HOLE 10 -	150	3
	HOLE 11 -	304	4
	HOLE 12 -	377	5
	HOLE 13 -	326	4
	HOLE 14 -	342	4
	IN TOTAL -	1,795	24
	ALL TOTAL -	4,297	57

To keep our score, we count the number of strokes we take to get the ball in the hole. The number of strokes is our score for that hole." Bessie restated.

"Remember, the holes we believe we can reach the target zone in one stroke, the short holes. We agreed that after the ball landed on the target zone, we should use no more than two strokes to putt the ball in the hole. For the course, count one stroke to get the ball onto the target zone, plus two strokes to putt the ball into the hole."

Bessie concluded, "We all agreed that we should require no more than three strokes to putt the ball in the hole on the shortest holes. Does that make sense, Barbara? Jonathan?"

"Aye. It does make sense. I remember that day, too. Deciding on the fair number of strokes to put the ball into the hole is an interesting idea. We did all agree to those numbers for each hole. I want to hear more about how you arrive at the scores." Barbara stated.

"Okay Barbara. We agreed that on the short holes, the course gets assigned a score of three. David and I decided to call the short holes, 'threes'. If the player puts the ball into the hole in less than three strokes, the player wins the hole. But if it takes four or more strokes, the course wins the hole in the contest against the course. If the player scores a three, the player and the course tie the hole." Bess answered.

"The longest holes require three good strong, accurate strokes for each of us to reach the target zone on a good day." David explained. "We agreed that a good player can reach the target zone on the long holes using no more than three good strokes.

Again, after the ball rests on the landing zone, we expect to putt the ball into the hole using no more than two strokes. By adding the three strokes to rest the ball on the target zone, plus the two strokes to putt the ball into the hole we sum three strokes plus two strokes, which equals a total of five strokes. So, we call these longest holes, the 'fives'. When we put the ball into the hole in less than five strokes, we beat the course on the 'fives'. When we score a five, we tie with the course."

"The remainder of the holes, those longer than the 'threes', but not as long as the 'fives', we call, 'fours.'"

"Are you following along with us? Is our explanation regarding the score for each hole clear to you, Jonathan?"

"Aye. David and Bessie, the scoring makes perfect sense. In addition, the idea is excellent. Your reasoning is also easy to follow."

"Easy to follow the scoring concept, aye. Yet somehow I do not believe beating the score for the course will be easy to accomplish." Robert observed.

"To beat the course requires great play." William added.

"However, if I match the assigned course score for a hole, I believe I achieved a great round. I think that matching the score assigned for the course is a cause for celebration. Matching the score set for the course is our goal. When we achieve our goal we feel good." Margaret offered.

"All right. From your comments, I see that you understand the concept of playing against the score for the course on each hole." Bessie resumed.

David explained, "Now, we want to make the contest for the player against the whole course. To learn the score for the course, we sum the total number of strokes from the holes that are 'threes', plus the total number of strokes from the holes that are 'fours', plus the total number of strokes from the holes that are 'fives.'"

"That sounds pretty complicated." worried Jonathan.

"Well, I guess that I made the score for the course sound complicated. For making this scoring method sound complicated, I apologize, Jonathan. However, once you begin to visualize each hole as a three, a four, or a five, I am pretty sure you will think differently." David sympathized.

Bessie helped, "Really, thinking about the holes in this manner is not complicated. When you gain experience playing against the course, while you keep score by counting your strokes, you will actually begin to think of the holes as threes, fours and fives."

"For us, assigning the hole as a three, a four, or a five, simplified the way we think about scoring the game. Especially when thinking of our score in a contest versus the score for the course."

"David illustrated the rationale for how we produced the fair score for the course." Added Bessie. "The course always gets the same score. Every time we play the game, the score for the course is the same. The course can never score better. By the same token, the course can never score worse."

"In stroke scoring, the player continues to assess each shot, must consider the choices available for the next shot, must select a shot and then must execute the shot. I see the advantage of competing against the course. To me playing against the course advances my spirit of competition." David explained

To differentiate and identify this means of scoring, we designated the term, 'stroke scoring'. Following our discussion, does the explanation make more sense, now?" Bessie asked.

"There is another advantage to 'stroke scoring'," David continued. "We can also use 'stroke scoring,' to play against each other, even if we are not playing together at the exact same time. We can play one player versus another player and employ the 'stroke scoring' method in a direct competition.

Or we can compare each player's score against all of the other players' scoring for that round of the game. At the end of the day, we can determine one winner. In addition to knowing who won first place that day, we will know who finishes with the second lowest score, third lowest score and so on. Eventually, we identify every player's score from first place to last place."

Bessie emphasized, "In stroke scoring, we keep a careful, honest accounting of the number of strokes taken for the entire round. Every stroke counts. At the end of each hole, we add the number of strokes taken for that hole to the previous number of strokes we have taken for that particular round of play."

"We won't know the winner of that round until the last player completes the round and states the score. What do you think of 'stroke scoring' and playing against the course?"

Chapter 91 | *1399* | Playing Versus The Course

"The player might choose to play safe for a particular stroke. Or maybe the player decides to take a risk. For example, the player may decide to try to hit the ball further than on a normal stroke. Because I know the score for the course, I consider that in my decision-making process. I decide to play a safe stroke, or I decide to take a risk on a more dangerous shot. Those decisions affect my strategy for the game on that particular day, at that particular time." Bess added.

"We would like to open a discussion about this scoring method. Can we start with this question? Do we all agree with the strokes that David and I assigned on each hole?' Bess asked. 'Jonathan, what do you think about these scores for each hole? Is the number of strokes for each hole fair for you? If you are playing well, are you able to make the scores we estimated for each hole?'"

Jonathan answered first, "I am the youngest of all the friends. At this time, I am the smallest lad. Of course, that also means I have the longest opportunity to continue to grow and get stronger." He chuckled. "We began our mission to design a game that would be fair to every participant. My opinion really matters for the purpose of this discussion. If I decide I can reasonably expect to make the score if I play well for each hole, then we can all reasonably expect to reach the hole in that number of strokes. I know I don't always hit the ball as far as Robert, or William, or David, or Heather, or Bessie, yet. However, all of you see that my skills are improving, and I am gaining strength rapidly. Every time I practice, every time I play the game, I hit the ball farther. In addition, I hit the ball straighter and with more control.

As I look over the yardage for each hole, I make an assumption that we are playing the game on a fair day. We can define a fair day as a day when the wind is not howling at gale force. If I also assume that I play to my capabilities, there is no hole that I think I cannot reach, in the allotted number of strokes. That assumption is provided, of course, that I make smart decisions. I select the right strokes. Then I execute the stroke. I agree with Marion. If I play well enough to make my score match the course's score, I met the challenge. In other words, if I come close to making that score, say I miss the score for the course by five strokes, I will feel very good about the way I played the game that day."

William commented, "Jonathan, just because I hit the ball farther than you now, does not mean that I possess a great advantage. Because I hit the ball farther, the times that I do not hit the ball squarely and accurately, I can hit the ball to a worse place than someone who does not hit the ball for as long a distance as I hit it. My ball could be in far worse shape for the second shot, because the ball did not come to a stop in a good place. If I can produce a score close to 54, I will feel very good, too. On the other hand, if I do hit the ball accurately and long, there is not one hole that I could not reach in the number of strokes the way David and Bessie assigned to the course's score. I agree with Jonathan, playing the game by counting my strokes versus the score for the course truly does offer a fair challenge to play the game."

David asked, "Marion and Heather, you two are the youngest lasses. Your opinion about playing against the course is just as crucially important as was Jonathan's opinion. The score is challenging to William and me. We know the score is a challenge. The question remains, is the score for the course fair to you? We want the game to be fair to every player, regardless of size, regardless of strength. You heard the thoughts from William and from Jonathan. You heard the rationale from Bess and me. We need to hear from you. What do you think?"

Heather began, "First, I agree with everyone. Attaining a score of 54 for the entire 14 holes offers a demanding challenge. On the other hand, that precise difficulty makes pursuit of the challenge worthy. We have to keep in mind that the course does not truly play the game. The score for the course is a standard. That standard was set in ideal conditions. For the course, the score is constant and consistent. The playing conditions will not matter to the course. To us as players, the way that the wind, the rain, and other changes in the weather affect and challenge us matters. We will continue to keep scores. We will keep scores whether we play against other as individuals or as teams. The weather and surface conditions will affect all players fairly equally. That means the further challenges will also be fair to competition between individuals and teams. So, I am good with the selections made by Bess and David. I agree with what William and Jonathan said about the Course Score."

"Well said, Heather." Marion chimed in. "True, we wanted fairness. Building challenges into our new game became as important as designing and constructing a game that was fair. William and Jonathan, I appreciate the points you made to this discussion. Those were thorough, well thought, and well-articulated points. I am in total agreement with the points you made. I do think that this concept of a score for the course may be an important consideration as we go forward. I have not pondered all the possibilities. I plan to apply considerable thought into what we can do when we play in direct competition with the Course's score."

We know what we expect to shoot for each hole. When we hit good shots on each hole, we have a target for comparison. If we make a 54 or less, we know we played the course quite well for that day. To keep score, all I have to do is count each stroke. If I take 54 strokes or less, I win. I beat the course. If I hit 55 strokes, or more, for the entire fourteen holes, the course wins. That stated, I believe 55 to be an excellent score. When I play, on some holes I beat the course. If I put the ball into the hole the number of strokes we designated to make, I win. On some holes the course beats me. On some holes, we could also say that the course and I match scores.

Matching the score for the course is the target. To match the expected score is a good score on a hole. If I can match the score on a hole, that means that I hit the target for which I aimed. In archery, the object is to hit the target. In fact, whenever we hit the target, we win. If I am able to hit the target on every hole for the course, I know I made a good score. In my mind, when I hit the target, I win.

"David and I introduced the concept of counting strokes to put the ball into the hole to compare the actual number of strokes to the expected number of strokes for that hole. When we employed the term, 'playing against the course', that is what we mean. By knowing which holes are threes, fours, and fives, we already know the number of strokes to make a good score. The course cannot change. The numbers of threes, fours, and fives will always be the same. Therefore, the course always scores the same."

"When I play against the course, to keep score is quite simple. All I have to do is count each stroke I take. To tally the number of strokes I take is a simple task. At the end of the game, after I finished all fourteen holes, I compare the number of strokes I took to the number of strokes we agreed for the course score. If I score the same number of strokes as the course, or fewer, I beat the course that day. The number of strokes, my score, tells me how well I played that round. If I score more than the number of strokes determined for the course, the course won the game that day."

The friends were silent. They felt satisfied. They smiled. Each pair of eyes sought each friend. They made deep eye contact with each other. They communicated without speaking.

Until, Marion asked, "Do you remember what day it is tomorrow?

Chapter 92 | 1399 | Michaelmas

"Aye!" sang the other eleven voices. "It's Michaelmas!"

"We did it!"

"We created a new game!"

"Remember when we set our goals?"

"Remember when we discussed what we wanted?"

"Remember when we decided what we did not want?"

"I remember when David and Bessie showed us that old ball."

"I remember when William spoke about 'Tug of War' and working together!"

"We shared our ideas, our skills, and our talents to arrive at consensus. We agreed to commit our energy to make a game. We wanted a game to challenge us. We have such a game."

So engrossed in their discussion were the lads and lasses that they failed to notice twelve adults walking towards them.

"Well, well. What have we here?" Father Weaver surprised the friends.

Mother Shoemaker teased, "I wonder what this crew has been up to."

"Since Lammas, I noticed these young ones have spent a lot of time out here on the Links with David and Bessie." Chuckled Father Shepherd. "I wondered if there were ten new shepherds. If so, Mr. Weaver, perhaps we ought to enlarge the flock."

"I have the same question. Mrs. Shoemaker." Reiterated Mother Tanner.

"I cannot take my eyes off the workmanship in these sticks." Father Bowyer admitted.

"I must agree. The joinery is amazing." Marveled Father Carpenter.

"The sticks look like they are custom fitted to each lass and lad." Observed Mother Bowyer.

"The finish is high quality. Look at the wrapping. Look at the application of lacquer. The finish is so smooth, I just want to wrap my hands around it." Mother Bowyer admired.

"Aye. The finish on the sticks are as smooth and beautiful as magic wands." Commented Mother Tanner.

Barbara, Russell, Heather, and Robert blushed. Praise heaped on their craftsmanship by the parents made them feel uncomfortable. Jonathan made sure everyone noticed. "Look at our friends the Bowyers and the Carpenters. They are all turning red."

"Jonathan," William soothed, "Let's respect their feelings. When some people are praised they feel embarrassed.

"I think you are right, William. I did feel embarrassed." Heather quickly changed the subject. "I think we should show our parents what the Shoemakers designed and created for the game."

Each lad and lass pulled out one of the wonderful, identical chicken egg size balls. Identical except for the color covering the balls the lasses owned.

Mother Shoemaker spoke first. "This is wonderful leatherwork. I cannot see or feel any stitches. How many pieces of leather do you think they used, Father?"

"Hmm, that is an intriguing question, Mother. It is difficult to say when I have not found the seams. The seams are so well sealed. They have been glued as well as stitched. Then there is a substantial lacquer coating. I could see a four piece, but if I were to design a ball this size and hardness, I think I would use three pieces. Well Marion, Jonathan, how many pieces did you use?"

"You are correct, Father. We did use three pieces. Two identical circles and a rectangle."

Father Tanner complimented. "The workmanship is impeccable."

"I love the colors." Mother Tanner added. The other mothers agreed.

Rhona praised, "Marion's stitchery is the secret. She makes the stitches so tiny. She finished off every ball. Jonathan showed us how to cut and drill the patterns to make identical balls."

"Thank you, Rhona. Mothers and fathers, you should know that making the balls was a total team commitment. Jonathan and I could make three or four balls in a day. When all the lasses came to help, we made a dozen balls in one sitting. Margaret came up with the idea for the colored balls. All the lasses agreed color was a grand idea."

"Alright. You made sticks and balls. What do you do with them?" Questioned Father Carpenter.

"That is the best part. That is the fun part of the game."

"Aye!" Shouted Jonathan. "We smack the ball with the stick! Mother you have to try this!"

"Let's get organized!" Bessie stated. "First, families group together. Lasses share your stick with your Mothers. Lads with your fathers."

"Robert and Heather, before we smack some balls would you talk everyone through the 'hammer grip'? Your mother and father already know how to grip a hammer." David smiled.

"Mothers and lasses stay here and make a line. Fathers and lads, step off 15 yards and make a line across from your family. Lasses, show your mothers how to hit a ball to your fathers. We will practice hitting balls by taking turns until everyone gets a feel for how to use the club to stroke the ball."

Mothers squealed with delight when they struck the ball. Fathers waited anxiously for their turns. Competitive juices flowed immediately. Laughter accompanied well placed shots. Teasing and encouragement the same for missed shots. Bessie and David moved the lines backward as the Mothers and Fathers improved their strokes quickly. When the lines reached 50 yards apart, Jonathan shouted, "Let's play the game!"

William called everyone into a tight formation so they could talk using a comfortable volume. "I think Jonathan is right. It is time to play the game."

"Hitting the ball with a stick is so much fun." Father Shepherd observed. "I thought we were playing the game."

"You mean there is more to the game than hitting the ball to each other. That was exhilarating!" Mother Weaver added.

"We agree! That is fun! But that is just a drill. That hitting is to get you warmed up. David and Bessie invented that fun drill for us." Barbara explained.

Russell said, "Playing the game is way more fun than the drill."

"I think we should start playing the game with Mothers and Fathers by using a scramble." Margaret offered.

"Why do we need a scramble? Did someone bring some eggs? I'm not even hungry a wee bit." Father Shoemaker joked.

"Dad…" Jonathan groaned.

"Well Jonathan," William laughed. "We can all see who you get your sense of humor from."

"Aye. That's true, William." Mother Shoemaker sighed. "At least you know Jonathan came by that sense of humor from his father, honestly.

"To play the game, we will use the skills you just practiced on the course. We will play as family foursomes. Each person will have a ball. Each team can share two sticks. This will be a scramble. Lasses and the lads will explain the concept as we play."

"Each family will play all fourteen holes. We have six families, six foursomes. We will start from six different holes. That way we will all finish the course about the same time."

The families enjoyed walking and talking while they played. Parents were impressed with how the target zones fit right into the natural beauty of the landscape. They appreciated how the Shepherds sculpted fairways to the target zones. Father and Mother Shepherd praised their children for expertly rotating the grazing areas on the Links.

The mothers and fathers loved playing the scramble format. Later, the families would play using other scoring methods. All could see advantages to each type of scoring. That first day, the parents were enthralled. They embraced their children.

Mother Weaver spoke, "Children stand here for a moment, while we parents have a chat. You can hit the balls if you want. But wait for us. We will be with you shortly."

When the entire twenty four person group reassembled by the Old Stone Bridge, Father Tanner spoke for the parents. "Lasses and lads, your parents have always been so proud of you. We trust you. Our trust, our faith in you has been well placed.

This game is wonderful. You succeeded in creating a fair game that is fun and challenging. We all look forward to playing the game again as soon as possible. You know what that means, don't you?"

The lads and lasses looked at each other. Marion spoke up, "I guess it means…we will schedule time to gather on the Links to play?"

"Aye, that's true. But it means more than scheduling. It means you are going to need to make twelve more sticks and two dozen more new balls. One dozen in white and one dozen in colors to match mother and daughter colors." Mother Tanner explained.

"But don't worry. When you make the equipment this time, you will show us how you did it. You will teach us. Then, we will help you." Mother Bowyer said.

"We are sure that our friends who live in St. Andrews will want to learn to play this game too."

"To play, they will need equipment."

"They will need to schedule a time to play on the course."

"Aye, not only have you created a new game, but you have also created a new market."

Mother Shoemaker asked, "Do you remember what day is tomorrow?"

"Michaelmas!"

Chapter 93 | 1458 | The Last

Brother Tanner

To the best of my recall, the narrative recorded on this parchment provides a most complete and thoroughly accurate account. I strove to depict the sequence of events beginning on Lammas Day and ending on Michaelmas Day in the year, 1399 Anno Domini. Twelve friends conceived and invented a game in St. Andrews. Together, we sought to create a scrupulously fair game. Our fair game later acquired the name, 'Golf'.

Development of golf continued throughout many years. Whenever we realized a need to improve fairness in the game, we met. Together, we worked to reach agreement regarding how to change the game. Each change in the rules moved the game of golf towards the direction of fair play.

Upon my soul, I testify the preceding writing to be honest and true. I offer the story, as my testimony. As God is my witness, my final task is complete.

By my hand, Thomas

Augustinian Canon

1458 Anno Domini   St. Andrews

Fragment

Epilogue | 2022

The Professors - Lecture Notes

And then twelve friends taught the new game to their friends!

The mothers and fathers thought playing the new game was fun. They loved to play the new game, too! The mothers and fathers taught the new game to their friends, too!

In 1457, because some leaders thought that the men were neglecting their Archery Practice to play golf, they spoke to the King. Those leaders convinced the King of Scotland to ban golf. The King decreed a ban on golf that year.

However, Scots still played golf.

Then, the King of Scotland learned to play golf.

The King lifted the ban on golf.

And the Scots resumed playing the fair game, their fair game, golf. And the Scots have never stopped playing golf. And the Scots will never stop playing golf!

Gunpowder produced a superior weapon to the longbow. Bowyers no longer made bows. Many bowyers became golf club makers.

In the ensuing six plus centuries, the fair game of golf attracted countless men and women, lads and lasses to participate. Through golf, the virtues of honesty and scrupulous attention to fair play continued to develop. The spirit of fairness the twelve dreamed for their game frames the written rules which continue to evolve for golfers everywhere.

It is safe to write that even though golf may not attract everyone to play the game, by the millions golfers enjoy participating. The Twelve Friends dream; to design, to invent, and to develop a new game succeeded. So long ago on the Links of St. Andrews, they brought their shared vision to life. Virtues and vision valued by the twelve lasses and lads in a game designed to be fair to all, continues to strengthen and evolve.

Golfers continue to enjoy participating with other golfers. There are many ways to enjoy the game. First, golfers relish the company of other golfers who share interest in the game. Golfers love to pit their skills in competition with others and with the course.

The tribe of golfers migrated from St. Andrews. Eventually, the diaspora of golfers reached the six inhabitable continents. Each continent boasts several courses. In between the continents, golf is played on countless islands.

The Voices

Bessie The Shepherd

Bessie's hair cascaded in long tresses blending tones of russet and sienna with chestnut highlights to her trim waist. On the Links, she frequently wore waist length braids. As a shepherd, Bess worked outside all day, all year. The sun kissed her face. Her complexion exploded in light freckles. The freckles enhanced her friendly, natural smile. Bessie stood 5'2. At age 14, Bess was the oldest lass. Her favorite color was light orange. Bessie was athletic and musical, a combination shepherds shared since Biblical times. She asked reflective questions. The periods of loneliness in her occupation invited her to indulge in daydreams. She knew how to help keep people on task. Bessie was extremely responsible. She put her excellent communicative skills into the practice of managerial skills. In partnership with brother David, Bessie managed the flock. Together, they supervised the collies to keep the flock safe and the Links productive. She was devoted to helping David grow.

Bess learned how her animals responded to different stimuli. When the flock grazed peacefully, she often pulled out her small flute. She used the musical sound from the flute to communicate with her flock, the collies, and David. Bessie loved to create poetry.

Dr. Christine MacGregor 2022 - Like shepherds for millennia, Bess carried a small easily retrievable musical instrument. The instrument functions to produce sounds to reach even beyond the range and pitch of their own voices. Shepherds the world over are in tune with the natural world. The oldest known musical instrument dates some 60,000 years ago. The ancient artifact began as a partial femur of a Cave bear. The bone was hollowed. It contains regular spaced drilled finger holes. Scientists created a reconstruction of the instrument. In the reconstruction, missing and damaged parts were replaced. When a flautist sent air through the passageway, the sound produced the music of a flute. Anthropologists observing this artifact concluded that the flute and the drum account for the earliest human instrumental music.

Brother Thomas -1458 - Bess mastered making music with her flute during the course of her years performing the lonely job. She taught David how to make music also. His talent matched hers. They found they could enjoy making new melodies and repeating a response across the Links. Frequently, Bess observed the birds which inhabit the Links. Birds interested Bess for a variety of reasons. She enjoyed their unique melodies. In her mind, Bess categorized the sounds of each species. She memorized and mimicked the birdsongs. She taught herself to sing, to whistle and to produce each bird song on her flute. Bessie's portable hand flute was always at hand. The ever-ready flute performed another sound delivering function. For a working shepherd, the most practical application from the flute occurred when she employed it as a whistle to command the collies.

David The Shepherd

David's light brown hair color mimicked dry straw. At age 13, light freckles decorated his smooth complexion. David stood an even six-foot height. His stature meant the friends 'looked up' to him physically. We also looked up to David because of his integrity. He never cheated. David was athletically precocious. His ability to run fast coupled with amazing agility served him well when the sheep required a guiding hand. A commanding speaker, David was blessed with a deep rich voice. He spoke clearly and deliberately. He never mumbled. His voice compelled us to listen. We always knew where David stood on any issue.

Yet, David was also a wonderful listener. The combination of careful listening and effective speaker always put David in the midst of any discussion. David was always focused and that helped to keep people on task. To change David's mind required factual evidence. He cited facts to make his arguments. This combination of clear understanding of facts, powerful speaking, and intense listening made David an excellent communicator. In a discussion or a fight, David was one lad you wanted on your side.

David applied creative approaches to solve problems. He was observant and reflective. He never hesitated to ask questions. With so many hours of time away from other humans, David was a dreamer. But he did not dream as an escape, David welcomed and shouldered responsibility. His dreams became visions.

David trusted Bess completely, though the two of them enjoyed teasing other good naturedly. Bess taught David how to be a shepherd, how to play the flute, and how to connect with the collies. They worked together on their own every day. However, there was still time enough for both of them to experience the frustrating loneliness shepherds endure.

The Shepherds found creative ways to stay in communication beyond the range of their own voices. They used whoops, and whistles and arm signals. Like Bess, David enjoyed creating music. Both played the flute. They loved to play duets.

The shepherds knew the geography of the Links intimately. They noticed every square yard. They knew the week when the sweet grass would appear. In their heads, they mapped out and conferred about the seasonal, weekly, and daily grazing patterns. Managing razing patterns kept the pasture healthy and productive.

Both Shepherds engaged in observations of the changing landscape. When sudden storms appeared, shepherds guided the flock into the safety of the numerous bunkers on the Links. Shepherds were no strangers to danger. Whenever danger lurked Bess and David adapted their behaviors to confront and manage the situation.

The Shepherds worked most closely with the Weavers. Together, the families shared ownership and the responsibility to harvest fleeces during shearing season.

Barbara The Bowyer

The first impression Barbara made fixated upon her shining ash blond hair. The color captured the luster of moonglow filtered through the veil of a translucent cloud layer. Barbara implored Bess to precision shear and shape her hair to a few inches above shoulder length. Barbara's bright silver blue eyes sparkled. Her smooth complexion enhanced a reflection of her joy. She stood 4'9. At almost 15, Barbara was the second oldest lass. Her favorite color was blue. However, when the lasses chose colors for their balls, like older girls everywhere, Barbara settled for bright orange so that a younger lass could choose first and select blue.

Barbara possessed very strong hands. To make the powerful longbow she worked with yew, the strongest wood. Such work using both hands developed strong fingers. To fashion arrows she developed highly skilled finger control and touch. Performing such work enabled Barbara to develop a high level of confidence in the combination of her physical skill and strength. The required skills she mastered to produce the longbow included making precision measurements, tracing, sawing, cutting, shaping, smoothing, preserving wood, shaping horn to fit bow shaft.

Barbara was a great listener. She was courageous. I think she was a natural leader. Barbara accurately grasped any situation quickly. She asked excellent questions which clarified our thinking whenever we confronted a problem. Barbara often showed us how to see and accept new and different viewpoints.

To make arrows, Barbara selected, cut, and shaped the cedar shafts. Barbara selected and trimmed goose and swan wing feathers to making fletching. She installed the fletching to the shaft by expertly applying glues and wraps. The arrow shafts must be accurately centered and knocked. Arrows and arrowheads must be joined and balanced precisely.

To make bowstrings, the family grew flax plants. They harvested flax plants and processed them into long fibers. The fibers were braided together to form a string that was strong enough to pull and bend a long bow.

I remember a moment with the entire group of friends. I shared an early memory about Marion dancing on her father's hand as a tiny girl during Festival. William interrupted me. 'Thomas, you are too young to remember, but Barbara and her father performed similar trick. I grant you that Marion is a superb dancer. Barbara also danced beautifully. But Barbara added acrobatics to the performance. She performed cartwheels and back walkovers on her father's open palm. To end her performance, Barbara made a signature move. When her father held his hand steady at waist height, she leaped into a double back flip. She landed and her feet stilled. She stuck that landing like the point of a knife into dirt. Barbara always received an ovation from her audience."

The Bowyers worked most closely with the Carpenter family. They also worked closely with the Tanners.

Russell The Bowyer

Russell's light brown hair grew thick and straight. His smooth fair complexion framed a friendly inviting smile. Russell stood 5'5. Over that summer, in the midst of a growth spurt, added 3 inches. At twelve and a half, Russell was the second youngest lad. Russell counted Jonathan and me, together the three youngest lads, as best friends. Russell was also very close with Robert the Carpenter. Russell's hazel eyes harbored astonishing powerful vision. At long distances, Russell saw objects clearly the rest of us didn't see. None of us were able to identify an object, which Russell described perfectly. We respected his clear vision. Often when unsure of a target, we asked Russell to tell us what he saw.

Russell was the best archer. He could launch arrows with astonishing accuracy. At ranges up to 50 yards, Russell consistently placed a three-arrow shot group measured within the span of half a hand. To launch arrows at long range, Russell matched the pace and distance of the top men archers.

Archers in Scotland functioned as a team. Russell modeled the part of a team player. Bowyers took pride in providing archers with the complete longbow weapons system to perform at peak level. Building a bow to fit an individual archer was a critical commitment to improve teamwork. To build a proper fitting, high performance longbow, Russell solved several problems. Russell was an excellent listener. Longbow production required several crucial decisions. Russell applied process to solve issues involved in the craft.

Russell's ability to focus served him well in all aspects. He focused on targets. He focused on shots. He focused on fitting an archer. He focused on producing a custom fit, high quality, durable, reliable longbow. Russell made precision measurements. He accurately traced, sawed, cut, shaped, smoothed, and preserve wood, particularly yew. Yew was a poisonous wood. It required carefully handling to keep the bowyer safe. Together with his sister, Russell built accurate, dependable arrows. They also produced strong bowstrings from the plant to the bow.

The Bowyers worked most closely with the Carpenters. Russell and Barbara also worked closely with the Tanners.

Heather The Carpenter

Heather's rich burnished golden hair captured the deep color of the first quarter hour or the last quarter hour of the day's sunshine in tight waves. The texture of her hair emulated the queen's gold crown. No one could ever recall when even the wisp of a single hair was out of place. Frequently, she wove her favorite color, bright yellow yarn, or ribbon into her hair. At age 13, Heather stood an even five feet. Her smooth white gold complexion glowed. We all basked in Heather's inner glow Part of Heather's charm stemmed from the fact that she never seemed not to recognize her beauty.

Heather's deep, luminous brown eyes invited friends to come near. She listened with her eyes. Every time I spoke with Heather, her eyes captured me. I experienced a magical feeling. In the rich dark brown pools, I observed my own reflection. I felt like I was seeing myself the very way that she saw me. I knew that when we talked Heather was pleased. Others in the group spoke of experiencing the same feeling. Heather valued each of us. Her personality was supportive. We knew Heather believed in us. We wanted to live up to her expectations. We never wanted to disappoint her in any way. Heather's quiet demeanor made everyone feel comfortable to be near her. We all wanted to be close to her.

Like all carpenters everywhere, Heather possessed very strong hands. The daily practice of the carpenter's craft enabled her to develop very skilled hands. For Heather, the result of combining skills and strength meant that the feeling of confidence in her abilities flourished.

Heather quickly grasped any situation. She possessed the vision to use carpentry to solve any need or situation. To the family shoppe, she brought creativity and art to complement the engineering solutions of construction.

The Carpenters worked closely with the Bowyers. They also maintained a close professional relationship with the Tanners. The Tanners who supplied the glues, stains, lacquers, and wood preservatives. Carpenters also worked closely with the Weavers on loom repair.

Robert The Carpenter

Robert's hair piled into sandy blonde curls. The curls framed a confident, friendly face. Robert always offered a ready smile that highlighted his ruddy complexion. At age 14, Robert stood 5'4.

The carpenter's daily repetitive motions included swinging a hammer and sawing through wood. Such repetitive movement developed powerful forearms that already bulged on Robert. All of the friends developed strong hands. However, Robert's arms and hands were the strongest for any of the friends. Carpenters employ specific grips to efficiently guide their tools. Proper grips allow carpenters to perform repetitive movement work for a full day.

In addition to muscle work, carpenters used their brains. They transformed raw lumber into useful articles. Robert possessed superior analytical knowledge to problem solve. His father taught Robert and his sister how carpenters approach problem solving from an early age. Carpenters take pride in the knowledge that Jesus worked as a carpenter. Robert was naturally quiet. When he did speak, the others paid attention closely. Frequently Robert's insight required explanation because of the sheer volume of technical knowledge he mastered. Robert enjoyed making clear explanations to the others so that they can understand his vision. His opinions were highly valued by the friends.

To solve problems and make quality products, carpenters learn and master specific skills. Those skills include wood shaping, precision measurements, accurate tracing, saw, plane, sanding, joinery, finish, lacquer, preserve, glue. Hands are skilled and accurate with a touch or a feel. He could translate his knowledge through his hands when he worked in shaping and joining wood. He possessed superior knowledge of wooden joinery, glues, lacquers, and finishes.

Margaret The Tanner

Any amount of light, from bright summer noon sunlight to the glow of evening's dying embers ignited fire within Margaret's striking copper red hair. Like a brightly polished copper mirror her hair shone. At age 14, Margaret stood 4'10. Tiny light freckles dotted the soft pale complexion across her pert little nose and spread across her high cheeks. Eyes colored deeply like precious emeralds pleasantly complemented the structure of her cheerful face.

Since age four, Margaret worked in the tannery. Among her many skills, she knew the entire sequence of steps to process leather from a freshly skinned raw hide to super soft and supple required to make fine gloves. Margaret specialized in custom leather processing. She learned the sequence of many steps to produce leather in various forms and degrees of hardness from soft and supple to strong and stiff. Margaret was highly organized. Margaret took the responsibility of taking inventory for the shoppe. She kept track of the various chemical solutions required in the shoppe and the vats rooms. She also set the schedule for the various stages and steps during processing. In addition, she procured the raw materials required to produce our superior glues and lacquers. At the time of our story, Margaret recently learned of new methods and dyes to produce striking new colors for leathers.

Worked most closely the Shoemakers. Shoemakers were the most important customer for the Tanners. They produced all the custom leathers the Shoemakers require. Shoemakers also ordered preservatives and glues. The Tanners also worked very closely with Carpenters and Bowyers to supply them with glues, lacquers.

Thomas The Tanner

At the time of the story, I stood 5'3. My hair was then the color of Ginger, a shade of red. However, the color of my hair did not quite match the luster of my sister's locks. Both of our faces were lightly freckled. Seemed like some kind of freckles go with every shade of red hair in Scotland. My eyes then and now are green. Missing left hand due to tragic childhood accident. Right hand is very strong. I was almost 13. Jonathan the Shoemaker and Russell the Bowyer were my two very best friends. We were the three youngest lads. We could talk about anything and everything under the sun. We may even have talked about other things also.

Margaret and I strove to learn everything we could about leather. Margaret specialized in glues and lacquers. I specialized in the production of parchment. Tannery owned the parchment contract to supply the Cathedral. Father and I worked diligently to supply a sufficient quantity of top-quality parchment. It was very important for the family to maintain that contract because the Cathedral paid with cash.

We processed leather to super soft and supple for fine gloves. We kept track of the various chemical solutions required in the shoppe and the vats rooms. To produce leather in various forms and degrees of hardness and stiffness required us to learn, practice and master many skills. Our profession demanded that we stay highly organized. At our tannery we specialized in custom leather processing. We procured the chemicals required to produce superior glues and lacquers.

In addition to the production of fine leathers, I worked to produce fine parchment. I worked with the two major customers for the Tannery: The Shoemakers and the Augustinian canons at the Cathedral.

I was the best artist in the town of St. Andrews.

Rhona The Weaver

Rhona's hair refracted the color of light-yellow honey. Her hair glowed like light from the warm summer sun. She instructed her close friend, Bess to keep her hair sheared to just shy of shoulder length. Frequently, Rhona pulled her hair up to secure it. When Rhona wore her hair up, I thought it looked like she wore a princess's crown.

However, Rhona wore her hair up for a practical reason. She always wore it up when she worked on the looms. Wearing her hair up, kept loose strands away from the yarns in the looms. Her skilled fingers moved nimbly across, over and through the warps and wafts in the loom. She moved her fingers so fast that my eyes found it impossible to follow the tasks of ten fingers moving independently. Rhona explained her reasons to keep her hair short, "Weaving stray strands of my own hair into the tapestry was disadvantageous."

At age 13, and 5'9 height, Rhona towered over all the other lasses. I know that her height sometimes made her uncomfortable. Only two lads were then taller than Rhona. Yet, in spite of the uncomfortable feeling, Rhona always carried herself regally. Like a queen, when she walked with perfect posture, Rhona floated above us.

Rhona's eyes were the eyes of an artist perfectly in tune with color. Some call the color of such eyes, hazel. Hazel eyes can seem sympathetic to other colors. When Rhona wore green fabric, her eyes seemed to be green. However, when she wore blue fabric, her eyes picked up the color blue. I found this attribute of Rhona's eyes especially endearing. As a fellow color artist, I recognized Rhona's true genius to color in her tapestry masterworks.

Rhona was an artist who produced tapestry. She could transfer any cartoon to tapestry. She already mastered the standard looms. Rhona was an expert on the new, large loom. She could weave precious metal threads of gold and silver into the tapestry. The scenes reflected the sunlight filtered through the stained glass to shine with life.

The Weavers worked most closely with Shepherds. Also worked closely with the artist, Thomas to produce artwork and design in tapestry. Rhona stayed in closest contact with Bess the Shepherd and Heather the Carpenter.

William The Weaver

William stood the same height as David, a full six feet. Unlike David's slim athletic build, William carried massive shoulders. He outweighed David by some twenty-five pounds. The additional weight was all muscle. William's shock of hair sparkled like the color of new fluffy snow on a bright clear day. His eyes were a piercing deep blue. His clear complexion tinted copperish high cheeks. At age 15, William was the oldest of us. William's voice sounded deep and manly, though not nearly as deep as David's. He spoke more slowly and softer than David as well. William and David were best friends.

The rest of us felt safe in any situation whenever David and William were present in the group. We knew that they had our backs. Both were polite and respectful. Both tall lads demanded that respect and courtesy be practiced for every voice, and every idea whenever we met together as a group. Respect and courtesy provided an opportunity for those of us who were younger and smaller to offer our ideas to the entire group. Together, William and David almost seemed as if they were guardians for civility in our group.

I always appreciated both of these young giants. I am sure that William and Russell shared my feelings. We spoke of William and David many times. William and David were both excellent athletes. David ran faster. Although William also ran fast. William had stronger arms and shoulders. William was the best at the caber toss. He also excelled at the shot put and hammer throw.

Weavers produced woolen cloth in various weights, colors, and plaids. William mastered every weaving technique by this time in his life. In the shoppe, William set up the looms. His father inspected and spoke with William at length about the process. Weavers produce and dye yarns. He programmed the loom for the weaver to produce the various woolen plaid patterns favored by local customers.

The Weaver family worked most closely with the Shepherds. Along with the Shepherds both families share ownership in the flock with the archdiocese. Ownership of sheep helped reduce the cost of raw wool. When the fleeces were harvested, William and Rhona shared shearing duties with the Shepherds.

William maintained close contact with the Carpenters. The looms were constructed of wood. Looms sometimes required repair and replacement. A close relationship with skilled Carpenters offered an economic advantage when loom parts needed timely repair.

Marion The Shoemaker

Marion kept her soft, shining wavy dark chestnut colored hair sheared to shoulder length. Below her bangs, the rich brown in her eyes helped her capture a speaker's attention every time she practiced her powerful listening skills. Tiny flecks of gold sparkles danced in her brown eyes. She charmed everyone near her.

Marion held her petite frame straight and tall. Standing 4'5 she was the tiniest lass. Although she was petite she was perfectly proportioned in every way. Marion turned her petite body into a significant advantage. Her skill in creating tiny, nearly invisible stitchery was legendary. She produced the tiniest almost invisible stitches. She could tie knots so small and so tightly, that no one else could approach the precision. Marion's complexion was fair and clear. She smiled easily and often. She invited us to share time with her. Marion was also extremely smart and an excellent problem solver.

Perhaps because of Marion's diminutive size, she projected her voice. When she spoke, she projected power. Partly that may have been the volume level she could attain. There was no shyness. She spoke confidently with no arrogance. Her speaking ability compelled us to listen carefully. We wanted to consider her every contribution to any discussion. Her real power inhabited the ideas she shared. She always encouraged others to participate and engage in the discussion. At age 12, Marion was the youngest lass. She acted as confidently as the oldest lass. Her confidence served her well. Her encouragement and enthusiasm helped make our group work effectively.

Marion began working in the shoppe at age 3. As a toddler and early walker, she always stayed near her father. As she learned to talk, her father taught her leatherworking skills. Marion mastered how to plan, to draw, to trace, to cut, to punch, and to stitch fine leather.

Among my earliest memories is watching Marion and her father. She was so tiny she stood confidently on her father's open palm of his hand. Watching a tiny little lass stand on a man's open palm was a magical sight for me. She performed even more magic though. She stood on two feet. She posed. She lifted one foot. She stood motionless on one foot. Then, she stood on her toes. She posed with such grace and confidence. I marveled at the amount of trust she placed in her father to hold her steady. She danced. She leaped into the air. She twirled. She always landed lightly on her father's palm. I remember seeing Marion and her father at fairs and festivals. When dancing music played. Marion grabbed her father's hand. She led him outside. He opened his palm and reached down so that she could step onto his hand. Her father lifted his hand. Marion rode his hand up as he lifted. He brought his hand to waist high. Marion posed. Then she danced to the music. She executed all the steps that the lasses danced.

Marion's appearance reminded me of a little doll. Fortunately for me and for all the friends, we knew Marion as a complete person. Great ideas, a clear and powerful voice, and the spirit to get the things done enhanced Marion's leadership abilities. Jonathan often spoke of lovingly about his great fortune to have Marion for his 'big' sister.

Marion and my sister Margaret were the closest of friends. The Shoemaker family worked most closely with the Tanner family.

Jonathan The Shoemaker

Standing 4'7, at the time of this story Jonathan was the smallest lad. At age 11, he was also the youngest lad. To my artist's eye, at this age, Jonathan's head seemed large and out of proportion. The proportions of his body changed in a few years. He added considerable height and significant muscle mass. He grew the rest of his body to proportionally match the size of his head. Jonathan's dark brown hair was similar in color to his sister Marion's. The wavy texture in his hair was also similar. Like Marion, Jonathan's complexion was fair and clear. Jonathan was my best friend. He was so much fun to be around. He was always challenging and always full of life. He possessed a great sense of humor. Good natured Jonathan could laugh at himself when others returned his teases.

Jonathan was a very smart lad. He knew how to capture and more importantly, how to keep listeners interested, and often enthralled, when he spun a story. Jonathan loved to talk. He was unafraid to turn up the volume to get attention. He told a great story. When he grabbed attention, he varied volume and pitch to match the content of his message. Jonathan is a compelling speaker. He always seemed to have something to say about any topic. We could not wait to see what he would say next. Jonathan loved to tease. Most of the time, he knew just what to say to get us to laugh. That laughter often opened our minds to what he wished to say next.

Jonathan was a hard worker. He could make anything out of leather. Because at that time Jonathan was young and small, his strength was deceptive. As a master leather crafter Jonathan developed highly skilled hands. His craft also helped him to become an efficient problem solver.

Whatever the activity our friends engage in, Jonathan was committed. He loved competition. Even though he was the smallest, Jonathan was very strong. Jonathan ran very fast. Although in straight line running, he is at a disadvantage in races due to size and body immaturity. But when playing a game of tag, his quickness and ability to change directions amazed even the oldest lads and lasses. Whenever we raced over hills Jonathan left everyone behind. He moved so fast that his feet did not even seem to touch the ground.

Dr. Christine MacGregor — 2022

A lecturer and teacher at St. Andrews University. Her field of Study is Scottish Medieval History from the end of Roman occupation until the Reformation.

To Dr. McGregor golf is a passion. As often as her daily schedule permits, she invests time in improving her game. Her dream life would include playing a full round each day. Whenever she can, she plays 18. Dr. McGregor stated, "I believe in the power of practice. I find the evidence of the ten-thousand-hour rule explained in Malcolm Gladwell's 'Outliers' convincing. Daily participation and practice guide my golfing pursuit."

Although Dr. McGregor golfs often on a regular basis with close friends, she finds satisfaction when paired with a person she meets for the first time at the first tee. Dr. McGregor finds truth in the statement, 'When I play with another golfer for the first time, I discover that golfer is a friend I had not yet met.'

Dr. McGregor loves golfing in Scotland. "There are many legendary courses. Many more courses are fun and satisfying." To her, The Olde Course at St. Andrews is a sacred place.

"Most satisfying to me," Dr. McGregor continued, "was the irrefutable historical fact that lasses were equally important to lads at the genesis of golf right here in St. Andrews."

Professor Greenwood — 2022

Professor Greenwood came to the University of Edinburgh in 2000. His specialty is Medieval Scottish History 1000-1550.

Professor Greenwood cannot remember a time in his life without golf. "My earliest memories connect with a sparkle of white. A shiny white ball descending, bouncing, and rolling to a stop on the brilliant green. My young brain questioned how did that ball get here? Our family lived near mid fairway of a par five. Soon, a golfer, sometimes a man, other times a woman appeared to locate the ball. Always the golfer smiled and laughed. Yes, I saw the golfers who had hit a good shot. Then they addressed the ball and performed a unique ritual. At the end the golfer completed a stroke to send the ball soaring into flight. To me it was magic. I was hooked for life. I wanted to be a practitioner of this special magic. Fortunately for me, I pursued the practice of golf for the rest of my life…so far."

"I feel blessed. To translate this ancient artifact which documents the creation of Scotland's game fulfilled a sacred calling for a historian who possesses a passion for golf." Professor Greenwood stated, "I am so proud to partner with Dr. McGregor to publish the wonderful story about how the fair game of golf was invented by twelve friends on the Links of St. Andrews. Let there never again be a doubt to where and how golf originated."

Addendum

Rules of Golf - 1744

The first known Rules of Golf were drawn up in 1744 in Edinburgh for the world's first 'open' golf competition at Leith by the Gentlemen Golfers of Edinburgh, who would go on to become The Honourable Company of Edinburgh Golfers.

THE FIRST SET OF RULES OF GOLF

Articles & Laws in Playing at Golf.

1. You must Tee your Ball within a Club's length of the Hole.
2. Your Tee must be upon the Ground.
3. You are not to change the Ball which you Strike off the Tee.
4. You are not to remove Stones, Bones or any Break Club, for the sake of playing your Ball, Except upon the fair Green and that only / within a Club's length of your Ball.
5. If your Ball comes among watter, or any wattery filth, you are at liberty to take out your Ball & bringing it behind the hazard and Teeing it, you may play it with any Club and allow your Adversary a Stroke for so getting out your Ball.
6. If your Balls be found any where touching one another, You are to lift the first Ball, till you play the last.
7. At Holling, you are to play your Ball honestly for the Hole, and not to play upon your Adversary's Ball, not lying in your way to the Hole.
8. If you should lose your Ball, by it's being taken up, or any other way, you are to go back to the Spot, where you struck last, & drop another Ball, And allow your adversary a Stroke for the misfortune.
9. No man at Holling his Ball, is to be allowed, to mark his way to the Hole with his Club, or anything else.
10. If a Ball be stopp'd by any Person, Horse, Dog or anything else, The Ball so stop'd must be play'd where it lyes.
11. If you draw your Club in Order to Strike, & proceed so far in the Stroke as to be Accounted a Stroke.
12. He whose Ball lyes farthest from the Hole is obliged to play first.
13. Neither Trench, Ditch or Dyke, made for the preservation of the Links, nor the Scholar's Holes, or the Soldier's Lines, Shall be accounted a Hazard; But the Ball is to be taken out teed /and play'd with any Iron Club.

John Rattray, Capt

The rules were drawn up at the behest of the City of Edinburgh Council, who had presented the silver club prize and insisted that there had to be rules for the competition. The competition was open to all gentlemen golfers in Britain, but only local players participated. This tells us that there were no prior rules, and maybe if it had not been for Edinburgh Council, the golfers would not have drawn up rules themselves.

Rules of Golf, signed by John Rattray Captain 1744-47 and 1751 with amendments by Thomas Boswell Captain 1758. The original is in National Library of Scotland. A thousand copies were made and distributed by Hon Co and are on display in the golf museum at St Andrews and club-houses of many old golf societies.

For centuries, the original rules were thought lost, but in 1937 they were re-discovered by Mr. CB Clapcott on two pages at the back of a Minute Book of the Honourable Company. The pages contained thirteen Articles and the signature of John Rattray, as Captain. As he was 'Captain of the Golf' in 1744-1747 and 1751, we cannot be sure what the date of these rules is, but as they were copied verbatim for use in St Andrews in 1754, we can be sure they applied at this time. ("Rules of Golf - 1744 - Scottish Golf History")

There is a later amendment clarifying rules 5 and 13 also written on the same document. It is signed by Thomas Boswell who was Captain of the Leith golfers in 1758, but who had previously won the St Andrews competition in a play-off in 1755.

The golfers at St Andrews, who would later become the Royal & Ancient Golf Club of St Andrews, adopted the Leith rules for their own competition in 1754. They wrote them into their minutes, with only a small amendment to Rule 5, but strangely they included references to 'the Soldiers' lines' and 'the Scholars' holes' in Rule 13 that only existed at Leith. In the eighteenth century, other clubs, including the Burgess at Bruntsfield Links in Edinburgh and those at Aberdeen and Crail also drew up their own rules.

List of Resources

TOPIC

Birds

Edwards, E. W. J., Quinn, L. R., Wakefield, E. D., Miller, P. I., & Thompson, P. M. (2013). "Tracking a northern fulmar from a Scottish nesting site to the Charlie-Gibbs Fracture Zone: Evidence of linkage between coastal breeding seabirds and Mid-Atlantic Ridge feeding sites". *Deep Sea Research Part II: Topical Studies in Oceanography*, *98*, 437-444, https://doi.org.10.1016/j.dsr2.2013.04.011

"Fulmar", *Oceanwide Expeditions*, http://oceanwide-expeditions.com, download, 6/2/2021

Shannon, L. "Meet the fulmars this summer in St. Andrews", *The Royal Society for the Protection of Birds*, http://rspb.org.uk, 5 July 2021

City, Castle, Cathedral —St. Andrews

"The Augustinian Order", *The Augustinians*, http://Augustinian.org download October 10, 2020

Brown, M., Stevenson K. (editors) *Medieval St. Andrews, Church, Cult, City*, The Boydell Press, Woodbridge, Suffolk, 2017

Brown, M., Stevenson K., "'Ancient Magnificence': St. Andrews in the Middle Ages: An Introduction", *Medieval St. Andrews, Church, Cult, City*, The Boydell Press, Woodbridge, Suffolk, 2017

Campbell, I. (2013). "Planning for pilgrims: St Andrews as the Second Rome". *The Innes Review*, 64(1), 1- 22doi: 10.3366/inr.2013.0045

Campbell, I. (2017). "The Idea of St. Andrews as the Second Rome Made Manifest", *Medieval St. Andrews, Church, Cult, City*, The Boydell Press, Woodbridge, Suffolk, 2017

Chen, J. "Thomas Becket Badges: Developments and Interpretations of His Cult Since the Twelfth Century", *The Pilgrim's Guide*, https://thepilgrimsguide.com, download, September 5, 2021

De Gray Birch, W. *History of Scottish Seals, Volume II Ecclesiastical and Monastic Seals of Scotland*, Stirling: Eneas Mackay, 43 Murray Place, 1907 p135

Ditchburn, D. "Religion, Ritual and the Rhythm of the Year in Later Medieval St. Andrews", *Medieval St. Andrews, Church, Cult, City*, The Boydell Press, Woodbridge, Suffolk, 2017

Ewan, E. "Living in the Late Medieval Town of St. Andrews", *Medieval St. Andrews, Church, Cult,*

City, The Boydell Press, Woodbridge, Suffolk, 2017

Fawcett, R. "The Medieval Ecclesiastical Architecture of St. Andrews as a Channel for the Introduction of New Ideas", *Medieval St. Andrews, Church, Cult, City*, The Boydell Press, Woodbridge, Suffolk, 2017

Hammond, M. "The Burgh of St. Andrews and its Inhabitants before the Wars of Independence", *Medieval St. Andrews, Church, Cult, City*, The Boydell Press, Woodbridge, Suffolk, 2017

Hammond, M. "University of St. Andrews Library, UYSL 110/6/4, *Medieval St. Andrews, Church, Cult, City*, The Boydell Press, Woodbridge, Suffolk, 2017

Hunter, F. & Carruthers, M. ed. "Pilgrimage in Medieval Scotland, 4.43", *Scottish Archaeological Framework*, www.scarf.scot download August 29, 2021

"Kings and Queens of Scotland", historic-uk.com

Lambert, T. *A BRIEF HISTORY OF ST ANDREWS, SCOTLAND*

Mason, R. "University, City and Society", *Medieval St. Andrews, Church, Cult, City*, The Boydell Press, Woodbridge, Suffolk, 2017

"Open Virtual Worlds", *School of Computer Science*, University of St. Andrews, https://openvirtualworlds.org download August 2021

Reid, N. "The Prehistory of the University of St. Andrews", *Medieval St. Andrews, Church, Cult, City*, The Boydell Press, Woodbridge, Suffolk, 2017

"St. Andrews Cathedral and St. Mary's Church, Kirkheugh", *Statement of Significance*, www.historicenvironment.scot st-andrews-cathedral-sos.pdf. download March 2021

Stephenson, K. "Heresy, Inquisition and Late Medieval St. Andrews", *Medieval St. Andrews, Church, Cult, City*, The Boydell Press, Woodbridge, Suffolk, 2017

Taylor, S., "From Cinrigh Monai to Civitas Sancti Andree: A Star is Born" *Medieval St. Andrews, Church, Cult, City*, The Boydell Press, Woodbridge, Suffolk, 2017

Taylor, S. "The St. Andrews Foundation Account", *Medieval St. Andrews, Church, Cult, City*, The Boydell Press, Woodbridge, Suffolk, 2017

Taylor, S. "The Augustinian's Account", *Medieval St. Andrews, Church, Cult, City*, The Boydell Press, Woodbridge, Suffolk, 2017

Taylor, S. "The Boar's Raik", *Medieval St. Andrews, Church, Cult, City*, The Boydell Press, Woodbridge, Suffolk, 2017

The Way of St. Andrews, thewayofstandrews.com, download January 2022

Turpie, T., "When the Miracles Ceased: Shrine and Cult Management at St. Andrews and Scottish Cathedrals in the Late Middle Ages", *Medieval St. Andrews: Church, Cult City*, The Boydell Press, Woodbridge, Suffolk, 2017

"Uniting The Kingdoms, 1066-1603, Scotland Regained 1297-1328", *The National Archives*, nationalarchives.uk.gov

Collies

"Herding Tests and Some Useful Commands for Your Dog", http://www.dogslife.com.au, Aug 24, 2018

Henry, B. "A Guide to The Livestock-working Dog", http://www.extension.unh.edu Aug 2003

"Border Collies: Born to Herd", Wall Street Journal, http://wsj.com.video.borntoherd Dec 26, 2010

Kane, K. "Impressive Border Collie Herds Sheep into Barn at Lightning Speed", http://rover.com Jan 2021

Libby, T. "Get to Know the Border Collie, a dog breed bordering on brilliant", *modern Dog*, moderndogmagazine.com download Aug 23, 2021

Golf Balls, Golf Clubs, Golf Courses

"A Short History of Golf: Ancient Golf 1457-1800", http://www.timewarpgolf.com/index.php?main_page=page&id=9, download 9/11/20

"Bunker and Water Hazard", *Scottish Golf History*https://www.scottishgolfhistory.org/origin-of-golf-terms/bunker-and-water-hazard

"Coloured Flags and 'Out and In'", *Scottish Golf History* https://www.scottishgolfhistory.org/origin-of-golf-terms/coloured-flags

"Fairway", *Scottish Golf History* https://www.scottishgolfhistory.org/origin-of-golf-terms/fairway

"Golf ball from Hairy to Haskell", *Scottish Golf History* https://www.scottishgolfhistory.org/origin-of-golf-terms/golf-ball-feathery-gutty-haskell/#Wooden

"Links Golf Course-Meaning", *Scottish Golf History* https://www.scottishgolfhistory.org/origin-of-golf-terms/links-golf-course-meaning

Chervenka, M. "Feather golf balls": *Real or Repro: Your Online Source for Identifying Fakes or Reproductions*

Hutchinson, J. "The Right Kind of Rough", www.blog.standrews.com Nov 26, 2015

"Geology and Geography of Links Golf Courses", *Top 100 Golf Courses,* https://www.top100golf-courses.com/news-item/geology-and-geography-of-links-golf-courses downloaded 2/19/21

"Golf Club History", *Golf Club Revue: Spotlight on the Tools of the Greatest Game*

Kavas, I. Barton, R. "A Brief History of the Golf Ball", *GOLFSUPPORT*, London, UK Published on 14go.9.2016 – Latest update 22.9.2016

Learn, J. "Three Leather Balls Represent Oldest Evidence of Ancient Eurasian Ball Game. Inside Science", *Inside Science.* October 15, 2020

Moir, G. "Taking the Rough with the Smooth," www.blog.standrews.com, Jun 17, 2013

Ryan, S., "Mother nature and St. Andrews: James Hutchinson's secret wars", *Golf Digest,* July 19, 2015. https://www.golfdigest.com/story/mother-nature-and-st-andrews-1 download 8/5/21

Taylor, B. "Environmental Management at St. Andrews Links", *Sports Turf Research Institute, (Ecology and Environment Department) St. Andrews Links,* https://standrews.com download August 2019

"You'll be Surprised by these Quirky Old Names for Golf Clubs", https://golfsupport.com/blog/old-names-for-golf-clubs/ download 9/11/20

History and Geography

Butler, A. "Scottish Highland Games: Events and History", https://study.com June 2019

Gersick, C. "Time and Transition in Work Teams: Toward A New Model Of Group Development", *Academy of Management Journal,* 1988, Vol. 311, No. 1, 9-41.

"Timeline of Scottish History 1300-1350", https://www.undiscoveredscotland.co.uk download 6/6/19

"Timeline of Scottish History 1350-1400", https://www.undiscoveredscotland.co.uk download 6/6/19

"Medieval Scottish Names Submitted", https://www.behindthename.com

"Scottish Girls Names", https://www.Scottish-at-heart.com

"Women's Given Names Early 16th Century Scottish Lowlands", https://medievalscotland.org

Manguel, A. *A History of Reading,* Penguin Publishing Group, October 1997

Mackyntoisch, A. "Names from 13th Century Parliamentary Records", https://heraldry.sca.org Dec 23, 2020

MacLellan, W. "Stature in Scotland Over the Centuries", *The Journal of the Royal College of Physicians of Edinburgh,*

MacQueen, D. "History of the Highland Games", *Transceltic,* http://transceltic.com, May 22, 2016

"Ultimate Guide to Scotland's Highland Games", http: cottages-and-castles.co.uk, 27 December 2019

Manuscript Verification

"Authentication of legal and administrative documents" – The University of Nottingham, https://nottingham.ac.uk/manuscriptsandspecialcollections/researchguidance/medievaldocuments/authentication.aspx

Bak, J. M. "An Introduction to Editing Manuscripts for Medievalists" Central European University, Budapest, BAKJM@CEU.HU 2012

Benham, J. "Translating Medieval Documents: Some Common Problems", *Translation and Medieval Documents, Voices of Law: Language, Text, and Practice.* Copyright 2018, Funded by The Leverhulme Trust

Cammarota, M. "Translating Medieval Texts: Common Issues and Specific Challenges", (Università degli Studi di Bergamo, Italia)

Corwin, V. "Medieval Book Production and Monastic Life", *Dartmouth Ancient Books Labs: Historical Background and "How-To" Projects in Paleography, Papyrology and Codicology,* May 24, 2016

Nesmerak, K., Němcová, I. "Dating of Historical Manuscripts Using Spectrometric Methods: A Mini-Review Analytical Letters", *Vol 45, 2012/03/01* **pH and Water,** us.gov. http://us.gov, downloaded May 6, 2021

St. Andrews Pilgrim Badge, Medieval, British Museum, London "The Burden of Writing: Scribes in Medieval Manuscripts", *Medieval Manuscripts Blog,* British Library, 03 JUNE 2014

Warren, M. *Modern Theoretical Approaches to Medieval Translation,* Dartmouth College, michelle.r.warren@dartmouth.edu 2019

Medieval Archery

Burbage, I., Gamstedt, E. K., Keunecke, D., Niemz, P. "Mechanical performance of yew (Taxus bacccata) from a Longbow perspective", deGruyter https://www.degruyter.com/document/doi/10.1515/hf-2012-0151/html download 6/18/21

'European Yew', *The Wood Database,* https://www.wood-database.com/european-yew download 6/18/21

Kaiser, R. "The Medieval English Longbow", *Journal of the Society of Archer-Antiquaries*, Volume 23, 1980

Grewcock, M. "How I Make Medieval Arrows for My Longbow", youtube.com, September 9, 2017

Head, R. "How to Make a Medieval Arrow for Longbow – Warbow", youtube.com, April 4, 2020

Thurfjell, H. "A Bowyer Talks About Authentic Longbows", *The Mary Rose Longbows*, https://archeryhistorian.com download August 12, 2020

"Learning More About Our Longbows", *The Mary Rose*, https://maryrose.org Feb 20, 2019

Medieval Carpentry

Clark, J. "The Debate of the Carpenter's Tools Continued", *Tools and Trades History Society*, Newsletter 118 Winter 2012, http://taths.org.uk download October 10, 2020

mac Alasdair, L. F. "A Carpenter's Chest: Tools of the 15th Century", *The Oak, The Arts and Sciences Newsletter for the Kingdom of Atlantia*, Issue #12 download https://bloodandsawdust.com October 10, 2020

"Medieval Carpenter", *Medieval Britain*, https://medievalbritain.com download October 10, 2020

Sellers, P. "Mortise and Tenon Joint by hand in oak", youtube.com, Dec 1, 2011

"Mortise and Tenon – A Primer for Joinery" (Educational Infographic), *Florida School of Woodworking*, http://schoolofwoodwork.com download October 10, 2020

Poole, M. "Antique Joints and Joinery", *Antique HQ*, http://antique-hq.com download October 10, 2020

Medieval Life

Andrewes, W. "A Chronicle of Timekeeping", *Scientific American*, February 1, 2006

Albright, M. "Michaelmas: The Day the Devil Spit on Your Blackberries", *National Geographic*, https://nationalgeographic.com download August 25, 2021

Bellis, M. "The History of Mechanical Pendulum Clocks and Quartz Clocks", *ThoughtCo*, www.thoughtco.com April 12, 2018

Benson, L, *The Riverside Chaucer*, Boston, MA Houghton Mifflin, 1987.

Bloch-Dano, E. *Vegetables: A Biography,* University of Chicago Press website

Chaucer, G. *The Canterbury Tales*

Chaucer, G. *The Complete Poetical Works*, 'The Minor Poems, IX The Former Age', download Bartleby.com December 13, 2021

Clanadonia. *Yo Bassa*, Scottish tribal pipes & drums band 'Clanadonia' playing "Yo Bassa" during St. Andrew's Day event 2019. Youtube, Jan 4, 2020. Download Dec 20, 2021

Clark, S. "Guide to Wild Food Foraging in Scotland", https://visitscotland.com, November 25, 2020

"Cruck Framed Buildings", *Canmore*, National Record of The Historic Environment, website canmore.org.uk. download. August 30, 2019

Eric, T. "Are Broad Beans the Same as Fava Beans?" *CULINARYLORE* November 19, 2014

Gilbert, R., "Medieval Dyestuffs, Dyeing and Colour Names", *Rosalie's Medieval Woman Website*, rosaliegilbert.com downloaded December 13,2021

Kennedy, S. "The St. Andrews 1559 Project" *History Scotland*, Digital Reconstruction of St. Salvator's, 2017

Loredo, P. "Bandages: Spider Webs Were Used As Bandages in Ancient Times", *Loredo Hand Institute Blog,* loredohands.com September 5, 2019

Romandor. *Romandor's Shepherd Fluiera*, Authentic Shepherd playing flute in Carpathian Mountains, Youtube, Nov 10, 2018, Download Dec 20, 2021

Sandles, T. "Blackberries: Dartmoor Brimbles", *Legendary Dartmoor*, https://legendarydartmoor.com download August 25, 2021

Swetinburgh, S. "The Hospital Experience in Medieval England", *History Extra*, March 2016. website BBC History Revealed, BBC World Histories Magazine

Shiraishi, A. *How to Solve A Problem: The Rise and Fall(s) of A Rock Climbing Champion*, Make Me A World, April 7, 2020

"The Ticking of a Clock", *Histories of the Unexpected*, www.historiesoftheunexpected.com September 18, 2019

"World's Oldest Clock? Probably", *Horologica,* www.horologica.co.uk, download August 29, 2021

Parchment

Brown, M. "Parchment Making", Cornell University Library Conservation, Cornell University, April 3, 2015

di Curci, Meliora "The History and Technology of Parchment Making" LochacCollegeofScribes: Parchment Making.html

"How Medieval Parchment is Made", *NOVA*, pbs.org October 12, 2020

Meyers, J. "The Ancient Art of Parchment Making", Workshop Art Department, Middlebury College, Middlebury, Vermont, July 6, 2015

"Parchment", *Making the Medieval English Manuscript: The Takamiya Collection at the Beinicke Library*, On-line Exhibits at Yale, exhibits.library.yale.edu

Sheep, Wool, Weavers

Baines, P. *Spinning Wheels, Spinners and Spinning*, B.T. Batsford, London 1977

Campbell, T. "How Medieval and Renaissance Tapestries Were Made", *Heilbrunn Timeline of Art History*, https://metmuseum.org February 2008

Hawkwood, J. "Wool Processing", *A Writer's Perspective*, Aprilmunday.wordpress.com

Keenlyside, J. "Patricia Baines, Spinning Wheels, Spinners and Spinning". Reviews/Comptes Rendus, https://journals.lib.unb.ca/index.php/MCR/article/download/17015/22935?inline=1 download 11.21.2021

Ryder, M. (1984). "Medieval Sheep and Wool Types". *The Agricultural History Review, 32*(1), 14-28. Retrieved August 16, 2021, from http://www.jstor.org/stable/40274301

"Sheep Breeds", *National Sheep Association*, https: www.nationalsheep.org.uk, download 8/20/20

Snell, M. "Medieval Methods for Making Cloth from Wool", *ThoughtCo,* May 25, 2019

Stage, J. "Medieval Looms", https://journals.flvc.org › article › download

"Wad *n.*". *Dictionary of the Scots Language.* 2004. Scottish Language Dictionaries Ltd. Accessed 12 Dec 2021 <https://www.dsl.ac.uk/entry/dost/wad>

Shoemakers

Carlson, I. "European Medieval Shoemaking History and Techniques", *Website of a Historical Polymath*, https://websiteofahistoricalpolymath.wordexpress.com download March 20, 2021

Knox, E. "History for Fantasy Writers: Shoemakers", *Mythic Scribes: The Art of Fantasy Storytelling*, https://mythicscribes.com download March 20, 2021

Morris, S. "Shoe", *Medieval London*, https://medievallondon.ace.fordham.edu download March 12, 2020

Wubs-Mrozewicz, J. "Shoes and Shoemakers in Late Medieval Bergen and Stockholm", *Collegium Medieval*, vol. 18, 2005, https: medievalists.net

"What is a Cordwainer?", *The Honorable Cordwainers' Company*, https://thehcc.org, download March 15, 2021

Tannery

Bartosiewicz, L. "Skin and Bones: Taphonomy of a Medieval Tannery in Hungary, *Journal of Taphonomy*, Prometheus Press/Paleontological Network Foundation, 2009 Volume 7 (Issue 2-3)

"Leather tanning – Medieval to Edwardian", http://mittelzeit.blogspot.com download July 29, 2019

Carson, G. "The Medieval Tannery", *The Ancient World in Review*, http://ancientworldreview August 17, 2017

"Medieval Tannery Discovered in Norwich", *Archaeology*, http://archaeology.com January 7, 2015

Trade and Taxes

Barnes, F. "The Taxation of Wool 1327-1348', Finance and Trade Under Edward III the London Lay Subsidy of 1332, Manchester 1918. *British History Online* http://www.british-history-online/ac.uk/manchester-unilondon-lay-subsidy/1332   download 8/14/21

Eberlin, A. "Changing Definitions of Flanders and the Netherlands-Part 1', https://flemish.wp.st-andrews.ac.uk/2014/1010/changing-definitions-of-flanders-and-the-netherlands-part-1 download 6/8/21

French, M. "Imports from Flanders in the Medieval Period: Urban and Rural People" November 28, 2014

Oram, R. "The Sea Salt Industry in Medieval Scotland", *History and Politics Journal*

Rhodes, B. "Rescued from the Ruins: The Surviving Manuscripts of St. Andrews Cathedral", website: https://www.special collections.wp.st-andrews.ac.uk. download 8/19/19

"The 'Bremen Cog' from the Hanseatic Era: 600 years of History to Marvel at", website https://www.dsm.museum

"The Medieval Cog Roland von Bremen", website https://www.Tallship-fan.de

Acknowledgements

Bill Greenleaf, son of a Norwood Hills Club Champion and my golf guru, knows golf. More importantly, Bill loves to share his passion for golf. Most importantly, Bill mastered the art and science of teaching golf. He connects with golfers to develop into problem solvers who find joy in the journey. With gentle, honest, caring guidance, Bill coaches golfers at every stage and every age. In our winter years, golf goals morph. Instead of the power and free movement we once took for granted when we played the tips, now we experience bodies breaking down infested with arthritis. We can still play if we move up to forward tees to accept the appropriate challenge on the course. Thank you Bill, for sharing your children's bedtime story with me, my friend. What a journey! What joy!

Michael Finkel, MD is one of the best read persons I ever met. He is also a terrific writer. I knew Michael would be an honest, thorough, tough editor. He proved me right. He invested much time and effort in the task. He challenged me to defend sentences, facts and concepts. I finally accepted that such minute attention had one purpose, improve the manuscript. Together we worked to edit a legible translation from the professors, from the lads and lasses, and from the one handed scribe who created his opus magnus. Michael moved the needle. I am grateful.

Normandy Folks-my friend, Buddy Lee, since grade three on Garfield School playground, pitcher and catcher, plus wife Becky who host a group connected by sports. Now golf, cornhole and table games with our spouses entertain us. Jack and Rande Wagner, Jamie (we get to call him that) and Dolores Rosell. My regular golfing partner, Jack Dulaney, worthy successor to his Norwood Club Champion Dad. Vietnam brother, Les Tettenhorst hosts us at legendary Norwood Hills CC, home of Ascension Golf Classic, a gifted teller of tales. Ned Abernathy, golf merchandiser (Ben Hogan, Maxfli, Ping, Srixon) encouraged the project. Whenever we gather we remember athletic contests exactly the way they happened six decades ago. We probably even remember things that never actually happened.

College Basketball Teammates-who use any excuse to form an old man golfing team. Don Brashears-golfing/fishing partner, advertising guru who found a golf course with sand greens. Dr. C.E. Mohn, retired educator, offered ideas to clarify the manuscript as if it were a dissertation. Randy and Nancy Hubbard host a group of old guys to celebrate our coach, Dr. Jim Leutjen. Golf interests us the way basketball once did. Grateful for our get-togethers.

Thank you to numerous beta readers for your comments and encouragement throughout constructive stages of the manuscript process.

Special appreciation to Sharon Wible, my legacy, brought her dream of publication to fruition this year who offered insight into the process. Thank you to Creative Publishing Partners.

This is a work of fiction set in a historical context. Any mistakes are mine alone.

Good Reads for Golf Aficionados

Books for Golfers and Golf Lovers

Boomer, P. *On Learning Golf*, Alfred A. Knopf publisher, Random House, New York, NY, originally published 1946, 32nd reprint 2008

Dodson, J. *Final Rounds: A Father, A Son, The Golf Journey of a Lifetime*, Bantam, 2003

Frost, M. *The Greatest Game Ever Played: Harry Vardin, Francis Ouimet and The Birth of Modern Golf*, Hyperion, New York, 2002

Frost, M. *The Match: The Day the Game of Golf Changed Forever*, Hachette Books, 2009

Healey, J. *Golfing Before the Arch: A History of St. Louis Golf 1896-1997*, 1997

Hogan, B. Wind, H. Ravielli, A. *Ben Hogan's Five Lessons: The Modern Fundamentals of Golf*, Simon & Schuster, 1985

Murphy, M. *Golf in the Kingdom*, Penguin 1971

Penick, H. Shrake, B. *Harvey Penick's Little Green Book Further Reflections on The Game of Golf*, Harper Collins Ltd., 1994

Penick, H. Shrake, B. *Harvey Penick's Little Red Book, Lessons and Teachings from a Lifetime of Golf*, Harper Collins Ltd., 1993

Rotella, B. Cullen, B. *Golf is Not a Game of Perfect*, Simon & Schuster, 2007

Shaw, J. *Out of the Rough*, Williams & Norgate, London, 1934

Book Club Discussion Questions

Book Club Discussion Questions for
"And Then There Was Golf: The Lost Legend"
by Dr. Jason E. Holmes

1

The title, 'And Then There Was Golf' alludes to Genesis 1, v. 3 "…and there was light…" Light is a vital life giving element in the Judeo-Christian Creation story. The book title is intended to connect to a world before there was golf. The elements for golf already existed, but there was no golf. Something happened. And then there was golf. Creation stories center around gods or humans who possess supernatural powers. This story however, centers on emerging adolescents. To create golf, what elements were necessary? What powers did the lads and lads bring? What powers were necessary for them to possess in order to create golf?

2

James II's Act of Parliament of 6 March 1457 banned golf and football. The Act is the earliest known written evidence for the game in Scotland. Why do you think that the author chose the specific dates of Lammas to Michaelmass 1399, as the exact time frame for golf's creation?

3

When the lads and lasses watch the Scottish games they realize many inherent unfair issues to the games. In a discussion they discover that they want to compete in games that are fair to all. They commit to design and produce a new game that is completely fair for all participants. In order to be fair, golf is a game which requires players to be completely honest. As Scotland emerged from feudal society into the beginning of a free market society, the parents of the lads and lasses were first and second generation business owners. Honesty and integrity are crucially important to build a reputation for reliability and managing a successful business. Golf continues to demand total honesty and integrity from its players. Why do you believe honesty and integrity are so crucial to golf?

4

Most golf historians subscribe to the possibility that a game arose on the Links near St. Andrews that could be recognized as golf. What elements do the St. Andrews Links possess that support the notion that St. Andrews is the birthplace of golf?

5

The professors go to great length to establish 'provenance' for the manuscript. The chapter discusses the means to check the material for authenticity. What tests did they report on for the parchment? What tests did the professors submit for the ink? Besides the parchment and ink, what other evidence did the professors consider in order to achieve a reasonable confidence level that the manuscript was the real thing? Were there any tests for provenance that were new to you? What do you think about the steps that historians employ as part of the process to determine the authenticity of a relic? Why is the real thing so important?

6

Translation is exceedingly important and tricky to connect ancient texts with modern audiences. The manuscript dates to 1458 which places it more than a century before the birth of Shakespeare. Since the mid-15th Century the English language changed considerably. Literal translations are difficult to read for several reasons. Identify and discuss some of the issues presented by the Professors involved in translating ancient texts to 21st Century readers?

7

For the story of the twelve lads and lasses to reach modern readers requires that one of them attain literacy and write the story. In the medieval world literacy rates were extremely low. Only royalty and select members of clergy learned to read and write. How did the Tanner son become the only one of the twelve to become literate? What event caused him to write the story? How did he access the materials, parchment, ink, pens and place to write?

8

Many golfers call The Olde Course at St. Andrew's Links sacred ground. For centuries religious pilgrims journeyed to the Cathedral. Beginning with the story of how a relic of Andrew the Disciple arrived there centuries after the martyrdom of the Saint. Historians identify the story as a "Creation Myth". Why does the story of how St. Regis/Regulus transported the bones from Greece to the East Coast of Scotland fit the criteria for a "Creation Myth"? How does the concept of 'pilgrimage' connect with the Cathedral and with The Olde Course?

9

Every story centers on conflicts or problems. What conflicts or problems are faced in this story? How do the lads and lasses respond to conflicts and problems? What strategies can you identify?

10

Sounds are important facets of the story. Identify several different sounds from the Prologue and first six chapters. Choose three sounds. Explain how the sounds are employed in the story. How were Bessie and David affected by the new sound? How did they know the sound was different? Why were they compelled to discover the source for the sound? David feels the sound is magical. Explain why you agree or disagree with David's feelings about magic.

11

After all the lads and lasses received their new balls and their new custom fitted clubs, they had a contest to see who could drive the ball the farthest. No longer did Bessie and David, the Shepherds drive the ball farther than any others. Thomas was surprised by the outcome. When he saw that the new long distance champions were from the same family, he reasoned they did something different from the others. What did he learn that the Carpenters did differently than any of the others?

12

How did the difference between the Shepherds' club grip and the 'hammer grip' employed by the Carpenters account for such a significant difference in the distance the ball traveled? Have you tried both the 'club grip' and the 'Hammer grip' when you hit the ball? How much practice did it require for you to experience that change?

13

Once the twelve lads and lasses commit to collaborate in order to achieve their goal, to invent the new game, they begin a transformation. From a group of individuals they build a successful team. Members of a team put team goals ahead of their individual goals. The lads and lasses agree to bring their best ideas, efforts and cooperative behaviors to achieve their goal. Barbara insists that the team follow the business principles which their parents practice in their own business. How does Barbara convince the team to set a deadline? Why do businesses set deadlines to complete the work?

14

Bessie adapts a behavior during moments …or sometimes hours of calm, which often occur while overseeing the flock. She is secure in the knowledge that the collies manage the flock with complete control. Should circumstances change, the ever vigilant collies will signal Bessie immediately that her control is required. Until she is needed, she permits her mind to wander and to wonder. During those daydreams, new realms of possibility open to Bessie. She wonders, 'Do animals talk? She composes poems. She observes animals closely. She catalogs animal behaviors. She wonders… what if? Her observations of birds are intensive moments of discovery. Following one such discovery on the Links, when Bessie wonders, 'what if', how does the golf ball change? The lasses perform a 'blind experiment' on their brothers. The results are conclusive. What happened? How were results of the 'blind experiment' shared with the lads? How did the lasses reward the lads for their involvement in the 'blind experiment'?

15

On highly effective teams Leadership is crucial. Leadership also revolves among team members based on the situation, according to who holds critical knowledge and skills for a particular problem or who has access to data and information. Team members trust each other to accomplish the goal. Each team member feels empowered to take over leadership of the team at a particular moment when their skills, knowledge or access is required. The lads and lasses faced a difficult problem of target visibility together. Only the three tallest can see the target. No one sees a solution until Heather looks backward in the opposite direction. The change in perspective sparks insight for Heather. She takes leadership of the team. What solution does she propose? How does she persuade the lads and lasses to share her vision and her solution?